ARTHUR

www.penguin.co.uk

ARTHUR

GILES KRISTIAN

bantam

TRANSWORLD PUBLISHERS
Penguin Random House, One Embassy Gardens,
8 Viaduct Gardens, London SW11 7BW
www.penguin.co.uk

Transworld is part of the Penguin Random House group of companies
whose addresses can be found at global.penguinrandomhouse.com

Penguin
Random House
UK

First published in Great Britain in 2024 by Bantam
an imprint of Transworld Publishers

A CIP catalogue record for this book
is available from the British Library.

ISBNs
9781787635197 (cased)
9781787635203 (tpb)

Typeset in 11.5/14pt Adobe Caslon Pro by Jouve (UK), Milton Keynes
Printed and bound in Great Britain by Clays Ltd, Elcograf S.p.A.

The authorized representative in the EEA is Penguin Random House Ireland,
Morrison Chambers, 32 Nassau Street, Dublin D02 YH68.

Penguin Random House is committed to a sustainable
future for our business, our readers and our planet. This book
is made from Forest Stewardship Council® certified paper.

Arthur is for Sally, Freyja and Aksel.
How lucky I am to have you.

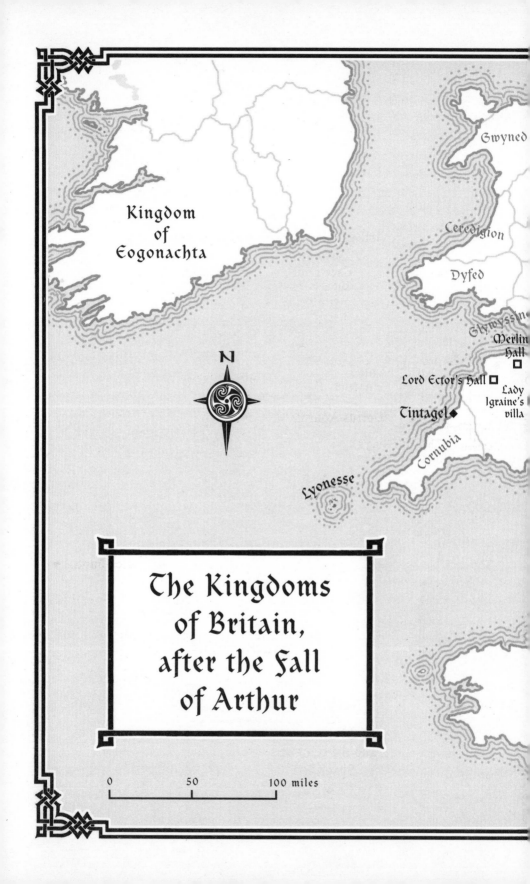

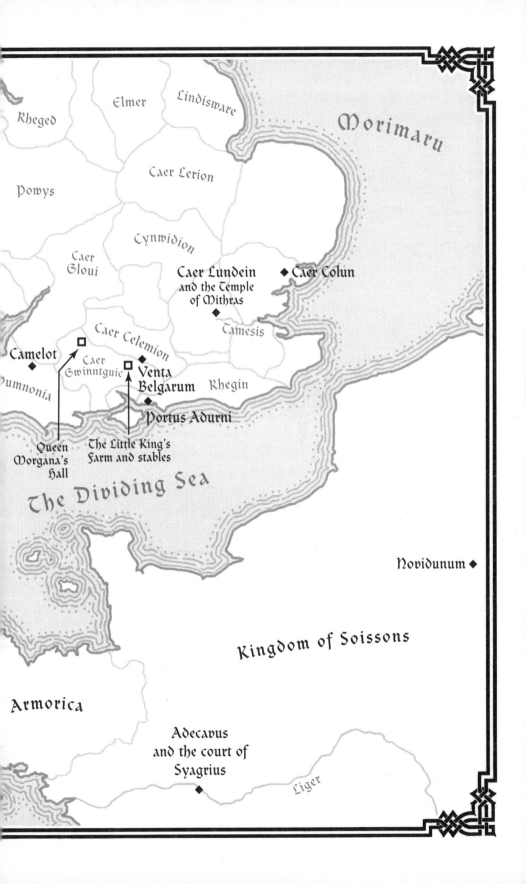

Prologue

THE BOY SHIVERED, BUT he was not cold. He had run through white-mantled fields and silent woods, his leather-soled shoes sinking deep in places, his blood in spate, pulsing in his ears: a ceaseless rhythm that he would not fall behind.

It was late in the day. The sun was low, a bronze disc, and the boy's own shadow lay stretched across the snow, tall and misshapen, like the spirit of the man he would one day become, looking back at the child he now was.

There!

He stood on a low rise, bare black oaks behind him, a valley below, breathing hard, so that clouds of fog wreathed his head, forming and dissipating with the rise and fall of his chest.

There they are!

He was far from home now and he knew his mother would be worried for him and angry at him for running away. There was a distant thrill in that knowing, but it was nothing compared with the fire that filled him now at the sight below.

He uttered a curse. A man's words from a boy's lips, but it felt right, for even a boy of just ten winters knows when he is about to witness something that might never be seen again.

He counted, taking his time because every one mattered.

'Seventy-eight,' he said at last, when he was sure. Seventy-eight men and horses, milling in clouds of steaming breath. Helmets and spear blades and ringmail as grey and dull as the clouds now moving in from the north, and the dark blood red of woollen tunics and cloaks and the dyed horsehair plumes flowing from their helmets. And round shields strapped on their left arms, painted red with a yellow ring enclosing a blue circle around the iron boss at the centre, so that it seemed each man carried the strange eye of some foreign god from distant, sun-scorched lands where Roman shrines were slung with smoke fragrant with myrrh, lavender and frankincense.

There was snow on the air now. The boy looked up, closed his eyes, felt for a moment the soft caress of it on his skin. Each snowflake landing like a mother's gentle kiss. Normally he would revel in the promise of a flurry, but this was no time for childish amusements. He opened his eyes and turned his face down to the valley, squinting as the snow came at him on a cool breath laced with leather and lanolin and the sweet, pungent scent of horses.

Those horses and their masters were moving, forming two lines facing west towards the setting sun. Men checking straps and helmets and pushing their cloaks back to free sword hilts. The animals nickering and neighing and pawing at the brittle snow with their iron-shod hooves. Perhaps they, too, felt the weight of the moment. Somehow sensed the passing of an age in the fading light.

The boy had never seen their like. Many folk did not believe they existed at all beyond tales gilded by firelight and fable, for they were said to have left the Dark Isles with the usurper Magnus Maximus. If that were true, then these horse soldiers were ghosts, or else the boy was still tucked in his furs and dreaming.

But no. Ghosts only walked abroad on Samhain, and one did not feel snowflakes on one's eyelids in a dream. What the boy was seeing was real, he knew. Flesh, blood and bone. The last of the horse soldiers. Men left behind at the western edge of a withering empire. The last equites Romani in a twilight time.

But it was not enough to see them at a distance and through snow blur, so he sucked a cold breath across his teeth, bent to tie the ankle thong of his left shoe which had worked loose, and ran.

He flew down the hill, light as the kittiwakes he had seen dipping to forage at the grey rolling furrows in Tintagel bay, his cloak reaching out behind, and his long, tangled hair untouched by the falling snow. He almost outstripped his own legs and fell, but his feet caught up and came down surely to the level ground, where he stopped and bent at the waist. Sucked in air slung thick with the rich smells of those men and horses: the fresh dung and urine of the animals – but not just the animals – that stained the white blanket unfolding on the land, and the horses' hay-scented breath and the sour tang of wine from the men themselves, and the onions from their last meal, and the old sweat in their tunics, and the grease which kept saddle and tack supple and kept rust off mail and blades.

A man at the rear had seen the boy and now others twisted in their saddles. He felt their eyes on him like heat but he stood their fierce gaze, even straightened under it and gave one dark-skinned soldier a nod, as of one man to another, and the soldier grinned.

The boy heard a murmuring and knew he was the cause of it, and then the one who had acknowledged him turned his gelding away from the rest and walked it towards the boy. His companions turned back to face their front and stretched their spines and necks to look over or between their fellow riders. For something was happening across the snow plain which the boy could not see from where he stood. Not that his eyes had any will of their own to tear away from the man and beast walking towards him now, the man sheathed in steel helmet and rings of iron, and the gelding clad in boiled-leather armour on head and breast, and steam rising from it like smoke.

The boy's breath caught in his chest. Fear scuttled up his back and nestled at the nape of his neck, but he held his ground, planted in that deeper snow so that he could feel the cold seeping into his toes and the small bones of his feet. He looked from the man to the spear gripped lightly in his right hand, its vicious blade accusing the snow-hazed sky, and he guessed that the spear, which he knew to be the legendary Sarmatian lance, was three times as long as he, the boy, was high. The rider could lower that spear blade and thrust it down with no more effort than a man spitting a fish caught in a pool at ebb tide.

Still the boy did not run, and the spear did not tip as the rider pressed his thighs to his mount's flanks and sat back, halting close enough that the smell of man and beast, of steel and leather and damp wool, came over the boy like memories.

'What are you doing here, boy?' the man asked, looking beyond him and up the hill as if seeking the boy's family. The voice was light, not guttural as the boy had expected, though the accent came as no surprise, for his skin was dark as burnt umber and the eyes held in them the ghosts of other lands and peoples.

'I wanted to see the horses charge,' the boy said. 'Is there going to be a battle?'

The soldier half turned to look at his companions, who were moving with practised ease, the whole company forming into three lines, knee to knee, spear points lowered now, the staves resting across their horses' backs in front of the saddles. Like this man, as well as the lance they all carried several light javelins in a case behind the saddle.

'There'll be a fight, boy. Has to be.' His breath fogged in the air and he lifted his chin. 'You should get back up there where it's safe. No place for a boy, this.' The horse snorted twin plumes of hot breath and pulled its great head around, seeming to glare at the boy through one of the eye-holes in the hardened leather shaffron covering its face. That head armour had been worked with cloth and oil until it looked like polished oak, yet there were deep scars and scratches in it still, just as there were dents and abrasions on the man's steel helmet and on the cheek plates which obscured much of his face.

'I'm not afraid,' the boy said, balling his fists at his sides.

One dark eyebrow lifted to the helmet's rim. 'I have a boy about your age.' His lips pursed. 'A little bigger, perhaps.' He glanced left and right at the falling snow and then, through that shifting confusion, at the wide valley floor which was almost featureless but for a few skeletal trees: crab apple and birch and, a distance off, three white willow, thick with snow, silent sentinels guarding some unseen waterway. 'Off with you, lad. Your people will be worried.'

The drone of a war horn carried on the thin air, and the boy knew it had not come from the equites but from the enemy somewhere beyond the swirling veils.

'I must go,' the horse soldier said. His hand came up to the helmet thong knotted beneath his chin, then he extended his left arm with the small round shield strapped to the upper part, as though testing his own limbs in their joints.

'Are you afraid?' the boy asked.

The man considered the question. 'A little,' he said. 'The enemy are many and we are few.' He turned his head and spat into the snow. 'Death comes to all men. But I would see my wife and son again . . . if the gods will it.'

The boy wondered what kind of father the man was. Wondered if he beat his son. If he rutted with women who were not his wife.

'Before you go . . .' The man reached behind himself, his free hand working nimbly at something, then he pulled a rolled fur back around and held it out towards the boy. 'It's bear,' he said. 'Keep you warm up there ... if you stay to watch.'

For a moment the boy just stood, wary of going closer, of accepting a gift from a stranger.

The man lifted the fur, then threw it at the boy, who caught it in two hands. 'I'll have it back after.'

'I will look for you,' the boy said, though he wondered how he would recognize this man among so many similarly armoured men and horses.

The man saw the question in him. 'I'll be the one without the rolled fur behind his saddle.' He half smiled, then once more lifted his chin at the hill behind the boy. 'Now, go.'

The boy nodded and turned and ascended, slipping now and then but never dropping the fur, which he clutched in raw hands. Only once did he look back to see the horse soldier walking his mount away to join the turma, his long red helmet plume swaying with the animal's easy gait. His cloak the colour of old blood. And when the boy came to the crown and turned and looked back over his own tracks and those of the rider, and at the white distance through his own clouding breath, his heart kicked in his chest and he felt his eyes swell, pulling at the taut skin of his face. For the enemy gathering there, two good arrow-shots away from the equites, was a war host. A mustering of warriors that any bard would liken in number to the leaves on a tree, or the pebbles on a sea-licked shore, or the stars in the black vault of the sky.

'Balor's eyes,' he said, the adult oath again feeling appropriate. He unrolled the bear skin and threw it around his shoulders, surprised that it smelled faintly of fish. He was cold now. The chill that had been all around him, yet kept off by his excitement, was *in* him now. Seeping deep into his flesh and seeking his heart.

'I should have asked his name.' The words shivered from his lips. Then the war horn sounded again, and the boy looked amongst the enemy swarm for their leader, for surely he must be a man worth seeing.

There! He caught a glimpse through the slanting snow. There, in the heart of the host which darkened the land like a stain. A big man amongst big men, swathed in furs like most of the others, and gripping a spear and shield as they did, but this one *was* their chieftain, he knew it. There was no telling what was beard and what was fur, but he wore an iron helmet, as did the thirty or so comprising his personal guard, his hearthmen. Most among his war host had no such war gear but wore leather skull caps or hats of fur, and the only iron they owned was that of their spear blades or axe heads.

But the boy had not run so far through this white day to see such as they. Low men. Farmers perhaps, or fishermen in their own land across the grey sea. Men desperate enough to take ship and make war in these Dark Isles. And so he brought his gaze back to the near distance, where a different race sat tall upon their noble beasts. Horse lords. Gods of war in bronze and iron. Warriors from a time now past, waiting in the snow like a dream fading with the dawn.

They cannot fight so many, the boy thought. *They should not fight*. And yet he wanted them to, and he was old enough to feel the shame in such a wish; wanting men to wade into blood when there could be no hope.

He gritted his teeth. 'There is always hope,' he said.

The leader of the horse lords was yelling commands which the boy could not make out, but he heard well enough the steel in that voice. The steel and the flint which sparked amongst the general's red-plumed companions and caught as fire. His muffled words rose in a crescendo, and every man roared, and the sound of it raised rooks from the far willows, those black birds rasping into the wan sky. The horse lords raised their spears, thrusting them skyward and clamouring still, and one man hoisted the turma's standard, which the boy saw was an ornate metal sculpture of a dragon's open mouth, behind which a long red cloth hung limply against the pole because there was but little wind.

'Draconarius,' the boy said, feeling the word in his mouth like a spell, for he knew that was the old name given to the man whose honour it was to carry that standard. And then the acclamation ebbed away as the front rank heeled their mounts forward and the whole contingent began to move.

The men of the enemy's front line were looking north, some of them holding their shields up against the snow. At first, the boy did not know why, but then it came to him. *They think this is a trap.* Those fur-clad warriors were looking for spearmen, an enemy war host coming up from the river or out of the flurries like vengeful wraiths. They did not trust that the seventy-eight mounted men walking their horses towards them were alone. But they *were* alone. The boy knew it. The horse lords knew it too, and still they moved forward, rising to the trot now, tearing up the white mantle of the snow plain and leaving warm breath hanging in shredding clouds behind them.

The boy looked up at the sky. It would be dark soon and he would have to walk home with no moon or star glow to guide him, only the ghost of light lingering on the snowy ground and hills. But he could not leave now, and so he pulled the bear fur tightly around himself and looked for the man who had given it. Perhaps that was him that he saw, riding in the rear rank, sitting tall in the saddle, his helmet's mane bouncing.

And then, at some signal neither seen nor heard by the boy, the equites Romani spurred their mounts into a canter and the turma moved as one, like a great cloud shadow rolling across the winter meadow, and the enemy must have known that this was no ambush by a force superior in numbers but something more desperate and perhaps more dangerous. Those men from across the sea had eyes only for those riders now, and they must have been gripped by terror at the sight.

Two hundred paces from the enemy, and the equites were galloping, the horses' hooves flinging snow and mud, the warriors each bringing his wicked long spear down two-handed across his mount's neck, trusting their four-horned saddles and the strength of their own legs to keep them seated.

'Kill them,' the boy muttered. He felt it in him like some hate-filled animal stirring in his gut, some creature that craved revenge for all the wrongs which the boy had suffered. He would see blood now. He would watch these farmers and leatherworkers, these men seeking land or silver or simply a new start, slaughtered by the horse lords of Britannia. By those sons and grandsons and great-great-grandsons of horse lords, stretching back some three hundred years to the Sarmatians whom the emperor Marcus Aurelius had stationed here.

Those low men tried to retreat now, but could not for the press of their countrymen, and so they held up their shields and cowered behind them, perhaps hoping the weight of their numbers would check the charge, absorb the terrible impact.

'Kill them!' the boy yelled, thrusting his fist skyward, hoping to be heard by men or by gods.

And then the turma was changing formation, even at such speed. It was like watching a murmuration of starlings, when flocks coalesce in an aerial dance, making and unmaking shapes against the waning daylight. The wings of the three ranks seemed to slow, while those at the centre galloped harder still, and with fluid grace born of long practice and marvellous skill the whole turma drew together again so that it formed not one front of three lines, but rather a wedge, or an arrowhead, the boy realized, aimed right at the centre of the enemy host. The place where their chieftain stood.

At the point of that arrow was the commander whose voice had carried to the boy, his own spear levelled as he led his men towards victory or death. Off his shoulder rode the draconarius, the shaft of his standard gripped in his right hand, the red pennant streaming from the dragon's head, and the boy was sure he could hear that strange thing hissing malevolently as the man spurred his armoured horse on.

'Now!' said the boy, and he flinched as though struck, as the point of that wedge hit the enemy mass and the rest followed, the sound of it like rolling thunder, and the splintering of shields and the screams of men and horses broke the day.

Those men at the fore simply ceased to exist, and the wedge sank deeper, and the war host shuddered as though it were one entity, a wave rolling over it, pushing every man backward into the man behind.

The boy had never heard sounds like this. Never such a noise. The shrieks of pain and the cracking of bones and the terrible wet sound of bodies being crushed and trampled to bloody ruin. The cries of the horses were almost worse than those of the men, and he knew that enemy spears were finding the soft flesh where the boiled-leather horse armour was not, and stomachs were being pierced. Guts spilled onto the snow. The boy fancied he could smell the viscera, sharp and metallic, even up there on the hill. The stark tang of bowels – men's and beasts' – disgorging dung. A taint on the air, on the boy too, which he might recall all the days of his life.

It was an abomination playing out before him and only him, as though he alone of his kin and kind had been called by some god of war as a witness, the intention of which he did not know, but that it must portend to his own future.

Bile had risen hot and bitter in his throat, but he did not think he would vomit, because he had not eaten since breaking his fast that morning. He spat, trying to rid himself of the foul taste. Yet, despite the horror of what he was seeing through the falling snow, he could not take his eyes from it.

The horse lords were pushing on, deeper into the enemy, spurring their mounts and thrusting down with their lances. Many had lost their spears and were hurling the shorter javelins into the press one after another. They could not miss, and men were impaled where they stood, but had no room to fall and were carried upright on the swell like men no longer alive and yet not fully dead. Some of the equites had drawn long swords and now they scythed them at heads and shoulders, and still others were laying about them with axes, and even across the distance the boy could see blood spraying and gobbets of flesh flying here and there.

He felt a sickness spreading in him. Souring his guts and thickening his saliva. He did not know what it was, but it felt like shame. He saw the leader of the equites pulled from his horse. One heartbeat that man was glorious in bronze scales, his helmet's red plume dancing as he hacked down with his sword again and again. The next heartbeat he was gone. Just . . . gone.

Then the draconarius fell, his horse's legs hacked away by men with axes, and a moment later the boy saw the standard being passed above the heads of the host, hand to hand, the pennant devoid of its glory now as the metal dragon head drifted across that dark sea like a timber from a wrecked ship, on its way to the chieftain further back.

But the horsemen ploughed on, the arrowhead deep enough now in the body of the enemy that the war host was being split, which the boy realized was their intention. That and getting to the chieftain to kill him and his hearthmen.

'Keep going,' the boy hissed, seeing that the point of the wedge was now less than a spear-throw from those helmeted men. *Just a little further.*

They would do it! Those lords of war in their red cloaks would cut their way through to the enemy's chieftain and butcher him, and then they would ride on, having ripped the heart from their enemy. The Saxons would break. They *must* break.

The thin note of a war horn drifted to him then. He looked to the north, towards the unseen river and the line of white willow. The sound had come from there. He squinted against the snow. He thought he saw something. Something dark through the haze, coming up from the river. He watched and waited and then they appeared and it seemed impossible that he could not see them before. Spearmen. Scores of them. More than a hundred. The horn brayed again and was answered by its twin somewhere amongst the main body of the enemy, and the boy's blood all but froze in his veins, bear skin or no.

'Balor help them,' he whispered, his body clenched by a terror he had never known, so that even his mouth and tongue were almost stupefied, unable to create proper sound. For this was why the Saxons had been looking north. Not because they expected more horse soldiers or those men's allies marching with spear, shield and hatred for the invader, but because they were hoping to see their own countrymen. Hoping to close the trap which they had laid. And now that trap *was* closing, because this new horde was wheeling to the east, towards the hill upon which the boy stood, the men at the extreme right running so that those nearest the willows were as the hinge, and the remainder were the gate now closing behind the horsemen. Sealing the breach which those brave riders had carved. Trapping them.

But there *was* still a chance. The turma was moving forward, still causing devastation within the enemy host. It was like a bear, ripping the guts out of its adversary with savage tooth and claw. The men's scale armour and ringmail, and the felt bindings and iron greaves on their legs, made them hard to kill, and their horses could not easily be brought down either, because of the leather armour on their heads and chests and the thick blankets or ringmail on some protecting their flanks and hindquarters.

Each rider is worth ten of these spearmen, the boy thought, the fight below him gaining a new and terrible intensity now because the horse lords had reached the Saxon chieftain and were driving desperately on, hacking and scything. The only way was forward, because the newcomers were massed thickly at their rear, attacking men and horses from behind, hurling spears at the riders' backs and darting in and out behind the horses, trying to hamstring the animals with their long knives.

The boy saw the Saxon hearthmen moving to make a shieldwall in front of their lord. Saw one of the horsemen lean back in his saddle and throw himself forward to cast a spear, which flew above that shield rampart and took the chieftain in his throat, causing his hearthmen to roar their anger. And in the boy's mind it was the dark-skinned man who had given him the bear fur that had thrown the spear.

But it was not enough. The hearthmen were surging forward now, heedless of their own safety, driven by shame, the boy thought, for having not protected their lord. And they threw themselves at the horse soldiers, and though many of them died in the act, faces speared, heads cleaved, enough got through to hack and hew at man and horse, so that the turma's momentum died, and even the boy, who had never seen a charge by equites Romani, knew that those brave and noble men were doomed.

They milled together, hauling on the reins, pulling their horses this way and that, seeking a way out, but there was none. The Saxons pressed in on all sides, like hounds closing on a wounded stag, blood scent in their noses, and the horses shrieked, eyes rolling white, teeth grinding at the bit, and were savaged where they stood.

Tears stood in the boy's eyes but they were not tears of sadness. He was angry. Angry at the commander of the equites for wasting those good men. He watched them die, those horse lords. Those gods of war. The clamour of it ebbed even as the light leached from the land, but he knew he would hear it always. He watched until it was done.

And when it was done, he wrapped himself tight in that bear fur, as if to hold every sound, every sight and every raw emotion to him, giving them no escape, and he turned from it all and walked into the darkening world, the snow silting his tracks until they were gone.

A Boy from the Fire

BERAN WATCHED THE FLAMES. They stretched and broke and hissed their secrets to the night, casting their bronze glow on birch trunks and ancient oak and the green leaves of the canopy above. Beyond the bloom of that fire the woods were dark and deep, as inscrutable as the day still to come, and so most of the men gathered around it kept their eyes on the flames, as men at war have always done since long before the druids dreamt of golden eagles and legions and new gods whose names were now fading in these Dark Isles.

Not that this could be called war.

'Give it here, Yann,' Red Tooth growled. 'Had more'n your share.'

Yann took one last pull on the wine skin, thumbed the stopper back in and tossed it across to the other man, who caught it and spat a curse as he weighed it in his hands.

'There'll be more where that came from after tomorrow.' Nabor was grimacing as he used a sliver of wood to pick something out of his teeth. 'We get the job done and we piss off. Lie low for a while and spend the summer drinking and whoring and doing whatever we want.'

Murmurs of agreement rippled around the gathered group.

'Tastes like goat's piss anyway,' Red Tooth said, handing the skin to Stenes beside him, who put his nose to the horn collar and sniffed the contents. He shrugged, drank deeply, then dragged a hand across his lips and rancid beard.

'Enjoy it while you can,' Beran muttered. 'Some of you will likely be dead this time tomorrow.' He leant forward and poked his knife into the charred remains of the boar which they had roasted earlier.

'Shut your mouth, old man.' Dyfnwal was glaring at Beran from across the fire. 'No one needs to hear that shit from you.' One of the horses tethered at the edge of the fire glow nickered and snorted as if in agreement.

'You can always rely on Beran to spoil the mood,' big Blandigan said, shaking his head as he took a stick from the pile beside him and tossed it into the fire.

With his knife, Beran levered a chunk of flesh and bone from the ashes and leant back against the birch stump beside which sat his weapons and a deer-skin sack containing the rest of his gear.

'If any of us gets a spear in the gut tomorrow, I hope it's you, Beran, you miserable bastard.' Red Tooth hawked and spat a wad of phlegm into the fire, where it sizzled and bubbled. If the others felt the same way they kept it to themselves.

'I haven't died yet,' was Beran's only reply, then he blew on the hot meat and gnawed carefully at it from the side of his mouth, still watching the flames. One of his front teeth had been hurting him for days and he knew he would have to pull it soon. Just one of the many pains he endured as a punishment for still breathing at his age. His left knee was swollen and hot to the touch and he spent most evenings and mornings kneading it like a man making bread, trying to disperse the fluid that gathered around the joint. His lower back was as stiff as a spear shaft and tortured by a dull ache that could only be chased away by ale or wine, and the knuckles and bones of his right hand were puffed up and hurt so much on occasion that he could barely grip a cup, let alone a sword.

Not that he admitted any of this to the sixteen men sitting around the fire or snoring in their furs hereabouts. They knew some of it. He was too long in years and too short in pride these days to keep the pain out of his face. Still, what could they say? They had seen younger, stronger companions killed and maimed, but Beran was still here, sharing their food and wine. Still pissing on the mood around the fire.

'Tell you something, Beran, if you die tomorrow, I'll be having that pretty sword you stole,' Red Tooth said. He was not the kind of man who could just let a thing go.

Beran glanced at the baldric and sword which lay beside him, rolled in leather to keep off summer rain or morning dew. Not the finest blade he'd ever owned, but not the worst, either. 'Bigger men than you have tried to take it while it was in my hand,' Beran said, 'so you're wise to wait till I'm dead.'

Red Tooth shook his head, gesturing at Blandigan to hand back the wine skin. The big man passed it over without complaint. 'No,' Red Tooth said. 'Death's too good for Beran. That's why he's still here when better men are not.'

Beran didn't disagree with that, but young Donan did. 'Shouldn't talk to him so,' Donan said, his honest face clenched in the play of flamelight. 'Should have more respect for your elders.'

Some of them laughed at this. Dyfnwal's eyebrows lifted at Blandigan, who pursed his lips and nodded, the two of them as surprised as they were quietly impressed. None around that campfire would have expected Donan to speak against Red Tooth, this being only Donan's seventeenth summer and judgement yet divided as to whether he had a man's portion of wits in his skull. Besides which, to Donan fell the tasks none of the other men in Nabor ap Nabor's mercenary band would willingly undertake themselves: scrubbing the mud and rust off their mail, fetching drinking water from streams or wells, gathering fuel for fires and the elm leaves and lichen they used to wipe their backsides. He didn't do much of the killing, Donan, but there were worse jobs than killing and most of those were his.

'Stay out of it, boy.' Beran shot Donan a look that should have been enough to silence him but wasn't, because even young Donan had drunk his share of the wine.

'I've seen Beran fight three men at the same time,' Donan went on, flames reflected in his eyes. He looked a simpleton then, Beran thought, with eyes round as coins and in each a tiny fire. 'Speared one in the side,' Donan went on, thrusting the imaginary weapon, 'cut the other's throat out, then put the spear into the third man's eye.'

'Aye, some shit hole in the north of Caer Gloui. I were there,' an older man named Hygwydd said. 'It were over in the time it takes to say it.'

Donan nodded. 'Beran was wild that day. Killed like the plague, he did.' He grinned to himself, pleased with the expression. He must have heard it somewhere.

'Enough, boy,' Beran snarled without looking up.

'Just saying what I seen,' Donan said. 'And that other time. It were snowing. We was half drowned in mead and that big bastard knocked over your cup. Looked like you'd wet your trews.' His smile was all teeth. 'So, you cut off his ear.'

'I said, enough.' Beran lifted his eyes to him now.

'Better do as he says,' Red Tooth told Donan. 'The old man needs his rest. Always tired because he has to piss five times a night.'

Some chuckles at this but not many.

'That'll do,' Nabor put in, throwing a meatless boar's rib at Red Tooth, who batted it away. 'I want you all rested. We've got work to do tomorrow.'

A faraway cheer drifted in on the breeze, making them lift their chins eastward for a moment. Then nothing.

'Days are too hot for work,' Dyfnwal groused, wiping greasy fingers on his beard.

'Who are we killing, anyway?' Blandigan's voice a low rumble issuing from the great cavern of his chest.

'People who other people want dead,' Nabor said.

'Saxons?' Red Tooth suggested. He was holding a green stick in the flames, watching the sap seethe and hiss from the end. 'Take our pick of them around here.'

Nabor sniffed. 'Not this time.' After a long moment he lifted his chin to Red Tooth. 'That a problem?'

The man considered this. Shook his head. 'Means nothin' to me. So long as we get paid,' he said, dropping the stick into the fire, then snatching the wine skin off the man beside him. He stoppered it and tossed it through the flames to Beran, who caught it. 'What say you, old man?'

Beran pulled the bung, lifted the skin to his lips and drank, the sour wine sluicing the taste of charred meat from his mouth. Red Tooth was right. He would be up several times in the night. Still, the wine dulled his many pains, so it was a bargain he had accepted.

He drank deeply. When it was finished, he laid the empty skin across the tree stump beside him. 'Fine by me,' he said.

'Maybe they're not coming.' Stenes spat onto the leaf mould. He was leaning against a trunk, idly running his pilfered Saxon long knife across a whetstone. It had been raining most of the night, and Beran had woken stiff, a chill in his bones, but Nabor had not let them get a fire going again because he would not risk smoke on the air giving them away.

'They'll come,' Nabor said, looking along an old drovers' path which meandered amongst the trees. 'They'll have no choice.'

Dyfnwal, on the last watch of the night, had returned to camp saying the sky in the east was aflame, which could only mean one thing: the Saxons were burning Caer Colun. And these men, loyal to no king or lord or any man other than Nabor ap Nabor – and to him only so long as he led them to coin and cunny – had looked at one another in the dark, the news hitting them like a blow, despite their having known Caer Colun's fall was inevitable.

Now, they were battle-ready in mail and helmets and leather armour, their spears and axes close at hand, the strings on their bows as taut as their nerves. While some were rigid with anticipation, others affected a posture of indifference. Such was the way with warriors before a bloodletting, Beran knew. Had seen it times beyond counting. The ones who could not keep still, and those who needed to empty their bladder or their bowels. The ones who laughed and threw insults around as if they were on their way to a tavern, not a fight. And those others who barely spoke at all, who kept to themselves, even fell asleep, seemingly without a care.

If you had never fought beside a man before, there was no way of telling from the way he carried himself whether he would do well and stand his ground, or run, or freeze, or foul himself through fear. But Beran *had* fought with these men. Had for two years lived amongst them, earning food and ale in the ruins of Caer Lundein, or haunting the marshes and the forests, sometimes killing Saxons for sport, sometimes killing men for pay. He knew them. They were not noble. They did not cling to lofty ideals, nor torment themselves with thoughts of the past or the future. They were more like animals, living for the day at hand. For food and drink and fornication. He knew what *they* were and he knew what *he* was.

For a while he sat amongst the bracken in the blush of the new day, watching a moth with red streaks on its black wings feed on a patch of yellow ragwort. He wondered what his old friend would have to say about that, what omen he would see in such a small thing, then he looked to the east because he smelled smoke on the air. The night's rain might have doused the flames of Caer Colun, but the place burned still. 'Camulodunum,' he murmured under his breath, invoking its Roman name like a spell for the lost. Camulodunum. The town had outlived the legions who built it. Had held out against the Saxon tides for more than one hundred years, but held out no longer. Its people were fools, Beran told himself, to think old Roman walls would keep them safe, especially since King Constantine had died in his bed some four years ago. The old warrior had fought the Saxons all his life. It was still strange to think he was gone. Many in Britain had imagined Constantine would still be leading his red-cloaked spearmen in battle long after the statues of Roman governors and generals that could still be seen in the land had crumbled to dust.

So, the east was lost. Most of the south too. The gods of Britain were long gone and the Saxons were the lords of the Dark Isles, and anyone who still did not accept that was a fool, or mad, or both.

He opened his right hand and closed it into a fist, wincing at the throbbing pain in the knuckles and joints. Bad most mornings but worse after rain. A stone's throw away, Donan waited beside a storm-felled tree, his back to Beran as he stood looking north-east into the forest, his spear gripped in both hands before him, moving his weight from leg to leg.

Beran pushed himself up onto his feet, cursing his knees, and walked past the ragwort, sending the red-spattered moth tumbling off into the mist. Donan's head lifted slightly at his approach, though he kept his eyes on the spaces between the trees.

'Thinking doesn't do a man any good,' Beran said.

'Ah, but you don't know what I'm thinking.' Donan's fingers were clenching and unclenching on the spear shaft.

Beran's fingers found a louse in his beard and crushed it. 'I don't want to know.'

Dawn sunlight streamed between the tall beech trees from whose bright green leaves the earlier rain dripped, a haphazard patter on the woodland floor. These warm, golden shafts of light raised a mist which hung here and there in veils, making it seem as though the ground itself smouldered. As if fire burned beneath, or some huge serpentine beast that harked from below the ground in some other realm steamed like a wet hound beside the hearth.

After a while, Donan said, 'I don't like this mist.' Sharing his thoughts after all.

'I do,' Beran said. He wore his tough leather coat over a long wool-len tunic, but no helmet for he could not abide the weight of one nor the way it closed him in, nor the quality it gave his voice when he spoke. Nor the memories. 'They won't see us till it's too late.'

Donan shook his head. 'Feels like an omen, and not a good one.'

Beran surprised himself with a rare chuckle. 'What do you know of omens, boy?'

Donan frowned. Lifted his right hand from his spear shaft, set the butt on the ground and started chewing his thumbnail. 'Maybe this mist is her doing.' He half turned to Beran. 'Queen Morgana.'

'Morgana?' Beran spat the name. Few men spoke of the queen without sounding like they were ridding their mouths of something foul.

'Aye, maybe this is her magic. To keep what we're doing hidden from the gods.' Donan looked at Beran from beneath his brows like a man who regrets what he has said and hopes it may have gone unnoticed.

Beran lifted his head and regarded the younger man. He was almost sure Donan was short of wits. Still, almost was not sure enough. Donan's eyes slid from Beran's and he turned fully away to stare into the forest again.

'What are you talking about, lad?' Beran put a hand on his shoulder. 'What has this to do with Queen Morgana?'

Still chewing on his thumbnail, Donan seemed not to have heard.

'Donan.' Beran batted the hand away from Donan's mouth, making the young man startle and turn to him, his face frozen in shock. Then it clenched into a scowl.

'I know who it is we're to kill, Beran,' he said. 'Red Tooth told me this morning. He got it off Nabor.' He shook his head. 'But I shouldn't say. Not my place.'

'Tell me,' Beran said.

'Can't.' Donan shook his head some more.

'Donan.'

'No, Beran. Can't.'

Beran reached out and grabbed hold of Donan's left ear, and the young man's eyes bulged. 'Tell me or I'll take this lug and sell it to that big bastard in Venta Belgarum who's missing one.'

Donan was all grimace but Beran held on to him.

'Thought we were . . . friends,' the young man said.

'We're not friends,' Beran said, giving the ear a last savage tug before letting go. 'And I won't ask you again.'

Donan straightened and put a hand to his reddening ear and blew out his cheeks before turning to glance back at Nabor, who was moving from man to man with a word here, a joke there. Playing the general to this company of thieves and murderers.

Donan's eyes came back to Beran. They were round beneath the rim of his leather skull cap, upon which a drop of water splashed, wetting Beran's cheek. 'There'll be gold and silver. Coin.' Donan grinned. 'Jewels. The treasures of Caer Colun. That's what we're here for, Beran. We're to make sure they get to Queen Morgana before King Cynric gets his hands on them.' He leant towards Beran, his tortured ear seemingly forgotten. 'Nabor says there can be no survivors. Not one, Beran. We're to kill them all.'

Beran's eyes scoured the younger man's. 'But you said there's one in particular we're to kill. Who is it?'

Donan grinned. 'Someone who won't take much killing.'

Beran reached out and grabbed hold of Donan by the neck of his tunic. 'Who, Donan?' Something made him look up, north-east through the rising mist and air now restless with buzzing insects. He growled a curse.

They were coming.

'Move!' Nabor hissed. They moved, every man careful not to disturb the forest floor as they took up their pre-arranged positions behind trees and furze either side of the old drovers' track. Beran stood amongst the shallow roots of a great beech, spear in one hand, his other arm cuffing at sweat which was already gathering at his brow and threatening to run into his eyes.

The day was warming quickly, the air thickening. Sweat crawled down his back between his shoulder blades and down his shins beneath the woollen leg bindings. He pressed his face against the tree trunk and closed his eyes, feeling the coolness of the smooth, damp bark on his skin, resting for a moment. Something about the smell – the green lichen perhaps – reminded him of the sea, carried him back across years. He pulled his face away and now he could hear voices and the scuffing of hooves and the creak of a carriage whose iron-shod wheels rolled over the ancient track like far distant thunder.

He clenched his jaw and took a long, deep breath, and it was all he could do not to edge his face around that trunk to catch a glimpse of whoever was unknowingly walking into their trap. How many would they be? Not too many warriors, he supposed, for most of Caer Colun's spearmen would be dead at the walls or in the streets, or fighting still, perhaps, as their homes burned or smouldered in the dawn. Some warriors, though, if they had snuck out of the doomed town with gold and silver and the treasures of that famed Roman fort. Or else that treasure would not get far in this land of thieves and cut-throats and Saxon war bands.

The old feeling then. A fluttering in the muscles of his thighs and upper arms. The quickening of his heart and the brightening of the day, as though he had previously seen the world through a linen gauze which now fell away. The old feeling before a fight. The years had taken much, and given much that was unwanted in return, but they had not dulled the old battle thrill, and now he let the spate of it course through his blood because he knew it would make him faster than his years.

From where he stood, he could see some of the others waiting silent and still behind other great beech pillars. The giant Blandigan with a spear in one hand, a long-hafted axe in the other. Red Tooth in his iron helmet from whose crown hung a fox's tail, his yellow-painted shield held so that it would not be seen by those on the path, and his right hand gripping a fine sword. Yann, crouching behind his own tree, grey in mail, a hand axe in each fist, and, furthest away, in a long tunic of iron rings and clutching spear and a shield covered in tanned leather, Nabor ap Nabor, who would give the signal.

The creak of the carriage was louder now. An ox bellowed and snorted, and Beran knew that at least some of the approaching party had passed Nabor and Red Tooth. He could hear talking, a man telling another of the Saxon he had killed on the town wall: a giant of a man with an axe as tall as he was. He could hear the clump and scuff of feet, men's and beasts', and the groans of the vehicle as it was pulled in and out of a hole in the path, and the squeak of its axle, and now even the buzzing flies which plagued the oxen and horses.

Beran silently commanded his body to obey him during whatever came next. He took a breath and let it slowly out.

One. Two. Three . . .

'Now!' cried Nabor, breaking cover, rushing in, and Beran strode out to see him thrust his spear into the neck of a warrior who had turned too late. Beran saw his companions falling upon the column, hacking and stabbing at red-cloaked warriors who all too late saw death coming out of the morning mist. The big Roman carriage had stopped, the ox-driver sitting upon it whipping the reins and striking the animals with a long goad, screaming at them to 'Go on! Go on!' But the oxen wouldn't move and instead stood lowing in their yokes, lifting their heads and muzzles, their glistening nostrils flaring as they inhaled the scents of fear and blood.

Red Tooth was snarling as he scythed a man down. Blandigan roared as he thrust his spear into a man's shield again and again, driving him back until the man fell and dropped his shield and tried to crawl away on hands and knees. The giant hurled his axe and it turned once, haft over head, and planted itself in the back of the man's skull, pitching him forward, dead before his face scuffed the earth.

'Kill them all!' Nabor yelled, pointing his spear. 'Anything that breathes.'

An arrow blurred past Beran's head and took a man in his eye socket, dropping him to his knees, where he screamed, clutching uselessly at the shaft. Beran walked past him to face a spearman whose fate was now entwined with Beran's own and perhaps had always been. The man stood on the balls of his feet, weight slightly forward, spear in his right hand, shield in his left, eyes glaring at Beran over the rim of that shield. He jabbed with the spear but Beran was still out of range and he saw sweat coursing from beneath the man's helmet into the beard on his cheeks. Saw the terror in the man's eyes. Confusion too, because this man from Caer Colun knew that these were not Saxons who had lain in wait to kill him, but Britons.

Beran closed the gap between them and out snaked that spear again, but Beran sidestepped and swept his own shaft to the left, knocking the man's spear wide as he himself stepped in, bringing the butt of his spear round two-handed to hammer it against the shield which the man had raised just in time. Both men stepped back, and the Caer Colun spearman turned his face and spat onto the ground and lifted his chin in a gesture that said he accepted death, but only for a price.

Around them it was a slaughter. Shrieks of pain and ruin rent the dawn. Blood flew in the mist. The rasp and clash of steel on steel. The wet *chunk* of flesh being cut. Beran despised the warrior before him, for what sort of man would leave his spear-brothers to die on Caer Colun's walls? Would abandon women and children to the lusts and cruelties and savage whims of the Saxons? And yet, Beran knew full well what sort of man. He rolled his shoulders and came forward, and their spear shafts met again, once, twice, a third time, then Beran feinted high, and the Caer Colun man bought the ruse and lifted his shield, so Beran dropped to one knee and thrust the spear up under the shield and into the belly behind. The man grunted and dropped his spear and staggered backwards, pressing his free hand to the wound.

Beran dug the butt of his spear into the dirt track and pushed himself up onto his feet, then walked to where the man leant against a tree, paling, dying, grimacing, his shield discarded now and both blood-slathered hands futilely pushing at a steaming swell of purple viscera that would no more return to its proper place than would any deed once done be undone. The man looked up at Beran, their eyes meeting briefly as Beran swept his spear, the blade ripping the Caer Colun man's throat in a crimson spray. He fell sideways and Beran turned to see Stenes sitting astride another man, working away with the long Saxon knife, and Blandigan standing before one of the oxen, bringing the poll of his axe down onto the animal's skull with a loud, splintering crack. The beast's eyes rolled white and its forelegs gave way and then the whole steaming, fly-bedevilled mass collapsed in a heap, pulling its companion's head down beneath their shared yoke.

'Not the oxen, you idiot!' Nabor ap Nabor bellowed at the giant, 'unless you want to haul that thing yourself! Balor's arse!'

Blandigan threw his arms and the long axe out wide as if to say he had only been following orders.

'Beran!' Yann called, and Beran spun to face a spearman who had somehow escaped the butchery and now saw a chance to blood the enemy. He was only three strides from Beran, spear gripped in both hands, its blade glinting in a shaft of sunlight, but Dyfnwal had already hurled his own spear. It streaked in the dawn, and Beran heard the *thock* as it drove into the man's chest, throwing him back off his feet.

Beran and others of the band looked around. Some had already begun scavenging amongst the dead for coins and brooches, weapons and buckles and good leather straps, and for anything to eat.

'They're running!' someone yelled, 'two of 'em!' and Beran and Blandigan looked up to see two men haring off into the trees in different directions, their red cloaks flying behind them, dry sticks snapping beneath their feet.

'Must've been hiding,' Stenes said, standing up from his kill and wiping his blade through a scrap of red cloth.

'Stay with the wagon,' Nabor commanded Red Tooth, then turned to Stenes and Dyfnwal. 'You two with me!' He looked at Konan. 'You get the other bastard,' he said, and Konan nodded and gestured at two others to follow him. They all discarded shields and threw off any heavy gear, then set off like hounds after a pair of foxes, loping between the trees and yelping with the thrill of it.

Beran turned back to the forest track and ran his eyes over the scene. No one could say Nabor ap Nabor's men didn't know how to kill. Beran counted fourteen men of Caer Colun lying dead or nearly dead among the beech trees and the strange fog hanging in the forest. It was a slaughter. Just two of their own had been killed, both men who had only recently joined them. It was usually the way of it. Last to join, first to die. Because the killing is easy, it's the not being killed that takes practice.

Tonight, wherever they found themselves on the road, they would drink to those men. They would drink and feast in the exhausted but exultant flush that hits a man after killing, when he knows it could be his own name on his companions' wine-slick lips. Then, the dead would be all but forgotten.

'You three,' Red Tooth said to Yann and the two standing nearest to him, 'go back up the track. It's going to take us some time to sort this mess out.' He gestured at the dead ox and its suffering twin, which was snorting and lowing in helpless rage, its fierce breath blowing detritus across the damp ground. Then he kicked a dead man, sending flies buzzing up from the red gash in the corpse's throat. 'We need to know if more of these Roman bastards are coming.'

'Why us?' Yann jerked his chin towards the carriage: a heavy Roman raeda the likes of which Beran had not seen for many years. A great big thing with sides and a canvas roof. 'You're not the only one who wants to know what's in there.'

'We'll wait for Nabor before we open it,' Red Tooth said. He pointed north with his spear. 'Now go!'

Yann tilted his head back, eyes narrow slits of suspicion, then grunted something to his companions and turned, and the three of them set off along the woodland trail, stepping over or around the dead men littering it.

Red Tooth barely waited until they were out of earshot, then turned to Blandigan and banged the blade of his spear against the side of the Roman carriage. 'Get it open,' he said.

Beran looked at Donan, who lifted his eyebrows and gripped his own spear like a man steeling himself to an unsavoury task, while Blandigan thrust his spear into the ground and approached the raeda, glancing at Hygwydd and Beran as he put a big hand on the door latch and lifted the axe in his other hand.

Beran and the others closed in around him, spears ready.

Red Tooth lifted his bearded chin. 'Open it.'

Blandigan lifted the latch and pulled the door open, and Beran saw darkness within and nothing more, because Blandigan leant forward to peer in, his huge body blocking the view, as the serpentine morning mist swirled around the giant's legs and up as if seeking a way inside the vehicle.

A man shouted, and Blandigan grunted and staggered back from the raeda, dropping his axe and lifting his big hands to his chest where they fast turned red and slick. A grey-bearded man tried to clamber out of the carriage, slashing his sword this way and that, but Red Tooth stepped in and speared him in the side, and the man grimaced and growled as Hygwydd and Donan took hold of him and dragged him clear.

Beran turned and looked at Blandigan stumbling off amongst the trees, clutching at the wound which would surely kill him.

'Bastard,' Hygwydd rasped. He had thrown the Caer Colun man onto the ground and now stood over him, his spear poised to finish the old warrior off, while Donan went after Blandigan. So Beran turned back to the raeda, lifted his spear blade protectively and peered inside. It took a moment for his eyes to adjust, then he saw amongst the piled boxes and oak chests two pale, frightened faces in the dark. A woman and a boy, their round eyes staring back at him.

Red Tooth shouldered him aside, growling, 'Out of my way, old man,' as he pulled himself up and into the carriage. 'What have we got here, then?' he said, his words muffled now he was inside the thing. A moment later the boy was flung out and Beran took hold of him by the neck of his red cloak, which was pinned at the shoulder with a fine-looking golden fibula that winked in a shaft of sunlight.

'Kill him, Beran,' Red Tooth shouted from within.

The woman screamed, but the sound was cut off, as if she was being strangled, and Beran looked into the boy's face and did not like what he saw there. Screwed up and red as a rowan berry, that face.

'Get your hands off me! Let me go!' he yelled in a thin, reedy voice, swinging his arms and his little fists, kicking out at Beran. 'Let me go!'

'Keep still, boy,' Beran told him, wincing as a small booted foot connected with his swollen right knee. 'Keep still, damn you!'

'Let me go, wretch! I command you!'

Hygwydd laughed at that. 'I think the little lord likes you, Beran.'

Beran shook the boy and again growled at him to keep still.

'Mercy on the child,' said the greybeard lying curled up on himself at Hygwydd's feet as though trying to stop his own life pouring out of the terrible spear wound in his side.

'Shut your mouth!' Hygwydd spat and jabbed the butt of his spear into the man's face, breaking his cheekbone. But the man took the pain, barely letting his eyes fall from the boy.

'Mercy on him, I beg you,' the man slurred through broken bones, bright blood spilling from the corner of his mouth into his grey beard. Then his eyes seemed to sharpen on Beran and, even in his pain, even as the shadow of death crept upon him, he tried to rise. 'You,' he said. 'You!'

'Stay down, you Roman bastard.' Hygwydd hit him in the temple this time. The man's head dropped to the ground, but still he turned his bloodied face, his eyes finding Beran's again. They were dulled from the blow. 'You know me,' he managed through a slack, bloody mouth. 'You know me, as I know you.'

Another scream from the woman – Beran assumed she was the boy's mother – inside the carriage. The whole thing was moving now, rocking like a boat on a swell, and the woman's terrified, plaintive cries seeped out through the canvas roof into the misty morning.

'How can it be you?' the dying man said, squinting at Beran now as though he did not trust his own eyes. Beran gave him no answer, but looked back at the boy who was still thrashing wildly in his grasp like a fish pulled from a withy trap.

'Friend of yours, Beran?' Hygwydd asked.

Donan had returned. He glanced at Hygwydd, then Beran. 'He's dead,' he said, indicating with his chin back towards the trees where Blandigan lay. He shook his head. 'Never thought I'd see that.'

'Forget Blandigan. You know who this little lord's father was?' Hygwydd asked Donan, pointing his spear at the boy.

Donan looked at the boy, scratched at a pockmark on his cheek and frowned, his bottom lip protruding. 'Someone more important than us,' he said.

'Course he's important, shit for brains,' Hygwydd said. 'He's King Constantine's son. Whelped on that young queen in there.' He nodded at the Roman raeda. 'The old goat.'

'Let me go or you'll pay!' the boy threatened them. 'Leave my mother alone or I'll kill you!' He kicked Beran's knee again, but the old warrior hardly felt it because his mind was reeling.

'How could you?' the grey-bearded warrior at Hygwydd's feet managed, the words slewing in blood and spittle. 'Why?' His broken face made for a terrible sight, the bones collapsing in on themselves.

'Ah, it's the way of the world,' Hygwydd replied, though Beran knew that the man had been talking to him and only him. Because the warrior *did* know Beran, and Beran knew him, no matter the years that had passed since last they had laid eyes on one another. 'You needn't concern yourself with it now,' Hygwydd said, 'for which you ought to thank me,' and with that he lifted his spear and thrust it down, the blade slicing deep into the man, right through him and into the ground beneath. The man died with a long sigh, his eyes never leaving Beran's. Never closing, not even when his heart had clenched and thumped for the last time.

'Kill the boy,' Red Tooth called from inside the raeda, eliciting another agonized scream from the boy's mother, which was smothered by Red Tooth's growling and then cut short by a blow.

'You heard him,' Hygwydd gnarred at Beran. 'No one left alive. Prince or not. Nabor's orders, or we don't get paid.'

Beran looked into that young face. The fear was obvious, and the anger, but there was something else too. Something implacable. An arrogance. A grim doggedness that ordinarily had no place in one so young, yet all but confirmed whose whelp this was.

'I said, kill him.' Red Tooth was climbing out of the carriage, pulling up his trews.

'Close your eyes, boy,' Beran said.

'Let me go!' the boy screamed.

So Beran shook him hard. 'I said close your eyes, damn you!' he roared, and there was enough steel edge in his voice to put a deeper fear in the boy now, because he went still and quiet and he looked into Beran's eyes, perhaps for the first time. There was a question in those eyes and Beran tried to answer it without speaking. He let go of the boy and the boy closed his eyes and lifted his arms and put them over his face.

'That's it, lad,' Beran said in a low voice.

'Do I have to do everything myself?' Red Tooth asked, drawing his sword and stepping towards Beran and the boy.

Beran turned and thrust the spear at Red Tooth, who twisted away but not fast enough, so the spear blade pierced his left shoulder and he yelled in surprise. Beran pulled the blade free and spun, but Hygwydd was on him, his own spear streaking for Beran's chest. Beran blocked the thrust with his spear shaft and scythed the blade across, ripping open Hygwydd's cheek and sending him reeling.

'Old bastard!' Red Tooth bellowed, lurching forward, and swung his sword, and Beran felt the blade cut through his leather coat and the wool beneath and the flesh beneath that. He stumbled backward and turned and hurled the spear, which flew through the rising mist and took Hygwydd in the belly. Then he twisted back, drawing his sword, upon which he caught Red Tooth's next swing, the ringing of the blades unnatural amongst the trees and twining woodbine. Even wounded, Red Tooth was fast and dangerous, but before he could strike again, Beran threw himself at the man, driving him back against the Roman carriage and bringing his sword up to thrust its wicked point into Red Tooth's stomach and drive it deep.

They were face to face, close enough that Beran could smell the man's sour breath and last night's wine, and something surprising too: sweet violet and rose. A rich woman's scent. An aroma that carried Beran back across the long hard years to another time.

'Why?' Red Tooth rasped, the hatred in his eyes replaced by confusion now, as Beran twisted the blade in his flesh and pulled it free. Red Tooth slumped to the ground, head lolling forward like a dead weight, his back against one of the raeda's big wheels.

'He's just a boy,' Beran said, gasping for breath.

A scream then, and Beran turned to see Donan coming at him with Blandigan's axe, his eyes wild as he shrieked. Beran sidestepped as the axe came down, embedding itself in the side of the carriage, then he swept his sword backhanded, taking Donan's head from his shoulders. For a heartbeat or two, the body stayed upright on its feet, blood spraying from the wound as the head rolled across the ground. It came to rest sidewards on the forest path.

'Fool,' Beran muttered, looking down at Donan's face and those eyes held open in a frozen expression of surprise. 'Why did you have to do that, you damned fool?'

He looked back at the boy, who had not moved, though Beran could see his face through a gap in his forearms and supposed he had seen the whole thing. 'Boy, see that bent tree over there?' he said, through gritted teeth because the wound Red Tooth had given him was announcing itself now. 'The one by the furze?'

The boy lowered his arms to his sides and nodded.

'There's a leather knapsack there. Bring it to me.'

The boy eyed him suspiciously, then looked at the carriage. 'Mother,' he called.

'I'll see to your mother, just fetch my gear,' Beran said. The boy didn't move. 'I said go!' Beran yelled, and the boy frowned, looked once more at the raeda, then ran off into the woods.

Beran pulled the door of the carriage wide enough to climb inside. The boy's mother was dead, as he had known she would be. Red Tooth had crushed her throat. There were scratch marks on the inside of the carriage where she had grasped and flailed in vain, and Beran wondered if he could have stopped Red Tooth before. He doubted it. Too late now. There she was. Long, black hair like a veil, half obscuring her white face. A dead queen of a dead town, lying in a heap amongst the bench furs.

Beran shook his head. The interior smelled of the violet and rose unguent which the young woman had worn on her pale skin, and it caught in Beran's throat, making him feel sick as he perched on the seat beside her and set to work with his knife, levering open one of the chests upon which the three travellers had rested their feet, judging by the dirt on the lids.

His eyes were not what they once were, yet by the morning light shafting through the carriage's open door he could see that he had found what he was looking for. Coin. Lots of coin. He grabbed a handful and with his other hand took one at a time, holding each up to the light to see what it was. There was a bronze sestertius of Antoninus, a silver denarius of Septimius Severus, and other various denarii. There were silver siliquae, and small silver-washed bronzes, and two gold solidi of Magnus Maximus. He put these and another handful into the purse on his belt. Amongst the piled coin there were necklaces, one of gold set with green emeralds, one of jet and ivory, and another of silver adorned with drops of amber. There were pearl earrings and bracelets of twisted gold, and twisted silver neck torcs and rings set with precious stones, and he imagined this dead queen's servants hastily filling these chests in the chaos of Caer Colun's fall. How many silver rings had been secreted away or slipped onto work-worn fingers amidst the turmoil? How many necklaces were pulled from the pile and fastened around necks which had never known silver or beads of glass covered with turquoise glaze? Those would all be in Saxon hands now.

Beran closed the lid and shoved the chest closer to the door before climbing out. The boy was standing nearby, watching him, but Beran ignored him and dragged the coin chest to the edge and tried to lift it. Too heavy. He'd never carry it. He pulled it out and it thumped onto the ground with a rattle, and he was relieved to see that the wood had not split. Then he bent and began to drag the thing across the forest floor, while the ox still yoked to its dead companion bellowed.

'Where's Mother?' the boy asked. Beran assumed the boy was afraid of him, which was why he kept his distance. Or perhaps he was more afraid of the Roman carriage. Of what was in that dark space.

'She's resting,' Beran said, not looking up. His back was already complaining, but he kept moving. Dragging the chest foot by foot towards the bent tree.

'I want my mother,' the boy said.

'I told you, she's resting. Leave her be.' He got the coin chest to the bent tree and the rotting remains of a beech, and positioned it behind the deadfall. Then he fetched Blandigan's axe from where it lay halfway between Donan's head and the rest of him, and went back into the carriage and took the dead queen's green cloak and returned to the chest.

'That's my mother's,' the boy said, flinty-eyed, his nostrils flaring. He was still standing there holding the knapsack, watching Beran, suspicious as a juvenile hawk.

'She said I could borrow it,' Beran replied, hacking at a leafy sapling with the axe. He laid the queen's cloak over the coin chest and put the sapling over it and moved it around until he was satisfied, then he went back the way he had come, scuffing at the ground with his boots, moving the leaf mould about to disguise the track which the heavy chest had made.

He heard voices and looked up. 'Come on,' he said to the boy.

The boy did not move. He was looking at the carriage.

'We have to go,' Beran said.

'I want Mother.'

Beran fetched his spear and went to the boy and gave him Blandigan's axe. 'Think you can carry this? Always useful to have an axe.'

The boy was glaring at him. 'You killed them all.'

'You can thank me later.' Beran turned and walked away. He had made five strides before he realized that the boy had not moved, so he turned back. 'If you don't come with me, they'll kill you.'

The boy narrowed his eyes. 'Will you kill me?'

Beran shook his head. 'I don't kill boys.' Still the boy did not move. 'Stay if you want,' Beran said.

They heard voices again, and the boy looked to the east. He lifted the axe slightly, his little hands clenching and unclenching on the haft.

'You want to stay and fight them, that's up to you,' Beran said. Then he turned and walked away into the trees. And the boy followed.

2

Belatucadrus, the Fair Shining One

'WHAT'S WRONG WITH YOU?' the boy asked. They had been moving west through the forest as the sun rose above the huge green canopies of beech and ancient oak, now and then dappling the floor with golden fire as a breeze moved through the leaves above.

'I'm just old,' Beran said. He knew the boy was wondering why they were not moving faster.

'You're bleeding,' the boy said.

'That too,' he said. 'I'll deal with that when we stop to rest.' Beran looked over his shoulder as he had done countless times already, half expecting Nabor ap Nabor and the others to be in sight behind them, all but salivating like hounds caught up to the fox. 'And anyway, you couldn't go any faster than this with those little legs.' He returned his gaze to the forest ahead, but could almost hear the frown on the boy's face.

'Will Mother be there? At the resting place?'

'No.'

After another few paces the boy said, 'Because she's still resting?'

Beran felt his own frown then. 'Yes.'

The boy seemed to be struggling with Blandigan's axe now. He had carried it a long way. The crescent head was thick iron and much wider than the span of Beran's hand, and the hardwood haft had been strengthened with metal bands, so whereas the axe had seemed fitting in the giant Blandigan's grasp, the boy's fingers reached barely beyond halfway around its handle.

'You're limping.' The boy was looking up at Beran beside him.

'Just the way I walk,' Beran said.

After a moment the boy took to walking with a faltering, laboured step. Beran knew he was mimicking him. 'When you're as old as me, you'll limp too,' he growled. 'If you live that long. Which I don't expect you will.'

The boy seemed to consider this. 'Why did your friends want to kill me?'

'They're not my friends,' Beran said. 'They were paid to kill you.'

'Silver and gold?' the boy asked.

Beran nodded. 'And wine. And . . . other things.'

'Then, why . . .' the boy let the unfinished question drift off on the warm air, but Beran knew it would be back. Sure enough: 'Why did you kill them? You could have been rich.'

Now it was Beran's turn to chew on his thoughts. 'I was rich once. I don't miss it.'

The boy's eyes narrowed as if in disbelief. 'Why aren't you rich now?' he asked.

'You talk a lot, boy.'

The air was thick with droning insects. Beran was damp with sweat but he kept up the pace which he knew would see his knees and ankles swollen when at last they found somewhere to make camp for the night. Better that than stopping to rest now, because Nabor ap Nabor would surely know what had happened and come after him. They would all come after him, and Dyfnwal might be a lazy, wine-addled murderer but he could track a snowflake in a blizzard. Nabor himself was even better.

'So, where are we going?' the boy asked after a while.

'Somewhere else,' Beran said. 'Away from the men that want to kill us. Away from Saxons. Away from the Queen.'

'My mother?' the boy said.

'Queen Morgana,' Beran said.

The boy was quiet for a while. Then he said, 'My mother is dead, isn't she?'

Beran considered the lie, but decided against it. It wasn't his job to be a father to the boy. 'Yes, she's dead,' he said.

'You lied,' the boy accused him. 'You said she was resting. You're a liar.'

'Been called worse,' Beran said.

The boy fell quiet again, this time for a long while, and Beran didn't mind it. Eventually the boy spoke again. 'If my father was alive, he would kill you and your friends.'

'I told you, they're not my friends. Thought I made that clear . . . you know, by killing them.'

The boy ignored that. 'After my father killed you, he would ride out with his best warriors and kill Queen Morgana for her treachery.'

Beran grunted. 'If your father was alive, he'd be older than the standing stones and creaking like a barn door in a storm.' Beran walked on but he knew the boy had stopped and so he stopped too and turned around, silently cursing the loss of momentum. His joints would not thank him when they began to walk again. The boy was standing there amongst the trees, holding up Blandigan's axe as though he meant to do something with it.

'My father was a great warrior,' the boy said.

'If you say so.'

'He fought the Saxons all his life. Fought with Arthur the Lord of War.'

'Your father tried to kill Arthur,' Beran said. 'One dawn at Tintagel. I was there.'

The boy eyed him suspiciously. 'I don't believe you.'

'That he tried to kill Arthur, or that I was there?'

'I don't believe any of it. You're an outlaw. A man who murders his own people. A man who kills children.'

'I didn't kill you,' Beran said.

The boy's hands were white on the haft of the axe. He took a step towards Beran and Beran thought he might actually swing that axe at him.

'I want my mother,' the boy said.

'I can't help you with that,' Beran said.

The boy's lip quivered. 'My father was a great king.' There were tears in his eyes. 'He killed more Saxons than you've ever seen.'

'Seen a lot of Saxons in my time, boy,' Beran muttered.

'He was a greater warrior than Lord Arthur. Maybe as great as Lancelot.'

A grunt escaped Beran's throat. 'We need to go, boy. We don't want to be standing here talking about the dead when Nabor ap Nabor and the rest of them get here.'

The boy looked behind him as a squirrel skittered up a tree trunk and vanished amongst the canopy. 'Who is he? This Nabor ap Nabor?'

Beran looked around, then fastened his eyes on the boy's eyes.

'You've seen what kind of man he is. Nabor kills for money. Not for Britain, or a king or lord. Not for kin and hearth . . . just for money.'

'Like you?' the boy asked.

That stung Beran a little. 'We need to go.'

The boy was eyeing Beran warily. 'Why should I go with you? You're an outlaw.'

'There are no laws these days,' Beran said. 'All that's long gone.'

The boy jerked the axe in his white-knuckled hands. 'I'm a prince. I will be a king.'

'A king of what?' Beran pointed to the north-east. 'Caer Colun is burning. The Saxons are kings of the ashes.'

The boy lifted his chin. 'A king is more than the lord of a town,' he said. 'He is the hope. Men will follow a king.'

In that moment the boy looked so like his father that Beran could not take his eyes off him. 'And that's why people want you dead, boy,' he said. 'The Saxons. Queen Morgana. Nabor ap Nabor. Plenty of other people who knew your father, I shouldn't wonder. All of them want you dead.'

The boy tilted his head on one side. 'But not you?' he asked.

'Not me,' Beran said. Then he turned and walked on. 'We need to go. Come or stay, boy,' he said over his shoulder. 'Makes no difference to me.' He walked on and did not look back, but he heard twigs snap and leaves crunch as the boy followed on behind.

They drank from a stream thronged with the bright little stars of yellow pimpernel, before continuing westward, not stopping again until the sun sank behind the hills before them and the light faded from the world. They rested a while in the gathering dark, amongst coppiced alder long abandoned. But they did not sleep; the boy because he was hungry and Beran because he knew they had not put enough distance between themselves and Nabor and the others. And so it wasn't long before they were moving again, their eyes having grown accustomed to the dark, aided by moon and starlight where the woodland canopy allowed.

Beran's knees were fire. His ankles molten iron. His feet ached, but most of his other ailments were absent, which was something. He knew, though, that when he stopped they would catch up with him, and then setting off again would be agony. *So, keep moving*, he told himself. *Keep moving and fool the body into thinking it is young again.*

35

'I'm hungry,' the boy said.

'I told you, I don't have any food,' Beran replied, looking for the stars to make sure they were still walking west. Two bats tumbled and flitted above, across a patch of dark sky.

'But I'm hungry,' the boy insisted.

'What do you expect me to do about it?' Beran growled.

The boy's face clenched in thought. 'You must be good at setting traps,' he said. 'You outlaws live here in the forest, don't you?'

'I can feed myself. Didn't ask for another mouth to feed.'

'I'm a prince.'

'A mouth's a mouth.'

Beran could almost feel the boy frowning in the dark from two feet away.

'We could set a snare like my father's hunters do. They catch hares and polecats and pine martens that way.'

'Not any more they don't,' Beran said. 'Look, boy, if we stop to set traps, we're more likely to catch one of the bastards who's after us. Or a Saxon. Or one of Queen Morgana's spearmen. We've got to keep moving.'

'So, we're going to Camelot?' the boy asked.

The name struck Beran like a blow to the chest. He stopped and the boy stopped with him. 'Why in Ban's name would we go to Camelot?' he asked.

'Because that's where Mother was taking me,' the boy said, looking up at him, and Beran realized he had not even considered where the fugitives from Caer Colun had been bound with their treasures and this heir to the kingdom. It made sense, of course, for where else was safe in Britain for the son of Constantine the Battle King? The man who had modelled himself on the Roman generals who once ruled in the Dark Isles, and who had waged war against the Saxons for the last sixty years.

'Lady Iselle wrote to my mother many times since my father died, begging her to go to Camelot where we would be safe.'

Another name, another blow. 'So why didn't you?' Beran asked. 'Your mother must've known Caer Colun could not hold out for ever. Even if the great Constantine had still been alive.'

'Mother said we would never abandon the people. Lady Iselle could not take all of them to live within Camelot's walls.'

'Well, your mother's people are slaves now, or dead. Or living beneath the sky like us,' Beran said.

'How long will it take to get to Camelot?' the boy asked.

'We're not going to Camelot.'

'But that is where I'm to go,' the boy said.

'Then go.' Beran lifted his chin to the south-west.

The boy looked off in the same direction. The forest was deep and dark and somewhere out there an owl screeched. His face swung back to Beran, dark brows crowding narrow eyes. 'I command you to take me,' he said.

Beran almost laughed. 'I don't recall swearing an oath to serve you, boy.'

'But I'm a prince.'

'So you keep saying. Still, you're not my prince, and your father was not my king.' He pointed his spear in their direction of travel. 'Now, let's go.'

They walked in silence for many miles, following the moon westward. Once, they heard the snapping of sticks and a rustling and they thought Nabor's men had caught up with them, so they waited, low and taut in the dark, Beran gripping his spear in readiness, the boy holding Blandigan's axe in his little hands, round eyes searching the gloom. But it turned out to be a roe deer foraging on a beech sapling, upwind and unaware, until something else in the forest spooked it and it ghosted away in the moon-silvered murk.

'We'll get our heads down,' Beran said, looking around for somewhere safe to rest. 'It'll be dawn soon enough but I need to sleep. Just for a while.'

The boy yawned and pulled his cloak of deep red around himself with a shiver and nodded. Soon, Beran found an ancient oak which was hollow, though it still boasted a clutch of gnarled branches thick with leaves.

'We're going to sleep in here?' the boy asked as he followed Beran, who was squeezing himself in through an opening in the sapwood.

'There aren't many Roman palaces hereabouts,' Beran said, dropping his knapsack inside the musty, earth-smelling place and leaning his spear against the inner wall. Slowly, he lowered himself down until he was sitting with his back against the wood, and the boy did the same, looking small and vulnerable in the shadowy interior of the once mighty tree.

Beran steeled himself, wincing as he pulled at the rent in his leather tunic and the woollen tunic beneath, lifting away the crusted blood until he felt the cool air touch the wound which Red Tooth had given him. He had known the cut was not deep. The blood had dried in a thick, dark crust, but he would have to wash the wound out and lace it with honey to clean it. A poultice of adder weed too, if he could, to help close the cut flesh.

Still, his body healed well, even at his age. It had always healed after wounds, so that he'd sometimes wondered if the gods played their part in it, keeping him alive. Prolonging the misery of his life, because the gods were cruel.

What gods? he wondered now, for the gods of Britain were long gone. Hounded by Roman gods and scattered by Saxon deities after them. Usurped by the insidious, creeping Christian god. Forsaken by the peoples of the Dark Isles and, with no druids left in the land, now never dreamt to.

'I'm hungry,' the boy griped, pressing a hand to his belly.

'You'll live.' Beran closed his eyes. He heard the boy climb to his feet.

'I'm going to find something to eat.'

Beran opened his eyes. 'Sit down.'

The boy loomed in that small, dark place, Beran's spear in his hands. 'I've hunted roe deer before.'

Beran grunted. 'You'll never get close.'

The boy frowned. 'I'll find bilberries.'

'Not in these woods.'

'I'll pick some yellow chanterelles,' the boy said. 'Mother cooks them in butter at this time of year.'

'Got some butter, have you?' Beran asked him.

'No, but . . .'

'Can't light a fire,' Beran said. 'Can't risk the smoke.'

The boy set his jaw, his eyes sharp as flint in the gloom. 'Well, I'll find something.' He turned to clamber out of the tree hollow.

'Sit down, boy.' Beran gestured to the spot where the boy had been sitting. 'You're not going anywhere.'

The boy was halfway out into the night when he twisted around and glared at Beran. 'Who are you to give me orders? My father was King Constantine. You are nothing but a thief and a murderer. A man without a hearth or lord. You are *nothing*!'

Before he knew it, Beran was up, the neck of the boy's red cloak snarled around his hand. 'You'll do as I say, you little turd.' He ripped the spear from the boy's grasp and threw him down, and he hit the ground hard. 'You little bastard! I never asked to be lumbered with you. You'll stay here until I say you can leave, and if you keep whining about food, I'll cut your damned throat, do you hear me? Do you have any idea the trouble you've put me to? Nabor ap Nabor is not the sort of man you want to cross. We'll have to sleep with our eyes open.'

The boy was winded. He lay on his side, his face turned down to the earth as he quietly gasped for breath. Or perhaps he was crying.

Beran looked out of the split in the tree to the night beyond, lending all sensory perception to his ears. The leaves of the trees whispered in the cool breeze, a soft susurration whose meaning men no longer understood. Nearby, some creature made its way along a trail, stopping now and then, sniffing for intruders it could not see. Beran turned and saw that the boy had dragged himself back to his place against the trunk wall. His eyes were on Beran. Hate-filled eyes. Eyes that Beran knew, though that was not the boy's fault.

'We'll eat tomorrow,' he said in a low voice, leaning the spear again and sitting in the dark. 'Get some sleep, boy. We'll find food tomorrow.'

The boy did not reply, though his silence was loud in that musty place. Beran made himself as comfortable as he could and, despite what he'd said about Nabor ap Nabor, he closed his eyes, hoping that dreams would not come. That memories would not find him.

'I never asked you to help me,' the boy said. 'I don't want you.'

Beran said nothing. He was already drifting away.

The villa was buzzing like a hive. Servants and slaves hurried this way and that, bearing amphorae of wine and precious olive oil from distant sun-baked lands, and earthen jars of butter, and fish oil for the lamps, and barrels of mead, and fowls that needed plucking, and joints of salted meat and bundles of clean rushes for the floor and furs for the beds, and baskets of onions, parsnips and beans, cherries, plums and sour blackberries. The air was fragrant with the smell of bread baking in the ovens and of the dried lavender hung from beams to sweeten the stench of the soldiers who would soon fill the small hall.

It was the end of the hungry time when rats and mice fight over the dust in the grain stores and folk must forage amongst wood and hedgerow for food. Now, men, women and children thronged the fields for harvest. From sunrise to sunset they worked with sickle and scythe, cutting and binding first wheat and rye, then barley and oats, breaking their backs to hoard precious grain while the weather was kind. Yet even these folk came in from the fields now, chattering like birds. Sweat-sheened and ruddy-faced from labour, and grey from the fields and plagued by flies but eager as children.

Because the great warlord was coming.

Uturius was what those who still pretended to be Roman called him. To most he was Uther ap Constantine ap Tahalais, warlord and prince, for his father had been king in Dumnonia for ten years before a Pictish blade sent him from this world to the next. Uther the Flame, bards whispered, Uther having burned seventy Saxon prisoners in the very ship in which they had crossed the Morimaru with spears and shields and heads full of dreams of taking this land as their own. Uther the Cruel, whispered others. Uther Crow, some called him, for he had a thirst for war and it was said those rasping birds followed Uther wherever he went, knowing that dead flesh would soon be found. Uther the Brave was how one of the songs had it, and no one would have dared dispute it or even speak whilst that song was on a bard's lips. Now, Uther, fighter of Saxons and brother of Ambrosius Aurelius, High King of the Britons, was coming, and the boy was afraid.

'Listen to me, Arthur,' his mother had said, taking his hand and leading him into the shadows beyond the bronze bloom of the nearest rushlight, 'you stay away while Uther is here.' She was bent over him, her fingers digging into his shoulders. 'Stay in the stables or go down to the stream,' she said under her breath, 'but do not come to the house. Do not let any of them see you. Promise me.'

He frowned, watching a servant strew meadowsweet and mint amongst the floor rushes. 'But I want to see the warriors, Mother,' he pleaded, turning his face back to hers. 'I want to see their swords and helmets. I want to hear of battles.'

'Listen to me,' his mother hissed, and he flinched because her fingers were hurting him now. There were tears in her eyes and he did not like that, and he began to feel afraid. 'You mustn't come here until they are gone. Be anywhere but here. Sleep in the barn and watch from afar if you must, but wait until tomorrow, when they're gone, before you come out.'

He clenched his jaw and balled his fists, angry at her for asking this of him. But he did not speak.

'Arthur.' She dipped her chin, her eyes riveted to his. 'Promise me.'

He waited another four beats of his heart.

'I promise,' he said.

Now, he stood at the end of the tree-lined avenue leading to the outer gate of the villa, watching spear blades and helmets glint in the morning light as the warriors of Dumnonia approached, raising the dust of the road in their wake.

At the head of the column was a knot of men on horseback and these held the boy's gaze like some spell or charm. They shone in bronze, steel and silver, these six, and even from that distance the boy knew which of them was Uther. To the boy's mind – and he knew that sometimes his imagination flew away with him – the battle god Belatucadrus, the Fair Shining One, cast that man in a glow distinct from that cast by the rising sun. Or perhaps it was the Roman god, Mars, who watched over Uther, for though Rome was fading from these Dark Isles like a dream, that god of war must have recognized a worthy warrior and been drawn to him even in his own waning.

Before he had run out to keep watch for the war band, Arthur had overheard folk giving their opinions as to the purpose of Uther's visit to the villa this day.

'Uther has come from killing Saxons and will choose more spearmen to take back to Tintagel,' a young tanner had said, as though it was obvious.

'He's just coming to bathe,' Brunor the blacksmith said, his own face slick with sweat and soot from the forge, 'for no doubt he'll be red with Saxon blood and reeking of Saxon piss.'

'I know what he's come sniffing for,' an old woman put in from her stool by the smokehouse where she sat at the quern grinding grain, her wrinkled, brown arm pulling the stone round and round. 'He's come to hump our Lady.' Her grin revealed a lonely tooth as the stones ground on, white flour spilling out from between them, dusting the cow hide beneath. 'Even the biggest warriors weaken for a woman like that. Aye, we'll hear the boards creaking tonight, mark my words.'

This got grins and nods from the others, but the thought sickened the boy, who affected not to notice when their eyes swung to him. He had heard such talk before and had hated Uther because of it, though he had never met the man. The thought of the filthy, grizzled warrior lying with his mother always brought the heat of anger to his cheeks. He wanted to protect her, even pictured himself challenging Uther, warning him at the end of a sword to stay away. Not that he owned a sword, but a spear wouldn't be hard to come by.

He did not think of such things now, though, as he watched the man approach at the head of his retinue. Did that make him a coward? Did it make him an unworthy son, to have put aside such thoughts so easily now that he was filled with awe by the sight before him?

They were less than an arrow-shot away. Perhaps close enough that Uther might make out his features, see the silver pin brooch at his shoulder and know that he was not one of the slaves, or the dog boy, or the son of one of the families who worked the land around the Lady Igraine's summer villa.

Best be away.

Just let me see his face, the boy silently asked. *Just a little closer so that I may see him properly.*

A dozen or so folk who had come in from the fields lined the road further out, calling out greetings to the spearmen, showering them with blessings and thanking them for defending Dumnonia against the Saxons, and against war bands from Powys, and the sheep thieves of Caer Gloui. Uther's men lifted their spears into the air in reply, grinning like conquering heroes.

A little closer.

He could see Uther properly now. The black beard and brows, the sharp nose and the hawk's eyes. He was broad and barrel-chested and thick at the neck, where a torc of twisted silver sat winking in the sun. His horse was as black as his beard and he rode it like a man who would rather be walking, though his ringmail and helmet, and the big dragon-painted shield strapped to the beast, would have weighed him down considerably were he on foot.

It was a cruel face, the boy thought. Or maybe just a hard one. Lord

Uther's brother was the High King, after all, and Uther was the right hand and sword of Ambrosius.

Those gyrfalcon's eyes, which had been watching the road ahead, now seemed to fix on the boy, and for two stuttering breaths the boy held that fierce gaze. Then he turned and ran back along the baked earth track between the old stone pine trees towards the villa.

He had tried to stay away. He had promised that he would, so he'd run down to the stream and checked the wicker traps and waded into the cool water to find they had caught three roach, two perch and four gudgeon, though he left them trapped. He swam for a while, scaring himself by imagining that the tendrils of slick green weed caressing his legs were the fingers of some misshapen creature or water spirit sent by Arawn to pull him down to the underworld. When he was shivering with cold, he climbed out and lay on the bank to dry, watching a hobby gliding high against the glare of the midday sun, and listening to the raucous chorus drifting to him from the rookeries in the near wood.

After that, he had skirted the timber palisade at the west end of the villa, close enough to hear Uther's spearmen on the other side of the wall, noisier than the rooks as they took their ease after the march, already deep in cups of ale and mead. They were setting up camp in the villa courtyard, for the Lady would not have so many filthy, rowdy men bed down in the house itself.

She had said the noise would bring on one of her headaches, but the boy suspected it was because she did not trust them with the Roman mosaic that was still mostly intact in the main room. The last time she had hosted spearmen in the house – a delegation from neighbouring Caer Gwinntguic – they had prised up two dozen of the little tiles when no one was around to see, so that when they had left, Igraine had discovered that the Roman goddess depicted in the mosaic had lost one of her breasts.

'It will be a warm night and they'll be used to sleeping outside,' she had told the servants.

'Will Lord Uther be sleeping outside, lady?' old Bricius had asked, one wispy grey eyebrow raised, and Igraine had given him the sort of look he deserved, for they both knew the answer to that.

At the western end of the villa the boy stood a while, listening to the rough voices within, hoping to hear Uther himself. He did not know

Uther's voice, but he thought that he would somehow recognize it when he heard it. Yet no voice stood out above another and he had promised his mother to keep away, so he had decided to go into the beech woods to look for sign of wolf or bear, though Iger the hunter had told him there had been no bears seen in Dumnonia since the legions.

Still, he could not wander so far unarmed. His mother would scold him for going such a distance anyway, but going into the great woods without a means of protecting himself? He would deserve the sting of the hazel switch across the back of his legs for that. Best slip back inside the walls and fetch a spear from the store.

How could he have known two of Uther's spearmen would be sharing a jug of beer by the door of the small brick building by the gatehouse where the bows and traps and the rest of the hunting gear was kept?

He had got past without them seeing him, knowing there was usually a spear or two in the larder, nestled between the beams of the low roof and hung with hare and pigeon, plover and goose. But there had been too many eyes around the house, too many busy feet and hands, which was why he now found himself standing behind the ancient wall hanging of woven flax which his mother had fastened in the dining room to keep out the draughts.

His feet ached from standing still so long. His whole body itched to move, but he fought it and held himself inert, keeping his breathing measured, in and out through his mouth because it was quieter. Even so, he could smell the greasy smoke from the fish-oil lamps and see around the edges of the hanging that the room was darkening as the diners feasted on all the treasures of the Lady's table. The boy had not eaten since daybreak and his mouth was slick at the thought of the roasted meats and mead, the fresh bread and olive oil, cheese and honey. Yet his stomach churned and he could not have eaten even were he at the table, because Uther was there. Twelve feet away, no more. His voice a low rumble, the words smothered by the delicate, trickling water sound of the lyre being plucked on the other side of the flaxen sheet behind which he hid.

The sound of that voice tightened the boy's stomach. Two winters ago, some hunters had caught a bear in the forests of far-off Gwynedd. They had been bringing the beast south, a rare and precious gift for King Ambrosius Aurelius, and had stopped at the villa to pay their respects to Lady Igraine. The bear had lost much of its savagery on its journey across the cantrefs and rounds of Britannia, half-starved and poked with spears and tormented by hounds, and yet when the boy had approached it, the creature had opened its pink mouth and given such a bellowing roar as had put ice in the boy's guts and clenched his heart. Hearing Uther's voice now had much the same effect.

Just keep still, he told himself. *They cannot sit here all night. Just keep still and quiet until there is a moment to slip away.*

Now and then he heard his mother, too, her voice the warm spiced wine to Uther's thick gruel. A few words here and there, though she and Prince Uther were not alone at the table and there were other voices weaving in and out of the thrum and the lyre's bright melody, the thumping of cups on the board and the scrape of knives on earthenware plates.

Goleuddydd, Igraine's younger sister, was there, and her husband Cilydd, whom the boy liked very much because Cilydd would let him handle his sword and heft his shield and, sometimes, would take him to Caer Gwinntguic to buy pigs and cattle for the estate, or iron to take back for Brunor to beat into sickles and blades, barrel hoops and arrowheads.

'Wine,' he heard Uther rumble, and not for the first time. The boy sensed one of the slaves pass close by, disturbing the wall hanging with an elbow and making him hold his breath because the lyre had fallen silent and, in that moment, he felt sure that everyone in the room knew he was there. That they could see him as a dark shape, perhaps, or see his feet beneath. Or else his mother's dog, Vala, was standing there, sniffing at the hanging, waiting for the boy to play with him, and any moment now one of the diners would pull back the sheet to see what Vala had found.

'General Gaus was an arrogant fool,' Uther growled, killing all other conversation.

'He's a dead fool now,' another man put in. 'Him and all his pretty horses.'

'I did not like the man but I could not deny the effectiveness of his equites Romani.' Uther said those last two words with scorn, and the boy resented it. 'If he'd have waited for my brother's spearmen, he and his men would still be alive and there would be Saxon blood in this bread. Saxon bone.' All other tongues were still then, and there was no sound in the room but that of a mouse scrabbling amongst the new sheaves of rushes on the floor. 'And you know what some are saying? That the king would not send spearmen, so Gaus had no choice but to fight alone. I swear by Balor, if I had been in Dumnonia I would have gone myself. I would have sent the Saxons screaming to their gods.' Uther grunted. 'Too late now. Saxon war bands are coming east. King Deroch cannot stop them, and without Gaus and his horse warriors riding along the southern shore watching for Saxon boats, it's too dangerous to stay.'

'I have my own spearmen,' Igraine said.

Uther laughed at that. A cold sound. 'You think two dozen old men can face down a Saxon wolf pack? A hundred of Lord Gorlois's men didn't stop me taking Tintagel from him, and ten fools with good shields ought to be able to hold that place.'

'Then leave some of your men here,' Igraine said.

The lyre's strings sounded again, eight notes like sunlight spilling through new green leaves, until someone hissed and the instrument fell silent again.

'I need every spear I can get,' Uther rumbled. 'No, wife. You must come back with me. We leave in the morning.'

'The men will be happy to see you come home, my lady,' one of Uther's men said.

'Tintagel is no longer my home, Lord Ector,' Igraine told him. 'It swarms with soldiers, like flies on dung.'

Something – a fist, the boy thought – slammed against the table. 'You cannot stay here,' Uther said. 'This . . . place is a rotting apple. A remnant of a time long gone. It will be nothing more than a pissing post for the Saxon dogs as they venture north from the Solent. And as they slink west from their ships on the beaches of Rhegin.'

'My lady, you will be safe at Tintagel, you and your people,' Ector said.

'I was not safe from your lord at Tintagel,' Igraine dared.

The boy felt the air in the room change at that, felt the silence fall, bitter as smoke from the fish-oil lamps. It was so quiet he was sure his own breathing could be heard.

'Gorlois was weak,' Uther snarled. 'Or perhaps he did not think what he had was worth winning for.'

'You are cruel, Uther,' Goleuddydd said, a tremble in her voice.

'You should be thankful for it,' he replied. 'All of you. My brother too. My name is known throughout Britain. In Armorica too. The Saxons fear me. The Irish fear me. The Picts fear me. We have many enemies . . . but they *all fear me*.'

'I am your wife. Should *I* fear you?'

Silence again but for the crackle of a reed in one of the lamps.

'Wine,' Uther growled.

The boy's thighs were trembling now. His heart was thumping in his chest and his palms were slick. He needed to empty his bladder and feared he could not hold it in much longer, so he put his hand down to his member and held it there, squeezing.

'So, wife. How long will you make me wait? How long will you play this game?'

'What . . . game, husband?' Igraine asked.

'There's another reason I have come, and you know it.'

'I don't understand,' Igraine said.

Uther sighed. 'Where is the boy?'

'Uther—'

'Bring me the boy.'

'He . . . he's not ready to—'

'Bring me the boy!' Uther demanded.

'He is not here. I told him to stay away, I swear it. He could be out in the woods or . . . anywhere.'

'You let him roam around the place unguarded? He is my son! You'd have him taken as a slave by some raider from Powys? Or skinned like a rabbit by some Jute or Saxon? I want to see him.'

'He doesn't know you.'

'Fetch him. I want him here in front of me before I finish this wine.'

'Please, Uther. Leave the boy alone. He's happy here with me.'

'I will not tell you again, wife.'

The boy was afraid, though more for his mother now than himself, and he reached out and pulled the wall hanging aside and took two steps, then stopped, his eyes finding those of his mother, who was sitting across the table from Uther.

'Arthur,' she said, eyes wide, a look in them he had not seen before but which he knew at once to be fear. He looked from her to each of the other five people on the benches, his gaze snagging a moment on a man with wild eyes before being drawn almost unwillingly yet inexorably to the big man at the other end of the table.

'What in the name of Taranis are you doing there, boy?' Uther said. 'Hiding like a vole in the rushes.' His dark brows loomed above dark eyes. 'Are you a vole?'

47

'No, lord,' Arthur said.

'Closer.' Uther beckoned him with a big hand, upon the back of which a livid scar ran all the way to the band of silver on his wrist. 'Into the light where I can see you.'

The boy took a step. Then another. He stood now in the golden bloom of one of the reed lamps, looking into those gyrfalcon's eyes. The face from which those eyes looked out was narrow and dark-browed. His cheekbones were high, his nose sharp, his lips thin. Black moustaches hung down either side of those lips but did not touch his beard, which was thick but combed and oiled into a point, like the blade of a spear used to hunt boar.

'You look like your mother,' Uther said.

'Lucky for him,' this other man said, this slightly built man with fire in his eyes, and to the boy's surprise Uther half smiled at that, lifting his cup in the other's direction.

'Were you spying on me, boy?' Uther asked. He had not taken his eyes from Arthur.

'I . . . no, lord.' He straightened and lifted his head. 'I wanted to see you, lord.'

Uther tilted his head to one side, half glancing at Igraine. 'Lord?'

'F . . . Father,' Arthur said.

Uther nodded. He stood from the bench and he was big in that space, though not as big as the bards' songs had it. 'A boy *should* want to see his father.' He lifted his chin with that blade of beard. 'Closer. I won't bite.'

The boy took half a step and now he could smell the man. The sheep oil in his clothes and the beeswax on his sword belt, over-tunic and boots. The sweat, old and sweet, sunk deep into the warp and weft of his clothes, and new sweat too, sour on his skin, and the wine on his breath which stained his lips and the corners of his mouth red. The boy could smell that, too.

Uther reached out and took the boy's chin in his hand, which was rough as elm bark. 'You mine, boy? Eh?'

'Uther!' Igraine stood and came to the boy and put her hands on his shoulders protectively.

'What? I just want to see if there's any of Gorlois in that face,' Uther said.

The boy made embers of his eyes and tried to make them burn the man, tried to hurt him for not treating his mother how he should have treated her.

'Off you go, Arthur.' Igraine bent down and kissed his cheek. 'Brisen will get you something to eat. But then go to your room.'

Uther lifted a hand. 'I'm not done with the boy.' His voice was a low snarl.

Igraine squeezed Arthur's shoulder and lifted her chin towards the door. 'Go on.'

Arthur glanced at Uther, who inclined his head and lifted his eyebrows. 'Stay where you are,' Uther said.

He wanted to stay. How could he protect his mother if he left her alone with this man? But he could see in her eyes how much his mother needed him to leave the room. And anyway, as much as he wanted to stay, he also wanted to disobey Uther. Wanted to defy him. He looked to the door.

'Don't do it, boy,' Uther said, reading his next move the way a good spearman knows when a thrust is coming.

Arthur clenched his teeth and felt his hands become hard knots at his sides as he walked towards the door, his feet swishing through the floor rushes.

'I said stay where you are!' Uther yelled, and in two strides he was on him, a big hand clamping onto his left shoulder like a falcon's talons gripping a young hare, and Arthur was flying backwards.

'Arthur!' the boy heard his mother cry out as he landed amongst the reeds, the breath driven from his stomach.

'You'll do as I say!' Uther bellowed. 'I'm your father.'

Arthur glared up at him. 'I don't want you,' he said.

Uther came fast upon the boy and loomed above him, his hand raised to strike.

'Little bastard,' he spat.

'No, Uther!' Igraine screamed.

'Leave him alone, Uther,' said the man with the fiery eyes.

Uther spun to face the man, pointing a finger at him. 'Stay out of it, Merlin,' he said.

Merlin glanced down at the boy, a faint look of amusement in his eyes before he turned back to his lord.

'No, Uther,' he said, 'I don't think I will.'

3

Tristan and Isolde

B ERAN WOKE TO FIND the boy gone. He clambered out of the
hollow tree, feeling like a man climbing out of his own grave, and
relieved himself against the old oak, blinking the sleep from his eyes
until his vision cleared. Then he stood awhile, pressing his hands into
the small of his back, looking east through the forest, his breath rising
in the cool dawn air. Pigeons greeted the day, cooing softly somewhere
above. Farther off, a raven kronked. He shivered.

'Where did you go?' he muttered.

He took his time fetching his things from inside the tree, stopping
now and then to bend and press his thumbs into the tight knots of his
knee joints, wincing with the pain of it. The boy had taken his spear
and left the axe. He wondered if the boy had woken early and gone
hunting, hoping perhaps to spear something for them to cook over a
fire. But as his body began to come back to him, the aches receding
like the morning mist, Beran knew the boy was not coming back.

'Where are you?' He slung his pack over his shoulder, gripping the
axe beneath the big blade. A red glow from the east was creeping up
trunks, and he felt the warmth of it on his legs. He knew he could not
stand there letting the day come upon him, so he turned and began
walking north. Maybe he'd go to Powys. Enough forest there to hide
out the rest of his life, whatever was left of it. The boy had made his
decision. And anyway, maybe the lad was better off without Beran
slowing him down. Just so long as he hadn't gone east in the dark. No,
the boy was a fool but even he wouldn't go back the way they had
come and risk running into Nabor ap Nabor and the others. He'd head
south-west, Beran was sure. No doubt thought he could slip through

Caer Lundein, Caer Celemion and Caer Gwinntguic without finding himself molested, enslaved, dead, or worse.

'Fool boy.' But the boy wasn't Beran's problem. 'Saved his life. Don't owe him any more than that.'

He's Constantine's son, a voice in Beran's mind said. *You know what that means.*

'If Constantine was here now, I wouldn't owe him anything either,' Beran said. Then he cursed, realizing he was talking to himself like some moon-mad old bastard. Not that the realization stopped him.

'Boy didn't choose his father,' he mumbled a short while later, passing a patch of gorse upon whose barbs some thistledown clung like wool, shivering in the cool breeze. 'Not his fault Constantine was a treacherous turd in the grass.'

Your fault that you hit him, though, said the accusing voice.

'Didn't hit him,' Beran replied.

What if Nabor ap Nabor catches up with him?

'Not my problem. I'm just an old man.'

What if Queen Morgana gets her claws on him? She'll cut his throat and curse his spirit.

'I told him to stay. He left. What can I do?'

He walked another ten paces before he stopped. He turned and looked back along the way he'd come. The little thief had stolen his spear. A good spear, that. Beran had carried it many miles. The blade always took an edge and the balance in the hand was just right, and he might not come across another spear like it for a long time.

'Boy should learn. You don't take a man's spear without asking.' He shook his head. 'Someone needs to tell the fool boy that.'

Then he was walking. South-west. 'Thieving little bastard,' he growled, knowing it was going to be hot later.

For now, though, the forest floor was still damp enough that he could follow the boy. He stopped now and again to study the signs. The beech trunk still slick where the boy had emptied his bladder. The print of shoe heel here. An overturned leaf. A broken cobweb still glistening with dew. Small indentations – barely visible, yet there all the same – from where the boy had struck the ground with the butt of the spear every fourth step.

By midday it was harder to be sure of the boy's trail, so Beran kept an eye on the sun's passage across the sky beyond the woodland canopy, hoping the boy was doing the same. He was hungry and knew the boy would be too, but there was nothing to be done about that now. Not with Nabor ap Nabor coming for them. He had meant to set off before dawn broke, but he had slept longer than he'd intended, and there was every chance that Nabor had found where they had spent the night and was now close behind. Nabor could follow a leaf blown on the wind and find where it came to rest.

In the late afternoon, he stopped by a stream and scooped handfuls of water across the cut beneath his collarbone, washing away the dried blood so that he could see if the skin around it was inflamed, which would likely mean the wound was infected. It looked clean, though he whispered a curse at Red Tooth for the biting sting of it, hoping the man's shade would feel that curse in the afterlife like a foul breath across his cheek.

It was early evening when he smelled smoke. The air was alive with the drowsy buzzing of insects. The undergrowth scratched and trembled with the activity of unseen creatures, but he had seen no sign of another traveller or hunter, nor any human but for the boy, until now.

He looked up and spied a grey gauze through a gap in the trees. He knew where that smoke was coming from. And he knew he would find the boy there.

When he came to the clearing he stood for a while amongst the trees, watching the place, his stomach growling at the smell of roast pig, onions and beans which hung in the air like the smoke barely rising from the roof to besmirch the reddening sky. It had been a shrine to some Roman god once, a place where long-forgotten rituals were enacted out of sight of others. Nowadays, the small Roman building of stone and brick was used as an oven, and beside it stood a timber and thatch building the size of a minor lord's hall, where travellers on their way to join the Roman road or cross the Tamesis river could find food, ale and shelter for the night. He had been there before with Nabor and the others, more than once. The last time, after they had killed a score of Saxons who had been raiding along the Tamesis valley. And so he watched now to make sure none of his erstwhile companions were amongst the half-dozen or so folk milling between carts and horses by the building's open door, or one of those returning from the latrine pit behind the building.

How this refuge was still standing at all beyond the protection of a guarded settlement was a mystery to Beran, although he knew that the man and woman whose place it was would serve anyone who could pay, be they Briton, Irish, Saxon or Jute, whether they believed in Arawn and Balor, Jupiter, the Christ, or Woden. And all men needed food and ale. Beran needed those things himself, so he stepped out of the tree line. Stopped again, because spearmen were coming through the woods on the other side of the clearing. Four of them. No, five. He did not think they had seen him and so he stepped back slowly and stood behind a snarl of bramble, gripping big Blandigan's axe in both hands.

Those spearmen broke from the tree line and now the folk outside the ale house saw them and some ran off into the woods, whilst others stood still and showed their palms in a gesture that told these new-comers that they were unarmed and sought no trouble.

'We're looking for a man and a woman from Cornubia,' one of the spearmen called out. With a gesture he sent two of his fellows around the rear of the ale house in case their quarry tried to make their escape through some other egress. 'Young, both of 'em,' he said. He wore a blue cloak and a good sword at his hip, this one. 'She has golden hair, a fair complexion and is known as a great beauty. The young man is about my height, though not as broad across the shoulder. His hair is dark and he wears it long.' His two remaining men were taking up positions by the door, spears levelled, as if they expected a fight. 'I know they spent the night at a round with a good turf wall half a day's walk west of here. I'm thinking they may be here now.' Blue Cloak tilted his spear towards the open door, then swept it back. 'If they are inside, send them out. We have not come to spill blood. Send them out and all is well. But, if any man or woman aids these fugitives, he or she shall be my enemy and there will be killing soon enough.'

A bull-necked man appeared at the door, showing empty hands, then stepped out into the late afternoon sun. He was followed by two women and three men, one of whom was so drunk he staggered and fell into the grass, slurring a torrent of curses. Still holding his hands wide, the bull-necked man approached the spearmen, glanced back at the tavern, then spoke to Blue Cloak. Beran could not hear his words but he knew well enough the kernel of it. The soldier nodded and waved the man and his friends away, then signalled to his spearmen that they were about to go inside and pull the mice from their hole.

'Tristan, son of Tallwch,' Blue Cloak called. 'We have come far, as well you know. But I have run you to ground. Do not make me walk so much as another step.'

He got no reply and so he lifted his chin. The other spearmen entered the tavern and Blue Cloak followed them.

A woman's scream from within the building sent starlings wheeling into the sky from the thatch where they had perched. Beran could hear Blue Cloak yelling commands and threats.

'You'd best not be in there, boy,' Beran murmured. There was a clatter of cups and the sound of earthenware breaking and more shouts, then the soldiers came back out, pushing folk before them at the tips of their spears. Among them, by Beran's reckoning, the dark-haired man and beautiful, golden-haired young woman whom the spearmen had pursued all the way from Cornubia.

The young man wore a mail hauberk over a pale blue tunic and rust-coloured trews. His sword scabbard hung empty. The woman wore a linen gown the colour of fresh cream, though dirty and frayed at the hem, and drawn in at her waist by a narrow leather belt.

They were young, these two, had perhaps seen less than twenty summers like this one, and they clutched each other's hands as they and the other five captives were pushed and jostled and lined up along the length of the ale house. The two spearmen who had gone around the back now reappeared, and Blue Cloak told them to go inside and fetch ale or, better still, mead.

'Mercy!' said a squat man in a stained leather apron, and Beran recognized him as the owner of the place. He was clasping his hands towards the nearest spearman. 'We thought you'd come to rob us. That's why we didn't come out.' He waved his arms towards the young man and woman. 'We served them food and ale but we don't know them. On my word, they're no friends of ours. Do what you want with them.'

One of the soldiers stepped in and thrust his spear stave against the man's throat, driving him back to the ale-house wall where he held him, the man gasping and reddening and wide-eyed with terror. His wife, as squat and round as her husband, was begging the soldier to let her man go, but the soldier was deaf to her pleas. He looked to Beran to be enjoying himself.

54

Blue Cloak barely acknowledged the interruption, having eyes only for the golden woman and her raven-haired man. 'Step away from him, my lady,' he commanded. She shook her head and said she would not, but the young man told her she must. With reluctance she let go his hand, and the young man took a step away from her, as though he knew what was coming. Blue Cloak spun his spear, stepped in and drove the butt end into the young man's belly, doubling him over.

The golden-haired woman cried out, but it didn't stop Blue Cloak, whose next blow struck the man between his shoulder blades and dropped him to his knees, where he gasped for breath.

'Do you know how many mornings I've woken stiff and dew-soaked because of you?' Blue Cloak said, as the young woman crouched beside her companion, trying to soothe him with word and touch. 'Damn traitor.' Blue Cloak strode forward and slammed the butt of the spear against the man's head. The woman screamed as the man fell sideways, and Beran thought he might be dead.

Not my problem, Beran thought. He'd find something to eat elsewhere. The boy was not here, and whatever was going on with this couple and these spearmen from far-off Cornubia, it was none of Beran's concern. He turned away, thinking to skirt around the place and pick up the boy's trail further on.

'Marrec! Look what I found!'

Beran turned back. Growled a curse under his breath. A spearman emerging from the ale house had the boy, one hand on the scruff of his neck, the other gripping his shoulder.

'I found a little lord!' the spearman announced, grinning as the boy struggled and fought in vain to break free.

'Get off me!' the boy yelled. 'Get your hands off me!'

'Keep still, you slippery little bastard,' the spearman snarled, taking his hand from the boy's neck long enough to slap him across the back of the head.

'Let me go!' the boy cried.

The blue-cloaked Marrec told his other men to keep their spears levelled at the prisoners while he considered the boy in the red cloak, who got another cuff around the head for all his wriggling.

'A little Roman lord,' the spearman who had caught him said, as though he had found some strange and mythical creature from the tales of bards.

'Who are you supposed to be, boy?' Marrec asked.

'Says he's a prince,' the other spearman said, wide-eyed. 'Says King Constantine was his father. Says the Saxons have taken Caer Colun.'

'I *am* a prince.' The boy was twisting and thrashing like a fish in a net. 'And you will let me go!'

'There you are,' Beran called out. He was walking across the clearing towards them, resting the axe on his shoulder like a man who has been splitting logs. 'Where have you been, boy?'

The boy was scowling at him.

'You have my thanks. You can let go of him now,' Beran told the spearman. 'It's not the first time he's run ahead of me, but I catch up eventually. Boy's always hungry.' He lifted his chin towards the ale house. 'He likes the pig liver and onions here. We both do.'

'He told me he's a prince,' the spearman replied, still keeping hold of the boy and eyeing Beran with suspicion.

'Ha!' Beran came to stand before them, his brows hoisted. 'A prince now, is he?'

'I *am* a prince!' the boy said.

Beran batted a hand through the warm air. 'Pay him no mind. Lad makes up stories like a damned bard.' He tapped a forefinger against his own head. 'Makes them up in his thick skull and tells them to himself day and night. I swear he ends up believing them.'

'My father was King Constantine,' the boy proclaimed, still trying to free himself from the spearman's clutches. 'The Saxons have burned Caer Colun! I swear it. My mother and I and some survivors escaped—' He stopped struggling and pointed at Beran. 'That man and his band of murderers attacked us. They meant to kill me on Queen Morgana's orders. Because I am the heir.'

'Best shut that mouth, boy,' Beran told him.

'Take me to Camelot,' the boy pleaded with Marrec. 'Lady Iselle will reward you, on my word.'

Marrec wore the face of a man who resents the interruption of his work, yet begins to smell an opportunity on the air.

'Stories,' Beran told him, shaking his head. 'Good ones, mind.'

'If you ask me, he's telling the truth,' the alewife put in, stepping forward and gesturing over to her husband, who had been allowed to breathe again and stood there holding his throat and wincing. 'Show him,' she said.

The man shook his head, scowling at her.

'Show him or I will,' his wife went on.

The little man spat into the grass, then spat even fouler words at his wife as he reached under his apron and pulled out something golden which shone in the rosy light of the low sun filling that glade. It was the boy's golden fibula, Beran saw, and he looked at the boy, seeing now that his red cloak was fastened at his right shoulder with twine.

'The boy had no coin so paid for his food and ale with this,' the tavern owner said, holding up the pin brooch for Marrec and all to see. 'No boy I know would have a thing like this. Fool could've eaten for a year.' Then he seemed to think better of showing the brooch off and hastily secreted it away whence it came. 'That and the red cloak,' he went on, 'like the spearmen of Caer Colun wear.' He spat again. 'Don't ask me what he's doing here, but seems to me he could be who he says he is.'

'He's not,' Beran said. 'I found the cloak on a corpse. We sometimes walk the fields of the dead.'

The Cornubian spearmen did not seem to hear him.

'We could take the boy to Queen Morgana ourselves,' one of them suggested to his companions. He was a big man and his face twisted so that his mouth seemed to be on the side.

'We've got our orders.' Marrec pointed his spear at the young couple kneeling on the ground beside the ale house. The man was not dead after all. But he was pale and bleary-eyed and his head was bleeding, though the woman was tending to the wound, mopping at it with her skirt.

'We have what we came for,' Marrec said, 'and should be gone before the king of these parts has us dragged to his court by our balls.'

'We'll pass a spear-throw from Queen Morgana's hall on our way home,' the other spearman said. 'Why don't we take the boy and see what comes of it? We can sell him to Morgana for our trouble. Or, if we meet Saxons on the road and things look bad, we can trade the boy for our lives. Either way, he's got to be worth something.'

'Emerit is right,' another of the Cornubians said. 'If Queen Morgana won't pay a fair price, we could take him to Camelot. Lady Iselle and Lord Galahad may have a use for the boy if he really is Constantine's son. Wouldn't that make him the grandson of High King Ambrosius?' His eyes widened as though he was only now realizing this. 'Makes him an heir to Uther Pendragon himself.'

'The boy's heir to nothing but a pole lathe, some chisels and our dwelling.' Beran held the axe out one-handed and pointed it at the boy, 'and I will take him now, for it seems his stories are jumping into your own heads like fleas from hound to hound.'

The man with the twisted face spat in Beran's direction. 'This old bastard just wants the money for himself,' he told the others. 'Can't be the boy's father. Old fuck like him.'

'Well, then how can the boy be Constantine's?' one of the others asked. 'He was as old as the sky when he died.'

'Because when you're a king you can hump whoever you like, you idiot,' the one holding the boy said. 'Constantine's queen was young and fair. So the bards have it. That right, boy?' He gave the boy a shake. 'Is your mother still a good-looking woman? Wager the old goat tupped her a thousand times before he croaked his last.'

Tears brimmed in the boy's eyes now.

'I'm the boy's grandfather,' Beran said, but no one took any notice.

'Let me go or you'll regret it,' the boy yelled.

'You came for us, not him,' the young man on the ground said, palming blood off his cheek and looking up at his captors. The cut in his head glistened wetly amongst his dark hair. 'Let the boy go with his grandfather.'

'Shut your mouth, traitor,' Marrec said, then jerked his spear at them. 'Up! On your feet!'

The couple stood, he unsteady on his feet from that blow to his skull, and the golden-haired young woman taking his hand in her own again to help him balance.

The spearman called Emerit took hold of the tavern owner and pushed him against the wall, his free hand ferreting under the man's apron until he found what he was searching for. He pulled the boy's fibula out and grinned, shoving the man hard backwards before secreting the little treasure somewhere on his own person.

'Thieving Cornubian bastard,' the tavern owner spat, at which the spearman half bowed and went to stand beside Marrec.

'We're taking these two and the boy,' Marrec announced, gesturing at the young man and woman. 'The rest of you, piss off.'

The remaining ale-house customers scurried away, not looking back as they vanished amongst the trees.

'No,' Beran heard himself say. 'You're not taking the boy.'

Two of the spearmen looked at each other, eyebrows raised. One laughed. Marrec regarded Beran in a way he had not before this moment. He was weighing him with his eyes. 'The boy is not yours,' he said, and lifted his spear and his empty hand. 'We all know it.'

'Even so, you will not take him,' Beran replied.

'Go home, old man,' Emerit called across the clearing, putting some flint in his eyes.

'We don't want to kill you, friend,' Marrec said. 'Seems to me you had your chance to get rich but you let the boy jump off the hook.' He turned a palm over. 'You're still breathing, yes? Turn around and walk away.' He pointed his spear into the west. 'Live to see another sunset. At your age, there can't be many more.'

Beran lifted the head of the axe towards the boy and the man still holding on to him. 'Let the boy go. I slept badly and I'm tired. As you say, I am old. My bones hurt. I just want to be on my way . . . with the boy.'

'Last chance, old man,' one of the spearmen said. 'Go now or I'll cut your throat.'

Beran looked at this man. He was young. So young. 'What's your name?' Beran asked him.

'Guithrit,' the spearman replied through a mirthless smile. He was puffed up with a confidence as yet unearned.

Beran nodded. 'I've known good men from Cornubia, Guithrit,' he said. 'I've stood in the shieldwall with them. I've bled with them.' He shook his head once. 'I don't want to kill Cornubians.'

The young spearman looked at his fellows, the Cornubians sharing grins or lifting eyebrows in surprise, perhaps even in admiration of the old man standing before them.

'He's got a pair of stones, this old bastard, I'll give him that,' Guithrit said.

Marrec's eyes were fixed on Beran's. 'You may have been something once,' he said, 'and you don't lack courage. But maybe you don't hear so well any more.' He turned his head and spat. 'I'm a fair man, so I'll tell you one last time.' His features hardened, the muscles in his cheeks tightening, lifting the beard covering them. 'Turn and walk away. Now.'

Beran did not turn. Did not walk away. The only movement he made was to straighten his spine and stand a little taller, though he felt the bones crackle within him. He expected to die there. What other outcome could there be? But he was not afraid. It would be a blessing really.

Marrec looked at Guithrit and nodded, and Guithrit gave a wolf's grin and lifted his spear and came.

The young spearman thought it would be easy. He did not break stride, but came straight for Beran. He feinted high, but thrust low, yet Beran read the move, sweeping the axe haft across to deflect the spear wide before swinging the axe head up across the man's torso to take him under the chin with a crack and spray of blood and gleaming shards of bone.

'Guithrit!' one of the other spearmen yelled as Beran straightened. The movement had come to him as easily as breathing, the speed of it like a swift darting overhead, and now the young man reeled off sidewards, clutching at his ruined face, blood flying everywhere, teeth spilling from the gaping red ruin of his jaw.

The man who had shouted glared at Beran, his eyes bulging, his face paling, then he came in a fury. He thrust with his spear, as Beran knew he would, which was why he had gripped the bloodied axe haft in both hands and stepped forward at the last moment, closing the distance between him and his attacker.

This the spearman had not expected, and Beran swept the haft up, deflecting the spear blade up and over his right shoulder, before twisting at the waist and punching the poll into the spearman's temple. The man stumbled backwards, momentarily dazed, but somehow kept his feet and held on to the spear. Not that Beran would give him time to gather his wits and use the thing, because in three strides he was on him and, gripping the big axe by the knob end of the haft, he swung it up and over his own head and brought it down, taking the man's spear arm off at the shoulder and cleaving his torso down to the cradle of his hips with a wet tearing sound.

The Cornubian keeled over and hit the ground a dead weight. Blood spurted and pooled on the clearing floor. Beran glanced at his first assailant, who was on his knees now, choking and gasping wetly, his eyes bulging with terror.

Marrec had not yet moved. 'Who are you?'

Beran jerked the axe to get a slick gobbet of something foul off the head, then turned towards the leader of the Cornubians. 'Give me the boy,' he said.

Marrec pointed his spear at the young Cornubian who was choking on his last weak breaths, blood foaming and bubbling at his mangled mouth and nose. 'That's my sister's lad,' he told Beran. 'And you've killed him.' For a moment Marrec watched the young man struggle, his teeth clenched in a grimace. Then he brought his gaze back to Beran. 'What'll I tell my sister?'

'You'll tell her nothing because you'll be dead,' Beran said, walking towards the man, gripping the haft of the axe tightly. He would have preferred a spear.

'We'll take him together,' Marrec called to his two remaining men, throwing one foot forward and crouching slightly, braced with the spear mid-height.

Movement over the man's right shoulder caught Beran's eye and he dared spare only a glance. Enough to see the brewer killing the spearman called Emerit who had robbed him of the boy's brooch, sticking a knife into his back again and again. The commotion turned Marrec's head and in that moment Beran lifted the big axe by the poll end of the haft, drawing it over his head before hurling it two-handed. The axe turned a full revolution in the air and the blade buried itself in Marrec's chest with a thunk, throwing him backwards off his feet. A choke, a noise that may or may not have been a word, and he was gone.

The grizzled spearman holding the boy looked suddenly lost and afraid. He shoved the boy aside so he could take hold of his spear with two hands and face Beran, who drew the long knife from the sheath at his belt and gestured with it, inviting the Cornubian to come at him. But Beran knew he would not get the chance to fight him, for the handsome young man with the dark, bloody hair whom these spearmen had come looking for had fetched Emerit's spear and now strode towards the last of the Cornubians.

'You should have let us be,' he told the man, who turned to his erstwhile quarry, realizing that his death was upon him. 'Why couldn't you leave us alone?'

The Cornubian had no chance to reply, and their spears clashed. A blur of quick thrusts and parries, the clacking of the staves and the metallic scrape of the iron blades, but the younger man was the better.

'Kill the Cornubian bastard,' the tavern keeper called out from where he knelt, pilfering from the man he had stabbed to death. His wife was searching the ones Beran had killed, and some of the folk who had been hiding amongst the trees came back into the clearing to see how the thing was going to end.

It ended when the younger man jabbed high twice, then thrust down with his spear, too fast for his opponent to block, and the blade pierced him in the thigh. The Cornubian shrieked and jumped back, looking down at his leg where his trews were wet with blood.

'Don't kill him, Tristan!' the golden-haired woman said through her hands, which she held against her face. 'I know his family. His wife and children. Don't kill him.'

The Cornubian looked up at Tristan, perhaps hoping to see pity in that handsome face. Or else perhaps he saw a moment's hesitation, for he turned and hirpled away across the clearing, trailing blood on the worn ground as he went.

'No, Tristan!' the golden woman called, but Tristan was already moving, pulling his spear arm back as he took three long strides and let fly. The shaft streaked flat and fast to take the man in the back between his shoulder blades, the spearhead burying itself somewhere inside him. No shriek this time, just a grunt as he fell forward. He flapped on the ground like a caught fish, the spear shuddering, and then went still.

'Cornubian bastards,' the tavern owner said again, pulling a coin from the clothes of the dead man he was robbing and holding it up to the light. 'We'll take them into the forest and bury them deep.'

Beran looked at the boy. The boy looked at Beran.

'I was hungry,' the boy said. Beran glanced at the young Cornubian lovers, who had thrown themselves together again now, like the surf to the shingle. They clung to each other as if they might never let go.

Beran looked back at the boy. 'Where's my spear?' he asked.

Beran ate a plate of pig's liver and onions and washed it down with a cup of beer, while the boy, who had eaten earlier, chewed on a hunk of bread with butter and honey which the alewife had given him to take his mind off the blood that had been spilled outside.

'A nasty business,' she said, ruffling the boy's hair as he sat on a bench beside Beran. 'We've not had a killing here since winter.'

'You've cost me, stranger,' her husband said from where he stood by the hearth, scrubbing at the blood on his hands with a scrap of cloth. Some of the tavern's erstwhile customers had drifted back in and sat drinking in the gloom and talking in low voices about what had just taken place. 'Those men lying dead out there would have eaten my food. Drunk my ale.' The man spat onto the cloth and rubbed with it, frowning in concentration.

'I didn't kill them all,' Beran replied, putting his cup to his lips and draining it.

'That's as may be,' the man admitted, 'but no one was killing anyone before you washed up here.'

'You've done well enough out of me,' Beran said, and the man could not deny that, for everyone had seen him flapping over the dead like a crow, scavenging finger rings and coins, knives and brooches and belts and cloaks and anything of value. The bodies of the Cornubians outside were near enough naked now, lying there under dark palls of flies because the tavern keeper said they would be easier to move in the morning when they were stiff. 'Like shifting timbers then,' he'd said to his wife, who'd nodded her agreement.

'Now I think of it,' Beran went on, 'you've done well enough to give the boy his brooch back.' He wiped his lips with the back of his hand. The beer was good here. Always was.

Some of the other drinkers went quiet, their eyes turning to Beran. The tavern keeper had stopped scrubbing at the blood and now looked up. 'The boy gave it freely in return for his food,' he said.

Beran looked at the boy, who gave a slight nod. 'I did,' the boy said, then he turned those young eyes on the tavern owner. 'But I want it back.'

A heavy silence fell over the place. The tavern keeper's lips twitched, his eyes narrowing.

Beran nodded. 'You heard the boy.'

For a moment the man hesitated, perhaps weighing up the possible consequences of denying the boy's request, but then he mumbled something foul under his breath and came over to the table and slammed the golden fibula down on the worn surface.

They ate quickly and Beran paid with a bronze sestertius, which also bought them provisions for the journey, including four flasks of ale, two loaves of bread, a cheese, some strips of smoked mutton, and the silence of the tavern keeper and his wife, should Nabor ap Nabor come asking questions. The boy headed outside to keep watch on the trees beyond the clearing while Beran washed his wound with wine and smeared upon it a poultice of honey and crushed yarrow leaves which he had gathered that morning.

He was putting his tunic back on when a shadow fell across the room. He looked up to see the young Cornubian called Tristan standing in the doorway, blocking the last of the daylight. Gods, but he was even younger than Beran had realized. His beard was wispy and patchy in places, and his shoulders still had some filling out to do.

'Thought you two were long gone,' Beran said.

The young man came in and sat on the bench across the table from Beran. 'My name is Tristan ap Tallwch,' he said.

'I heard.' Beran put the last of the food into his knapsack on the bench beside him and pulled the drawstring tight.

'And you are?' the young man asked.

'What's it to you?' Beran growled, placing the knapsack on the ground by his feet.

Tristan looked back towards the open door and the approaching dusk beyond. 'That boy out there, is he who he says he is? The son of King Constantine?'

'He's just a boy,' Beran said. 'Makes up stories like a damned bard.'

'His people were ambushed while fleeing Caer Colun,' Tristan went on. 'His mother was killed.'

Now he had Beran's attention. 'Keep your voice down,' Beran warned him, glancing around to see who might have heard. 'What else has he been telling you?'

Tristan raised an eyebrow and tilted his head towards the door. 'Singing like a little bird, he is.' He smiled.

He was a cocky one, this lad. Beran would give him that.

'Isolde has a way with people,' the young man said.

Beran grunted. 'She didn't manage to stop you spitting that man out there, did she?'

Tristan ignored this, sliding Beran's beer cup aside and leaning forward. 'The boy says you're taking him to Camelot. To Lady Iselle.'

'Again, what's it to you?' Beran asked.

'We can travel together,' Tristan said. 'You fight well.' Beran waited for the *for an old man*, but it did not come. 'And, as you have seen, I know one end of a spear from another.' Tristan sat back and turned his palms uppermost. His hands were smooth and unscarred. 'Safer to

travel together,' he said. 'At night, you and I can take turns on watch.'
He nodded towards the open door. 'Let them sleep.'

Beran picked up his cup and drained it, then stood up from the table
and picked up his knapsack. 'You have spearmen after you. Spearmen
all the way from Cornubia, meaning you've made an enemy of King
Mark. Why would I travel with people who are being hunted by a
king?' He took his spear from where it leant against the wall and walked
to the door. Good to have it back. 'Got enough enemies of my own.'

'You can't keep watch all night and you can't trust it to the boy.'
There was a little urgency in Tristan's voice now. 'Lad's just lost his
mother and needs a woman to care for him, not an ill-tempered old
bear who knows more about killing than he does about a boy barely
ten summers old.'

'You're not much older than he is,' Beran said, and walked out of the
tavern. He stopped just beyond the threshold and looked at the sky to
judge how long they would have before nightfall. He breathed in the
still, warm air, which was sweet with honeysuckle and thyme and the
smoke from the alewife's cook fire and laced with the rich, fluting
song of a blackbird.

'Come on, boy. We need to go.' The boy was standing with the
golden-haired woman. They were talking, both smiling. Beran realized
he hadn't seen the boy smile before.

'I told you,' Tristan said, coming up behind Beran and regarding the
boy and the woman, 'Isolde has a way with people. The boy likes her.
Anyone can see it.'

The boy and the woman were walking over to them now, still in
conversation. Beran was aware that he was staring at the woman but
he did not look away.

'Prince Erbin thinks the four of us should travel to Camelot
together,' the golden woman said. Barely a woman. Just a girl but three
summers ago, Beran reckoned.

'Prince Erbin?' he said, hauling his eyes over to the boy, who gave a
slight nod. It struck Beran that he had never asked the boy's name.

'And don't I get a say?' Beran asked.

The golden woman pursed her lips and lifted her chin. 'Are you a
prince?' she asked. Gods, but she was beautiful. As weary as he was, as
old as his eyes were, Beran could still recognize a beautiful woman

when he saw one, and he doubted then that the Cornubian spearmen stiffening outside would be the last to lose their lives over her. Whatever the reason King Mark had sent men to bring these two lovers back to Cornubia, he would send more, until this fair-skinned, golden-haired woman stood beneath his gaze once again. Who was she to him? he wondered.

'The boy is my charge,' Beran said. 'But he's not my prince.' He lifted the head of Blandigan's axe towards the woman. 'Who are you? And why are you running from King Mark?'

The woman's eyes flicked up to Tristan, and Beran turned just in time to see the young man shake his head at her. 'A madness has come over the king,' she said, looking back to Beran. 'He sees enemies where there are none.'

'There are always enemies,' Beran said. 'More likely a king does not see them where he should.'

'What is your name?' the woman asked.

'His name is Beran,' the boy said.

She nodded. 'We are grateful to you, Beran.'

'I'm just here for the boy. Nothing more,' he said.

'But we'll be safer together, Beran,' the boy said. Those eyes fixed on Beran's own were full of hope. Beran almost despised it. 'You saw Tristan's spear-throw,' the boy went on. 'He is a great warrior.'

'Takes more than a lucky throw, boy,' Beran said. But, despite himself, he was thinking about what Tristan had said, about how he could share the night watch. There was something to be said for that. Many was the night when Beran could find no sleep, for the aches of the body and of the mind, too. But when sleep did come, wouldn't it be of some comfort to know that someone was tending the fire? That he wasn't going to wake up on the end of a Saxon spear, or with Nabor ap Nabor's blade at his throat? It wasn't the dying that would trouble him, but the things Nabor ap Nabor would do to him first would be . . . disagreeable.

He grunted. 'I need to go to Caer Lundein first.' He looked from the woman to Tristan. 'There's someone I need to see. Someone I need to say goodbye to. After that, I'll take the boy to Camelot.'

The boy frowned. 'It's not safe in Caer Lundein.'

'It's not safe anywhere, boy,' Beran said. 'We go to Caer Lundein, I do what I need to do there, then I'll take to you to Camelot, because that's what your mother wanted.'

The boy considered this. 'And my friends can come?' he asked.

'Friends now, are they?' Beran asked, glancing at Tristan and Isolde.

The boy nodded, his expression firm.

Beran shrugged. 'Who am I to stop them?' He hefted his knapsack, axe and spear and set off towards the tree line at the edge of the clearing, far beyond which the sun was setting, the molten copper light of a summer evening ebbing from the world.

And the boy, the golden woman, and the dark-eyed young man went with him.

4

Morgaine

THEY MADE CAMP BESIDE the old Roman road to Caer Lundein, its cracked and ancient stone burst through with weeds and grass and tugging at Beran like a fractured memory. The boy seemed beguiled by Isolde, the two of them having walked much of the way hand in hand and chattering like birds, which had amused Tristan. Beran did not begrudge them their newfound friendship. He was just glad to be spared the boy's questions, though he wished he could stopper his ears rather than having to listen to half a dozen tales of King Constantine the great warlord. Constantine the scourge of Saxons. Constantine the brave, who held Britain against the invaders in the years since Arthur fell at Camlan and vanished like a dream.

Darkness was in the trees now, only kept at bay by the small fire which crackled and popped as Tristan sat on his haunches beside it. The younger man fed sticks to the flames, but was always watching the trees. They had not eaten since the ale house, preferring to save the food till morning, and now Beran sat running a whetstone along the crescent blade of Blandigan's axe.

'He's a sweet boy.' Isolde was looking down at the boy who lay asleep with his head on her lap, his pale cheek bronzed in the fitful copper firelight.

'He's a thorn in my arse,' Beran grumbled. 'And if he talks about *the great Constantine* all the way to Caer Lundein, I'll cut out his tongue and feed it to the crows.'

'Shh,' Isolde frowned at him, laying a delicate hand over the boy's ear.

'What have you against the boy's father?' Tristan asked, tapping a curved piece of bark on the ground to knock the woodlice off before adding it to the fire. 'He's been dead four years.'

'Constantine thought he was the new Caesar,' Beran said. 'You Cornubians fed his ambitions. Your own king was the first to bend the knee to him.'

'King Mark had little choice,' Isolde said. 'Cornubia cannot make an enemy of Dumnonia, whoever rules there. And in those days Constantine was riding around Britain getting oaths from every lord who sat in a hall. Years before he threw the Saxons back and made his court in Caer Colun.'

Tristan snapped a stick and pushed both pieces into the fire. 'Isolde is right, Beran. By then, Constantine was the only battle lord keeping the Saxons at bay. If not for him, King Cerdic and a handful of lesser Saxon kings would have driven us all into the western sea.' He looked over at the young prince sleeping in his lover's lap. 'And Arthur, for all his victories, was never proclaimed, never made king in Dumnonia.' He nodded at the boy. 'That boy's father was the last hope. A battle king when we needed one.'

'What do you know of it?' Beran asked him. 'Fought the Saxons, have you?'

Tristan looked back into the flames. 'No,' he said.

'No,' Beran echoed. 'I didn't think so.' He spat onto the whetstone. 'Constantine was an arrogant bastard, and any man who trusted him was a fool.'

'You knew him?' Tristan asked.

'I met him.' Beran held the stone still against the cheek of the axe.

Satisfied that the fire had taken, Tristan scrambled back onto his cloak, which he had spread on the forest floor, and lay on his side watching the flames and the night beyond, his head supported by his right arm. 'Then why are you helping the boy?' he asked Beran.

Beran wanted to close his eyes. 'You ask a lot of questions for someone who hasn't told me why he's being hunted by the King of Cornubia.'

The young man and woman shared a look, and Beran saw Isolde give a slight shake of her head.

Beran shrugged. 'It's your business,' he said, examining the axe's edge and testing it on his thumbnail.

'So why risk your life for him?' Tristan asked, nodding towards the boy. 'You couldn't have known the innkeeper back there was going to stab that soldier to death. Or that I would fight, come to that.'

'You call that fighting?' Beran asked.

Tristan's brow lifted. 'The man made a run for it. I'd wager you weren't inclined to chase after him.'

Beran grunted.

'You know what I think?' Tristan said.

'I don't care what you think,' Beran said.

Tristan ignored this. 'I think that without our help, those men would have butchered you, and you know it. Why would you get yourself killed for the son of a dead man you hated?'

Beran lifted the whetstone to his mouth and spat on it again. 'Keep asking me questions and I'll take the boy and go. Leave you two to find your own way to Camelot.'

'You're doing it for silver,' Tristan said. 'I understand that. They'll make you a rich man. A great reward for saving a prince. A boy who may be a king one day. Who may be a famous warlord like his father before him.'

Beran owed this young man nothing, least of all an answer. He held his tongue.

'No, my love,' Isolde said, slowly shaking her head as she watched Beran. 'That's not it. Beran is not doing it for silver. Don't ask me how I know, but I do. I know that much.'

Beran lifted his head and looked at her, and for a moment he wondered if she had the sight. If she could read him the way he had seen priests of long-dead gods divine the future from the livers and glistening entrails of beasts. This way might not require a death, but it was deadly enough for all that.

He felt some shadow of the old ache pass like a cold breath through his guts. This young woman across the fire from him would not be the first to weevil into his thoughts. Into his soul. He had known others with that talent.

Tristan frowned, lifting his chin. 'What is it then, Beran, if not for riches?' His eyes were narrow in the flame glow. 'For hope? For Britain?' He jerked his head towards the boy sleeping soundly on Isolde's lap as she stroked his unkempt hair. 'Do you look at the boy and see the saving of Britain?'

Beran knew he was being teased. Being goaded by a stripling in his first beard who not so many years ago was doubtless wetting himself and crying at bad dreams. Still, he looked at the boy, this son of Constantine, and his mind summoned the image of the child's mother, despoiled and lifeless in that Roman carriage.

'I see a boy,' he muttered. 'Just a boy.' A breeze rattled the oak leaves above their heads, and Beran looked up at the sound. A shiver ran through him, so he returned his focus to the axe and ran the whetstone along its edge. 'Just a boy,' he said, under his breath.

Arthur watched Prince Constantine through the haze of dust which the fighters' feet raised from the sun-baked ground. Standing at the High King's right shoulder, chin lifted as though he sought to smell a different air than those around him, Prince Constantine looked like a younger version of Ambrosius. Arthur did not know his cousin's age, just that he was several years older than himself. Fifteen. Sixteen perhaps. Taller than Arthur, and broader across the shoulder, so that Arthur was curious as to whether the body beneath that breastplate of boiled leather matched the stomach and chest muscles represented upon the armour. Perhaps so, and perhaps it accounted for the arrogant set of his cousin's face. That and being the first-born son of the most powerful king in Britain.

'See there, Arthur,' Ector said, pulling Arthur's attention away from Prince Constantine and back to the spectacle before them. Ector nodded at the shorter of the two fighters circling each other, swords and shields raised. 'Mabsant is being played like a lyre. He'll lose badly if he keeps letting Calobrus draw him in like that.'

Arthur had already noticed this and other flaws in Mabsant's style. Even so, his father's champion had not lost this fight yet, for all that High King Ambrosius's man was terrifying to behold with his ox's shoulders and those small boar's eyes in a face that had been broken once and hated the world since.

'See his sword arm. How he overextends the wrist.'

'But he *is* fast,' Arthur said.

'Aye, rushing to defeat,' Ector said, though not loudly, because

Prince Uther himself stood but a little way off amongst the crowd, his teeth bared, flashing white against the dark of his long moustaches. 'Calobrus is as fast and stronger too. More importantly, he has that which can't be taught. A knowing. It's in him, deep as marrow in bone. Like the way a stag knows to begin the rut when the first leaves turn to copper and gold. He's a killer, is Calobrus.'

The adversaries drew apart from each other, breathing hard and arming sweat from their eyes. Mabsant was winded, his broad chest heaving, face flushing red with exertion and heat. Arthur knew that real fights, where men sought their own survival by another's death, rarely lasted so long. A flurry of blades and a thump of shields, and one man would land a blow that sealed the other's doom.

Unless, of course, those men were clothed in fish-scale armour or ringmail coats, as worn by those horsemen Arthur had watched ride to their deaths with General Gaus when he had been but a young boy. Such armour was rarely seen nowadays, though he had been close enough to one such coat to run his hand down the bronze scales, captivated by it. By the feel of the little plates, innumerable in their overlapping rows, and cold as water. Awed by the skill of the craftsman who had made it when Britain's oaks swayed beneath the breath of Roman gods. The scale coat belonged to his father, but Uther would not wear it in battle; he said that dressing like a Roman would offend the old gods of Britain to whom men owed veneration and in whose name he fought the Saxons. Still, Arthur had loved it.

'Watch carefully now, lad,' Ector said, 'and bear in mind what I've been teaching you. About keeping your sword close to your body when you parry, and not leaning forward so your heel lifts and puts you off balance.'

The fighters came together again in a fast flurry of limbs and the ringing and scraping of steel, as Mabsant parried Calobrus's blow, then struck his shield boss. The warriors slammed their shields together and stood, legs braced, each bearing the other's weight and holding there, taking a moment to rest, their faces close enough that they would smell the previous night's wine on the other's panting breath.

'Take him, Calobrus!' Prince Constantine called, and those around him cheered and began striking their own shields with their spears.

'Show him what you showed that sack of shit Acwellen when the sky turned red!' shouted one of the High King's spearmen, as more in the crowd hammered their shields, so that a thunder rolled across the gathering, making rooks in the far trees rasp in chorus. They had all heard the story, how Calobrus had challenged King Hengist's champion to single combat, as the war host of High King Ambrosius faced the Saxons by the sea in southern Caer Gwinntguic two summers past. The way the bards sang it, Belatucadrus, that god of war whom even the Roman soldiers had worshipped in Britain, appeared to Calobrus, telling him to challenge Hengist's man before all the greatest warriors of the land. And the sky had reddened: an omen of the Saxon's blood which Calobrus would spill. Men spoke of it still, in Lord Uther's hall and in the wheat fields as they swung their sickles, in the training yard where they practised sword and shield craft, and in the forests as they hunted boar and stag. For the fight had lasted the time it takes to fletch an arrow, so that by the end both men had been almost too tired to stand, but Acwellen had bled a river from his many wounds and, when the two men had stepped back to catch their breath, the Saxon had paled and fallen sideways like a great ash after the last bite of the axe.

This fight, though, was getting stale by the reckoning of some, and Arthur supposed it was because there was no blood yet to brighten the late summer day. The fighters were using blunted swords, for neither Lord Uther nor High King Ambrosius would risk serious injury to his man in an exhibition fight. Still, a broken arm or rib, or a shattered cheekbone, or some other wound was more than possible despite both men being swathed in wool, mail, and iron helm in the sultry heat which had hung idle for days so that only a storm could scrub it from the world.

'Enough games, Mabsant,' Prince Uther yelled. 'Put my brother's man on his arse where he belongs.' This got rumbles of agreement from some, and Mabsant glanced at Uther and nodded, but there was something in his face. Arthur saw it, even with his boy's eyes.

'Mabsant knows,' Arthur said in a voice barely above a whisper, not taking his eyes off the big man. *He knows he's outmatched.*

'What's that, boy?' Ector said, but Arthur had not meant the words for him, and he watched Mabsant's face, seeing the defeat there even before the decisive blow. Then, as if by some unspoken agreement, the two men threw themselves apart again, each resuming his fighting stance in readiness for the next clash.

When I am a warrior, they will never see my fear, Arthur thought.
'Finish it!' the High King called to his man.

Calobrus hammered the pommel of his sword against his shield and
strode forward, and the crowd roared.

Mabsant went to meet him, turning Calobrus's sword aside once,
twice, the crowd clamouring like the rooks across the stubble field, but
then Calobrus took a step back and dropped his shield a hand's
breadth. Perhaps Mabsant believed he could win then, for he pushed
off his back foot, thrusting high, but Calobrus brought his shield up
and over, hammering it down onto Mabsant's sword. Had Uther's
champion's feet been firmly planted he might have stepped back and
recovered. Instead, he stumbled forward and threw up his shield, but
Calobrus had already swept past him and now swung a backhanded
cut which struck Mabsant on his back, sending him sprawling face
first into the dust.

The High King's men jeered and laughed, while Uther's men cursed
or grumbled, one of them even hurling his cup across the makeshift
arena, wine spattering in the sunlight like a bard's depiction of blood.

'Get up!' Uther bellowed. 'Up, you mutton-headed bastard!' Mabsant climbed to his feet and turned, but Calobrus was on him, driving
him back with a savage combination of strikes, several of which beat
Mabsant's desperate defences, hitting his left shoulder, his right forearm, and the last tonking against his helmet. Arthur winced and some
around him *ooh*ed because that blow would have shattered Mabsant's
face bones had it struck a hand's breadth lower. Yet, to his credit,
Uther's man kept his feet.

'Hold, Calobrus! Enough!' The High King's voice cut through the
roars, stilling every tongue. Calobrus nodded and stepped back from
Mabsant, rolling his shoulders as if he was only just warming to the
task at hand, though the fight was won.

'No! Keep fighting!' Uther yelled. 'Fight, damn you!' He turned to
his brother. 'My man does not yield,' he said, then he spun back to
Mabsant. 'At him, or I'll fight him myself!'

Mabsant turned his head and spat blood and growled a curse, pum-
melled his shield and took a purposeful stride towards Calobrus, but
Ambrosius's champion kept his feet planted and looked at his lord,
awaiting the High King's orders and his alone.

'This isn't good,' Ector muttered, as others in the crowd shared dubious looks or watched King Ambrosius and Lord Uther. Arthur sensed a change in the air. It was still and heavy and threatening, like the feeling before a summer storm.

'It's over, brother,' Ambrosius said.

'I can still fight, lord king.' Mabsant rolled his big shoulders and lifted his chin.

Ambrosius ignored him. He was looking at Uther, and he raised a hand to still the murmurs rising amongst the spearmen around him. 'Your man is beaten. He fought well, but no one wants to see him maimed.'

'Mabsant tripped,' Uther countered, pointing to a tussock of grass amongst the worn, sun-baked earth. 'There. Lost his balance, nothing more. Or is your champion the kind of man to claim another's bad luck as his own skill?' Uther turned to face his own men. 'Perhaps that Saxon sack of shit Acwellen tripped and fell too, hey?'

The High King's spearmen did not like this, and there arose amongst them a rumble which Arthur felt in his guts. Calobrus, too, had taken offence, judging by the flint in his eyes as he regarded Uther. Yet he was wise enough to hold his tongue, knowing that this had little to do with Mabsant or himself. Whatever now tainted the air was between brothers.

'Calobrus has earned his wine and will not fight again today,' High King Ambrosius announced, his voice raised for all to hear so there could be no misunderstanding.

Uther threw out his big hands. 'Someone else then,' he said. 'If not Calobrus, let us have another contest. We have all gathered for it. What about Prince Constantine?'

All eyes turned to the prince, who lifted an eyebrow but gave no other outward sign of what he thought of Uther's suggestion.

'My son will fight him,' Uther went on. 'Where's Arthur? Where's my son?' It did not surprise Arthur that Uther had not noticed him, though he stood but ten paces away. Yet enough of Uther's spearmen knew where he was, enough heads turning in Arthur's direction to cause their own breeze. He heard Ector curse under his breath.

'There you are,' Uther said, his dark eyes finding Arthur at last, and Arthur felt the scorch of his father's scrutiny as he had on every occasion of their meeting. 'You'll fight Prince Constantine, won't you, Arthur?'

'No, Uther,' Ector growled, though not loud enough for Uther to hear it. 'No, don't do this.'

Arthur was aware of men moving around him like a tide, and then Uther was there, looming before him, all muscle and leather, sweat and ale, and strangeness.

'He's a little older and taller, your cousin,' Uther said. 'Stronger perhaps. But you are my son, Arthur.' Uther reached out and gripped Arthur's shoulder with a powerful hand. '*My* son.'

'He's not ready, Uther,' Ector said, loud enough this time to be heard.

Uther took his hand from Arthur's shoulder, crossed his arms over his broad chest and glared at Ector, his chin lifted so that his long moustaches bristled in the warm breeze. 'Not ready?' he said. 'Then what have you been teaching the boy these last years?'

Ector frowned. 'I only mean he's not ready to fight Prince Constantine. Not here, lord. Not like this.'

Arthur felt the heat rise in his cheeks at that and glanced at his cousin through the crowd. Constantine was looking back at him, a half-smile warping the tight line of his lips.

'Listen to me, Ector, and listen well,' Uther went on, his voice like the rolling snarl of a dog before it gives to barking. 'You and Merlin swore to me. You to instruct the boy in weapon craft, Merlin to . . .' he flapped a hand, 'do whatever it is a druid does. You swore that between you, you would make a man of the boy while I'm off killing Saxons. Now you tell me he's not ready?'

'I won't see the boy hurt,' Ector said. Arthur knew his foster father was risking Uther's famous wrath with that, and he admired the courage in the statement. Stronger than any admiration, however, was the resentment he felt at the implication that he was not up to the match.

'I'll fight him, Father,' Arthur heard himself say. 'I'll fight Prince Constantine.'

Uther grinned savagely, then spun back around to face the High King. 'You hear that, lord king? Arthur wants to fight your boy.' The spearmen of both lords cheered and clamoured, and the far-off rooks in the tall trees imitated them. 'What say you, brother?' Not that Ambrosius could stop the thing now, for all that he had won a score of great battles, had received the acclamation of a dozen kings of Britain, and was, men said, beloved of the gods.

Ambrosius Aurelius, the High King, this warrior defender of the Dark Isles, looked at his son, who nodded as men slapped him on the back and growled words of encouragement. Then Ambrosius turned back to Uther and lifted his hands to show his palms. 'If they want to fight, they can fight. With my blessing,' he said.

Uther nodded, still grinning even though he must have heard the big spearman beside Constantine telling the prince to knock the scrawny little turd's head off quickly so they could start on the wine skins awaiting them in their host's hall.

'My son!' Uther bellowed, gripping Arthur's shoulder again and shaking him like a man disturbing an apple tree to see the fruit rain down. 'My son, Arthur!'

Resigned now to that which he was powerless to stop, Ector inclined his head to Arthur, the way he did whenever the words that would follow carried particular import. 'You can still stop this foolishness, lad. You don't have to do this.'

Rather than tell Ector he was wrong, Arthur clenched his jaw, turned and strode to where Mabsant still stood waiting to see how things turned out. The big warrior nodded and handed Arthur the blunt sword and his battered shield without saying a word, then walked away as the crowd moved as one, recreating the small arena as it had been before.

Men were cheering again, half of them for Arthur, half for Prince Constantine, but as Arthur locked eyes with Constantine across the empty space, the sound receded until it could have been the distant sea throwing itself upon the Tintagel shore.

'Here. Put this on,' one of his father's men said, offering him a padded woollen tunic which stank of sweat and lanolin, and which drowned him when he pulled it over his head. 'And this,' the warrior added, handing Arthur a rust-spotted iron helmet; a helmet borrowed from a smaller warrior than himself from the look of the thing.

Arthur put the helmet on, catching the stale sweat smell of the yellow-stained quilted linen liner. The world around him receded further still, all sound muffled now but for his own breathing, the volume of which was louder, and the pulsing gush of blood in his ears; an effect which was new to him because in his practice bouts with Ector he wore only a skull cap of hardened leather.

He turned his head this way and that, getting used to the weight of the helmet, the crowd blurring past his eyes in a sea of faces and bright-coloured tunics, silver brooches, torcs of twisted metal, and slender cloak pins. And he thought he heard Uther say, *Don't you disgrace me, boy*, but the words might have sounded only in his own head, as he made a series of practice cuts with the sword, whose leather grip was damp with Mabsant's sweat.

Constantine had given his own belt and scabbarded sword to a retainer and now stood holding the champion of Dumnonia's sword and shield as naturally as if they were his own. The helmet which Constantine wore *was* his own, though, and there was not a spot of iron rot upon its surface. Indeed, the sun glinted from it now the way it always did in the songs and tales which bards spun on ale-drowned nights in the halls of the kings and lords of Britain.

Arthur had learnt of such things from Ector who, being sworn to Uther, shared wine at his lord's table. And he'd heard tales from Merlin, too, for being a druid Merlin travelled the land, receiving hospitality at any hearth or cook fire, be it that of a king or a mendicant, Briton, Pict or Irish. There were always songs of warriors, just as there were always songs of battles and of beautiful women, and though Arthur did not like admitting it to himself, his cousin, standing there tall and broad-shouldered, feet hip-width apart in a fighting stance, looked as much a warrior as almost any amongst his uncle's or father's retinues. He lacked only their beards and battle scars, Arthur thought, and that distant look he had recognized in some warriors who had seen terrible slaughter and played their part in it. The absence of these made his cousin look even more like the young hero in some fireside tale.

'Are you ready, cousin?' Constantine asked him.

Arthur nodded. The thick tunic was much too big for him. It was heavy and the arms were stiff, so that he feared they would slow his sword work, but it would serve well against the impact of a glancing blow, and he was quite confident that his opponent's blunt sword would not bite through it to cut his flesh.

'It ends when one of you throws his shield down and says the words, *I yield*,' Ector said, loud enough to be heard above the thrumming crowd.

'My son will not yield,' Uther said.

But Ector had not finished. 'Or else it ends,' he called out, 'when either Prince Uther or King Ambrosius says so.'

'Enough talk, Ector,' Uther told him. 'Let us see if you have taught the boy anything useful.'

Ector raised his hands and stepped back, and Arthur drew a long breath and took three steps towards Constantine. His mouth was as dry as ash but it was too late to get a drink now, and he watched his cousin's eyes for any indication of what his first move might be. Would Constantine be aggressive, coming at him like a crashing wave? Or would he choose caution, getting Arthur's measure before fully committing to the fight?

'We're counting on you, boy,' a spearman called. One of his father's men.

For all his size and the years he had on Arthur, Constantine came forward slowly, sliding his booted feet across the ground, his shield held close against his body, the flat of his sword kissing the leather-bound rim of that shield, its point accusing Arthur. Or condemning him.

'He's over here, Arthur ap Uther,' a man behind Constantine called, rapping a knife hilt against the metal boss of his shield. Men on both sides laughed at that, because the helmet was so big on Arthur that its rim kept falling over his eyes.

'Careful, Prince Constantine; if you hurt the boy his mother will have your balls between two rocks.' This raised more laughter. Arthur felt the fire in his blood, hating these men for bringing his mother into it. Hating his father, too, for taking him from her and yet not wanting him, either, but sending him away to be raised by other men. These laughing spearmen, who drank his father's mead and shared his hearth and fought for him and loved him, did not know his son. Arthur knew he was a stranger to them, a boy who had spent too many years being mothered and now was nestled beneath a druid's wing, which made them resentful of him.

Well, they would not expect this. Neither would Constantine, who was still two spear lengths away, edging left and eyeing Arthur over the top of his shield. Arthur rushed him, putting his shoulder against the inside of his shield and slamming it into Constantine's shield, hoping to throw his cousin off balance and cause an opening. But Constantine had set his feet in time, and he was the heavier, so Arthur felt no give in him, and his own bones rattled under the impact of the collision. Constantine anticipated the sword which Arthur swept low beneath their shields, their dull blades ringing in the bright day. Arthur pulled his sword arm back and this time brought it up and over his shield, bending his wrist to reverse the strike, and again the swords sang, but then Constantine shoved against his shield, throwing Arthur back, and now Arthur was retreating, his opponent hammering his shield, so that Arthur felt the marrow in his forearm quivering with slow pain. He would feel it keenly enough later.

'You . . . made . . . a mistake . . . cousin,' Constantine said, in between strikes, still forcing Arthur back under the weight of the onslaught.

Arthur had no strength to waste on words. He pulled his shield away and slid to the right and scythed his sword at the passing blur of his adversary. But Constantine got his own shield round in time, then punched the pommel of his sword into Arthur's face, sending him spinning, as the crowd cheered or gasped or cursed, and Arthur's legs turned to water. He staggered and fell, a furnace-like heat raging in the bone on the right side of his face.

'Up, boy! On your feet!'

His father's voice. He got up. Through the aqueous blur of his vision, he saw Constantine coming for him, so he swung wildly, but his cousin sidestepped and countered with a low blow that filled his right thigh with a crushing pain. Arthur struck out again. Missed again, and a new pain flooded his back, blooming from a point on his left shoulder blade. He staggered forward, his right leg tingling, numbing, rejecting the commands he gave it, and he knew he would be dead by now had their swords been edged.

'Say the words, Arthur!' Ector called. 'Say the damn words!'

'Stay out of it!' Uther commanded Ector. 'The boy is not beaten yet.'

Arthur straightened, turning back to face his opponent. The shield felt impossibly heavy in his left hand, dragging his arm down towards the ground. He could barely see out of his right eye and he did not know why, and so he lifted his sword arm, touching the back of his hand to his face, and realized that the flesh of his right cheek had already swollen horribly, forcing his eye closed.

'What are you waiting for?' Uther called, his voice the only one on the warm breeze now. The other men were silent, their rowdiness subsided. It seemed they had seen enough. 'Fight him, boy!' Uther bellowed.

Arthur had to turn his head full round to regard Ector with his good eye. Ector shook his head. Arthur turned back to look at

Constantine, whose brows were drawn together in a disapproving expression as he gave an almost imperceptible shake of his head.

Arthur shifted his weight, testing his right leg, and was relieved to find it would bear him. He grimaced at the pain in his shoulder, leg and face, leering at his enemy through his left eye. Then he lifted the sword and charged.

He did not even see the blow that put him down.

He lay there, coming back to himself and the world like a swimmer kicking upwards to break the surface. And with this re-emergence came pain. Flooding his whole body all at once, though it was as nothing compared with the dragging weight in his stomach. Humiliation.

'You're alive, lad. You're all right.' Ector's voice seemed far away. 'Let's have a look at you.'

He lifted his face from the dirt, which was also in his mouth so that he turned his face and spat brown saliva. He raised his good eye and saw the High King's spearmen congratulating Prince Constantine. Saw many of them, including his father's men, walking away to find new diversions in the hall and sluice dry throats with ale. Which was worse, he wondered: that they had seen him lose so badly, or that it seemed they had already forgotten the whole thing?

'The boy has embarrassed me,' Uther growled at Ector. 'And I blame you.'

'We will work harder, lord,' Ector replied, helping Arthur up onto his feet and carefully removing the helmet. 'Given time it'll be a more even match, hey, Arthur?'

Arthur lifted his chin and glared at his father, but Uther would not look at him. Or could not.

'I need wine,' Uther said, turning away from them both, 'an amphora to forget what I've just seen, and another to drown out my brother's crowing. Damn you.' He strode away after the king and the rest of them. 'I expect better from you,' he called as he went. Whether to him or to Ector, Arthur did not know.

Ector muttered something under his breath and tossed the helmet to the spearman who stood awaiting its return. The man caught it, nodded and turned to follow the others. 'Shouldn't have fought him, lad,' Ector said. He lifted Arthur's chin and turned his face to examine the injury, Arthur having to close his good eye against the glare of the afternoon sun. 'Hmm. It's not pretty but you're young. It will heal. No damage to the eye itself, lucky for you.' He let go of Arthur's chin and grunted. 'Shouldn't have fought him, Arthur.'

'I had to,' Arthur said, but there was little conviction in the words.

'Did you? Hmmm, well, I expect Uther's Lughnasadh gift will be lighter by a swine and a cask or two of ale because you *had to*.' With only a handful of days before the late summer ceremony, Arthur doubted Lord Uther would take the trouble to see to it that Ector received a thinner harvest gift than usual just because he, Arthur, had been beaten with the practice swords by his older cousin. But then Ector knew Uther better than he did.

'Next time I'll win,' Arthur said. Ector's mouth moved to form a reply but then his lips clamped shut on it and he just stared at Arthur, who held his foster father's gaze with the eye he could see out of.

'Ah, I need a drink, too,' Ector said at last, as though a cup of good ale was the only thing that could rinse away the whole sorry business. 'If I were you, Arthur, I'd stay out of his way. The pity of it is that I don't have a choice.' With that he shook his head again and turned and walked towards the hall, from which the sound of boisterous men rose like the smoke leaking from the golden thatch.

Arthur was glad when they had all gone, leaving him alone beneath the low summer sun, as a warm breeze billowed a cloud of dust up from the stubble field. He screwed up his face, lifting a hand to his swollen right cheek and feeling the heat from it. Slowly, he rolled his left shoulder, wincing as pain lanced in his back, then lifted his shield arm, which ached terribly from his cousin's thunderous blows.

'That was not a fight the bards will sing of, Arthur,' he muttered to himself, the various pains in his body eclipsed by the wound to his pride. Then he saw something – or someone – through the blur of his slitted right eye, and turned his head. His good eye made out a girl, a young woman, leaning against the rail near the stables. Watching him. Her hair was a tumbling mass of copper curls which looked like flame in the late sun. Her skin was pale, white as the patch on the stola of the Roman goddess Juno at his mother's villa where, over the years, hands had rubbed off the blue paint. He could see her aquiline nose and deep eyes, and the shadows pooled beneath the knife-sharp cheekbones, and he knew he had never seen her before. But now he felt an invisible twine stretching across the distance between them, tight as a lyre string. It played a note in his mind, that string, and he could no more ignore it than scorn his own body's need to breathe, so that he realized he was walking towards her before he had even thought why, or what he would say when they came face to face.

Not that the red-haired girl had any intention of letting him speak first.

'I have never seen someone lose so badly. You didn't land one decent hit on Prince Constantine.'

'He's taller than me,' Arthur said. 'He has a longer reach.'

'And he's stronger, obviously,' the girl said, 'so why didn't you keep your distance? Circle him and keep him moving, keep him guessing while you dart in and strike his forearm here.' She flattened her left hand and chopped it against her right arm. 'That would hurt. Make him angry. More likely to make a mistake which would give you an opening.'

'What do you know about swordplay?' Arthur could feel the scowl on his face.

'Not much,' the girl admitted, then she lifted her chin, 'but I know how to bring down that swelling. You won't be able to see anything with that eye if we don't.'

'I saw *you* well enough,' Arthur said, immediately fearing he had sounded too eager with that. But this girl *was* striking. He had never seen her before, nor anyone like her. 'I mean, you stood out because, well, everyone else is gone,' he said, lifting his right arm in the direction of the hall. She almost smiled at that, a slight pursing of the lips which lifted those sharp cheekbones higher still.

'I can make a poultice with snake weed.' She looked to the west. 'There is some growing in the river meadow. And there is betony at the margins of the stubble field. We'll boil it in milk, if you can get some. Drinking that will help with the pain.' She pointed at him, and he felt more conspicuous than he'd ever felt. 'And it will help with that,' she added. 'Betony is good for the eyes.'

'I told you, there's nothing wrong with my eye.' Arthur turned his face, not wanting her to see the swelling, which he could feel growing still, the skin tightening, pulling at his nose and twisting his already misshapen right eye.

Damn Constantine.

'So, you don't want to go down to the river meadow with me?' she asked him.

His stomach tightened. Her eyes looked dark, almost black because the low sun was behind him now, casting her in shadow. But those eyes were in him like fish hooks. 'Well, I suppose if you can stop this turning purple and black, I would be grateful,' he said. 'I don't want to give my cousin the pleasure of seeing it.'

The girl's hands vanished into the mass of curls and she swept the flames back, tying them behind her head with a cord he had not seen her holding. 'I said I could help with the swelling, not the colour.' She tilted her head and regarded him. 'Though perhaps a paste of wheaten flour and rose water would hide it a little.'

'Thank you,' he mumbled, gingerly rolling his left shoulder in its socket. 'Where are you from?'

'Caer Lot, far to the north,' she said. 'A long way from here, Arthur ap Uther.'

Her use of his formal name surprised him, but more than this there was something in the way she spoke it. A taint. As though it had not tasted good in her mouth.

'And do you have a name?' he asked.

She lifted one thick copper eyebrow. 'Yes, we have names in the north.'

'Of course, I—'

'I'm Morgaine,' she interrupted.

'Morgaine?' He had never said the name but he had heard it said. Heard it whispered, mostly, by his mother or her steward, old Bricius. Even once by Merlin, when Arthur had found the druid in one of his dreaming awake states by the fire one black winter night. He had not known who this Morgaine was, or why her name was never spoken aloud, but now here she was, close enough that he could have reached out and touched her. And if he had already found himself caught in her spell like the roach and perch in his wicker trap, knowing her name only tightened her strange hold over him.

'Your father killed my father, Arthur,' she said. 'I was curled up in my bed furs, fast asleep one mist-shrouded night, when Uther came. He slaughtered my father and took Tintagel from us.' Her eyes narrowed. 'I was too young to know what was happening, but I have dreamt of it since. Of blood. Of screams lost in the suck and plunge of waves breaking on the shore.'

Arthur felt her words like one of Constantine's sword blows, only he felt this in his stomach. A twisting blow that left him short of air.

He knew nothing about that of which she spoke. Had never even questioned how Uther had come to be Lord of Tintagel. All his life it had simply been so. 'I . . . I was not born until after,' he said, as though in defence of his own part in whatever wrongs this girl believed she and her people had suffered at the hands of his father, Uther ap Constantine ap Tahalais. Uther the Flame. Uther the Cruel.

'I know that, of course,' she said. She spoke further, but Arthur did not hear it because his mind was racing.

'So, my mother is your mother?' He said it as a question but he already knew the truth of it. It explained the whispers. Though there was much he still didn't know.

Morgaine nodded, her eyes never leaving his. Her fierce stare felt like a weight on him, though it was not unpleasant, more like a thick blanket on a cold night. At last, she looked away to the west and started walking. 'Come, Arthur,' she said, without looking back. 'Let us go down to the river meadow and find that snake weed.'

For a moment he watched her. She seemed to float across the worn grass like late evening mist. For several heartbeats he wondered if he might still be face down in the makeshift arena, some blow to the head having summoned this red-haired girl like a fever dream.

And then he followed her.

5

In Honour of Mithras

I T WAS A RAIN-FLAYED night when they came to the walls of Caer Lundein. What moon there was barely hazed the thick cloud veiling it, lighting the world no more than can a flame behind a sooty horn lantern illuminate some long-abandoned hall where fires once leapt to melodies played on lyre and flute. When he had come here as a younger man, Beran had found himself intoxicated by the possibilities of the past. He had tried to picture in his mind how Londinium had looked when the Romans ruled in Britannia. When coin and wine and expensive oils and Rhineland glass and fine red tableware and imperial edicts flowed into the ancient capital, and legionaries patrolled the walls. Now, the buds and vines of civilization which the Romans had cultivated in these Dark Isles were ashes and ruin, and Caer Lundein little more than a doomed enclave, a greasy, guttering flame in a land which was forgetting.

And Beran had all but forgotten, too, which was how it had to be.

'How will we get in?' Tristan asked above the ceaseless hissing of the rain. They had stopped to take in the section of wall protecting Caer Lundein's north-west, the four of them soaked to the marrow and shivering in the chill, murky night. Even in the gloom they could see shapes moving atop the wall: the handful of militiamen who guarded this section, some of them holding skins over their heads against the downpour.

'You can climb if you want, young man like you,' Beran said, walking on, the old wound aching as it always did in wet weather, 'I'll use the door.'

He led them down into a stinking ditch and up the other side, slipping on mud and half falling and cursing at his sludge-covered hand, then over rubble, the remains of a once great building that had been pulled down and piled onto Caer Lundein's defences. They climbed and stumbled over the bones of the past, and the rain lashed down, as though its purpose was to wash away the last remnants of Rome from this part of Britain.

Then the boy stopped and grabbed hold of Beran's sleeve, pointing up at the wall with his other hand. 'They've seen us,' he said.

The others looked to Beran, and Tristan stepped in front of Isolde, holding his spear across his body.

'Who's down there?' a voice from the wall called. 'Announce yourself!'

Somewhere out in the dark, a dog was barking.

'Cynric, King of the Saxons,' Beran growled up at the night-shrouded figure.

There was a moment's silence but for the seething rain and the dog, then, 'Beran, you old shit.' A bronze glow chased the night from that section of the rampart, the flame faltering in the downpour. Beran could smell the pitch feeding that firebrand. 'Another step and we'd have put spears in the lot of you,' said the voice.

'Balls, Kollr!' Beran called back, lifting his chin to the south. 'You couldn't hit the river if you fell out of a boat. Open up.'

Kollr leant over the wall, thrusting the sputtering torch further out as he peered down at them. 'Who's that with you? And where's Nabor and the others?'

'My friends have come to honour the god,' Beran replied. 'I haven't seen Nabor for days. Expect he's somewhere up to his eyes in whores or Saxons. Now let us in before we drown out here.'

The boy was still staring at Beran, the whites of his eyes bright as coins in the flame glow. 'It's all right, boy,' Beran breathed, low.

The flaming torch disappeared, Kollr barked a command and they heard the *clump* of heavy beams being lifted from their brackets behind a door so barely visible in the darker shadow beneath the stone wall that the others seemed surprised it was even there.

The iron hinges of that stout little door wailed as it opened.

'Welcome to Caer Lundein,' Beran said, and they followed him into the city.

He led them through the ruins of Londinium, the young woman and the boy holding hands, Tristan following behind, alert, hackles raised, ready to fight.

'Grip that spear any tighter and you'll find yourself unable to hold a cup later,' Beran told him. 'Easy, lad, you're safe enough here.' He found the younger man's vigilance irritating, not least because it clearly unsettled the boy. But mostly it rankled because Beran could not remember that feeling himself, of being so possessive of life, of wanting above all to endure, either for himself or for someone else.

After twenty paces he glanced at Tristan again, seeing the man's knuckles still chalk-white around the spear shaft, his eyes sifting the rain-slashed dark for enemies, and Beran shook his head but held his tongue. As irksome as it was that the young man did not take him at his word, Beran allowed that he and Isolde must have felt like hunted animals since fleeing Cornubia. Beran knew that feeling well enough himself from his days with Nabor ap Nabor being dogged by Saxon war bands through the forests. That life could wear a man down. Or else it could make him taut as a drawn bow and liable to jump at every rustle in the trees. That was Tristan. But there was fire in him. That was clear enough, and Beran had not been gone from the world so long that he did not see that King Mark would have to kill this young man before he could take Isolde back.

Yes, Beran knew who she was. The truth of it had seeped into him like the rain in his bones. It was in her bearing, young as she was. She wore it like an ermine robe. Beran had known of her by another name: Esseylt, which was the way the bard who had sung of her and King Mark had it last Imbolc, when Beran watched the folk of Caer Celemion celebrate the end of winter with cups of white ewes' milk and cleansing fires. And perhaps he had not realized before now because he was an old fool.

'I have never seen anything like this,' Isolde said, looking this way and that as they navigated paths through the rubble and between the empty shells of buildings that yet stood. 'How did men build such things?'

'You should see Camulodunum,' the boy said, gesturing with his free hand. 'We have roads like this, only without so many holes. We have stone houses and temples, and much of it looks as it did before the legions left, not like—' he cut himself off as he remembered Caer Colun's fate. The Saxons had burned it. Men from across the Morimaru had stormed the Roman walls and slaughtered his people, and men of Britain had murdered his mother. The boy fell silent, turning over the still smouldering ashes of all this in his mind. Beran thought he should say something to fill the sudden silence, but he could summon no words of comfort and so they walked on amongst the innards of that dead place, the only sound their footfall on the broken path they trod.

Besides, perhaps it was better that the boy could see the darkness all around and feel the chill in his very bones. Better that he had never known the time before, of hope and courage, when men yet dared to talk of throwing the invaders back into the sea. When Beltane fires licked the skies to ensure that the sun would always return to ripen the crops, and bards travelled from hall to hall singing the songs of Britain, and druids yet dreamt to the gods. All gone now. All of it long gone, like a field of flowers and morning mist from a childhood memory.

A pair of spearmen were walking towards them, shoulders hunched against the rain. Beran felt Tristan behind him tense, could all but hear the young man's heart thumping, but the guards walked past without paying them much heed, though they nodded to Beran, who nodded back. They passed the headless statue of some long-dead Roman official, and a house half swallowed by briars, and took a wide berth around two snarling dogs fighting over some scrap of flesh. Somewhere to the east, a woman was screaming in the night. It was a sound to chill the blood, and Beran heard Tristan telling Isolde that he would not let anyone touch her.

'Careful here,' Beran cautioned, as they walked between the ruins of two houses which were both taller than the height of five men. 'A child was killed here last winter.' He lifted Blandigan's axe, pointing with it. 'A tile slid from the roof and smashed her skull.' He snapped his fingers. 'Just like that, she was gone.'

'Poor thing,' Isolde said, the four of them looking up warily, though it was too dark now to see those overlapping tiles of fired clay which had always put Beran in mind of the fish-scale armour so rarely seen these days.

'Aye,' Beran sighed. 'Here's me, can't seem to die, and that poor girl barely gets to live. The Fates are cruel bitches.'

They walked on, but for Isolde who lingered in that place for a moment, as though she were trying to commune with the girl who had lost her life there, then Tristan turned and called softly to her and she hurried to catch them up.

'Stay together,' Beran told them as they came to a camp comprising a dozen tents of goat leather which he could smell even through the rain drumming against those hides and hazing the lamplight glowing at the entrance of each. 'This lot will take heads first and ask who they belonged to after.'

A man emerged from the nearest tent, breath fogging in the cool night air as he mumbled curses at the rain, thrust his spear's butt into the ground and relieved himself against a plinth of glistening marble.

'Whose men are they?' Tristan asked in a hushed voice, sweeping his sodden hair back from a face which Beran suspected had not been so gaunt before he had made an enemy of his king and been hunted for it. The thought soured Beran's guts like some memory of a rancid meal.

'They're the men who hold Caer Lundein, or what's left of it,' he said. 'Men of Rhegin and Ceint who have fled the Saxons. Some men of Powys and Caer Gloui who come for the coin. Even a few Saxons man the walls nowadays.'

'And who is their lord?' Tristan asked.

'The spearmen of Caer Lundein don't have a lord,' the boy answered before Beran could. He had spoken with distaste, as well he might, being the son of a king, Beran thought, for kings and lords had need to call spearmen to their banners, and those men gave their blood to the soil, father and son, father and son.

'They serve the council,' Beran said. 'Old men who still think this is Rome and they the senate. They negotiate now and then, buy peace between us and the Saxons south of the river. Even trade with them across the bridge.'

'Trade with the Saxons?' the boy said, looking horrified.

'Aye, sometimes,' Beran said. 'If they can remember which warlord they've a treaty with, mind. But we're killing each other again before long.' He swept the long axe towards the clutter of tents. 'These men are paid to hold the walls, so that's what they do.'

The sound of Caer Lundein's defenders laughing and shouting as they ate and drank and played dice hung like fog in that place, muted by the deluge, yet drawing Beran's memory back and back to long ago. He had fought with men like these. Soldiers, not murderers and thieves like the men he had lived amongst these last years.

'Right,' he said, lifting Blandigan's axe again, this time pointing with it to the ruin of a Roman temple whose entrance steps were guarded by a pair of ivy-sheathed columns. 'Here we are.'

'What is this place?' Isolde's voice sounded flat and dull as the door clumped shut behind them, a peal of thunder rumbling in the world beyond as they descended, their progress lit by flickering lamps placed on every third step.

'A temple, once,' Beran said, relieved to be out of the rain, 'for Mithras.' The reeking smoke from the fish-oil lamps was making the boy cough, though he had buried his nose and mouth in the crook of his elbow. 'A warrior's god,' Beran added, watching his footing in the gloom, his eyesight far from what it had once been. There was a time he could watch hawks soaring high above the world and follow them in the stoop, arrow-swift as they took some prey on the wing. A lifetime ago. 'The legions brought Mithras to Britain. His cult endured long after they returned to Rome.'

'My father was an initiate,' the boy said. 'Of the lion class. He had a cup with the lion's head on it. A bowl too.'

'That does not surprise me,' Beran muttered, sweeping the last of the rainwater from his face and ducking as he descended the last few steps, coming to a place where the ceiling of damp, crumbling plaster was low and the passageway more narrow.

'That you, Beran?' a voice said. A man rose from a stool, stooping slightly as he brought a spear to bear, but he straightened and lowered the weapon as his eyes confirmed the identity of the shadow-played figure before him. 'Haven't seen you for two moons or more,' he said, then grinned. 'Hoped the Saxons might have got you at last.'

'Age will get me before a Saxon blade will.' Beran swept an arm behind him to introduce the others. 'My friends have come to lighten their purses in the name of Mithras.'

The guard frowned. 'Haven't seen them before,' he said, his gaze lingering on Isolde. 'And I would remember a face like that.' Still staring at the young woman, he said, 'Lord Guivret know you're bringing them?'

'Move aside, Ulfin, and he'll know soon enough,' Beran said.

The guard considered this, perhaps thinking that Lord Guivret did not pay him enough to get on the wrong side of Beran. 'Suppose he will at that,' he said, turning to thump his fist against the door five times and growling at whoever was on the other side to open up.

When the door opened, smoke billowed about them, fragrant and sweet, tendrils reaching into the passage down which they had come and filling Beran's nose to vanquish the stench of his wet woollen clothes.

They stepped into that place and Beran turned to the others. 'Don't touch anything, don't offend anyone,' he said, seeing how their eyes were wide with awe and bright with reflected flame.

A soft whistle escaped Tristan's lips. 'I have only seen one other place like this,' he said. 'A house near King Mark's hall, where the Christians gather.'

Beran grunted. 'You won't find many Christians here,' he said, his gaze following theirs to take in this shadow-pooled, windowless chamber with its two lines of columns like sentinels either side of the central aisle, its stone benches sitting in between those columns, and its strange statues. One depicted a man armed with a sword standing within what might have been an egg, and another was a warrior with sunbeams emanating from his head, and the largest sculpture – at the end of the chamber, raised on a pedestal altar of marble and torchlit so that by the flickering light it seemed to move – of a man wrestling a bull, one arm around the massive animal's neck, the other holding a blade to its throat. The man and the bull were painted in colours that were still bright after so many years: his flesh-coloured limbs and green tunic, his red cloak and brown cap, and the bull in his grasp as white as the full moon.

Beran was trying to see the old temple anew, as if through the eyes of his three companions. Not for the first time, he reflected that he had seen many wonders in his life. The great Wall far to the north. Palaces of marble, baths of steaming water wider than a lord's hall, in which he and his wife had bathed together. Proud stallions clad in shining lea-ther, snorting and pawing at the summer grass, tossing their manes, eager to run. Great arenas built by long-dead emperors, where champi-ons fought for the entertainment of thousands of imperial subjects. A library crammed with books and scrolls, the combined knowledge of great minds. War bands glittering in mail and scale armour beneath a low winter sun. So many wonders, yet even the memories of them were tainted now, unclear like the image in an old mottled mirror.

'It feels like we are in the earth,' the boy said in a small, breathy voice. 'I mean deep in the earth, in a place of gods.'

'There are no gods in Britannia, boy,' Beran said. 'Not any more.' Yet even as he said the words, he felt the weight of that cave-like place, of the ancient and worm-holed roof beams, and the earth above pressing down on him, of the strange rituals and mysteries that must have taken place where they now stood, and which took place still, on occasion. For all that he believed the gods had flown these Dark Isles, or faded like a bloodstain in the soil, he yet felt there might be some danger in saying as much, though he was long past fear on that score.

The boy frowned at him. 'But you told that spearman on the wall that we had come to honour the god.' His words trailed after themselves in that cavernous space.

Beran cocked an eyebrow at the boy. 'Just an expression. You'll understand soon enough.' He set off down the central aisle, the others walking at his shoulder, Isolde and the boy touching each of the columns they passed. 'Thought I said don't touch anything,' Beran mumbled.

'There's no one here to see,' Isolde replied, stopping beside the statue of some Roman deity and pressing her palm against the god's cheek.

'Well, that's about to change,' Beran said, as he led them behind the pedestal altar with its sculpture of Mithras slaughtering the bull, and took hold of the iron ring handle of a stout door. 'Keep hold of the boy.' He turned the handle and pulled the door open. Ahead lay a narrow tunnel upon whose white plastered walls shadow and light danced to the silent tune of a through-draught that tickled the flames of rushlights.

'Where are you taking us?' Tristan asked, moving aside to allow a staggering drunk coming the other way to pass. Beran did not reply. There were other passages leading off on either side, but he led them along the main one, towards the clamour of voices and the stench of sweat and piss, cooked onions and garlic and acrid fish-oil smoke and people. They had to step over a man slumped against the passage wall, snoring into the cup which he held on his chest, and soon after the tunnel ended. They emerged into the main chamber which was thronged with men and women, and foul smelling, and ill lit by tall iron tripods whose oil-filled bowls spewed black smoke to the low, soot-stained ceiling. Beran glanced back and saw the boy was pressing his hands to his ears.

'Stay close, boy.' Beran was pushing through the clamorous crowd, forcing a channel for the others to follow. Some swore at him as he muscled his way amongst them. Most did not seem to care, so intent were they on the spectacle for which they had all gathered, and for which silver, coin and wine had been wagered.

'Finish him, Melis!' a woman's voice shrieked above the din.

'End the old black bastard!' a man yelled.

Beran shouldered his way to the forefront of the press, pulling the others into the space he had made, and the three of them stood there beside him, taking in a scene which Beran knew they would never have expected down there in that underground vestige of some Roman cult. A man with skin the dark brown of chestnuts and short, iron-grey hair was fighting a younger, broad-shouldered, bull-necked opponent, the two of them naked but for loincloths and linen knuckle wraps, their skin glistening with oil and sweat.

The men had been grappling, but neither had gained the advantage and so they broke their hold on each other and drew apart, breathing hard, wiping sweat and blood from their eyes as the crowd bayed for violence. The dark-skinned man noticed Beran and gave him a bloody grimace, and Beran nodded back. Then the other, bigger man lumbered forward and swung his fist, but the dark man ducked the blow and scythed his right fist into the big man's left ear, to the obvious delight of many in the crowd.

'Who is he?' Tristan asked.

The big man shook off the blow and came again, throwing a combination of punches which his opponent took on his raised forearms and ribs before the two grabbed hold of each other again and clung on in the roar from the ring of bodies around them.

'His name is Palamedes,' Beran said.

'He's a Saracen,' the boy said in awe. 'The Saraceni formed the equites in the army of Theodosius the Great,' he told Tristan, who seemed equally captivated by the dark-skinned fighter. 'My father said they were great warriors.'

Beran grunted. 'Tell that to Melis there.' The bull-necked man had wrapped his brawny arms around Palamedes and was lifting him off the ground. Those great arms and powerful chest and shoulders began squeezing the life out of the Saracen, so that Palamedes was gasping for breath, and Beran half expected to hear the snapping of his ribs even above the noise in that chamber.

'I've something to do,' Beran said. 'Stay put. I'll find you after.' He looked down at the boy, who was looking at him, eyes suddenly betraying fear. 'You'll be safe with Tristan.'

Isolde put an arm around the boy's shoulder and gave Beran a look that said, *You'd better not be lying. You'd better not abandon him now.*

'I won't be long,' Beran told her, eyes scanning the crowd, as someone bellowed at the bigger fighter to knock the dark-skinned man back to whatever sun-scorched land he had come from. The faces around them were twisted in savage glee, or in anger at the thought of their anticipated lost wagers, or pinched with grim sympathy for the man being crushed so that his eyes were bulging in his paling face. 'Just stay put,' Beran told the others, before turning his shoulder into the press of bodies.

'You're not going to wait to see if your friend wins?' Tristan called after him. Just then, Palamedes created enough room in the other man's grip to lean back and whip forward, slamming his forehead down onto the big man's nose, making his opponent cry out in rage and let go of him. Palamedes dropped and scrambled on hands and knees across the straw-strewn floor, out of the other's reach.

'I've seen it a hundred times,' Beran called back, gesturing to Tristan to keep his eyes on the boy. He pushed on around the inner edge of the throng, towards the man who would make the most money this night whoever won the bout taking place before him. A man who might easily go unnoticed amongst such a crowd, but once noticed was rarely unremarked upon, and not only because he was no taller than a child of seven summers, but because he was the lord of this subterranean place, this mostly forgotten temple to a long-vanished god. Guivret the Small, some called him. Others called him the Little King, and when he saw Beran twisting and shoving his way towards him, the Little King did nothing to disguise the foul words that Beran read on his lips.

'Not here,' Guivret said, turning away from the contest and hirpling off on his stout little legs. Beran had to lengthen his own stride to keep pace, easy as it was now to pass through this rough rabble of Mithras because two men cleared a path for the dwarf lord, pushing folk aside with the shafts of their spears.

They walked through a knot of grizzled-looking warriors gathered around a man on a stool playing a crwth, his stubby fingers surprisingly nimble across the strings as he sang along. An old tune but new words. Something about the great warlord Arthur, and how he had not died after the great battle at Camlan but would come again, a flame relit in the darkest time.

Shouldering his way through, Beran fished a bronze coin from the pouch on his belt and tossed it to the man, whose hand jumped from the instrument to catch the coin. He nodded at Beran.

'Sing something else,' Beran growled, walking on. Behind him, the tune changed to a merrier one.

They were soon in another tunnel, this one so low that Beran and the two spearmen had to bend over and walk stooped as old men. *I am an old man*, Beran thought, touching the blade of Blandigan's axe to one of the many low columns of thin red brick that lined this tunnel, a passage which had long ago carried hot air to heat the building that once stood above their heads.

Guivret came to a crude door and opened it, and Beran followed him into a cell which had been carved out of the bedrock itself, its arched ceiling high enough for Beran to stand tall again, his back already complaining from being bent. The ceiling and walls were damp as always, as though the Tamesis was slowly seeping into the place, and the rock was scarred here and there with Roman writing, names of the long-dead perhaps, or prayers, or even curses, Beran thought, whose meanings were lost now, though once perhaps they had held power.

The spearmen did not follow Beran into the room, instead making their way back along the passage, he presumed, to take up guard positions where they and their spears could stand straight.

Beran watched Guivret approach a table, upon which a loaf of bread sat beside a jug and four wooden cups. Beran could smell that the bread was freshly baked, even over the stink of his wet clothes and the stench of the main chamber that lingered yet in his nose. He said nothing, his stomach rumbling as Guivret lifted the jug and filled two cups, pouring the wine from a height so that the stream of it was the colour of garnets by the light of the beeswax candle behind.

In the shadows cast across the far side of the room, a bare-breasted woman lay half-swathed in skins on a Roman *lectus genialis*, watching Beran with sleepy eyes. He had never seen this one before. Dark skin, hair as glossy as a black stallion's mane and lips the same colour as the wine. Not that any of this would hold Guivret's attention for long, he knew.

The lord of the temple of Mithras put the jug down and lifted both cups, extending one towards Beran, an eyebrow arched in suspicious disapproval. 'What I lack in height, I make up for in cleverness, Beran. Few around here would disagree. So, tell me, if you would, why am I wasting good Galician wine on a dead man?'

Beran leant the axe against the rock wall and took the cup, nodding in thanks and bringing it to his nose to breathe in the wine. Berries and plums. Oak and leather. He closed his eyes and for a heartbeat he was young again and strong and in love.

He opened his eyes and watched Guivret over the rim of the cup as he tasted the wine. Let it wash over his tongue and around his mouth a moment, before he swallowed. 'You know, then?'

Guivret glared at him. 'Of course I know. Bad news travels fast.' He swirled his own wine around in the cup, watching it as a druid might watch some potion he was mixing. 'Nabor paid a boy to ride here while the bodies of the men you killed were still warm.' He sipped his wine. 'He thought you might come back here. Said that if you did, I am to string you up by your feet until he comes.' He shrugged his solid shoulders. 'The men you killed work for me as often as not. Your actions will cost me dear, Beran.'

Beran felt a chill in his stomach in spite of the wine. 'Is that your intention? To hand me over to Nabor?' He feared for the boy, he realized. He feared that he had made a terrible mistake by bringing him here.

Guivret eyed Beran and scratched his bearded neck. 'I don't take orders from cut-throat scum like Nabor ap Nabor. Besides, he can deal with you himself. I expect he's not far behind you.' He drank again, dragged his hand across his lips and pointed a wine-stained finger at Beran. 'But I would like to know why you betrayed your own men.'

'They are not my men,' Beran said.

'You know what I mean.' Guivret tilted his head to one side. 'Who is the boy?'

'Just a boy,' Beran said. He went over to the table and picked up the loaf and tore a hunk off.

The Little King frowned. 'If you're going to drink my wine and eat my bread, Beran, then do me the courtesy of not treating me like one of your halfwit sellsword companions.' Seeing Beran chewing must have whetted Guivret's own appetite, because he hurried over to

Beran, snatched the loaf from him and bit into it. 'Who is the boy?' he asked through a mouthful. 'He's of good stock. Well fed and bright-eyed. Haughty as a little prince, you might say, even half drowned by the rain and sloshing about with a miserable old wretch like you.'

He could read people, could Guivret, and more than once Beran had wondered if the little man could read him. 'He is the son of King Constantine and Queen Brendana,' Beran said. Easier to be honest. 'We were supposed to kill him. On Queen Morgana's orders.'

Guivret's brow furrowed. 'So, he *could* be a king one day. With that blood in his veins, maybe even a new Pendragon.' He lifted his chin and scratched his thick neck. 'Of course Morgana wants him dead. The old witch still burns a candle for a Britain where her grandson sits on the high seat.' His lip curled as he said, 'Melehan ap Mordred ap Arthur. That smug fool seeks to rule above all the kings, including the Saxon ones.' Then he half smiled with the satisfaction of having seen it all clearly. Whistled. 'That boy out there is their only blood challenge to the line of the High Kings, Uther, and Ambrosius before him.' He bit off another hunk of bread, thinking whilst he chewed. 'I wasn't expecting this when you washed up like a turd on the foreshore, Beran.' His squared-off jaw was working hard on that bread. 'Some teary-eyed bard out there is squawking that this boy of yours could be the one who unites Britain and throws the Saxons back into the sea.'

Beran had never known Guivret to nurse such grand hopes for Britain, nor even much hatred for the Saxons, come to that. But the man had an Agassian hound's nose for opportunity, and Beran could see silver glinting in the Little King's eyes now.

'Or he could just be a boy who grows into a man,' Beran said, 'which can't happen if he ends up as dead as his mother in some forest hereabouts.'

But Guivret was still thinking as he chewed. 'So, you decided to kill everyone *but* the boy?' he asked.

'Not everyone.' Beran shrugged. 'Just those that would have killed him and me.'

The dwarf flapped a dismissive hand. 'You risked your life for this boy. You betrayed your own for him. And now you bring this trouble to my door?'

'I don't kill children,' Beran said. His mind spooled back to the ambush in the forest and the greybeard who had been Queen Brendana's bodyguard. He had known Beran for what he was. And for *who* he was.

How could you do this? Why?

His stomach soured at the memory. Or perhaps it was just the wine on an empty belly.

'And the other two out there?' Guivret gestured with the half-eaten loaf to the door. 'The young lovers. Who are they? What have they got to do with it?' He raised an eyebrow. 'She is a beauty, eh? Even an old bear like you can see that. Perhaps I can convince her to stay here. She would live like a queen.'

The girl lying on the Roman bed made a sound that told them what she thought about that, but Guivret ignored her.

'They're nobody,' Beran said. 'But yes, they're in love. They like the boy and the boy likes them, so I said they can travel with me.'

'The boy is tempting.' Guivret scratched his cheek. 'The girl too.' He shook his head. 'But I'd struggle to stop Nabor killing the little prince. And the girl . . .' He sighed. 'Seems to me she likes tall, pretty men. It would be . . . upsetting if she didn't yield to my charms.' With a look he dared Beran to mock him, but Beran held his tongue, let his eyes say nothing. 'No, I need you gone, Beran. Gone like you were never here.'

Beran nodded. 'Came to get my things.'

'You can't come back.'

'I won't.' He finished his wine and placed the cup on the table. 'We'll be gone by first light. Can you get us across the river?'

Guivret nodded. 'If it means I can be sure I've seen the back of you.' He frowned then. 'Emmeline will take it hard, though I'll never know why she's so fond of you.'

Beran grunted. 'She's better off without me.'

Guivret gave a snort of agreement. 'Where will you go? What are your plans for the boy?' Before Beran could weave the lie, the little man waved a hand through air now fragrant with the earthy aroma of honey from the expensive candle. 'Don't tell me. Better if I don't know.'

Beran fetched the axe and gripped it by the throat.

Guivret lifted his chin. He knew that weapon well enough. 'So, Blandigan is dead?'

'He is, but I didn't kill him,' Beran said.

'Shame,' Guivret said.

Whether he meant it was a shame that Blandigan was dead, or a shame that Beran hadn't been the one to kill him, Beran didn't know. And he had no time to ask, because echoing down the tunnel from the main chamber came the sound of people shouting.

Because the Saxons had come.

6

The Black River

BERAN THUMPED ON THE door. 'It's me. Open up. Hurry.'
The door opened and Emmeline stood there, her grey hair
swept back from her face and bound tight, so that all the years of her
life lay easily there, mocking him with their honesty.

'What's happening?' she asked, her creamy white eyes seeing nothing, though she knew well enough who had come. She took his arm
and ushered him into the dark room she had shared with him nights
beyond counting over the last years.

He found the flint and steel and tinder where they always kept
them, and soon an oil lamp crackled with a new little flame.

A bowl full of oats, butter, milk and honey sat on the table, a spoon
standing up in the mixture where she had left it. A shame they would
not have time to wait for the oat cakes to bake, he thought.

'The Saxons have crossed the river. A lot of them,' he said.

Her face tightened. 'Too many?'

'I don't know.' Beran was already on his knees, opening the chest
containing his belongings, which Emmeline had allowed to take up
space in her little room down there in the catacombs beside the temple
of Mithras ever since he had come to Caer Lundein, returning to the
world like a shade on Samhain eve.

He took out a frayed cloak. 'Maybe the garrison will push them
back across the river. Maybe not. We won't be here to find out.' Then a
pair of trews and two tunics, one of wool, the other bleached linen. He
laid these garments aside. Then came a belt, a leather flask, a sheath
and knife whose blade had all but forgotten the touch of a grindstone,
a waxed leather hood, three woollen socks and a shedding wolf pelt.

He could hardly see by the one small lamp flame, but he knew these things by touch.

When the chest was empty, he drew the knife and used it to ease up the boards of the false bottom, removing them one by one until he found the purse of coin, rings and precious stones. All that remained of his earnings. Not much for the blood he had spilled, he thought, weighing the purse in his hand before tying it to his belt and tucking it away.

'Is it true, Beran?' Emmeline asked. 'There's a whisper. That you turned against Nabor. That you killed his men.'

'I've done worse,' he said. Emmeline knew that, of course. She had scrubbed enough blood from his clothes. And yet she had fed him and washed him. She had trimmed his hair and beard and given him more than he deserved. He had never known why.

'Get your things,' he said over his shoulder. 'We travel light.'

'If not for the Saxons, you'd have left me here, wouldn't you?' she said. An accusation from the shadows. 'Would you have even said goodbye?'

'I'd have said goodbye,' he said, though now he was there with her, he did not know if that were true. It would have been easier to spend the night, then slip away in the dawn.

'And if I'd have chosen to go with you? What then, Beran?'

'I wouldn't have expected you to come with me,' he said, sweeping his hand across the bottom of the chest. 'Not out there.'

'And now?' she asked.

For a heart-stopping moment he could not find what he was looking for.

'Now, neither of us can stay,' he said, reaching for the lamp and bringing it closer.

He could feel her thinking in the gloom. After a moment, she said, 'You know they will come for you. A man like Nabor; he'll kill you, Beran.'

'Not if the Saxons kill me first.' He saw it then. The thin strip of green ribbon folded long ago around its secret. He could hear men shouting, could hear the hobnails of shoes against the flagstones of the temple floor. Perhaps even the clash of blades, yet he could not be sure, for that was a sound often in his ears whether real or not, like the distant crashing of waves always being in a seashell.

'Where will you go?' she asked.

'*We'll* go west,' he said. 'To Camelot.' He reached down but stopped, not daring to touch that last remaining thing. As though it were a flame. 'There's a boy. I've given him my word that I'll take him there.'

'A boy? What boy?'

He steeled himself and closed his hand around the folded ribbon.

She grabbed his shoulder. 'What boy, Beran?'

Just as well she could not see him now, he thought, holding the past tightly in his hand.

'A boy who didn't deserve what Nabor had planned for him,' he said.

'But Camelot, Beran?' she said. 'I can't go all that way. Not fast enough. Nabor will catch up with us and he'll kill you. You know he will. Sure as ice in winter.'

He lifted the thing to his nose and he closed his eyes and he breathed it in. It still carried her scent. Faint now. Almost not there at all. But it was her. His bones ached these days and his eyes were dimmer than they were. He needed to piss three times every night, and food did not taste as he remembered it, but his sense of smell was still sharp, and now it had talons that tore through his chest and took hold of his heart, near stopping it. Slowly, he unwound the ribbon. There was no need to do it, but why not rip his heart clean out now he had started? It had been years since he had felt anything at all, other than the aches of his old body, so this was almost ... exquisite. Unknown and yet so familiar. Like the lingering emotion of a dream whose images have faded away.

'You need to go, Beran,' she said. 'Need to go now.' She took up her blackthorn staff from where it leant against the wall. 'Leave all that,' she said, gesturing with that staff, though she could not know what he held. 'Can't go back, Beran. Can't ever go back.'

Perhaps she was thinking of the man she had lost years ago, not killed by Saxons but taken by some fever. Everyone had their wounds.

'I know,' he said. 'Don't think I don't know that.'

Emmeline loved him in her way. He knew that, too. She had taken him in when he was nothing but the burden of his own ghosts. When all he had to offer was violence. The times she had stitched his cuts, her fingers all the more nimble, perhaps, because of her blindness; and as those wounds closed, so he had opened up to her a little. They had kept each other company whenever Beran found himself in Caer Lundein. The blind woman and the old man. Like the thin ends of old roots entwining in the dusk.

The ribbon unwound now, he looked at the silver ring gripped between his finger and thumb. Warm, as though it still held the heat of the flesh it had caressed for so many years. Burnished and smooth. Yet sharp as a blade to him.

'Come on, let's go,' he said, standing and wrapping the ring back into the green ribbon. As green as it had ever been, that ribbon. It had not faded as he had faded, but was as fresh and bright as when it had tied hair as black as a crow's wing. Blue as a beetle's shell. The burnished copper of beech leaves at the season's turn.

He had come back to say goodbye. And for the meagre coin he had earned and not yet spent on food and drink and other things. For the ring, too, perhaps. But he knew then that he could not take the ring. Could not carry such a thing as that, even now, after so long. With a subdued sigh, he put the ribbon-bound ring back into the chest, tucked into the corner where the silver-grey hairs from the moulting wolf's pelt had gathered, and pushed the boards of the false floor roughly back in place before closing the lid. He stood, turning to Emmeline.

'Come,' he said, handing her his old wolf's pelt, which she put around her shoulders, deftly tying the leather thongs which she had woven into it herself.

'My flask,' she said, turning back into the dimly lit room as he opened the door. Cries of panic and alarm coursed through the tunnels, washing over him.

He listened intently for thirty beats of his heart, trying to discern any telltale sounds of violence between and among the voices. No metal clash, no nearby hammering of fist or weapon on barred door; there was time yet, but barely.

He turned to urge haste, and found Emmeline close beside him. She took the hand he offered her and they left the small room, following the tunnels back the way he had come. They met Tristan and Isolde and the boy coming the other way, their eyes wide in the gloom.

'We have to get out, Beran,' Tristan said. 'The Saxons are everywhere.'

Beran saw an unspoken accusation in the boy's face. 'What is it?' he asked him.

'I thought you'd left us,' the boy said.

'You thought wrong, boy,' Beran said.

'The guard, Ulfin,' Tristan went on, 'he was shouting that the spearmen of Caer Lundein were building their shieldwall a spear-throw south of here. Said there were Saxons already in the ruins above our heads.'

Beran muttered a curse. 'Follow me,' he told them, 'and stay close.' They nodded, then he turned to Emmeline, putting a hand on her shoulder, feeling the bony nub of it beneath that old wolf pelt. 'I'll guide you,' he said.

She shook her head. 'I want to stay, Beran. I'll only slow you down.'

'No, you won't,' he said. 'You're younger than me, remember?' He forced a smile which Emmeline would never see, though she had once told him she could hear a smile creaking in his lips. 'And Tristan here is from Cornubia, where he has been living a soft life at the court of King Mark. If anyone is going to slow us down it will be him.'

Tristan frowned at him. 'You know who I am?' he asked.

'I know,' Beran said. 'But now's not the time for all that.' He took up his cloak and Emmeline's hand, closing her hand around a fistful of the cloak's hem. 'Don't let go.' It had been a long time since she had left the ruins of Caer Lundein, and Beran knew that the world beyond was terrifying, infinite and unknowable to her. 'And trust your footing,' he told her. 'I'll keep to even ground where I can.'

He led them a different way this time, through the main chamber, which was all but empty now, then along a tunnel which had long ago carried water from the Tamesis to the most important villas and baths nearby, where they had to progress on hands and knees through damp weeds and ancient sludge. The boy found it easy. The young lovers made light enough work of it too, but for Beran and Emmeline the going was slow and arduous, and Beran wondered if his knees would ever allow him to stand straight again, assuming they ever came to the end of that shaft.

At last, they spilled out into the night a long way from the temple of Mithras, all of them squeezing water from their cloaks and trews, Beran and Tristan seeking any dry corner of cloth upon which to wipe blades, lest the iron rot set in.

The rain had stopped but the sky was thick with cloud still, so that it was very dark, and there was a swirling wind which had the boy shivering in his wet clothes. That wind gathered up the sounds of fighting – the clash of blades, the thump of shields and the cries of men – scattering them into the night like leaves of sound, making it almost impossible to tell where the battle was unfolding. Beran knew, though. He had told the men of the Caer Lundein garrison where their defences were most vulnerable. Down by the old docks, he had said, where the river had silted, and folk walked out across the mud with their eel traps. That silting made the crossing narrower. With a good elm bow a man could shoot an arrow from bank to bank at that point in the Tamesis's snaking course. He had once known a man who could have thrown a spear across it. The old Roman wall there should be repaired, he had told them, for that is where the Saxons will make their big push when it comes. But they had not listened. Not to him. And why would they? He was just an old man. He was like a rusty blade himself, some hard thing of iron but ragged and worn and unneeded.

'Where now?' Tristan asked. He gripped his spear and he gripped Isolde, their clasped hands making a pale knot in the gloom. The wind gusted, whipping Isolde's hair across her eyes and bringing with it a ragged cheer from the throats of warriors on Caer Lundein's walls or amongst the ruins.

Beran looked back to where he knew men were hacking and stabbing, pushing and panting for breath, every living one of them, be he of Rhegin or Ceint, Powys or Caer Gloui, or some mouth-warping Saxon village from across the grey sea, driven to butchery so that he might live to see another sunrise or hold a lover again. Or a child.

'This way,' he told them, setting off. Bats whirred above their heads. To the west of them, dogs barked incessantly. Beran had once had a dog himself. He knew that a dog's senses were sharper than a man's and that they would know there was trouble long before their owners did. 'We're going down to the river,' he said.

Tristan stopped, and so Isolde and the boy stopped too. 'But the Saxons hold the land south of the river.'

Beran stopped and turned and looked at him. 'You want to go back that way?' He pointed Blandigan's axe to the north. Another shout went up. Perhaps one side had broken the other's shieldwall. Perhaps not.

Tristan looked at Isolde, who gave a slight shake of her head.

'No,' Tristan said.

'Didn't think so,' Beran said, continuing on, Emmeline at his left shoulder, holding on to his cloak with one hand, her staff with the other. After a heartbeat, the others followed.

'We'll go upriver. Get away from all this,' Beran told them. 'Either the Saxons will be thrown back to their palisade on the other side of the Tamesis and will be licking their wounds until Samhain ...' He reached out and took hold of a twig which had become snarled in Emmeline's hair. 'Hold still,' he said softly, easing the thing free. 'Or they'll win,' he continued, tossing the twig away, 'in which case they'll be looting, rutting themselves senseless and using Caer Lundein as a pissing post come morning. Either way, they won't care about a little boat making its way upriver in the dark.' He hoped that was true.

'A boat?' the boy asked, through shivering lips. He was looking at Beran with round eyes. Isolde pulled her cloak tighter round her neck against another gust, her own eyes boring into Beran's, so that he cursed inwardly at this new life that would have him explain his every quiet thought to others.

'We need to get upriver,' he said, 'and I don't swim like I used to.' He was peering into the south, wondering if his old eyes were missing things: the whites of a man's eyes, a polished iron blade, dull in the night. The copper glow of a campfire around which men would be huddled in the damp dark – anything that would tell him that there were Saxons down on the river's edge, guarding the boats they had crossed over in, perhaps, or older men waiting as a reserve should they be needed at the walls.

'I can swim.' The boy looked from Tristan to Isolde. 'Like a fish, Mother used to say.' His face hardened then, as though he had just remembered that his mother was dead, the knowledge catching him by surprise like a kick to the stomach.

'Then if there's no boat, you'll have to swim for the both of us, boy,' Emmeline said, her face turned in his direction, her eyes white as pebbles tumbling in on the tide.

'There'll be a boat,' Beran assured them, leading them on through the dark.

They passed a clutter of half-collapsed timber-framed buildings whose mossy, mouldering thatch bristled in the wind. Then came onto a wooden wharf whose thick pilings disappeared into water which was flecking white under a racing sky.

'Careful, it's slippery,' Tristan said.

'Rotten too,' Beran warned, guiding Emmeline around a jagged hole where someone's foot must have broken through the timber quay. There had been a time when vessels came up the Tamesis laden with Spanish olives and Syrian wine. Once, he had even seen a great ship with a white sail, which had somehow navigated the treacherous shifting sands of the Tamesis estuary. As a boy, he had stood amongst scores of men and women who buzzed like bees as they watched dark-skinned crewmen unload the precious cargo onto this very wharf, the ship rising at its mooring to reveal its green-slimed belly. Now, the tide ebbing as it was, the wharf looked more like the skeleton of some great and ancient beast washed up onto the shore.

'There!' the boy hissed, 'down on the strand.' He was pointing, but Beran could see only the black Tamesis mud and the black water beyond, and beyond that, the indistinct line of the far shore, where the shivering shape of trees met the charcoal sky.

'I see them,' Tristan said, to Beran's irritation.

'Saxons?' Beran looked at Tristan rather than trusting his own eyes in the darkness.

'No. A man and a boy, I think,' Tristan said.

'Look, they have a boat,' Isolde said.

Beran swore under his breath. He crouched at the edge of the wharf, his knees popping, then jumped down onto the muddy foreshore, his boots sinking deep. 'That's no boy,' he said, gently helping Emmeline down onto the strand beside him. 'That's the man whose boat we're getting on.'

'Don't just stand there, Beran, help us with this!' the Little King called, flapping his short arms in Beran's direction. He and Palamedes were floundering in the mud, trying to pull the small boat round as they dragged it towards the lapping fringe of the wind-rippled river.

Tristan and the boy plunged through the mud to help, but before Beran could follow, Emmeline tugged on his cloak. He turned back to her, the wind whipping her hair – the same colour as the wolf pelt – back from her pale face.

'I'll not be going with you, Beran,' she said.

'Of course you are,' he said, taking her by the arm.

'No, Beran. Listen to me now.' She thrust the staff into the Tamesis mud and it stuck there like a branchless tree. Then she grabbed hold of Beran by both arms and he felt the strength in her. 'There's nothing for me out there,' she said, lifting her chin and her sightless eyes to the west. 'Nothing but tripping on your heels and slowing you down.'

'You're no slower than I am these days,' he said, though he knew she was right. She would slow them down, and somewhere, perhaps in the woods, or maybe at some round at which they'd stop for shelter or provision, Nabor ap Nabor would catch up with them and he would kill Beran and the boy. *Sure as ice in winter.*

'You go now, old man,' Emmeline told him, her voice competing with the wind. 'You promised that boy and now you must keep that promise, do you hear?'

Beran glanced over his shoulder. They had dragged the boat down to the water and the Little King was already aboard, Palamedes and Tristan holding the ropes while Isolde and the boy looked back at Beran, waiting for him and Emmeline to join them.

Beran lifted his free hand and pressed it gently against Emmeline's cheek, and she pushed her face against that hand, hard against the tough calluses on his fingers, as though greedy for his touch, as though she knew she would never feel it again.

'I'll take you back, find somewhere safe,' he said, lifting his chin in the direction from which they had come. 'A place to lie low until you know who holds the walls.'

She shook her head. 'You're old, but you're no fool. They're waiting and you must go. I found my way in this dark world before I met you, Beran, and I'll find my way when you're gone.'

He did not know what to say to her then, though he knew he must let her go back alone. He opened his mouth to speak but now she pressed her fingers to his lips. Even in the wind-whipped night he could smell the honey from the oat-cake mixture on those fingers. 'Before you go off across Britain with this boy and these two young Cornubians . . .' She took hold of his right hand in both her own and pressed something against his palm, and he did not need to look to know what it was. Her white eyes seemed to search his. 'I know what I said, that you can't go back. And it's true, none of us can. Still, we take the past with us into the future.' She turned at the sudden rasping call of a corncrake which had burst from a clump of reeds and taken to the air, all rufous wings and long trailing legs in the murk. 'For we carry it with us, Beran.' She brought her sightless eyes back to his. 'We must,' she said, 'or else we cannot know who we are or how we came here.' She squeezed his closed fist. 'Do you understand?'

'No,' he said, 'I don't.' And yet he held tightly that ribbon-bound ring, though it could have been an ember spat from some baleful fire, singeing his skin and his soul too.

'I think you do,' she said.

'Beran! We are leaving, with or without you!' Guivret called, and Beran turned his head to see the lord of the ruined temple balancing in his little boat, waving an arm.

'Go,' Emmeline said, letting go of Beran and stepping back.

He lifted her hand to his lips and kissed it. 'Go north, keeping the wind on your right cheek. Find shelter and wait. The Saxons won't linger in the ruins, they'll go back across the river.' He did not know if that were true, but he hoped it was.

She nodded. 'Never known you to talk so much. Go on now!' She flapped a hand towards the river.

He nodded in turn. Took that hand and kissed it again and turned and plunged down the muddy strand, his knapsack over his shoulder, Blandigan's axe in one hand and the ribbon-bound ring in the other.

'And look after that boy,' she called after him. 'You were a little boy yourself once, Beran. Try to remember that.'

'Aye, when Eiocha was born of sea-foam,' he mumbled into his beard, doing everything he could not to slip in the sludge and fall on his backside as he made his way towards the boy, who was watching his progress keenly, Isolde holding him close, her hair flying like a war banner.

'You're just leaving her there?' Isolde asked him as he threw his sack into the boat.

'It's none of your concern,' he said. 'Get in. Tide's ebbing still and we'll be rowing against it.'

The boy jumped aboard, the boat tipping dangerously as he sat down in the thwarts, because it was not properly afloat yet, but still half cradled by the Tamesis mud. Beran gestured for Isolde to follow, but she found her way blocked by Guivret, who stood with his legs planted shoulder-width apart, one hand on the hilt of the Saxon long knife which hung in a scabbard from his belt on two straps.

'Never said I'd take these two, Beran. Just you and the boy.' He lifted his free hand and fluttered stubby, ringed fingers at Isolde and Tristan. 'Not unless they pay me. They're trouble. I can smell it on them.'

'Where will you go?' Beran asked him.

Guivret gestured vaguely to the south. 'To my horses first, then down to Portus Adurni and to Benoic. Cross the sea with us, Beran. I'll pay you well, and I could use your sword.' He tilted his head towards Palamedes. 'The Saracen will be pleased with the company.'

'I doubt that,' Beran said.

The Little King looked from Beran to Isolde. 'Silver. Or you and your handsome friend will have to find another way.'

'I can out-row Beran,' Tristan said, still holding the stern rope.

'I don't doubt it,' Guivret said. 'But Beran and I are old friends.'

'Don't give me that horse dung,' Beran said. 'You and your boat would have been gone had the boy not seen you.'

Guivret threw an arm up in the direction of Caer Lundein's walls. 'How was I to know the Saxons would attack? I could hardly go looking for you in the middle of all that. And anyway, when I agreed to get you across the river, I was drinking my second-best wine and trying to get rid of you so that I could enjoy the company of my new friend.' He glanced from Isolde to Palamedes, who was already sitting on a row bench gripping a pair of oars. 'Did you know she was born in Carthage?' he asked.

Palamedes shrugged as if to say maybe he did and maybe he didn't.

'They are coming with us,' Beran told him.

Guivret narrowed his eyes at Beran. 'For a price.'

Beran turned to Isolde and Tristan. 'Get in.'

The Little King pulled the Saxon knife from its scabbard and pointed it, first at Isolde, then Tristan. 'I said no. This is my boat, not his.'

'Put that away before you hurt yourself,' Beran growled.

Guivret's eyes bulged and he turned to Palamedes. 'Why are you just sitting there? Do something, you savage! What do I pay you for?'

Palamedes looked at Beran, who saw that one of the Saracen's eyes was swollen almost shut from his fight in the temple chamber. 'If they want to come, let them come,' Palamedes said. 'But we need to go now.' He nodded towards the shore where flames were flying in the night.

'Saxons,' the boy said.

Those flames were torches and they were coming down to the river. 'Get in,' the Little King told them all, and so they did.

*

Tristan used an oar to push them out into deeper water, and then the little boat was free. He sat on one of the two benches and rowed, keeping time with Palamedes. The boy and Isolde huddled in the stern, whilst Beran and Guivret crouched in the bow, their quarrel forgotten now that the enemy was close.

They all watched the shore and those bobbing firebrands, and the rowers had barely made six strokes when warriors appeared on the wharf, the rumble of their voices shredding in the wind as they looked across the water.

Beran's gaze lingered on Emmeline, who yet stood just beyond the water's edge, the dark shape of her lingering just beyond the fitful glow of those torches. He wanted to shout to her, to warn her about the spearmen who were but a stone's throw from where she stood. It seemed they had not seen her yet, though surely Emmeline must know that the men were there.

'Not even Saxons would hurt a blind woman standing in the mud on a night like this,' Guivret said. 'Why get their boots filthy?'

Beran knew the Little King was trying to put his mind at ease, yet his stomach knotted this way and that as they slipped away on the dark river, leaving Emmeline behind. The night had fallen across her like a black cloak now, so that she was lost to his sight. He felt that loss like a weight of guilt, like something tainted in his gut, and sickened he looked in vain for her still, as the flames from those men's torches tore at the gloom.

It was slow going because the great river was still flowing back into the sea, but Palamedes and Tristan were strong, neither man wanting to be the one to let his oar-stroke wane. Now was Beran glad for Tristan's company, because he knew he would have been puffing already and dead soon enough from a burst heart if he had tried to keep up with the Saracen.

There were some other boats on the dark river, small craft pushing westward, filled with the families of garrison men, Beran supposed. Families who had decided to risk escaping Caer Lundein by water, which told Beran that the Saxons must have breached the river palisade in numbers and were likely killing and looting amongst the ruins north of the temple of Mithras.

After another ten dips of the oars, the boy said, 'They're following us, Beran. Look.' No doubt they all knew the truth of it, but the boy was the only one who chose to say it aloud. For the wind-flayed torches were still visible now and then, glimpsed in the gaps between the warehouses, wharves and quays of the waterfront.

'They'll give it up soon,' Beran said.

But they did not give it up, and Beran knew that despite the muscle which Palamedes and Tristan were giving to the oars, they were not moving fast enough against the current. Guivret knew it too.

'They'll have us at the bridge.' The Little King was careful not to let the others overhear.

'They might,' Beran admitted. 'And with any luck they'll see that we're not men of the garrison or merchants fleeing in a boat piled with amphorae of wine. We're nobody.'

Guivret gave him a wry look. 'Speak for yourself,' he said. 'And don't forget, I know who the boy is.'

'You do, but the Saxons don't.' Beran twisted to look over the bow in case he could see the old, rotting Roman bridge in the gloom.

'Just a little further,' Guivret said.

Palamedes and Tristan rowed hard. Sometimes their oars chopped at the river when the wind whipped furrows that rolled past their little boat in the dark, but mostly their strokes were long and true, pulling against the dark water, defying the easterly flow towards the great estuary.

Beran had not been on this stretch of the river since he was around the boy's age, before the Saxons had grown in numbers and when the Tamesis was still thronged with flat-bottomed boats which could beach on the foreshore at low tide. Boats which swept downriver to Rutupiae or Dubris and the larger ships waiting to export the treasures of Britain: wool and cloth, silver and lead, bears, fierce hunting dogs and cowed slaves. And vessels which had crossed the Dividing Sea in the summer to sweep up the Tamesis, laden with bronzes and sculptures, pottery, ceramics and glassware, silks and even marble of various colours, imported by those rich lords who yet clung to dreams of a Roman Britannia that was already crumbling around them.

All gone now. All of it of no more substance than a memory which may just have been a dream. Hadn't they been fools to think they could cling to the past? How many men had died for it fighting the Saxon tide? How many women made widows or taken as slaves? How many children left to play in the ashes?

'What shall we do?' Tristan said through gritted teeth as he leant back in the pull. 'They're faster on land than we are on the river.'

'Should we cross over to the south bank?' Isolde asked, looking from Beran to Guivret, then peering across the white-flecked, wind-furrowed water.

'Can't even see the other side,' Palamedes said.

'No,' Beran said. 'The south bank will be crawling with Saxons. Thick as flies on blood. The river narrows soon. If we make it past them at the bridge, they'll leave us alone.'

'You hope,' Tristan mumbled.

'We'll find out soon enough.' Guivret was pointing ahead. 'There it is.'

Beran saw the old bridge looming in the murk, could smell the burnt charcoal tang of it, where more than one fire had tried to consume its stout timbers. And whilst that bridge was mostly a ruin like so much of Roman Londinium, it yet spanned the river from bank to bank, low enough to prevent tall-masted ships from venturing any further west.

The boy stood in the boat and pointed. 'There they are! Look, Beran, there they are!'

There was a gash in the fast-moving cloud, so that a wash of moonlight lit the landing stage where vessels moored to be loaded and unloaded, and it was onto this timber deck protruding far into the river that spearmen came running, their shouts and the *clump* of their feet on the boards carrying across the water.

'They can't reach us,' Guivret said, gripping the side of the boat and watching the men on the landing stage who were cast in the bronze glow of their own flaming torches.

'Get down, boy,' Beran growled. 'Stay low.'

'I've seen that one before,' the boy said.

'Do as he says!' Palamedes cursed in his own tongue. 'Down, boy.'

An arrow hissed past the boy's head, and another plunged into the water a spear's length from the boat. The boy dropped back down into the thwarts, looking at Beran with wide eyes.

'Listen to Beran, Prince Erbin,' Isolde said, pulling the boy into her and placing a protective hand on the crown of his head. There was screaming in the night. A sound to curdle the blood in one's veins. They all hunched into themselves, keeping their heads low, though Tristan and Palamedes did not stop rowing.

'But I've seen one of those men before,' the boy said. 'In the forest when they ambushed us. I looked through a crack in the carriage and saw him.'

'You sure, boy?' Beran was peering at the indistinct shapes on the landing stage.

'Young eyes, Beran,' Palamedes said. 'Lad sees like a hawk compared to us.'

'But are you sure, boy?' Beran repeated, frustrated that the distance was too great for either flame or moonlight to help his own eyes make out their faces.

'Beran!' someone shouted across the water before the boy could answer. 'Beran, you traitor! You dog!'

'Not Saxons then,' Tristan said.

'Just row,' Beran murmured.

'Who are they?' Isolde asked.

Beran wished they had a shield or two then. 'Everybody stay down,' he said.

'Beran, you old fuck!' yelled the voice. In the distance there was a great crash, as of oaken beams collapsing, followed by a roar of flame, and sparks flying up into the night sky above Caer Lundein. 'You can't outrun me, Beran!' the man bellowed.

Ignoring his own advice, Beran stood to get a better look, his legs braced, tightening the core of muscle that still sheathed his stomach after all the years.

'There you are, traitor!' Nabor ap Nabor was pointing his spear at Beran. He held something in his other hand, but Beran could not make it out. 'There you are, you old bastard traitor.' His men now stood at the edge of the platform, two of them loosing arrows which streaked in the dark, their white fletchings catching the moonlight. 'You left something behind, Beran! Here!' With that, Nabor took two steps and swung his arm and hurled something out across the water. For a heartbeat, Beran caught a glimpse of moon-silvered hair and pale skin.

'Was that . . . ?' Isolde could not speak the rest of the words. She looked pale and afraid in the moon glow.

'Don't look at it,' Tristan hissed at her. 'Don't look, my love.'

Beran's guts had drawn tight. 'I'll kill you,' he said under his breath. 'I'll kill you!' he bellowed at the near bank. 'I'll kill all of you!'

Nabor threw his arms wide. 'Here we are, old man!' he shouted. 'Come ashore, Beran. We'll end this. On my word the boy won't suffer.'

Tristan's bared teeth showed in the murk as he rowed. 'Who would do that? What kind of man?'

'Nabor ap Nabor.' Palamedes' voice was a low rumble.

Beran watched Emmeline's severed head bob amongst the rolling black water, her face turned up to the night sky. But soon, thank the gods – if there were any gods that remained in the Dark Isles – it was lost to his sight.

He looked at Nabor, who was striding along the landing stage, more than keeping pace with their boat. 'I'll kill you for that, Nabor,' he said, his blood hot beneath his skin and prickling in his scalp, his pulse gushing rhythmically in his ears.

There were others on the wharf now, too. He could see them, men, women and children clinging to their belongings and climbing into small boats and pushing off into the river against the flow. Behind them, Caer Lundein was aflame, the clouds stained with fireglow, as though steeped in blood. The tang of smoke was in the air. Fear too.

But none of that mattered to Beran. He would give the Saxons Caer Lundein in return for Nabor ap Nabor, not that he was anyone to make such a bargain.

'Get down, Beran,' Isolde said. But he did not get down. He was deaf and blind with rage. His old heart was thumping in his chest, a drumbeat demanding that he attack, that he jump over the side and swim to the shore and kill Nabor ap Nabor. One foot was already up on the sheer strake, and he gripped Blandigan's axe by the throat and he burned to spill blood. It was the old rage. The one which had at times writhed in him like a malevolent creature, the two of them wading through blood together as crows croaked in leaden skies and the earth shook with the battle clamour of thousands.

'Sit down, Beran, you old fool!' The Little King was pulling at him, trying to get him back down into the boat. 'Step over the side and you'll sink like a quern stone. You know it as well as I do.' He was squat and strong, was Guivret, and he took Beran's cloak in two hands and yanked on it, hauling Beran backwards so that he fell down into the thwarts with a thud, the boat bucking and rolling with the disturbance.

'They have a boat,' Palamedes said. And Beran saw that they did. Nabor's men had pulled a knot of townspeople from an old Roman hippago, the sort of vessel used to ferry horses across the river. Six men were taking to the three pairs of oars, eager as hounds after a stag. Nabor himself was climbing aboard, yelling orders that were lost in the wind.

Guivret punched Beran's shoulder. 'What was I thinking? I should have let you jump. We're too heavy. We'll never outrun them.'

'Lay a hand on me again and I'll throw you into Nabor's boat from here,' Beran said, but the Little King seemed not to hear. He was looking at their pursuers, his eyes hard, his face pinched with the knowledge of what would happen to him if Nabor caught them. 'Row faster,' he told Tristan. 'Row faster and I'll pay you when we get to my farm.'

'You don't strike me as a farmer,' Tristan said, bending forward, plunging the oars, hauling them through the dark water. The promise of silver was as nothing to him. What added draw were riches to any man whose lover's life was a spear-throw from the grave? He pulled and pulled, his oars clutching the Tamesis and dragging it past their hull as though he could do it for ever. And Beran looked at Isolde, who sat in the bow with the boy, her eyes round with fear, her hair almost white beneath a wash of moonlight that silvered the water. The young man rowed for her and her alone, Beran knew. Tristan was young and his heart was strong, and he loved Isolde. And Beran envied him for that.

7

A Fate Sealed

'LOOK THERE.' LISANOR POINTED with one hand whilst gently pull-ing on her reins with the other. Her little bay mare snorted twin plumes of freezing breath and tossed her head in the fog of it as Lisa-nor dismounted, her boots crunching the stiff grass. It was bitterly cold, a crisp day beneath a startling blue sky, and thin as a skein of ice on a pail of water.

He had waited for her by the holly thicket where only a few berries remained, red droplets of blood amongst the glossy green spines, his legs shivering with the expectation of what was to come. He watched her now walk across the clearing, in awe even of every dark footprint amongst the hoary tufts, his throat thick with desire and guilt. 'We came out for mistletoe, not bones,' he said, lifting his hands from the reins of his pony, cupping them around his mouth and huffing warm breath into them. 'What is it? Polecat?'

'Fox,' she said, squatting by the white skull and running a finger across the arch of the gaping eye socket. The bear skin drowned her, and she had wrapped a pine-marten pelt around her neck, covering the lower part of her face, so that from a distance she looked like one of King Uther's hunters or some grizzled woodsman, but for the braid of hair which lay upon the dark pelt like a golden rope.

'Well, I suppose Merlin will find some use for it,' he said.

She stood and carried the skull back to her horse, which waited patiently, steaming in the raw day and doubtless enjoying not being plagued by flies.

He had given her the bear skin at the season's turn, and Merlin had raised an eyebrow at Arthur the first time he saw it around her shoulders, but had not shared his thoughts on the gift.

'Let me see.' He gestured at the goat-hide bag suspended from her saddle, into which the fox skull was bound. He urged his mount forward and she opened the bag so that he could see inside. There was a roe-deer antler, a yellow brain fungus, cones from pine, larch and alder, a pheasant's feather, and the blue and black feather of a jay.

'Such treasures,' he said.

She closed the bag and slapped his leg. 'Don't tease me, Arthur ap Uther.' She was frowning up at him. Her nose was red with cold and her breath clouded between them and he could smell in it the honey and oats she had eaten before riding out to meet him.

He grinned. 'I'm not teasing,' he said. The blood rushed to the part of his leg where she had touched him and gushed up to his groin. 'But if you don't find his precious mistletoe, he'll make some foul potion with that fungus and make you drink it as punishment.'

She pulled herself up into the saddle and clicked her tongue, and her bay mare walked on.

'Not if we leave tonight,' she said, looking straight ahead.

Perhaps his ears were iced over, for it took a moment for that to seep through. He heeled his mount forward to catch her up, the thump of his heart in his chest as loud to his ears as their horses' hooves on the iron-hard earth. 'Now you're teasing,' he said.

'Why not?' She turned to look him in the eye. 'Have you changed your mind? You've been asking me to leave with you since last Beltane.' Her expression gave nothing away, but part of him thrilled to the idea, even if she *was* just toying with him.

'Of course I haven't changed my mind,' he dared, then leant out of the saddle and took her hand in his. 'You are all I think about. You make my blood tremble like . . . a butterfly's wing.'

She laughed at that, and the blood that was in his groin flooded his cheeks. He let go of her hand and returned it to the reins.

'I'm sorry,' she said, trying to tame her smile. 'Don't look so hurt, Arthur. No one expects you to be a bard with honeyed words and the voice of a song thrush.' She hardened her face in a way that he suspected mirrored his own expression. 'You are the son of a warrior lord. You must be strong and brave and fierce in battle,' she said in deep and serious tone. 'You are a prince of Dumnonia. You may even rule one day, if your cousin dies or cannot lead spearmen in battle.'

'Not if we leave Dumnonia,' he said. 'I won't be a prince or a king. I'll live as a tanner or a blacksmith's apprentice. Perhaps one day I'll have my own forge.' He could imagine himself in the leather apron, hammering red-hot metal on a good anvil stone. 'Are you sure you would be satisfied with a soot-stained smith for a husband? Instead of a prince?'

'Meet me by the hut at the old hawthorn tonight, when the night guards light their fires. Then you'll know whether or not I will be satisfied to leave Merlin's hall and run away with Dumnonia's worst bard.'

Ector's farmstead was a fair distance from Merlin's hall, and there was no direct line of sight because of the beech woods, but Arthur reckoned the night would be clear, so he would see the glow in the sky from the sentries' fires.

'What about Merlin?' he asked. 'What if he sees you sneaking out?'

'Merlin will be in his cups on such a night.' She smiled. 'Hot spiced apple wine. He won't notice me.' Her smile seemed sincere and his stomach rolled like the breakers at the foot of Tintagel, where the great Uther ruled.

'There!' She pointed to a skeletal apple tree whose gnarled and leafless branches were white with frost feathers. Amongst those branches there was what appeared to be a green nest, some miracle of verdant life flourishing in defiance of winter.

'What does he need it for?' Arthur asked. 'Has he got sores on his arse again?'

'Arthur, have some respect,' she chided him, clicking her tongue and walking her mare towards the old apple tree. 'There's a girl in Moridunum who is tormented by some god,' she said. 'I have seen it, Arthur.' Her eyes were wide now. 'This poor girl. When the god is in her, she jerks and shakes and no one can stop it. Her whole body, like a mackerel on a hook.'

'Which god comes to her?' he asked, trying to imagine a girl shaking like that.

'Merlin doesn't know,' she said, 'but the mistletoe makes it harder for the god to hold to the girl for long.' He looked up at the mistletoe. It was rich in berries as white as milk.

'Merlin wants her to live in his hall so that he might speak with this god in his way.' She shrugged. 'And do whatever a druid does.'

'Well, I don't believe it,' he said. 'Why would a god do that?' His father had spoken of being visited by Arawn, King of the Otherworld, who told the child Uther that he would grow to be a great warrior and that no blade would kill him. More than once, Arthur had secretly hoped that Arawn's prophecy would be tested. 'What use has a god for a little girl?' he asked, exhaling hot breath into his cupped hands again, a shiver running from his lower back all the way up to the top of his head.

'Don't ask me; I'm not a druid.' Lisanor slipped off the mare's back and looped the reins over a low branch of the apple tree. 'I *do* know that we must be careful cutting it free,' she said, drawing a sharp little knife from a sheath on her belt and pointing with it at the mistletoe. 'None of it must touch the ground, or else that is a bad omen.'

'I don't believe in gods taking up in little girls and I don't believe in omens either,' Arthur said. He smiled as he watched her climb up into the tree. 'What use has a blacksmith for omens? He needs a strong arm, a good hammer, a hot flame.'

'Well, you just sit there daydreaming about hammers while I do all the work,' she said, pulling herself along one of the stouter boughs. No easy thing with the bulk of that bear skin catching on the crooked branches around her. Frost floated down from those branches, glittering in the clear day, and he watched Lisanor reaching out towards the mistletoe, her breath clouding around her face; a face that he would kiss before she returned to her tasks at Merlin's hall and he to Ector's barns, where he should have been helping Cai gather up all the dung from the stables to be mixed with marl and piled up for spreading on the fields. He could imagine the look on Cai's face even now as he shovelled steaming dung into a handcart, cursing Arthur for his absence.

Time alone with Lisanor was worth Cai's ire. Was worth anything, Arthur thought, as he dismounted and walked his fell pony closer. 'Be careful,' he said.

'It's not the first time I've climbed a tree,' she said.

Finding her balance, one leg either side of the bough, she reached out with both hands, her left seeking in the clump of mistletoe for the stem, her right gripping the knife, whose blade misted with Lisanor's breath on that frigid day. 'Got it,' she said, making the cut. But she had reached too far and now she overbalanced, her body half rolling off the branch.

He shouted her name as she dropped the knife and let go of the mistletoe in order to grab hold of that winter tree, and he flung out a hand for the falling green tangle and caught it.

'Well done, Arthur!' she called, easing herself back along the bough until she was low enough to drop the rest of the way, her boots thumping on the frozen earth. 'Would you have caught me?' she asked, her cheeks flushing red. She came to him and wrapped her arms around his shoulders and kissed him, and his blood gushed in his veins and the muscles in his thighs trembled with it.

'Of course,' he said and meant it.

They stood entwined by the winter tree for a long time, the fog of their breath mingling and drifting on the thin air, but they were not cold.

'We'd best be getting back.' Her words were hot on his lips and sweet in his mouth.

'We can stay a little longer.'

'No, we can't. But I'll meet you tonight. I promise.'

His stomach tightened at the thought of the two of them leaving Dumnonia together, shedding their lives and the expectations of others. Of Merlin and Ector. Of his father. Even of himself.

Lisanor broke the embrace first and took his hands in hers. 'When the guards light their night fires,' she said. He nodded and they mounted and turned and rode west.

He did not mention the single white berry, white as a blind eye, that had broken from the mistletoe and still lay where it had landed, disguised against the frosty grass.

His teeth were rattling in his skull despite the two cloaks he had wrapped around himself before riding out into the biting night, his progress slow now because he would not risk the pony sweating and then getting too cold. The sky had not stayed clear as he thought it would, but the low cloud that had brought flurries of snow in the late afternoon had reflected the glow from the fires at Merlin's hall, so that he had known when to set out. Now, he turned his face up to the sky and felt the soft sting of ice, and he hoped Lisanor was warm enough as she rode to the hut by the old beech.

'Are you glad for the extra blanket, girl?' he asked the pony, rubbing her neck. The pony was hardy and her winter coat was thick, and she snorted as though treating his comment with derision. 'Ah, you don't mind the cold, do you, girl?' he said, patting her with his other hand, trying to get the blood into his fingers. Steaming breath shot from her nostrils and she snorted, and he smiled at her pride and told her that he would give her a few handfuls of oats when they got to wherever they were going, because his mother had once told him that a fell pony stays warm so long as it is fed.

'Did you hear that?' He turned his head sharply, eyes sifting through the dark. It had not sounded like a man. A badger amongst the furze perhaps. Or even something smaller. Yet it served as a reminder to remain vigilant lest he arouse the curiosity of some shepherd by his huddled flock, or another traveller abroad in the winter night. Not that any traveller was likely to be out here on a night like this.

He sat up straight and twisted in the saddle to look behind him. Then he looked to the east, at the great swath of dark beech forest and the glow from Merlin's fires bronzing the low cloud, his alertness giving way to a pang of guilt twisting in his stomach at what he and Lisanor were doing.

The old man is not so hardy, he thought, rubbing the horse's flank again. Not that Ector was old, not really. But he had complained some days ago of the cold sitting in the walls of his house, and of the damp seeping into the bones in his flesh, and this midday had taken to his bed with some illness. His eyes had been clear, and there was no fever, and Ector himself had said the illness would pass, but Arthur knew the man deserved better than for him to slip away at such a time and without saying goodbye. Since taking him in at Uther's command, Ector had treated Arthur with kindness and respect beyond even that owed to the son of a lord and grandson of a great king of Britain.

Still, there had been no choice. Ector would not have allowed Arthur to leave any more than Merlin would brook the idea of Lisanor and Arthur fleeing Dumnonia to live in the woods together like a pair of swineherds or cut-throats, or like forbidden lovers hiding from the eyes of men and gods. No, this was the only way, he knew, and the thought of Lisanor was enough to subdue that writhing serpent in his belly. He grinned despite the cold hurting his front teeth. *We'll be warm soon enough*, he mused, imagining the two of them under thick furs, her flesh touching his, a fire crackling nearby. Her scent. Her pale skin, smooth to the touch. Her breasts both soft and hard against his cupped hands, and the secret parts of her, hot and silken and just as eager as he.

He shifted in the saddle. There. He could see it now, the old tumble-down herder's hut and the lone tree beside it that had somehow survived the axe of the folk who had sheltered in that hut over the years. He could see no light from flame or horn lantern, but that did not worry him. Lisanor would be careful. It was not unheard of for Merlin or Ector to send spearmen out should a sentry report a flame in the night, for raiders from Dyfed or Glywyssing were known to cross the Hafren in search of cattle or folk to take back to their misty strongholds as slaves. And sometimes Saxon boats stalked Dumno-nia's southern coast, landing hot-blooded warriors who came to test the spears of Britain before vanishing like the ebb tide on a shingle beach.

He came to the place and dismounted and tied the pony to the hawthorn by halter and lead rope, murmuring soft words to the animal and rubbing its back to straighten out the blanket. Then he stood a while beneath the bare and brittle branches of that spreading tree, huffing warm breath into his hands and recalling the first time he and Lisanor had met in that hut. Hard to fully grasp the memory now. It had been early summer, after the Beltane fires had lit the night, their great flames flapping like the war banners of ancient heroes, and they had lain amongst the long grass beneath the hawthorn's tangled crown and white flowers. They had each shared confessions: Lisanor to having taken it upon herself to run messages from Merlin to Ector just so that she might catch a glimpse of Arthur at his labours, and Arthur to feigning interest in the gods and in Merlin's stories of the history of Britain before the Romans in order that he might lay eyes on Lisanor at the druid's hall.

They had laughed at each other, the breeze fragrant with the sweet smell of cut grass and carrying the lowing of cows in full milk, the cattle roaming the pastures again after the sparse winter fodder.

Hard to imagine the sun's warmth on his skin now, on such a night as this.

'Where are you?' he said to the darkness in the south. She should have been here by now. He clasped his arms around himself and rubbed his flesh, telling himself that Lisanor was simply delayed. Per-haps she had been given some task, such as making up Merlin's hearth fire or fetching the druid's spiced apple wine. Or perhaps there had been a spearman near her place of egress and she had been forced to wait, shivering in her bear skin until the way was clear. But she would come. She had promised she would. And so he waited.

Lisanor did not come. He waited through the heart of the night, and only when the new day crept upon the world in a pale cloak far in the east did he give up hope and mount the pony, his body as stiff as a spear, his flesh numb and his heart sick. He was no longer shivering, as though even that animal part of him which he could not control had given up and abandoned him. He could not hold the reins with his unfeeling hands, nor grasp at some small hope that she had broken her promise unwillingly. Not now. She had not come. She was false. He meant nothing to her.

The pony carried its leaden burden through the pre-dawn stillness, remembering the way, or perhaps following some scent of woodsmoke and habitation which the young man on her back could not discern.

She does not love me.

Sleet arrowed across the darkling world and he all but closed his eyes against it, sitting astride his horse like a dead weight, his thoughts confused, blurry, unformed. His world now as tenuous and as vulnerable as the feeble day bleeding into the eastern sky.

What now? If she is false, what now?

They saw him before he knew he was home. Recognizing the pony and its rider's red cloak, two spearmen hurried from the gate, one of them taking off his own cloak and throwing it over Arthur's hunched shoulders whilst the other took the bridle as though the pony would lose its way without him.

'You've been out in this all night?' the cloakless man said. Arthur did not look up but he knew the voice belonged to old Cleor.

'Cold enough to freeze your piss,' the one leading his pony said, the fog of his breath trailing behind him in the gloom. Even half frozen and in the dark, Arthur would have known Galehaut by his limp. 'Where have you been, Arthur?'

He did not answer.

'And what's all this?' Cleor said, patting one of the bulging leather bags which Arthur had stuffed with clothes, food and the other supplies he and Lisanor would need to start their life together.

'Lad's spit has iced up,' Galehaut said. 'A cup of hot wine will loosen his tongue.'

They passed through the gate and Arthur lifted his head for the first time and saw, through the sleet and blurriness of his vision, Merlin. He was swathed in pelts and standing by a brazier which hissed and spat, its ailing flames casting the druid's face in a bronze glow as he held his hands towards them.

'What's he doing here?' Arthur said. His first words and they came out slewed, each running into the next, like the muttering of a drunkard.

'Merlin? He's here with his draughts and potions for Lord Ector,' old Cleor said. 'Came last night. You must have been gone before he turned up.'

They stopped a few feet from the fire, and Arthur climbed down. His legs almost gave way because he could not feel them beneath him, but he steadied himself against the pony, which snorted and tossed its head.

'I need to feed her,' he said, rubbing the animal's flank.

'Leave that to me, lad.' Galehaut lifted his chin in the direction of the hall. 'You need to warm up.' With that he led the pony off to the stables, and Cleor headed back to the gate, leaving Arthur standing there staring at the flames in the brazier.

'The kind of morning that makes you wish you'd stayed in your bed furs, hey, Arthur?'

Arthur lifted his own hands to the hissing fire but said nothing.

'Arthur, there you are.' He turned to see Morgaine coming from the doorway of Ector's hall, holding a cloak above her head against the icy rain. 'Have you been outside all night?' she asked, coming to him and letting the cloak drape around her face so she could put her hands on his arms and rub them back to life. 'You poor thing, you're stone cold.' Her hair spilled out from beneath that cloak in tendrils of flame, and he looked at her.

'I'm fine,' he muttered, wanting nothing more than to get to his room. 'What are you doing here?'

She glanced at the druid behind him. 'Merlin brought me. To help tend to Lord Ector.'

'Morgaine's knowledge of herblore is prodigious,' the druid said. 'But then, she is a far more willing student than some others I could mention.'

'Come, Arthur, let's get you warm,' Morgaine said. He nearly asked her if she had seen Lisanor the previous evening, for she and Morgaine were friends, but he did not want to give Merlin the satisfaction and so he said nothing. 'Come.' Morgaine took his hand as though to lead him back towards the hall, but Arthur held his ground and lifted his chin towards the hall in which Ector lay shivering.

'Does he know?' he asked.

Merlin was rubbing his hands together above the fire, his eyes reflecting the flame. 'That you spent the night out there looking for cherry and willow bark to help ease his coughing? No, we don't need to bother him with that. Besides, Morgaine and I brought everything we need.' He looked up from the burning brazier and their eyes met. 'Get warm and then get some sleep, Arthur,' Merlin said. 'You and Cai will be at your weapons later. Spears, I believe. And it seems Cai is angry with you for some reason, so you'll want to have your wits about you.'

Arthur held the druid's eye a long moment, then he turned and went with Morgaine.

'Put her out of your mind, Arthur,' Morgaine said, filling his cup once more. The spiced apple wine was no longer hot, but it was still good and so he drained the cup again, watching Morgaine as she kneaded the muscle in his calf. 'Does this feel good?' she asked him, her eyes lifting to glance at him through a wavy veil of red hair.

'Yes,' he said. His throat was thick and his head was swimming from the cold, or perhaps it was the wine. She had told him that the best way to warm himself was to take off his damp clothes and get beneath the furs, and so he had done it, though he had not expected her to stay with him, or to burrow beneath the pelts and put her hands on his benumbed flesh and try to impart sensation and life to it.

'You are sure you did not see her?' he asked. 'Do you not both eat at Merlin's table? Sleep in the hut beside his hall?'

Her thumbs burrowed into his slowly softening calf. He winced.

'Why do you want to talk about her now?' Morgaine asked, sinking her thumbs deep into some gristly knot.

He growled a curse. 'I preferred it when I couldn't feel anything,' he mumbled.

Her lips bowed a little. Not a smile, but almost.

'You have soot,' he said. 'Above your right eye.'

She lifted her head and flicked her red hair away from that eye and leant forward, wordlessly inviting him to deal with the sooty stain.

And so he licked his thumb and gently swiped at the mark until it was gone. She didn't thank him, just went back to work on his calf muscle, letting her hair fall across her face once more.

'Well?' he said. He leant over for the jug on the table and filled his own cup and hers too. Now he could taste a bitterness that he had not before. Wormwood perhaps, to balance the sweetness of the apple and honey.

'Did you see her?' he asked. Beneath the furs, her hands moved up. Working into his thigh. Gently stroking the big muscle upwards, then retreating lightly down the sides of the leg.

'I saw her,' she said. 'But we spoke only of the weather. And of how she had nearly fallen out of a tree whilst picking mistletoe for Merlin.' Her hands went still. 'Forget about Lisanor,' she said. 'You don't need her, Arthur. Gods, but you are like a bee in the lavender about that girl.' She reached out one hand to lift her cup and take a mouthful of wine. Her bottom lip glistened with it by the rushlight.

Her hand returned to his thigh and he felt the ghost of the cup's warmth. 'You could have frozen to death waiting for her. You're a fool, Arthur,' she said, her hands sweeping slowly up. Then down again.

She was right. He was a fool. He had waited all night, like some hound obediently awaiting his master's return. But Lisanor had never intended to meet him. Her words earlier in the day had been lies woven to humiliate him, because she knew that she was the lavender and Arthur was the bee. He was as a plaything to her. Well, no longer.

'Does this feel good?' Morgaine asked, not looking up at him now.

He swallowed. 'Yes,' he said.

Her hands moved up again. Just a little.

'And this?' she asked.

He cleared his throat. 'Yes.'

His head felt heavy and so he lay back on the furs and listened to the crackle of the rushlight flame and the scrabbling of a mouse in the thatch above, and the rhythm of Morgaine's breath.

'This?' she said. Her voice was soft and quiet.

'Yes,' he whispered.

Afterwards, he had fallen asleep. When he opened his eyes, the rushlight was out but there was daylight leaking in through the cracks in the walls where the timbers had twisted over the years. Lord Ector's dogs were barking in the courtyard, the steward, Orri, growling at them to stop because his skull was throbbing from too much ale.

Arthur knew how the man felt, grimacing at the thought of the empty jug on the table by the bed. He sat up and pushed himself back against the wall and looked down at Morgaine sleeping beside him. Waking now, coming upon the world slowly, like a winter sunrise. Her hair lay thick on the furs and there was a flush in her cheeks, blooms of pink felwort in snow. An impossible thought. A thing that could not be. Could never be.

'Did you sleep?' she asked, smiling up at him.

He felt sick.

'A little,' he said. 'I—'

He stopped at the sound of footsteps outside, but whoever it was continued on their way to Ector's hall and, before he could speak again, she said, 'We drank too much wine,' then she pushed herself up so that she was sitting beside him.

'We did,' he agreed.

'It was good, though, wasn't it?' she asked, turning to look at him, dipping her head, wanting his eyes to find hers. She was not talking about the wine.

He would not give that to her. He knew it was petty, cowardly even, after what they had done. But he could not give her that.

'Arthur?' she said. 'Why won't you look at me?'

'I have to go,' he said. His limbs were all his own again and they demanded movement and he obeyed, throwing off the red-deer hides and sheep skins and fumbling for his trews where they lay on the wattle mat beside the bed. They were still damp, but he put them on.

'It's still early. Ector is abed and Merlin will be close to his hearth,' she said, sweeping those copper waves back from her face. 'Meaning we are as free as birds a while longer.'

'I have to go,' he said, slipping his tunic over his head and sitting on the edge of the bed to pull on his boots, which were still sodden and cold.

'You're going to see her, aren't you?' Her lips were a tight line and the bones of her cheeks might have severed a strand of hair or two had she not brushed it back.

'I have to see her,' he said.

'Why?' She spoke the word like a challenge, and he resented her for that.

'I need to know why she lied. Why she promised to meet me if she had no intention of coming.'

She sighed. 'It doesn't matter now, Arthur.'

'It matters to me.' He had one boot on but was struggling with the other.

'You can't see her,' Morgaine said.

'She'll be at Merlin's hall. I'll set off now, before anyone misses me.'

'You're not listening, Arthur,' Morgaine said.

With a grunt the boot was on and now he stood up and turned and looked at her.

'You can't see her, because she's gone.' Her breath misted silver in a chink of pale daylight lancing through the wall.

His stomach lurched. He felt suddenly dizzy, as though the hut was spinning around him. 'What do you mean, gone?'

Morgaine shrugged, then pulled the bed furs up to cover her shoulders. She frowned. 'I don't know. But you will never see her again. Merlin made sure of it.'

'Merlin?' His mind whirred like a thrush in a cage. 'What has Merlin to do with it?'

'He has sent Lisanor away,' she said. 'Believe me, Arthur, you will never see her again. But you will be happier for it, I know you will.'

'So, we—' He broke off and closed his eyes for a moment as he reordered his thoughts. 'She would have come?' he began again, opening his eyes and fixing them on Morgaine. 'Would have met me like she promised?'

Morgaine nodded. 'Yes, but—'

Arthur raised a hand and she fell silent. 'Merlin stopped her,' he said. 'And now he's . . . sent her away?' The sickly feeling had passed, and in its place was anger, swelling and twisting and seeking a way out.

'Merlin knows what's best for you, Arthur. You didn't think he would allow the two of you to run away together? Allow you to cast aside your birthright and everything he has dreamt for you?' She held her hands clenched on the furs over her knees. 'He has dreamt of your future. He says the gods speak to him of you, Arthur.'

'Damn him! And damn the gods!' he said, then pointed at the bed on which they had coupled in the dawn. 'And what will the gods say of this? Of what we have done?'

She folded her arms and looked up at him. 'It just . . . happened,' she said.

But he wasn't listening now. He was thinking about Lisanor and how she was not false after all but would have met him by the hawthorn at the old shepherd's hut. Would have kept her promise.

'How did he know?' he asked her.

Morgaine held his eye, but also held her tongue.

'How did he know?' he said again, this time giving each word the same weight and tone.

For three heartbeats Morgaine seemed unsure how to answer, but then her eyes hardened and she lifted her chin, and Arthur thought he had never seen anyone look more like a queen, and that included Queen Amena, his uncle the High King's young wife, whom he had once seen in the great hall at Tintagel.

'*I* told him, Arthur,' she said, casting it at him like a blade, though she was sitting in his bed, naked beneath the pelts.

Arthur was reeling now. 'But you said you had not spoken to her about our plans.'

'She said nothing about them, but I am not blind, Arthur. I knew the two of you had met yesterday. It was in her face when she returned.' Her lip curled. 'I could smell you on her.'

'You craven witch!' he snarled, and stepped forward and backhanded the empty wine jug, sending it smashing against the wall. Morgaine flinched, but the movement was minimal. 'Where has Merlin sent her?' he asked. He lifted his hand and pointed a finger at her. 'Tell me, Morgaine.'

She shook her head. 'I don't know. I swear it, Arthur. Why would Merlin tell me?'

He stood there, not knowing what to say or what to do, knowing only that he felt as though his guts had been ripped out of his belly.

'I will never forgive you for this,' he said. 'Never.'

They held each other's eyes a long moment, tears in hers, rage vying with contempt in his, he knew, until he could look at her no longer. He turned and opened the door and stepped into the pallid, unmade day.

8

The Saxon Lands

THE ROMAN HIPPAGO WAS faster than Guivret's boat, its six oars chopping into the river and driving it on, so that it was not much more than a good spear-throw behind them when the gash in the fast-moving cloud healed over, plunging the world into darkness again.

'Lord Guivret! Where are you going?' It was Nabor's voice, coarse enough to tear through the gush of the river around the boat's prow and the uneven breath of the wind across the water. 'You owe me silver and wine. I won't be forgetting that,' he called. 'Don't think you can scamper away from me, you little bastard rat. Silver and wine, Little King!'

Guivret's hand fell to the white hilt of the Saxon blade at his belt. 'Fool if he thinks he'll ever piss my wine up the wall again,' he said, and pulled the long knife from its sheath, then stood and pointed it across the water, though Nabor and his boat were invisible in the murk. 'Come and get it, Nabor! I'll cut out your eyes and shit in your skull, you pus-filled maggot!' He hawked and spat over the side of the boat. 'I'll open your guts and send you screaming to the afterlife!'

Beran thought he heard laughter in the dark off their stern, through the hiss of the wind and the splash of oars in the foam-flecked river. 'I'll cut off his balls and give them to him in a wine cup,' Guivret snarled, sliding back down onto his backside lest he be thrown overboard.

'These horses,' Beran said, as the little man sheathed the seax with quick hands. 'I'll buy two from you.' He glanced at Tristan, who was sweat-sheened and grimacing, his stroke never faltering. 'I'll buy four,' he corrected himself. 'Don't need hot bloods or coursers, so long as they can get us to Camelot.'

Guivret was still peering into the dark, trying to discern how close Nabor and his men were now. 'Buy them with what?' he asked, turning to Beran now. 'You seem to be travelling light.'

'I have money,' Beran said, thinking of the chest of coins and silver and precious stones which he had hidden in the forest the day he made an enemy of Nabor ap Nabor. 'More than I could spend in the life I have left.'

'You have that much?' The dwarf's eyes were narrow.

Beran nodded. 'But not here.'

Guivret tilted his head and scratched his bearded neck. 'You'd best not be lying, Beran,' he said.

'There!' the boy cried out. He was on his feet, pointing over the stern, but he ducked as an arrow streaked in the night and was lost to the river beyond. 'They're so close!'

'Can't go any faster,' Tristan growled through his teeth.

'At your age . . . I could have rowed faster . . . with one arm,' Palamedes said, heaving for breath, his dark skin glistening with sweat. The two of them breathed like forge bellows, a relentless rhythm that was answered by every chop of the oar blades in the dark water.

Beran couldn't see the Roman boat, but he took the boy's word for it. Nabor was gaining fast.

'Palamedes! Palamedes ap Esclabor!' Nabor's voice carried on the wind like the rasping of a crow. 'My fight is not with you. Give me Beran. He's nothing to you. Give him to me, Palamedes. Or kill him!'

Palamedes' eyes met Beran's in the gloom.

'Kill him for me, Palamedes,' Nabor yelled. 'Whatever the Little King is paying you, I'll pay more. Hear me, Saracen? Kill Beran. Do it now!'

Palamedes plunged the oars into the Tamesis. Leant back in the pull. Bent forward and plunged them again. 'I can't do that, Nabor,' he called over the stern as he pulled, sweat dripping from his beard. 'You want him dead, you'll have to kill him yourself.' The Saracen held Beran's eye for another three strokes, then looked back to his task. Words were not needed between them.

'Then you'll die with the rest of them,' Nabor bellowed.

Beran looked at the north bank and back towards the old Roman heart of Londinium. There were three distinct gauzes of copper light hanging in the night sky, spreading west like a false dawn. The Saxons were burning Caer Lundein, setting fires in the timber dwellings, storehouses and granaries, and Beran's mind flickered with the cleansing flames of a hundred Beltane fires. Perhaps all the land of Britain would have to burn, he thought, before the old gods would return and raise a people from the smouldering embers. He could imagine his old friend saying such a thing, and he wondered if there was any chance the man could still be alive somewhere under the same dark sky.

'We're coming up on another boat,' Isolde announced. She was on her knees looking out over the bow, the boy beside her.

'Saxons?' Beran asked. He could see the boat with his own eyes now, the great swath of sail paler than the night around it, the stern darker. It had to be twice the size of Guivret's boat. Larger still, perhaps.

'No,' she said. 'I don't think so.'

Beran nodded. He would trust her young eyes. 'Put that boat between us and Nabor,' he told Tristan and Palamedes, who adjusted their stroke accordingly, turning their bow to favour the south shore so that they would come up on the other vessel's port side.

'I see you, Beran!' Nabor shouted. 'You're a dead man. You and the boy are dead.'

Tristan and Palamedes hauled on the oars, and before long they drew alongside the bigger boat, close enough to it that Beran could have reached out with Blandigan's axe and touched its hull. He saw faces peering down at them, women and children and an old man with white hair. From the shouting aboard that vessel he knew there must be some men too, but it seemed they were busy fighting with the sail, trying to harness the wind. No easy task on a night like this where it seemed to gust from different directions. That wind was a murmuration of starlings swooping and twisting and whirling.

'Closer. Bring us closer,' Beran told the Cornubian and the Saracen as he made his way from the stern to the bow, clambering around the men, trying not to ruin their stroke.

'What are you doing, Beran?' Guivret blurted. 'Any closer and we'll foul the oars.'

Beran ignored him. 'Closer,' he told Tristan and Palamedes. 'Get us alongside. That's it. Nearly there.' He steadied himself against the side of the boat, Blandigan's long axe in his right hand. 'On my word, ship oars.'

'What's happening, Beran?' Tristan was rowing as hard as ever. 'Tell me what's happening, damn you!'

'Just do what he says,' Palamedes growled.

Beran waited four more strokes, then said, 'Now!', and they pulled the oars into the boat, and Beran leant over the side, holding out the long axe, and hooked the beard of the blade over the other vessel's sheer strake and pulled, grunting with the effort.

'Beran?' Guivret was on his feet now, looking up at the other boat, the Saxon knife in his hand. Looking up at the faces of the people looking down.

'Who are you? What are you doing?' one of those folk said. It was the old white-hair, and he was jabbing a spear down at Beran. 'Let go of our boat,' he demanded in a voice as creaky as the ropes on his vessel.

'Keep your voice down, old man,' Beran hissed, his arms straining, one leg braced against the side of the boat as he pulled.

'Ha! Who are you to call me old man?' White Hair said, thrusting weakly with the spear.

'We mean you no harm but we're coming aboard,' Beran said, pulling his head out of reach of that jabbing blade. 'And get that spear out of my face,' he told the man, and this time he could hear in his mind his old friend laughing at the thought of him being finally sent to the afterlife by this feeble old goat. 'Our boat is holed, so we're coming aboard. We have a boy and a woman. We mean no harm, may the gods curse me if I lie.' The spear blade withdrew and so he turned to the others, lifting his chin at the boy. 'What are you waiting for? Up you go.'

'We can't just board their boat,' Tristan said, though he'd already discarded the oars and had one hand on his knapsack and the other on his spear.

'I told you, do as he says,' Palamedes purred in his deep voice. 'And be quick.'

Isolde, who was holding the boy's hand, nodded at Tristan, and they all gathered their gear and stood in the thwarts, balancing as best they could as Beran kept the two boats kissing, and the larger vessel's sail pushed them on against the Tamesis tide.

'You're the Little King,' said a voice. One of the younger men had joined the women and children and the old man at the side, his long moustaches trailing in the wind as he stared down wide-eyed. 'Lord Guivret,' he said.

'The same,' Guivret admitted, then patted the purse at his belt. 'And I have coin, if you will have us.'

The man disappeared, and Beran thought he might return to the side with a spear of his own, but he did not reappear at all. Instead, a big man with big shoulders came and reached down to Guivret, who lifted his hands and allowed himself to be pulled up and into the boat.

'Hurry,' Beran urged Isolde. Up she went, followed by the boy, then Tristan, then Beran himself, and lastly Palamedes, who hauled himself up as the Little King's boat drifted away into the dark.

The folk whose boat they now sailed on kept their distance, their eyes on Guivret mostly, for he had earned a reputation in Caer Lundein, even amongst those who did not venture into his underground world. Besides which, Guivret's small stature had always drawn people's gaze, as surely as a pure white foal or a dancing bear, so that he was long used to it, and it had been some years, by Beran's reckoning, since anyone had bled or had a bone or two broken for staring.

The man with the long moustaches, who seemed to be the leader of these folk, came to stand beside Beran, Tristan and Palamedes at the starboard side, the four of them looking out to where the oar blades of Nabor's unseen rowers bit the river, lacing the dark water with ribbons of silver.

'It's working,' Palamedes said. The moon was veiled and they sailed through a shadow world, yet Beran could see that Nabor's boat was turning to port. Because Nabor had seen Guivret's boat racing north, back towards Caer Lundein, and perhaps he thought Beran was trying to outrun them by letting the ebb tide carry their smaller boat down-river. And so Nabor had no choice but to turn his own boat around and go after it.

'You knew they would follow it?' Tristan asked. 'How could you be sure they would even see it?'

Beran shrugged. 'I didn't know,' he said, 'but what choice was there? They would have caught up with us. There would have been blood. Most of it ours.' Nabor's boat had turned with the river's flow and was already slipping out of sight, swallowed by the darkness.

'And even if we couldn't outrun them on this,' Palamedes said, 'we'd have the advantage of height.' He grinned. 'We would kill them as they tried to board.'

Beran nodded, and Palamedes slapped Tristan on the shoulder. 'I told you to listen to Beran,' he said. The two of them were still breathing hard, drawing the night air into their lungs and looking out over the Tamesis. 'Didn't I tell you?'

'You did,' Tristan admitted, glancing at Isolde by the mast. She was talking to one of the womenfolk, her arm around the boy's shoulders. 'But I'm beginning to think we were safer before we met him,' he added, pressing his thumbs into his palms and blowing on the pads of his fingers, which looked raw and swollen from gripping the oar. Not for the first time, Beran marvelled at the soft life Tristan must have lived down in Cornubia, far from the Saxon war bands, protected by King Mark's spears. Tristan had never stood in the shieldwall. Had never chased a pack of wolves from the forests where the dead lay in heaps, or ridden into the blood fray on a war horse and scythed men down like summer wheat. How different a man's life could be.

'Isolde says you have the Morrigán on your shoulder, Beran,' the young man said softly, as though that goddess of war was even now perched there in crow form and he feared offending her.

Beran glanced at Isolde, and though he outwardly shrugged off her observation about him, as one might rid a waxed cloak of rain, yet the words chilled his insides. 'The boy is my charge, not you, Tristan ap Tallwch,' he said, turning back to the young man. 'You're free to go your own way whenever you choose.'

Tristan looked over at Guivret, who was staring eastward, down-river, perhaps regretting the loss of his little boat. Beran guessed what the young man was thinking. That he and Isolde would travel not to Camelot after all, but to Portus Adurni and then across the sea to Benoic, where they could go to ground and King Mark would never find them, and they could love each other in peace.

Benoic. Beran had been there many years ago. Had loved the son of a king of Benoic as a brother, and hated him like a sworn enemy. His thoughts of that land across the Dividing Sea were curtailed by the man with the long moustaches.

'You lied,' the man accused him. 'About your boat being holed.'

'I did,' Beran said, thinking that if this man wanted to make some-thing of it, he would soon be sinking to the bottom of the Tamesis. And perhaps this thought somehow jumped flea-like from Beran's mind into his accuser's, because he glanced at a young boy and girl who were sitting huddled together amongst a coil of rope amidships. His own children, no doubt. And he frowned. 'You're still going to pay me?' he asked.

'Not me, him.' Beran pointed the axe at Guivret.

The man lifted his chin, finding his courage now he knew he did not have to deal with Beran and that axe. 'You'll pay for your passage, lord or no lord, just as you said you would,' he called to the Little King.

Guivret pulled his thick beard through a little fist. In Beran's experience, he was a man of his word, but that did not mean he tolerated being spoken to like that.

'I'll pay you to take us as far as the river goes before it turns north,' he said. 'The valley where a smaller river pays into the Tamesis. There is a place there, of ancient earthworks which once guarded the north bank.'

'I know it,' the man said, 'but we're not going as far as that.'

Guivret's hands went to the purse at his belt. He examined what he had pulled out then tossed it towards Moustaches, who caught it deftly, though not before Beran had glimpsed a dull gleam of silver in the dark night.

'The earthworks,' the dwarf said.

The man nodded. 'Yes, lord.' He closed his fist around the coin before returning to join his companion at the tiller.

Beran and Guivret looked at each other, both acknowledging with nothing more than a nod that they had, between them, bought some measure of respite. Then Beran felt a presence at his back and turned to see the boy standing looking up at him with narrowed eyes beneath protruding brows.

'I heard what Tristan said. About the Morrigán,' he said. 'My mother told me a story of that goddess. There was a great hero who had fought against the Romans. He won many battles and earned great fame. But after many years he grew weary of war and turned his back on the world, choosing to live a hermit's life. But the Morrigán found him. She took the form of a beautiful woman, begged him to return to battle, to lead as he once had. She promised him there would be peace in Britain after one more fight.'

Beran grunted. 'There will never be peace in Britain,' he said.

The boy raised a hand to ward off the interruption, and in that gesture Beran saw Lord Constantine in all his proud arrogance. 'And so the hero went to war again,' the prince said, 'but it was a trick.' He looked suddenly very grave. 'We all know that the Morrigán is greedy only for death.'

Beran nodded. The boy continued. 'The battle lasted three days and nights, but it went badly for the hero. At the end he saw a crow picking at the dead littering the field. But the hero knew it was really the goddess, taken crow form.' The boy threw an imaginary spear. 'The hero cast his spear, killing not the goddess but a real crow which was pecking at the eyes in a corpse beside her. The Morrigán was angry that a mortal man had dared to make an enemy of her. She flew up into the grey sky and came down and landed on the hero's shoulder, so that all the Roman soldiers would know that here was the leader of the Britons. One hundred spears flew then and the hero was slain.'

Beran had heard the story before, or a version of it at least, though he did not say as much to the boy, who stood there frowning still, waiting for Beran's reaction.

'Get some sleep, boy,' Beran said. 'It will be morning soon and we've a long way to go.'

They sailed the rest of that night, following the snaking coils of the Tamesis through a dark land that belonged to neither Saxon nor Briton, but ebbed and flowed like the river itself between warlords. Beran slept deeply and well, soothed in slumber by the gentle motion of the boat, and even the usual aches and pains of his body were quiet, as though his very bones were grateful for the chance to rest, safe upon the wide water.

He woke in the pale dawn, thinking he had emerged from the claws of a dream about the Morrigán. Then, as the fog of sleep drifted from his mind, he realized it had not been a dream of the goddess of death, but the raucous *kaah* of rooks in a small wood of elm and ash along the south bank coaxing him awake.

'We thought you had died.' Palamedes tossed Beran a hunk of bread which he would not be able to eat until he had emptied his bladder over the side.

'Still here,' he said. He was damp and cold and he shivered.

The boy and Isolde were sitting across from him, huddled together in a thick woollen cloak, the boy's eyes still heavy, though he smiled at Beran.

'But I'll gladly die in my sleep, old friend,' he added, shifting to push himself upright and wincing at the return of his stiffness. 'Soon as I've got the boy to Camelot.'

Guivret and the man with the long moustaches were at the tiller, talking together in low voices and pointing out landmarks. Tristan was still asleep, wrapped in his cloak on Isolde's other side and snoring softly.

'How do you two know each other?' Isolde asked, looking from Beran to Palamedes.

Beran looked at Palamedes, who lifted one eyebrow, intrigued to see how Beran would answer.

'We fought together,' Beran said, bending and straightening his left leg. The knee was badly swollen. 'A long time ago.'

'A *long* time ago,' Palamedes echoed.

Isolde and the boy looked at him. 'In Arthur's time?' the boy asked.

Palamedes eyed the boy and nodded. 'Yes. I fought for Arthur.'

The boy's eyes widened. 'Did you meet him?' he asked. 'Arthur and my father were cousins.' There was pride in his voice and he was fully awake now.

A half-smile played on the Saracen's lips. 'Of course I met him,' he said. 'I told you, I fought for him. I rode with him against the Saxons, when the thunder of our horses' hooves rolled through the earth and had our enemies' bones shaking in their flesh.'

The boy's lips pursed then, his expression one of disbelief. 'Then it is a wonder you are still alive, Palamedes,' he said, 'for my father said that Arthur was reckless in battle. That he thought his shining horse warriors were as gods, and that many good men died for his ambition.' He frowned. 'My father and Arthur were not always friends. But other men say Arthur was the greatest warlord who ever lived. What do you think, Palamedes? Was Arthur as great a warlord as some say?'

Beran muttered a curse. 'Enough talk of Arthur,' he said. 'Lord Constantine too.' He looked at Palamedes. 'Both are long gone now.' He pressed a thumb into the soft swelling around his knee joint. 'And he is a fool who believes old stories from men who have got their own memories mixed up with dreams and bard song and the blather of folk who have never been close enough to a Saxon to smell the mead on his breath.'

The boy ignored him. 'Were you a horse soldier like Palamedes, Beran?' he asked.

Beran's bladder was fit to burst, so he hauled himself onto his feet, wincing at the pain in his back and knee. 'Do I look like one of Arthur's horse lords, boy?' he asked. He could hardly stand straight.

The boy shook his head. 'No,' he said, seeming disappointed. He thought for a moment, then he said, 'But you were young once. You were—'

'Enough now, Erbin,' Isolde said in a quiet voice, as Beran walked to the stern. 'Or Beran's foul mood will set in for the day. But when we're safe, we'll sit by a leaping fire with wine and music, and Beran and Palamedes will tell us stories all the night.'

'Do you promise?' the boy asked her.

Beran looked over his shoulder for the woman's reaction, and saw Isolde smile at the boy. He was surprised, given the pain in his limbs and the pressing urge low in his stomach, to find himself wondering at her beauty. And then she spoiled it. 'What say you, Palamedes?' she said. 'Will you tell us how it was to ride with Arthur in the before time?'

Beran murmured another curse and looked across the misty water.

'If there's enough wine, I may even sing of it,' the Saracen said.

Beran began to piss, another shiver running through him, his eyes watering in the dawn's thin breeze. He watched the northern bank slip by, and the rooks leaving their roosts and clamouring up into the ashen sky, and the meagre tendrils of smoke drifting from isolated dwellings that he could not see beyond the trees. And then he saw the timbers jutting from ancient earthen ramparts, a line of black stakes still standing like sentinels against any approach from the south, as they had for twenty generations. An eternal bulwark against the ghosts of Roman legionaries which might still march across these Dark Isles beneath the gilt glow of unseen eagles.

There were gaps where some of the stakes had fallen or been hauled from the earth and long since lost to the river, and some were shorter than others, giving the impression of a mouth of broken teeth grimacing in the first light, a warning perhaps, to any upon the river: *Turn around and go back. Go back while you can.*

'Did you know that the king of the Catuvellauni tribe, whoever he was, built this breastwork of stakes to defend his land from the great Roman emperor Julius Caesar?' Guivret announced to the others.

Beran turned around and limped back to where his cloak, knapsack and weapons lay on the deck. 'Caesar was no emperor,' he said, bending to pick up the hunk of bread.

'Beran's right,' the boy said. 'Just like Arthur was no king.'

Guivret batted their words away with a hand. 'Am *I* a king . . . really?'
he asked. 'Look at me, taking flight like a thief!' He showed them his
own food. 'Sharing bread with a cut-throat, a Saracen, two runaways
and an arrogant boy whom people want dead.' The boy scowled at
Beran, who gave him a look which said that Guivret wasn't wrong.

The Little King turned and, like the rest of them, watched that
ancient rampart slide by, each stake the trunk of a young oak tree, fire-
hardened and sharpened and enduring still, when so much in the land
had been lost. 'But Caesar,' the Little King went on, 'we know his
name! To this day, we give it breath and wonder at the man's achieve-
ments.' He bit into the bread and chewed, his beard jerking up and
down. 'Do you think anyone will remember the name of Arthur ap
Uther?' he scoffed. 'Will we remember Arthur in even so few as twenty
summers from now?'

Beran spat a wad of half-chewed bread over the side. 'Might as well
be eating my boots as this,' he said, before anyone could answer Guivret's question. Then he tossed the hunk of stale bread out over the
water. Because he was no longer hungry.

Down came the sail as the steersman brought the boat into the reeds
along the bank, sending a pair of marsh hens clattering up, clucking
angrily as they careened off to land amongst the vegetation further
downriver.

The folk whose boat this was would go no further lest they ground
the vessel on that very same ford where Caesar's legionaries had waded
across the river into the teeth of tribal resistance. 'We've come further
than is wise,' the man with the long moustaches told Guivret, 'for we
shall have to wait for tide or wind before we can follow the river back
east again.' He was watching the woods of the south bank as though
he expected to see Saxon spear wolves stalking its fringes like wraiths
in the mist.

'You have helped us,' Guivret told the man, getting his attention
with another silver coin, which the man took without a word. 'When
the Saxons are sluiced out of Caer Lundein like rancid slops, come
and find me at the temple of Mithras. I will feed you and your family
at my own table.'

The man gave this the look of scepticism it deserved, then shook
the hand which the Little King offered him. Nabor ap Nabor or no,

Beran could not envisage things going back to the way they had been, with Guivret ruling his little underground kingdom, earning silver from bloody bouts fought in the name of some long-vanished Roman god. Besides which, knowing that Guivret and Beran were disembarking on the southern bank, the man must have thought they would be killed or taken as slaves by Saxons soon enough, though that was none of his concern. He had been paid, as Guivret said he would be, and that was that.

They clambered down the gangplank, through the reeds and onto a grassy bank lined with white willow whose leaves draped in the water. Beran took the opportunity to cut a sliver of bark from that tree, which he tucked into his belt. Then they set off into the mist, and it was not long before they were amongst hornbeam and oak, rowan and hazel, the rising sun warming their left cheeks whenever it found its way through the shivering canopy above.

By noon, they had not seen another living soul, and Tristan suggested that all the Saxon warriors south of the river must have been involved in the attack on Caer Lundein.

'Even were that true, we don't want to run into any Saxon women either,' Palamedes warned. 'They can be more fierce than their men.' As he walked, he spun his spear in front of him, passing the stave between the fingers of his left hand, which mesmerized the boy. 'I once saw a Saxon woman bite off a man's ear because he hit her child,' the Saracen said.

Isolde ruffled the boy's hair. 'If anyone hurt you, I would bite off their ear, too,' she told him, which made the boy smile.

'Do you have children, Beran?' Isolde asked him.

Beran thought of a young woman in the marshes. A woman as wild as a hawk, as fierce as a wolf, as brave as any warrior who ever stood their ground in a bloodletting.

'I have a daughter,' he said. He felt his stomach cinch tight, like a saddle girth around the barrel of a horse.

Guivret seemed surprised. 'You have never spoken of her,' he said, and though Beran looked straight ahead along the forest track which foxes and badgers and smaller animals had made over years, he felt the dwarf's eyes on him. A heavy gaze for a little man.

'Is she alive?' the boy asked.

A blunt question, though Beran did not begrudge it from a boy whose father was dead and who had been mere feet from his mother as she was murdered. To the boy, having family who yet breathed and felt the sun on their face was not something to be assumed.

'Yes, she's alive,' he said. 'Far as I know.'

As wild as a hawk. As fierce as a wolf.

'What is her name?' Isolde asked.

He did not want to think of her. Did not want to summon her face to his mind like some druid at Samhain sitting in the flame-licked dark inviting spirits through the veil. Once you lit a fire, you could not control where the smoke went. Thoughts were like smoke, Beran knew. They went where you did not want them to go. And he knew that thinking of his daughter would lead to a place where he could not follow. It would lead to *her*.

'Are you certain you know the way?' he asked Guivret, rather than answering Isolde's question. 'We don't want to stumble into some Saxon camp.'

'Does a bee know the way to its hive?' Guivret was smiling. 'Trust me, Beran. My father and his grandfather, and his great-grandfather before him, have been selling horse stock here since the legions left. Where do you think Arthur got his best war horses?'

Beran caught Palamedes' eye at that, though neither interrupted the Little King. 'My ancestor rode with the Ala Prima Thracum,' Guivret went on.

'The First Wing of Thracians!' the boy said, clearly proud of his ear for the Roman tongue, and Beran saw Constantine in his mind, arrogant in his Roman breastplate and red cloak, the skin of his cheeks and chin raw from the razor's edge. Smoke goes where it pleases, he thought.

'Just so, Prince Erbin,' Guivret said. 'Gods, Beran, but this boy has too much clever in him to be wandering the land with the likes of you.'

'If we run into a Saxon wolf pack, maybe the boy can speak to them in Roman,' Beran said. 'Maybe that will stop them from taking our heads and feeding them to their pigs.'

Isolde put her arm around the boy and pulled him to her as they walked. 'Ignore him,' she said.

Guivret armed sweat from his forehead and the flattened bridge of his nose. 'More than three hundred years ago, my ancestor stayed behind when the quingenaria was shipped across the Dividing Sea to fight in Germania,' he said, then flapped a hand at the warm air. 'Perhaps he was in love with a beautiful woman.'

'Or perhaps he deserted his sword-brothers because he was a coward,' Palamedes said. This brought a look from Beran, but the man avoided his eye.

Guivret shrugged, incapable of taking offence on behalf of a long-dead ancestor. 'He knew horses and it made him rich,' he said, 'and my people stayed here selling horses ever since.'

'But this is Saxon land now,' Tristan said, 'so how is it that you still have a farm hereabouts? How can you trade without the Saxons taking all you have?'

'You don't know the Little King,' Palamedes told him, 'but you will.'

Tristan stopped abruptly and raised his spear, and the others stopped too, but then they saw the creature whose movement had caught Tristan's eye and startled him. A squirrel, the red-brown of iron rot on a blade, was perched on a tree stump, clutching an unripe hazelnut. The creature was completely still now, as though it believed that the interlopers could not see it so long as it did not move.

'It makes no difference to *him* who rules the land,' Guivret said, as they moved on. 'Roman, Briton or Saxon. So long as he can hoard his acorns and nuts and run from branch to branch.'

'You see,' Palamedes said, '*now* you are getting to know the Little King.' For this he earned a laugh from Isolde, a rare smile from Tristan.

'The squirrel that is only thinking about his acorns does not see the owl in the branch above him,' Beran said, taking the long axe from his left shoulder and hooking the head over his right.

It was a while before anyone spoke again.

They walked south, keeping their eyes open and their blades near their hands, and whenever they saw smoke above the trees or smelled it on the air, they discussed where the dwelling might be and gave it a wide berth.

The day had grown warm, the air fragrant with comfrey and woodbine and alive with insects streaking here and there, so that if Beran did not know the truth of it, had he not seen the glow of fires above Caer Lundein and heard the clash of blades just the previous night, he might have been tricked into believing there was peace in the land. But there was no peace, and nor would there ever be, so long as men hungered to take by sword and spear that which was not theirs.

Not that it was his concern. Not now. He was walking south, deeper into land ruled by Saxon lords, which was not a clever thing to do, but at least it would make it harder for Nabor and his men to follow. The Saxons knew Guivret the Little King. They bought his horses and so they let him live, but they would not extend that mercy to a warrior like Nabor ap Nabor, a man who had sent dozens of Saxons to the afterlife to drink with their forebears in the hall of their god Woden.

Just keep going, old man, Beran told himself. He would get horses at Guivret's farm and he would take the boy to Camelot because he had given his word. And then he would find a tree to sit beneath in the late summer sun, and he would close his eyes and he would not open them again.

By the early evening, they had come to rich farmland bristling with barley and oats that had not yet been harvested for the want of three days without rain. They saw some folk a way off, with no sign to tell whether they were Saxons, or Britons who had been allowed to stay and work the land for their new lords. Either way, they kept their distance, staying amongst trees where they could, and avoiding the spines of higher ground where they would stand out against the skyline.

The swelling in Beran's left knee was better than it had been, but after a day's walking his hips ached and his lower back too. He cut off a small piece of the willow bark and chewed it, and it helped with the pain. He had learnt many things from his old friend, of the properties of flowers and plants, and the secrets of herblore that could fight off illness and discomfort. Of all the memories which sometimes broke through the surface of his mind, like gnarled roots seeking through hard, dry earth, these at least he did not resent, nor stamp them back down whence they came.

Their shadows stretched out beside them, black and tremulous and slithering over the uneven ground, like spirits unwilling to abandon the living. A short while later, they came into a copse of hornbeam, birch and maple, whose understorey was of elder, its umbels of white flowers transformed to bunches of blood-red berries.

'My mother makes elder wine,' Isolde told them, pulling some berries off their red stalks as she passed a small tree. 'But you must pick the flowers in full sun or it will be sour,' she said, a distant look in her eye as she held the fruit to her nose. Tristan reached out and took her hand in his, and Beran saw her give him a sad smile.

'We will be drinking wine soon enough,' Guivret assured them, 'and not elder wine but pressed from grapes that have ripened beneath a kinder sun, far in the south of Gallia. I tell you now, you will not have tasted better.'

A *hoom* escaped Beran's throat. 'That's some boast,' he said.

'You doubt me?' Guivret asked, looking amused.

Beran shrugged. 'I've lived a long time. Drunk a lot of wine,' he said, thinking how a cup or three of wine now, any kind of wine, would help douse the fire in his lower back. 'Once shared a cask with a Frankish king,' he added, regretting the words as soon as he had spoken them, for he could almost hear the creak of eyebrows arching.

'A king? What king?' the boy asked. 'And how did it taste?'

'Ah, don't believe his stories, boy,' Guivret said. 'Why would a king of Frankia let a lowborn cut-throat like Beran anywhere near his wine?' He pressed a thumb against the side of his nose and shot a wad of snot into a clump of bracken. 'More likely Beran cut some Dumnonian lord's throat and stole his wine, and his woman too, which is how he ended up a ruin in the ruins of Caer Lundein, working for me. He and Nabor are coins struck from the same die.'

Beran said nothing to that. He did not have the breath to waste trying to bend another man's opinion of him. The boy, though, did. 'No,' he blurted, 'Beran is not like that. He is not a killer like Nabor. He saved me. That day in the forest, they would have killed me like . . .' He stopped and Beran looked at the boy and saw his face tighten, saw his lips fasten on the next words before they could be spoken. He swallowed. 'Like they killed my mother,' he said. 'They would have slaughtered me like an animal if not for Beran.' He looked up at Beran, their eyes meeting. 'Beran stopped them. He fought three men to save my life.'

Beran dipped his head, not in acknowledgement of his role in the boy's survival, but at the courage it had taken to speak of his mother. The boy nodded back.

Guivret sighed. 'And now we must sleep with one eye open lest we wake to the cold touch of Nabor's blade,' he said, clearing his other nostril.

'Not if the Saxons kill us first,' Palamedes put in. 'Or Queen Morgana does.'

'The sooner we get to Portus Adurni and take ship the better,' Guivret said. 'Thirteen mares, four stallions. All my remaining stock. We'll take them to the coast and across the sea to Benoic. I know men who will buy good horses.'

'You're selling four to me,' Beran reminded him.

Guivret wafted a hand in Beran's direction. 'You want to stay here, that's up to you. Palamedes and I will grow fat and rich in Benoic, while you and the boy blow around Britannia like leaves on the wind.'

Tristan and Isolde caught each other's eye then, and Beran knew he would be buying only two horses from Guivret after all, and that the young lovers would cross the sea with Guivret. To Benoic.

'It will be dark before long,' Tristan said. 'How much further?'

'Can't you smell the horses?' Palamedes said, grinning. His left eye was still swollen and Beran knew he must look terrifying to anyone who did not know him.

Then they came out of the trees onto a sloping meadow where purple cranesbill, white meadowsweet and corn chamomile shivered in the evening breeze. And there below them, nestled at the foot of the slope, sat a clutter of buildings, stables, animal pens and a paddock in which the Little King's horses stood cropping the sweet grass.

9

No Gods of Britain

Palamedes held Conall against the plastered wall, a knife pressed against the steward's fleshy neck.

'I thought I was doing what was best, I swear it, lord,' Conall protested. The colour had drained from the Irishman's fat face, sweat was beading on his balding head, and his hands were shaking by his sides. Clearly the steward did not expect to be alive for much longer, and from what Beran had pieced together in the short while they had been under that roof, he had no reason to think the man pessimistic. Just as well the boy and the lovers were outside, admiring the horses.

'Tell me again why you thought me dead,' Guivret said. He was pulling at his beard with both hands, as if that was the only way to stop himself from drawing the Saxon long knife at his belt. 'If I were dead, you Irish sack of dung, my shade would have come here and pissed in your pottage. I would be haunting you now, you treacherous bucket of pus.'

'Eadwig gave me no choice, lord,' Conall whined, his face turned to the wall, his eyes fixed on Palamedes, as though to break the Saracen's gaze was to invite the cut that would end him. Bright with fear, those eyes, putting Beran in mind of the pig which the steward had had slaughtered earlier at Guivret's command, before things had soured. 'Lord, please,' Conall said, and Guivret gestured at Palamedes to ease off with his blade so that the Irishman might speak more easily. Conall managed a small nod of thanks.

'Last full moon, Eadwig was here,' he went on. 'He bought the spotted mare. Told us that King Cynric had united the tribes. That the Saxons were gathering and Caer Lundein would fall.' Conall's eyes flicked to Guivret, then Beran, then back to the knife beneath his chin. Guivret gestured again, and again Palamedes lowered the knife, though not by much. 'And he came the morning before last, saying that the attack on Caer Lundein would happen that night. There was no time to warn you, lord.'

'So, you thought you would sell my horses to Eadwig, and for half their worth, because I would be lying dead in the ruins of Caer Lundein and you might as well get rich?'

'No, lord,' Conall said. 'Of course not.'

'And you sent my spearmen north because you would not pay for them. With *my* money!'

'They would not stay, lord, once they heard that the Saxons were gathering to take Caer Lundein. And why pay them to stay if we had no horses for them to guard?' Conall seemed now to be avoiding Palamedes' eyes. He knew he would find no mercy there. 'I would have kept the money safe in case you returned,' he said. 'And I would have got a better price, of course, but Eadwig said I could either sell them to him for what he was offering, or he would take them and pay nothing.'

'That Saxon shit,' Guivret spat. 'And you say he'll be back tomorrow?'

Conall nodded. 'At daybreak.'

Guivret turned to Beran. 'This fat fucking toad was a slave before I took him in. Sold at the great market where the Liffey meets the sea. Thin as a birch he was then. Now look at him! And this is how he repays me.'

'What else could I do, lord?' the Irishman pleaded. 'You know Eadwig.'

Beran had gone to the window and moved aside the flap of animal hide covering the hole. He was watching the boy sitting on the back of a small mare which Tristan was leading on a rope halter, the two of them cast in the late summer bronze of the dying day. The boy was smiling.

'This is what you get for doing business with Saxons,' Beran told Guivret.

'Oh, the wisdom of Beran,' Guivret muttered. 'And yet everything was in its place before you returned.'

Beran watched the boy leap from the horse and land well. Saw Isolde laughing and clapping, and Tristan patting the mare and telling her what a fine horse she was.

'So I'm to blame for the Saxons now, am I?' He turned back to Guivret, who was still glaring at Conall, the thick fingers of his right hand twisting a gold ring on the middle finger of his left.

'I'm saying that the gods that cursed my birth and yours are playing games with us,' the dwarf said.

'You flatter yourself, Little King, if you think gods take any interest in us.' He didn't waste his breath by sharing his thoughts, that there were no gods watching over the Dark Isles any more, other than perhaps those gods which had come with the Saxons, like dark clouds following ships across the Morimaru, or like packs of wolves on the heels of a war host.

'Lord?' Palamedes said, for his knife still lay beneath the steward's chin. At Guivret's signal, Palamedes lowered the blade, let go of the man and stepped back, and Conall seized his chance to hurry away, mumbling that he needed to empty his bowels, if it wasn't already too late.

'We could take the horses and go, make a run for the coast,' Palamedes suggested, sheathing the knife. 'I'll wager the boy can ride, being King Constantine's boy.'

Guivret looked at Beran, inviting his opinion.

'This Saxon, Eadwig, will have men watching the farm,' Beran said. 'Because if you don't trust the Irishman, do you think a Saxon will? Besides, it's been a long day. I'm tired. We all are.' His hips and back were agony. His right elbow ached from the weight of the long axe, the knuckles of his hands were inflamed and his feet were swollen like a couple of leather helmet liners left in the rain, so that he feared he might never get his boots off.

'We take a risk by staying,' Palamedes said. 'Eadwig leads a handful of spearmen. I have never seen him without them. And now we don't have any.' He looked from Beran to Guivret. 'Whatever arrangement Eadwig has made with Conall, he might decide that his days of having to pay for your horses are over.'

'He might,' Beran admitted. 'But how far do you think we'll get in the dark, riding through Saxon land? Not just us but the nine horses we'll be leading? There's no way of doing that without being noticed. They'll think we're a raiding party.'

Palamedes shrugged as though to say he had given all the advice he had to give, and that it mattered not to him what they chose to do.

Beran looked at Guivret. 'If you want to take your horses to Benoic, you're going to have to renegotiate with Eadwig.'

Guivret considered this. 'I've dealt with him since before that boy out there was born,' he said, looking at the door. 'When he sees I'm alive, he'll regret trying to rob me like a hound on its hind legs eating from the table while its master is away.'

Beran nodded. 'It's decided then. We stay.' He pressed his thumb into one of the swollen knuckles of his other hand, moving it this way and that, feeling the give of fluid beneath, where once had been sharp, unyielding bone. 'Now, where's that wine you promised us?'

The Little King had been as good as his word, and his wine was as good as any Beran could remember passing his lips. He could not remember ever having tasted better, not even courtesy of King Childeric of Frankia, though he did not say as much to Guivret.

They were sitting on furs around the hearth, slurping down steaming bowls of bean, turnip and swine stew, the meat so tender that it did not hurt Beran's jaw to chew it, as even newly baked bread would these days.

'Your horses are very fine, Lord Guivret,' the boy said with a curt nod and a subtly condescending expression beyond his years. As though the relative safety of the present situation had emboldened him to remind Guivret that whilst the dwarf might be called Little King, and lord, he, Erbin, was a real prince by anyone's measure. The grandson of Ambrosius Aurelius, High King of Britain no less.

'I am honoured, young prince.' Guivret humoured the boy with a warm smile before blowing on his spoon and sucking at the hot liquid. His thick beard glistened with it.

Tristan and Isolde were sitting farther away, in the corner of the room, talking in low voices as they devoured the food. Beran thought it unlikely that those two had ever grown so hungry down there in Cornubia at King Mark's court.

'And you, Beran?' Guivret said. 'What is your opinion of my stock, for what it's worth?'

Beran shrugged, using the edge of his spoon to tease apart a hunk of flesh against the side of his bowl. 'What do I know of horses?'

'Come now, old man.' Guivret waved his spoon, looking at Tristan and Isolde as if hoping to draw them into the conversation. They

seemed too preoccupied. 'We all heard you say you fought beside Palamedes in the old days, in the great battles against the Saxons.'

'I didn't say that,' Beran muttered.

'But you must have seen fine horses? Even if only as you trudged
through their dung behind men like Palamedes here.' He pointed his
spoon at Palamedes, but the Saracen was too busy scraping the last of
the food from his bowl to take much notice. 'My horses have not been
trained for war, of course, have not galloped into battle ...' Guivret
picked up his empty cup and struck it against the empty bowl. 'Have
not smashed through a Saxon shieldwall to leave in their wake a litter
of snapped bones and bloody meat.' He put the discarded bowl down
in the fragrant floor rushes and picked up the wine jug. 'Still, most are
of the bloodline of those very animals which the Romans brought to
Britannia, and *could* be trained for war.' He poured the wine into his
cup. 'If there were still men alive who knew the ways.' He lifted the cup
towards Palamedes. 'The Saracen here could do it, perhaps, but he's too
valuable to me for his skill with a blade to be letting him go off and play
with horses all day.'

Palamedes was digging something from his teeth with the nail of
his little finger. 'I had more chance of living to a good old age when I
was fighting for you in the temple every other night than I do out
here,' he said.

'But you were losing that fight two nights ago,' the boy said, the
firelight reflecting in his wide eyes.

Palamedes grinned at him, the flesh under his left eye taut and
tumid and glistening with a sheen of sweat. 'I was just letting that
thick-skulled fool think he had the upper hand, Prince Erbin,' he said.
'You would have seen me win if not for the Saxons.'

'They cost us dear, my friend,' Guivret added, thinking of the lost
wagers.

Beran was enjoying the food very much. He was glad Guivret had
not ordered Palamedes to kill Conall, for he doubted the Irishman's
wife would have balanced the sage, garlic, rosemary and pepper so well
after that.

'The dun mare with the white on her left foreleg is drooling,' he said.
'Favours the right side of her mouth. Sores, most likely.' He spooned
more stew into his mouth. He felt their eyes on him but he looked only
at the boy. 'Did you see the white mare with her ears pinned back?' he

asked him. The boy nodded. 'That means she's in pain. Don't know what's hurting her, but something is.' The boy looked at Guivret, and Beran continued eating. 'The smaller of the two chestnuts will go lame soon if you don't take the stone or thorn out of her hind right hoof.' He swallowed. 'The silver has a weak back. She would have carried a man in scale armour once, but no longer. The black stallion could be a good horse but he's resentful because no one is brushing his coat as well as he deserves.' He shrugged, wondering if there was any more stew to be had. He had not realized how hungry he was. 'The dapple grey with the high neck, short belly and long head will fetch a good price, though,' he said. 'Is there more of this?' He lifted his bowl. 'Oh, and the dun with the cobwebbing on her forehead was hollowing out her back when the boy was on her. Whoever has been riding her, they're not fitting the saddle properly, or else the saddle itself is not right for her.'

There was a moment of silence but for the hiss and pop of the fire, and the scraping of Beran's spoon against his bowl.

'Is that all?' Guivret said. The Little King was staring at him, as was the boy, his mouth hanging open. 'Anything else I should know?' the dwarf asked.

Beran thought for a moment. 'Your stables face west when they should face south, and your hay is damp,' he said. 'Well, is there more?' He lifted the bowl again. 'And pass me that jug, or would you drink it all yourself?'

He had known he would pay the price for the three jugs of wine he had shared with Guivret beside the dying fire when the others had gone to their bed furs. This was the third time his bladder had woken him, and he stumbled through the dark and opened the door as slowly and quietly as he could, so as not to wake anyone.

The night was clear and cool, and the sky was impossibly vast, awash with stars beyond number, one for every soul that ever gazed upon them. One for *her*, he thought, then cursed himself for thinking it and for letting the wine seep in far enough to float the bones of the past.

The dewy grass was cold beneath his bare feet, but it felt good after the day's walking. At least they would have horses to take them the rest of the way, he thought. He sensed movement to his right. Bats. Flitting in the dark around him. Shadows amongst shadow. As a child he had been able to hear their squeaking, but now they were silent and ephemeral, like the ghosts which people said walked at Samhain when the veil thinned.

He stood looking up at the stars as his bladder emptied. One of the stabled horses nickered softly and another snorted as if in reply. Somewhere in the woods to the west, an owl *hoo*'ed. Closer, in the copse beyond the horse paddock, a fox was barking and wailing like a widow's lament, as Beran's stream spattered on the ground. Afterwards, he shivered and stood for a moment eyeing the ridge to the south, a black shoreline against an ocean of stars, wondering if there was a Saxon spearman up there now, watching in the night, keeping an eye on the Little King's horses.

He turned back to the steading, hoping he would be able to sleep through until dawn, but the sound of voices stopped him dead. He reached for his sword on instinct, but it was not at his hip, and so he made do with holding his breath and looking over to the hay shed beyond the pig pen. He saw two figures in the shadows and he knew them. Tristan had his arms outstretched, his hands on Isolde's shoulders, and even in the gloom Beran's old eyes could see that all was not well.

None of his business why the young lovers were not asleep by the hearth embers. He turned away.

'Beran? Is that you?'

He turned back to see the young man coming towards him, while Isolde hurried off in the direction of the house, heeling tears from her eyes as she went.

'Tristan.' Beran nodded in greeting.

'What are you doing out here?' Tristan asked, chin raised, his tone suspicious. 'Are you spying on us?' The young man's face was taut, his neck stiff.

'I was having a piss,' Beran said.

Tristan tilted his head. 'Again?' he said. 'I saw you earlier. You fed the fire on your way out.'

Beran shrugged. 'Wait till you get to my age,' he said. '*If* you get to my age.'

Tristan pointed an accusing finger. 'Were you listening?'

Beran straightened. 'I told you, I came out because I needed to piss. Now get your finger out of my face, boy.'

Tristan frowned, but lowered his hand. 'How long have you been standing there?' He folded his arms across his chest. 'What did you hear?'

'Nothing, thankfully,' Beran replied. 'The last thing I want in my ears is some lovers' quarrel. I need to sleep.' He turned and would have walked away but for Tristan's hand, which had closed around his upper arm. 'What are you doing?' Beran said, turning back to face him.

'Beran, it's just that …' Tristan left whatever it was unsaid, and Beran pulled free of the man's grip.

'I'm going to bed,' he said.

Before he had made three steps, the young man behind him said, 'She's with child, Beran.'

Beran stopped. Turned around. Saw Tristan's face, cold beneath the cold stars.

'Her bleed is late.' Tristan shook his head. 'She brought blood moss with her from Cornubia.' He looked ashamed then. 'I had not thought about it, but then I saw the bag with the moss. None had been used. Not since we left home.'

Beran stood there, just looking at the young man, whose face was turned towards the house, as though he expected to see Isolde standing there.

'She's sure?' Beran asked.

Tristan nodded. 'She said it has been nearly three moons since her last bleed.'

'Why are you telling me?' Beran asked. 'As I said, I came out to piss, not to get involved in whatever is going on between you two.'

Tristan took a step towards him. 'She's afraid,' he said, pressing a hand to his own stomach. 'She doesn't know how she will carry a child, living like this. Like outlaws.' He swept an arm out towards the dark rise to the south and the world beyond. 'Or where we can go when it's time. Who would help her deliver the babe?'

'I'm tired,' Beran said. 'And none of this has anything to do with me.' He turned to walk away, but Tristan grabbed his shoulder again and this time Beran twisted, knocking the other man's arm wide, and stepped in and threw his hand around Tristan's throat and drove him backwards across the worn ground, until the young man's back struck the side of the hay barn.

Tristan lifted his right arm and brought it down hard on Beran's forearm, breaking his grip, then pushed himself off the shed wall, shoulder into Beran's chest, forcing him back. 'You selfish old bastard,' he growled, a hand up at his own throat as he coughed and spluttered for the breath which Beran had denied him.

Beran pointed a finger at him, in echo of Tristan's earlier gesture. 'Lay a hand on me again and I'll kill you,' he said. 'Damn you, boy! You call *me* selfish?' He had tried so hard to keep it all buried. Had tried ever since he had learnt who the young lovers were. But now Tristan had hauled it from him, like the roots of some old plant which were never supposed to be exposed to stars or sun, air or sight. 'What have you done, boy?'

Tristan half turned his head away, though kept his eyes riveted to Beran's. 'What have *I* done?' His anger was muddied by confusion now.

'Isolde is not your wife, Tristan,' Beran said. 'She is another man's wife. A king's wife.' He let those words hang in the night air between them. 'Your uncle's wife,' he added finally.

Tristan's lips tightened, the muscles in his face drawing like knots in the flesh of his cheeks. 'I love her. She loves me.' As though it were so simple as that.

Beran gritted his own teeth.

Roots being pulled up from the dark, dark earth.

'And what of your uncle? Does he not love her?' he asked. 'And what of your duty to your king? What of Isolde's faithfulness to her lord and husband?'

Tristan looked up at the night sky as if seeking answers amongst the riddles written there. He let out a long, stuttering breath and brought his gaze back to Beran. 'My uncle did not appreciate what he had,' he said. 'But I love her. I *love* her, Beran. Every breath I draw is the whisper of her name. For years, every moment we were not together was a taste of death to me.' He grimaced. 'I cannot live without her.'

His words were a blade in Beran's chest, cold and sharp and piercing bone harder than scale armour, sinking into tender flesh beneath. Flesh that bled still, that quietly wept foul poison even after all the years.

'I love my uncle the king,' Tristan said, 'but I could not stay and watch them together. It would have killed me.' He looked into the west. 'We had to leave. We had to run. Any man would understand.' He lifted his hands and cradled the back of his own head and blew out a long breath, his eyes coming up to Beran again. 'You would have done the same, Beran.'

'No.' Beran shook his head. 'You have betrayed your lord, Tristan. You hungered for his wife and you took her for yourself.'

'That's not how it is,' Tristan said.

'You have disgraced yourself and dishonoured your king,' Beran said.

'No.' Tristan was shaking his head.

'And if Isolde has a child,' Beran went on, 'that child will always serve as a living reminder to King Mark of the blade which you have thrust into him. You, who should have loved him. You, who he himself has loved.'

Beran looked into the west now, imagining the King of Cornubia looking out across his land, wondering where the young lovers were, picturing in his mind Tristan and Isolde together beneath the stars, flesh on flesh, while he sat alone with his wine and his bitterness and his shame.

'We love each other, Beran,' was all Tristan could say.

Beran felt unsteady on his legs, as though the ground beneath him was falling away, or as though he were on a boat and could not find his balance. He lifted a hand, finger outstretched, not a threatening gesture this time but one of warning. 'It is poison,' he hissed. 'You have poisoned all three of you.'

'No,' Tristan said in a small voice. But Beran was walking away. 'No, Beran,' the young man said in his wake.

Beran cursed under his breath as he walked back through the dark, the stars above indifferent to all who gazed upon them. The gods of Britain gone now, their power as faint as the scent in the air after rain. The hopes of a people crumbled to ashes and dust, like bones in the fading embers of the funerary fire.

He knew he would get no sleep now.

'Damn you, boy!'

The jug flew and Arthur lifted an arm to shield his face, the jug smashing against it, shards hitting his right cheek as he turned his eyes away.

'Useless, stupid, gods-cursed cunt of a son!' Uther bellowed, spittle flying from his mouth, glistening in his black beard as he strode across the hall in front of his high seat, stirring the old, damp floor rushes and the hanging hearth smoke, which attended his wake as though the man himself smouldered. 'You hag-ridden lump of rancid horse dung!'

'Father, I—'

'Silence!' Uther's voice was thunder in that place, or else it was the plunging crash of waves on the Tintagel rocks below the great warrior's clifftop fortress. He stopped mid-stride and swung his baleful eyes to Arthur, who kept his hands by his sides, resisting the urge to wipe away the trickle of blood that he could feel on his cheek below his right eye. He would not give his father that pleasure. 'Ungrateful toad!' Uther spat, pointing a finger at him.

Uther put the sole of his boot against a brazier of burning coals and pushed the thing over, spilling the coals across the rushes and sending a wave of sparks, smoke and ash across the floor. 'Fool!' he bellowed. 'You shame me!'

Three slaves appeared like wraiths in the gloomy fug, hurrying to gather up the coals in iron pots and animal skins lest Uther, warlord and, some said, King of Cornubia, should burn down his own hall. Not that the reeds were likely to burst into flame, damp as they were from wet shoes and wet hounds, rain having hissed from the grey sky for three days straight since Samhain.

Uther paid the slaves no heed but snatched a cup from the long table and hurled it at Arthur, this time throwing wildly and missing him by a spear's length. 'She is your sister!' he roared. 'Your sister, Arthur!'

'Half-sister,' Arthur said, but if Uther heard he showed no sign of it. The warlord drove a finger against his own chest, burrowing it amongst the thick fur that covered his shoulders. 'Is there something twisted inside you, boy?' He bared his teeth. 'Something foul and rotten?' He took two strides towards Arthur and stopped himself, and threw his arms wide. 'Well?' he screamed. 'What's wrong with you? That you would bed your own sister?' His flushed and mottled face twisted as though the words he spoke were venom.

'Half-sister,' Arthur said again, under his breath this time.

'That you would put a child in her belly!' Uther went on, turning and striding to his great high seat carved of oak. When he got to it, he turned back and threw up an arm and gripped the chair's tall back, his hand bone-white, as though holding on to the chair was the only way to stop himself throwing something else, perhaps even one of the slaves on their knees by the upturned brazier. 'You are my son!' he cried. 'Have you not your choice of cunny from here to Caer Gwinntguic? Are there not a score of women within a spear-throw of my hall who would open their legs for a silver coin or a jug of wine?' He pointed across the hall. 'And you chose her?'

Arthur turned his head, glancing at Morgaine, who stood across from him, silent and inscrutable, her hands placed protectively over her stomach. Arthur had not yet had a chance to look at her properly, but now he looked. His eyes moved down from her pale face and the waves of red hair, as wild as fire, down to the slight swell of her belly. He had not seen her in four moons, but there was no mistaking it. No hiding it, even from a man's eyes.

'I was drunk, Father,' he said, flooding with guilt and sickening shame to think that Morgaine was carrying his child. That it was growing within her even now. That she might feel the flutter and twitch of the quickening.

She returned his gaze, but he could not read her thoughts, and he wondered if she felt that shame, too, for that which she carried inside her. For what they had done together that freezing dawn when he had returned numb and stiff, and she had warmed him with wine and her own flesh. Looking at her now, he could almost recall her scent in his nose, the taste of her, and something stirred in his groin. He looked away.

'You were drunk.' Uther's voice was now the low growl of a war hound straining at the leash. He seemed to be trying to subdue the rage that trembled in him. 'So you tupped your own sister?'

Arthur flinched at that. 'I would not have done it had Merlin not sent Lisanor away,' he said. 'I loved her, Father.'

Uther clenched a fist and brought it down on the back of the chair. 'Love! Ha!' He lifted his chin, his black, spittle-webbed beard glistening by the light of the hearth fire. 'And what do you know of love?'

Arthur did not answer that. He looked down and saw a mouse shivering in the rushes beneath a mead bench.

'Well?' Uther said.

Arthur looked up, and Uther extended an arm, inviting his son to enlighten him.

'Where is Lisanor?' Arthur asked. 'Why will nobody tell me? Where did Merlin send her? I want to know what happened to her.'

Uther seemed taken aback. He narrowed his eyes, as if trying to decide what effect his next words would have. '*I* had Merlin get rid of the girl,' he said, laying that out like a challenge, his eyes never leaving Arthur's.

Arthur had not expected that. It landed like a blow. He felt the blood begin to simmer in his veins and he took a breath and let it pass slowly out between his lips. Then he swallowed. 'Why?' he said.

'Why? Because you are an embarrassment to me,' Uther said. 'Following some ploughman's daughter around like a puppy drooling for its mother's teat. I need to make a man of you.' He swung an arm, scything through the smoke. 'Had I known you would swive your sister instead, I would have had Merlin poison your pottage and be done with you.'

He turned on Morgaine then. 'And you,' he snarled. 'Do not think I am ignorant of a woman's wiles. What was your scheme, girl?' He shook his head. 'You are not my daughter, but there is enough of your mother in you, I can see. Tempting men with that nettle bed between your legs.' He eyed Morgaine the way most men looked at Merlin, with a mixture of curiosity and suspicion. 'You have more clever in you than Arthur, girl,' he said. 'Why would you let the fool put his seed in you?'

Again Arthur looked at Morgaine.

'Arthur was sad, lord,' she said, glancing at him. 'He needed me. I comforted him.'

'Comfort?' Uther snorted. 'That is one word for it. And look at your reward.' He pointed at her swollen belly. 'The child will be cursed for the incest in his begetting. That is how the gods punish us.' He glared at her. 'Go now,' he said, 'and if I hear of you and my son lying together again, I will burn you, girl. You and the cursed child you carry.'

Morgaine stood a moment longer, glaring back at the warlord of Cornubia and Dumnonia, enough flint and steel in her eyes to make sparks. Then she looked at Arthur, as though giving him a chance to speak up for her, but Arthur had nothing to say, and so Morgaine nodded and turned and swept out of that smoky hall.

It was raining hard now. Lashing against the roof and the timbers of the west wall. It was a foul day. The kind of frigid, grey day that soaked into the bones and the spirit.

'Now, Arthur,' Uther said, when it was just the two of them but for the mice in the thatch above their heads and in the rushes beneath their feet. 'Listen well. I'm going to tell you what will happen.' He went to the hearth and held out his hands, clenching and unclenching them above the flames. 'You will not tell anyone about the child,' he said. 'You will never speak of it. Never.' He rolled his great shoulders like a man steeling himself to some task, a feat of strength perhaps. 'When the child is born, I will . . . deal with it.'

Arthur's stomach clenched. His head felt as it did after strong wine. 'You will have it killed?' he asked.

Uther had been looking into the fire, but now he turned his face to Arthur. 'I told you, if the child lives, it will be cursed. You might also carry that ill luck for the rest of your days. Certainly the shame of its existence will cling to you, like mud to a boot. Do you understand this, Arthur?'

'Yes, but—'

Uther stopped him with a raised hand. 'I will not kill it,' he said. 'No blade will touch it. No poison or noose.'

Arthur shook his head. 'I don't understand.'

Uther looked up and frowned and put out a hand. A drop of water splashed against his palm because rain was seeping through the thatch there. 'I will have it taken out upon the lake,' he said.

'You will have it drowned?' Arthur did not want to believe what he was hearing.

'I will put the infant's life in the hands of the gods,' Uther said. 'Let them decide its fate.' The warrior lord growled for a slave to attend him, and three heartbeats later a thin, hunched man materialized from the shadows behind the wall hangings at the hall's rear. Uther said something to him in a low voice, and the man hurried out of the hall.

'And Morgaine?' Arthur said. 'What about her?'

'She will be sent away, Arthur. Somewhere she cannot spin trouble for you.' Now he turned his gaze back to the flames and the damp, seething wood. 'You are my son, Arthur. I do it for you.' He bent and picked up a fire iron and pushed a log deeper into the flames, where it hissed angrily. 'Morgaine will not get her claws in you. I will see to that.'

Only now did Arthur lift a hand to his face and thumb off the blood that was already drying on his cheek. 'And me?' he asked. 'What happens to me?'

Uther's lip curled in his black beard, as black as Arthur's was fair.

'It's time you became a man, Arthur,' he said. 'Come the summer, the High King will call my spears to Dumnonia. I will go to kill Saxons. I'm good at it. But there will always be more Saxons to kill. And there will come a day when I am too old to lead spearmen into the butchery.' He nodded to indicate his oaken chair. 'Do you think you could be the sword of Britain then?' Uther's eyes seemed to weigh Arthur like a pair of scales. 'You will have to kill our enemies,' he said. 'You will have to break a Saxon shieldwall.' He lifted a brawny arm and pointed at Arthur. 'Yet I see nothing in you that makes me think you could lead men in battle. Nothing.'

Just then the door thumped open and Arthur turned to see a man come into the hall. A big man. Broad and scarred, his face weathered by war and cruel-looking beneath a beard the colour of iron rot on a blade. 'Lord Uther,' the man said, dipping his bald head, from which he palmed rain, flicking it away, before fixing hard eyes on Arthur. He wore ringmail and carried a large and heavy-looking sword at his hip.

'Arthur, this is Cadwain,' Uther said. 'I believe Lord Ector has taught you as much as he can about sword and spear work. But Cadwain here will teach you more than this. He will teach you how to win. He has soaked the lands of the Eogonachta with blood. He has killed two dozen men in single combat.'

'The Irish do not fight in the shieldwall, Arthur,' Cadwain explained. 'Each warrior seeks to undertake a duel with a worthy opponent.' His lips warped within the red bush of his beard. 'They come at you, screaming and wild, and they don't feel pain, but they die like any other man.'

Uther nodded at Cadwain. 'He will forge you into a blade that may one day be of use to Dumnonia.'

Cadwain looked Arthur up and down. 'Can you fight, Arthur ap Uther?'

Arthur straightened. 'I can fight.'

Cadwain grunted. 'We'll see, won't we? One thing I do know is that I'm going to work you so hard you'll wish you were an ox yoked to the plough.' He sniffed and knuckled snot from his nose. 'Maybe you can swing a sword. I daresay you can throw a spear. Good shoulders. You're strong, I can see that. But when I've finished with you, you'll be more dangerous than famine and disease, fire and winter.' He grinned then, but his eyes remained as cold and grey as the day outside. 'But before any of that, how are you on boats, Arthur?'

Arthur looked at Uther, who was holding his hands above the hissing hearth again. 'I want you far away, Arthur,' he said. 'And I don't want to see you again until there is something in you that I recognize.'

There was a roaring deep in Arthur's ears, like the sound of the tide washing into the cave on the beach far below Uther's hall. It was the hate inside him rising. Welling up and swirling and threatening to spill over or else drown him in the dark.

'Where are you sending me?' he asked.

It was Cadwain who answered. 'Lyonesse. We leave with the tide.'

Arthur almost laughed then, but the sound that escaped his mouth was broken, ill-formed. 'I can't just leave. What will Ector think?'

'I will send word to him,' Uther said.

'Does my mother know?' Arthur asked.

Uther's lip pulled back from his teeth. He stepped up to Arthur, who tried not to recoil, but kept his feet planted and his shoulders squared, though he had to partly turn his face away from the warlord, whose bristling beard prickled against his cheek and the new cut there. 'You and Morgaine both came from her womb,' Uther hissed into his ear, so that Cadwain could not hear. Arthur could smell the swine fat in that beard and the ale on his sour breath. 'Do you think she wants you anywhere near her after what you have done?'

Uther stepped back and tilted his head in a gesture that invited Arthur to answer, but Arthur clenched his teeth and his hands. He clenched down on the rising hatred inside him and he said nothing. And maybe his father saw his silence as weakness, further proof of his unworthiness, or perhaps the warrior saw it as an opportunity to stick the knife in one last time and twist it.

'Go with Cadwain and prove yourself to him,' Uther said. 'Earn this man's respect while I kill Saxons. Make something of yourself, Arthur, or don't ever come back here.' The Lord of War lifted his stinking black beard in the direction of the hall's door, beyond which the rain lashed and the sea hurled itself upon Tintagel's shore to break in furious gouts of white spume. 'Now get out of my sight.'

And so, he turned and walked away, bile thick in his throat, shame and anger warring in his heart, and the burning fire of their eyes upon his back.

10

Beran and the Boy

'THE SAXONS ARE COMING!' The boy was as excited as a puppy and as welcome as a pail of freezing water in the face. 'Wake up, the Saxons are here!' He was going from furs to furs, shaking each of them awake.

'Is it morning already?' Tristan mumbled, Isolde stirring beside him.

The boy came over to Beran, who raised a hand to ward him off before the boy could prod or poke him. 'I heard you,' Beran said, sitting up groggily and coughing. There were no flames in the hearth but it was still smoking, and the smoke hung in that place thick as unwound burial shrouds. 'Believe me, boy, Saxons are not worth getting excited about.'

'How many?' Palamedes asked, yawning.

Beran blinked and rubbed his eyes, trying to decide whether he had slept or not.

'Seven.' The boy was almost bouncing from foot to foot. 'They look big.'

'Everyone looks big to you, boy,' the Saracen said, climbing to his feet and stretching his arms behind his broad back.

'I know how he feels.' Guivret had appeared in the doorway, looking like he had been awake for a while. 'I'll deal with Eadwig. Let's not have any trouble. You hear me, Beran? This is business. Let's keep it friendly.'

Beran coughed again. 'It's nothing to do with me,' he said.

Guivret nodded and went back outside, and Palamedes followed.

One thing to be said for the Little King was that it did not seem to matter how much wine he drank, it never showed on him the next day.

Beran, on the other hand . . . He felt as though his brain had swollen inside his skull and was threatening to crack it open and spill out.

'Here.' The boy handed him a cup of ale.

He took it and drank, hoping it would rid him of the headache.

'I want you to stay out of the way,' he told the boy.

The boy frowned. 'But I want to see the Saxons,' he protested.

'You've seen them. Now find somewhere to hide and stay there until they're gone.'

'No,' the boy said.

'No?' Beran was taken aback. He winced at the throbbing in his head. It was too early in the day to have to deal with a petulant prince.

'Listen to Beran, Prince Erbin,' Isolde told him. 'People are looking for you. Better if we don't take any chances.'

The boy thought for a moment. 'All right,' he said, downcast.

It struck Beran that Erbin had accepted instruction far more readily from Isolde, so he nodded her his thanks. The look she returned was cold. Perhaps Tristan had told her about his conversation with Beran, not that he wanted to think about any of that now, with his head splitting open and a pack of Saxons at the door.

He creaked to his feet, putting on his sword belt and turning his head this way and that to work the knots out of his neck. 'Isolde, best if you stay out of sight too,' he said. And not because people were looking for her and Tristan, too, but because she was a beautiful young woman, and he knew what men were capable of.

Isolde looked from Beran to Tristan, who was putting on his tunic.

'He's right,' Tristan said, picking up his spear. 'Stay inside.'

Palamedes appeared at the threshold. 'They're here, Beran,' he said.

Beran nodded and went outside, blinking in the dawn, coughing out the hearth smoke and breathing in the fresh morning air with its scent of long, dew-laced grass and meadow flowers, cut with the sweet musk of the horses. How many such dawns had he seen in his life? How many more would he see? He felt like a lone ash in a coppice wood. Forgotten. Overlooked. Somehow missed by the woodsman's axe. The dawn was the same as a thousand late summer dawns before it, yet the world had moved on, and he was still here.

'Keep your mouths shut and leave it to me,' Guivret said as he, Palamedes, Tristan and Beran stood with spears against the paddock fence, watching the Saxons coming down the slope in the weak morning light.

'This your first close-up look at a Saxon?' Palamedes asked Tristan.

'The Lady Iselle sent King Mark seven heads last Beltane,' he said. 'But yes, these are my first breathing Saxons.' He gave a nervous smile, and looked at the Saracen. 'I've seen more men with skin as dark as yours in Cornubia than I have Saxons.'

'Then you are a lucky man,' Palamedes said through a grin.

Each Saxon carried shield and spear, two had swords at their hips, and all wore a scramasax, the long Saxon knife, in a horizontal sheath on the front of their belts. None wore helmets or mail. This was Saxon land, won with blood and steel, they were confident, and the day would grow too warm for armour when they had little to fear.

'You still live, Little King,' said the Saxon who must surely have been Eadwig, when he was but two spear lengths away. One of the two sword-armed men, he had a fair beard and lank fair hair, and he smiled at Guivret as though he were greeting an old friend.

'Of course I live, you Saxon fiend,' Guivret said, holding out his short arms. 'The attack on Caer Lundein failed. Did you know? Hundreds of your kinfolk lie dead in the ditches.' He shook his head as if at the memory of it. 'It was a great slaughter, Eadwig. I would wager that the tribes are even now turning against King Cynric for leading them to ruin.'

Eadwig eyed the dwarf with suspicion, as one of his men, an old warrior with close-set eyes and but a few wisps of hair on his sun-browned scalp, spun Guivret's words into the Saxon tongue for the others. Another man, in a thick fur whose rancid stink Beran could smell from where he stood, touched the small wooden hammer hanging at his neck.

'So, yes, I am alive,' Guivret went on, as the Saxons spoke amongst themselves, appearing to deride the dwarf's news for the lie it was, 'which is good news for you because it means we can do business together again.' He turned to Conall, who was standing nearby. Rivulets of sweat were running down the steward's fleshy cheeks into his black beard. 'Fetch ale for our guests,' Guivret told him.

For a moment, the man just stood there. 'Well?' Guivret said.

The steward nodded and hurried away, calling to a skinny stable boy to help him.

Guivret shook his head. 'Fat swine sometimes forgets who is master here.'

Eadwig raised a fair eyebrow, then pointed his spear at the house from whose thatch grey smoke leaked to stain the brightening day.

'Why you here if attack . . .' He lifted his chin and scratched his neck while he searched for the word. 'If attack . . . fail?'

Guivret curled his lip. 'Because, my friend,' he said, turning his head and spitting, 'the stink of dead Saxons puts me off my wine.' He took a deep breath. 'I came here for the clean air, Eadwig. And because . . .' now he gave the man a wry smile, 'it seems that if I am not careful, that Irish swine Conall would sell my horses for less than half what I could get for them across the sea.'

Eadwig scratched his beard now, finding in it a louse which he pulled out and crushed between finger and thumbnail. He looked at Beran and Tristan, then laid his gaze back on Guivret, flicking the louse away, discarding it as he discarded Guivret's lie about the Saxon defeat. 'Now King Cynric holds Caer Lundein, your horses worth less to me.' He shrugged. 'My people have now many horses. Harder for me to sell yours.'

'Harder still if you don't have any,' Guivret replied. 'Can't sell what you don't have.' He turned his face to the east, where a tideline of pale gold seeped up into the blue. 'I wonder, Eadwig . . .' he swung his gaze back to the Saxon, 'if our days of doing business together have come to an end.'

Eadwig considered this as he watched a wasp land on the shaft of his spear below the blade. It seemed to be trying to eat the ash, where the wood was stained dark. Then the Saxon leant the spear towards Beran and Tristan, and the wasp flew away. 'Who they?' he asked.

Tristan's handsome face was pale, his knuckles white on the shaft of his spear as he glanced at Beran, who shook his head, warning the young man against saying anything.

'They are my friends from Caer Celemion,' Guivret said, wafting ringed fingers towards them. 'They have offered me a pound of silver for the black stallion and more for the dapple grey.'

Eadwig laughed at that, looking back to the house. 'Where is Conall?' he asked. 'I more like making business with him.'

'I'm sure you do,' Guivret said, as Conall and the stable boy came back laden with mugs of ale for the Saxons.

'I will buy all your horses, Little King.' The Saxon took the offered cup and sniffed its contents. 'My people moving north.' He smiled. 'Many people. Need many horses.'

Guivret inclined his head. 'For the usual price,' he said. 'No less.'

Seeming content that the ale had not been mixed with hemlock or nightshade, Eadwig drank deeply. His men followed his lead, gulping down the ale and dragging hands across their lips and beards, belching and muttering amongst themselves. They were bored. Just as well Isolde was somewhere out of sight, Beran thought.

'For price Conall agree with me,' Eadwig said.

'No,' Guivret said.

The old Saxon with the close-set eyes did not need to turn that into the Saxon tongue for his spear-brothers to understand it. A plaintive cry drew Eadwig's eyes up to the pale blue sky. Beran looked up and saw a pair of ravens attacking a hawk, the black birds kronking noisily as they drove the mewing hawk westward. He guessed that Eadwig was seeing some sort of omen in that battle above the realm of men, for Woden was sometimes called the god of ravens.

'We know each other long time, Little King,' Eadwig said. 'I give you what I agree with Conall.' He shrugged. 'Or I take.'

Hearing these words spun into the Saxon tongue, Eadwig's spear-men tossed their empty cups onto the ground and squared their shoulders. Conall gestured at the stable boy, who went amongst those warriors, pale and trembling with fear as he picked up the cups.

Beran glanced at Palamedes, who gave a slight shake of his head.

'I take and you get nothing,' Eadwig went on, 'and maybe we burn this place.' Again, he pointed his spear at the house and hay shed. 'Maybe we make fire here and take the black stallion to give for King Cynric.' He glanced at the stable boy, who had dropped one of the cups and was fumbling to gather it up. 'Maybe give slaves, too.'

Beran watched Guivret's face change, nostrils flaring, the veins in his neck straining beneath the skin. It was a sight that amused the Saxon leader; he snorted and tilted the cup of ale at Guivret. A mocking toast. Then he threw his head back and tipped the warm ale down his throat, holding the cup in place to drain every last drop. It was long, that arrogant final quaff. Long enough for the dwarf to pull the seax from its sheath, take three strides longer than his legs should reach, and plunge it into Eadwig's side before the Saxon knew what was happening.

'You come here and threaten me!' Guivret yelled, pulling the blade out and punching it back in, as Eadwig stood there, wide-eyed, blood welling at his open mouth.

Palamedes' spear streaked, embedding in a Saxon belly, and the man squealed like a pig and clutched the shaft and dropped to his knees.

'You Saxon shitting whoreson!' Guivret was yelling, stabbing Eadwig again and again, as Beran took two steps and thrust his spear at another Saxon, who blocked the thrust with his own shaft and punched the butt end into Beran's chest, knocking him backwards. Beran closed the gap and feinted and thrust again, his spear blade slicing into the Saxon's shoulder, making him bellow in pain. He looked at the wound, growling curses, or the names of his gods, or vows of vengeance, as Beran glanced at the chaos all around. Tristan's spear was stuck in the old Saxon's thigh, three foot of shaft sticking out either side, the Saxon just staring down at it as though unsure what to do next. Conall was staggering away, clutching his belly, from which bright blood spewed onto the grass.

Beran's man came at him, jabbing with his spear, exclaiming with every thrust, and it was all Beran could do to parry each attack as he edged backwards under the onslaught. The Saxon was faster and stronger and now he lashed his spear down onto Beran's shaft, knocking it out of his hands. Then he grinned and pulled the spear back in readiness to drive it forward into Beran's chest, to banish the breath from his lungs.

A hawk's scream then, and something flew at the Saxon, driving a spear into his ribs, and it was the boy, and the boy let go of the spear and staggered back, his eyes wide and wild, teeth bared like some cornered animal.

'Get back!' Beran bellowed at him, gasping for breath as he drew his sword and strode forward and took the reeling Saxon's head off his shoulders. The head landed heavily and rolled so that the lifeless eyes stared up at the dawn sky, as the man's body collapsed and landed beside it.

'Look!' The boy was pointing, and Beran turned to see one of the Saxons running, harefooting for the rise from which they had come, leaving his spear-brothers to their fate.

'Get away, boy,' Beran barked, but the boy was rooted to the spot, looking around as though spellbound by the bloodletting. Palamedes was working with his sword, holding a fur-clad Saxon at bay, while Tristan and Guivret were jabbing at the other remaining Saxon, who was blocking desperately with spear and shield and shouting after his fleeing companion, no doubt cursing him for a coward.

Guivret's seax found an opening, scraping a furrow of scalp from the back of the Saxon's head. 'I'll kill you, you dog! You pissing maggot fuck!' he roared, his beard strung with frothing spittle, the corners of his mouth thick and white with it. The Saxon turned his head this way and that, trying to fend off his attackers, a raw scrap of flesh and hair bouncing and flapping and spraying blood.

'Beran,' Palamedes called, pointing his sword after the runaway, who was now halfway to the top of the hill and bathed in the red blush of the rising sun.

Beran sheathed his sword and ran, his knees grating in their sockets, his ragged breath loud in his ears but not so loud as the rhythmic gush of his own blood in his head. He pulled open the stable door and went into that gloomy, sweet-smelling place, passing each stall until he came to the black stallion.

'Come on, boy,' he said, breathing hard as he untied the halter and stroked the animal's flank with one hand, and put his other to the stallion's nose to let it smell him. 'We have work to do.' The stallion neighed and tossed its head and kicked out once, but Beran held his ground, telling the animal in a quiet voice that he meant it no harm. He knew the stallion had smelled blood on the air and heard the shrieks of the dying. Now, the animal sensed the violence in the man who had come into its stall. Yet it yielded to Beran's touch and voice and, perhaps, to something deeper still, which Beran could not name. It let him lead it outside, into that red dawn. Let this stranger take hold of its thick black mane and swing himself up onto its back as though he were a young man again.

'There's a good boy,' Beran told the stallion, stroking its withers and leaning forward to pat its strong neck. He trotted the horse across the sun-baked earth, seeing that Palamedes had killed the man in the rancid fur and was striding over to help Tristan and Guivret butcher the last remaining Saxon who had stayed to fight.

'Palamedes,' Beran called, holding out his hand. The Saracen tossed his spear to Beran, who caught it smoothly and kicked his heels, the stallion breaking into a canter. He'd been right about the stallion. It was a fine beast, swift and strong, and its hooves drummed the hard earth, and he held on for his life as they came to the slope, the horse driving on and up, snorting, barely slowing.

'Good boy!' Beran called, feeling the stallion's muscles bunch and release, seeing its flattened ears twitch at his voice. 'Good boy now!'

When they came to the crest, he saw the Saxon. The man was

running still, ploughing through the long grass, stumbling now and then, his spear discarded. Beran kicked his heels again and leant forward, lifting his seat and urging the stallion to even greater effort, and the stallion obeyed, galloping now, the four-beat rhythm of its hooves replacing Beran's own heartbeat, its sinew and muscle and great strength redeeming Beran's weakness and frailty and all his long years.

Twenty paces. The stallion's hooves hardly touched the ground, and Beran moved with the animal, each of them feeling the thrill of it in the other, so that they were like the first and third strings of a lyre, sounding their notes in harmony, and the song was of the golden past.

The Saxon tried to look over his shoulder whilst running, and almost fell, and Beran thought he heard the man yelp like a fox run to exhaustion, though he did not slow.

Ten paces. The wind in Beran's face dragged tears from his eyes. Hairs from the stallion's mane whipped his cheeks. They came up on the left of the Saxon and, holding round the stallion's neck with his left hand, Beran leant to his right and levelled the spear, then thrust down, his momentum driving the slender blade into the man's back, between the shoulder blades.

The man fell forward into the grass and Beran leant back, bringing the stallion up, wheeling him round and round and eventually to a stop. 'You're a fine boy,' he said, heaving for breath, sucking it in like a bellows and rubbing the beast behind the ears as he walked it back to the body lying amongst the pink willowherb and purple betony. 'You're too good for the dwarf,' he told the stallion. 'He doesn't deserve you.' He leant out and pulled the spear free and laid it in front of him across the stallion's neck, and for a while he sat there, letting his weight settle onto the animal. There had not been time to saddle the horse, but he had not needed it. And now, without even a blanket between them, he could feel the stallion tense up, as if it were preparing to run again, or hoping to, so Beran leant back, and the stallion understood that it would not gallop again.

'Too good for those Saxons too,' he told the stallion, feeling each great breath and the swell of its belly as it blew, and the tremulous joy in its flesh. For Beran, it was as though all the years had rolled back like the tide. His blood was rushing in his veins. The battle thrill was in his muscles, quivering there, thrumming like the wings of small birds.

'Too good for me,' he said after a while, leaning forward to speak those soft words into the stallion's ear. Then he clicked with his tongue and urged the horse forward, and it blew and neighed at the dawn and tossed its head.

The others were looting the dead Saxons when he walked the stallion back over the crest of the hill and began down the slope, but they stopped what they were doing when they saw him. The boy ran across the paddock and up the foot of the slope, calling to Beran, asking if he had killed the Saxon. By way of answer, Beran lifted the spear and the boy saw Saxon blood slick on the blade.

'I didn't know you could ride like that,' the boy said.

Beran knew that the battle thrill was smothering a dozen pains at least, including the blow he had taken to his chest. It would all come crashing in on him later. For now, though, he was a horse lord again and could see it in the boy's eyes.

'And I didn't know you could use a spear like that, boy.' He felt the smile on his lips, felt the rareness of it.

The boy grinned proudly and pulled his shoulders back and patted the stallion which was still blowing from the run. And together they walked down the hill.

'Smell that?' Guivret asked, swaying gently in the saddle, his chin raised as he breathed in the air. The sun was low in the west, throwing shadows, theirs and the horses', across the ground and the swell of ancient burial mounds cloaked in blue harebell.

'Smoke?' the boy said.

Guivret shook his head. 'Something else,' he said.

The old Roman road leading to Portus Adurni was overgrown with grass and weeds and chamomile, which the boy was loath to see, he being from Caer Colun where Roman buildings still stood, and statues of emperors and gods still kept watch over the town's inhabitants, and the roads were still smooth.

The boy turned his face this way and that, sniffing loudly, his top lip hitched, which made Isolde laugh. 'You look like a mouse sniffing a piece of cheese, Prince Erbin,' she teased, sitting her dun mare stiffly, for she had ridden but little in her life and almost not at all since becoming King Mark's queen.

'I don't smell anything,' the boy said, 'just the horses.' But he lifted himself in the saddle and sniffed again anyway.

The breeze was coming up from the south, warm in the dusk, whispering through the tall grass of the chalk downland all the secrets of the long, long summer. And Beran had long since caught the salt tang in it. 'It's the sea,' he said. 'We're close now.'

'No, Beran, it's the smell of silver and coin,' Guivret said. 'The smell of opportunity and prosperity.'

But Beran smelled the sea, and for him the scent carried memories. It bore the weight of the past, just as the sea itself carries vessels laden with cargo, and Beran could no sooner turn these memories away, could no more prevent these vessels beaching on the shores of his mind, than he could stop breathing. And so the memories came unbidden, one after another, as unwelcome as the Saxon ships that scraped up the grey shingle of Britain's southern shore.

'You should come with us, Beran,' Guivret said soon after. He had already persuaded Beran to ride to the coast with him, to help protect him and his horses. In return, the Little King would pay for Beran and the boy to take ship west, to Tintagel, where they could hire a retinue of spearmen to escort the boy through Saxon-held land to Camelot. With any luck they could avoid raiding parties, Queen Morgana's scouts, and anyone else who would see them dead.

'No, I shouldn't,' Beran said.

'Why not? I will pay you to ride my horses at the markets.' Guivret was shooing at flies that were bothering his little mare. 'When folk see what you can do, or more importantly what my horses can do, they will be willing to pay more. They will line up with their mares to have the black stallion sire their foals. I don't doubt he could cover three mares a day.' He grinned at Palamedes. 'Like his lord and master,' he said.

'I told you, I'm taking the boy to Camelot,' Beran said. 'It's the only place he'll be safe.'

Guivret sighed. 'Ah, you are a stubborn man, Beran. You could live out your days in comfort. Wine, food, women. But you turn your back on it.' He shook his head. 'I don't understand you.'

Beran shrugged. 'I promised the boy.' He looked at the son of Constantine, who looked back at him with brows drawn together, as if he still did not fully trust Beran to keep his word.

'As I said, stubborn.' Guivret lifted an imaginary cup. 'Well, I will raise a drink to you both from my hall in Benoic,' he said, 'for all that you will likely be dead in some ditch by then, or have your heads mounted on Saxon spears.'

'Don't listen to him, Prince Erbin,' Isolde said. 'It's just his way of saying he'll miss you.' She gave a sad smile. 'We all will.'

Guivret chuckled at that. 'The only thing I'll miss is the silver and coin I used to make in the name of Mithras.'

'*You* used to make?' Palamedes said, looking askance at the dwarf. 'It was my blood, my broken bones that paid for your wine and whores.'

Guivret wafted his words away as though they were a horse fly. 'And I will miss Elissa. Did I tell you, Beran, she is from Carthage?'

'I expect she's telling some blood-reeking Saxon the same thing right about now,' Beran said, which earned a smirk from Palamedes but a grimace from Guivret.

Still, Beran could not help but admire the dwarf's confidence. In a matter of a few days, Guivret had lost his little kingdom and his farm and made an enemy of the Saxons, with whom he had done business for years. Now he had no choice but to cross the Dividing Sea and try to rebuild his fortunes in another land, and yet he seemed to relish the prospect. So, they were each riding one of his horses, and all but Isolde led two more, these spare horses laden with saddles and tack, food and wine and all the supplies which the Little King refused to leave behind for the Saxons to fall upon like crows to the stubble.

'And what will happen when you reach Camelot?' Isolde asked.

'That is not my problem,' Beran said.

'Lord Galahad and the Lady Iselle will welcome me,' the boy said. 'I know they will.'

'And you really think Beran can get you there?' This from Tristan, who had barely spoken a word all day, and none to Beran.

'I'm the only chance the boy has,' Beran said, before the boy could answer. 'His father was King Constantine. His grandfather was High King Ambrosius.' Beran heard a *kark* and looked up to see a heron sweeping southward across the sky. He touched the iron ring of the stallion's headpiece to ward off the ill omen in it. 'If I do not get him to Camelot, the Saxons will kill him. Or Queen Morgana will. Or Nabor will.' For a while he watched the heron's slow and solemn flight, and he wondered if the bird was the spirit of Emmeline, come to torment him for abandoning her on the bank of the Tamesis. But then he discarded the idea as something his old friend the druid might have said, and he smiled at that.

'Beran still believes in Britain,' the boy said. 'That is why he is not running away to Benoic. He still believes that one day we will beat the Saxons.'

Beran felt Palamedes' eyes on him then. 'I believe nothing, boy,' he said. 'Other than a man's word. And I gave you my word. That's all.'

'Beran is a man without hope, Prince Erbin,' Tristan put in. 'He does not understand what it is to hold a dream to your heart. Or to fight for something you love. To do whatever it takes.'

'I would be careful if I were you, Tristan,' Palamedes murmured.

But Tristan ignored the warning. 'Beran is bitter as wormwood. If he has ever loved anything or anyone I will be surprised.' Beran knew that the young man was goading him, but he did not reply. Nor did he answer Guivret's unspoken question, for the Little King was looking at him too, one eyebrow raised, waiting for an explanation of the Cornubian's sourness since they had set off.

Beran said nothing, because he was thinking about what he had seen up on a hill to the east. 'We're being watched,' he said.

'I see them,' Palamedes said.

'Where?' Guivret's head was swivelling like an owl's.

The Saracen lifted his chin. 'Against the tree line up there on the escarpment,' he said, 'where the white rock breaks through.'

'Yes, two riders,' the boy put in. 'Do you think they're Saxons?'

Beran thought he saw the glint of a spearhead in the last light of the day.

'What do we do?' Tristan asked.

'We keep going,' Beran said.

'Want me and Beran to ride up there and see who they are?' Palamedes asked Guivret.

'Hasn't there been enough killing today?' Isolde asked. She looked pale and unwell. 'I still have the screams of poor Conall's wife ringing in my ears.'

'There will be no more killing today, my love,' Tristan said with a weak smile that did nothing to mask his own fear.

Images of that morning's bloodshed came to Beran's mind. The big Saxon who had been faster and stronger and who might have killed him if not for the boy. He remembered the boy's cry, like the screech of a hawk. Remembered the thrill of mounting the stallion for the first time and chasing after the fleeing warrior and spearing him in the back. The copper stink in the dawn air. Conall's wife trying to push the Irishman's gut string back into his belly, her hands bright with blood as though she were butchering a swine for the table. He shook his head, to shake loose the picture as much as offer his dissent.

'I'm not riding up there,' he said. 'I agreed to guard your horses, Little King, not go looking for trouble.'

Up ahead, some four arrow flights away, a wide swath of woodland filled the horizon, blocking their view of the sea beyond and falling into shadow now, as sunlight drained from the world. Oak, hazel, birch and pine, the taller trees dark with a thousand bulky nests and their inhabitants. The rooks' voices, age-old and coarse, carrying to them on the breeze, sounded to Beran like condemnation.

He glanced back up at the riders on the hill. They had not moved, but still sat their horses near where the chalk rock showed pinkish red in the dusk, like a wound in the shoulder of the bluff.

'If it was Nabor, there would be more than two,' Beran said.

More rooks, and some jackdaws by the looks, were passing over-head, cawing raucously, beating for their roosts before darkness fell. They congregated above the trees, flocks of hundreds, swirling and twisting in black cauldrons of noise. Not crows, yet close enough, and Beran could not help but think of Isolde saying that he had the Mor-rigán on his shoulder.

'What if they are Saxons?' the boy asked. His hands were busy on the reins, fingers and thumbs worrying at the leather tack, rolling it over and twisting it back, and Beran knew the boy was reliving that morning's slaughter in his mind. Knew it might fester in him like a wound gone bad, because boys only ten summers old should not have to thrust spears into men's ribs and then see their heads lopped off, the stumps of their necks spraying blood like some druid's offering of death to the new season. It was a memory that could putrefy in a person. Beran knew all about the way memories could do that. But he also knew there was nothing he could do about it.

'If they're Saxons, they won't attack until they outnumber us,' he said. 'They could just be scouts, watching the road to see who's going in and out of Portus Adurni.' He knew it must rile the Saxon warlords of the lost lands that they had won so much in the south and east, had taken Caer Colun and driven their spears into Caer Lundein, Caer Celemion and Dumnonia, and yet warriors of Britain still held some of the old Roman shore forts. Noviomagus still held, if only just. So too Portus Adurni, as far as they knew. They would find out for sure soon enough.

'Beran's right,' Guivret said. 'We keep going.'

They rode on and came into the wood, eyes sifting the trees for any signs of ambush. Beran warned them to keep their movements slow and to try to stifle any fear, because the horses they rode would sense it and might in turn spook the animals they led on ropes.

It was cool and darkling amongst the trees, and loud with the uproar of the rooks above, so noisy that it drowned out their own voices when they spoke. So they did not speak, but rode on with their own thoughts.

The clamour amongst the tree tops was ceaseless and mesmerizing, like the sound of a fast-running stream, and it filled Beran's soul like brackish water. It was the call of all those who had come before, all those he had never known, and all those he had known and lost. It was rich, dark earth and ancient, twisted trees. It was dreams and pain, birth and death. It was blood, but not just his own blood, and he knew that the people of this land, as far back as the first folk who ever gathered dead-fall in this wood to make a fire, had succumbed to the spell of the rooks.

I should be gone, he thought. *But I am still here.*

When they emerged from the other side of the wood, there was still some vestige of light in the world. A shiver ran through Beran, from his thighs to his scalp, as though some part of him knew it had passed through a veil, that his body of flesh, blood and bone had emerged from an ancient realm in which his spirit yet lingered.

Why am I still here?

'Look!' the boy exclaimed, his voice hauling Beran from the mire of his thoughts.

'I have never seen anything like this,' Tristan said, glancing at Isolde, who was looking straight ahead, her eyes as wide as his.

'As magnificent as it was on the day the legions took ship and left,' Guivret said, a grin nestled amongst his beard.

'My father told me that Noviomagus is even bigger, the towers even more formidable,' the boy said in a tone that suggested he suspected King Constantine of embroidering the truth. That such a thing as he claimed simply could not be.

'Your father was right, boy,' Guivret said, then nodded, 'but this will do for us.' He clicked his tongue and urged his mare to walk a little faster, the two horses tied to his saddle trotting on behind.

Palamedes did the same, catching up with his lord. 'Come on,' he called over his shoulder. 'I know a place where the food is as good as the ale.'

They rode through the gloaming, towards great walls of rough-hewn flint and limestone slabs rising above the plain and overlooking the harbour and the calm sea, above which gulls shrieked and wheeled in the day's dying light. A bastion of Britannia that stood in spite of three generations of Saxons who had rolled up the shingle beaches of these Dark Isles. Though, where once it had been one of many such forts protecting the southern shore like a shieldwall, now it held no pretensions of turning away Saxon boats, harboured no ambition beyond its own unlikely survival.

Portus Adurni stood, and Beran believed the boy would be safe there. And that was enough.

The folk of Portus Adurni did not call Guivret lord, nor treat him with deference, as those who dwelt amongst the ruins of Caer Lundein and the temple of Mithras did. But neither did they treat him with contempt or mock him for his short stature, as they might have mocked another dwarf. They knew him as a horse trader and a man of ambition. As a merchant who sometimes came to the fort to take ship across the Dividing Sea and returned with a heavier purse than when he left. They knew his ebony-skinned bodyguard too, knew of his skill with blades and with his bare hands, by the Saracen's reputation if they had not witnessed it with their own eyes. And so the group found lodgings easily enough that first night, though not before they had sought out a man called Meriadec, whom Guivret paid to stable the black stallion, the dapple grey, and the next three most valuable of his horses. There were no more empty stalls, but Meriadec gladly put the remaining eleven horses in his paddock outside the fortress by the south-east corner, and swore to have a pair of spearmen guard them day and night until such time as Guivret returned for them.

When this was done, they followed Palamedes to a tavern by the south gate, where Guivret paid for a meal of oysters and freshly baked bread, ham pickled in brine, beans and turnips and a hard cheese that Beran said tasted older than the boy, though he ate a goodly wedge of it.

Guivret said that in the morning he would go to find a woman named Rivanon, who was one of the wealthiest merchants in Caer Gwinntguic and certainly the richest in Portus Adurni.

'She will arrange passage for us and the horses,' he told Tristan and Isolde, then looked at Beran. 'And she will know of the first ship heading west to Tintagel. Chances are it will be her own ship, the *Osprey*.' He picked up a loaf of bread, tore a piece off and dipped it in a dish of olive oil and fish sauce. 'Either way, I will buy you and the boy passage.'

Beran nodded. 'Thank you.'

Guivret dismissed him with a flap of his hand. 'A deal is a deal,' he said, chewing, a drop of oil glistening in his dark beard. 'And Rivanon will give me a fair price. She owes me.'

It was dark when they laid their furs and blankets on the flagstone floor of what had once been part of the barracks for the legionaries who guarded Portus Adurni. The walls were of stone and the roof was clay tiles, and it was cold in that place, though the night beyond was not. Taking a flame from a sentry fire, they lit three fish-oil lamps and sat in the gloom, passing around a skin of wine from Gallia, as the soldiers who once found themselves in this most northern land of their empire must have done in that very building hundreds of years before, as Guivret pointed out.

'Maybe the Saxons will leave one day, too,' the boy suggested. But they all knew that the Saxons would never leave. Their blood had watered fields that now bristled with wheat and rye, barley and oats. Their language had laid claim to the flowers and the birds, the trees and the beasts of the forest. Their gods had come with them and they were warlike gods and they had all but vanquished the gods of Britain.

'There are still men in Britain who will fight,' Palamedes said. 'But they need a leader.'

'There are no leaders now,' Beran said, wrapping himself in his cloak and lying back and closing his eyes.

'There is this boy here.' Palamedes nodded at Prince Erbin. 'His grandfather was the High King. He is the hope of Britain.'

'He's just a boy,' Beran said, without opening his eyes.

'Men will fight for you, Prince Erbin,' Palamedes said, undeterred.

Beran grunted. 'There are more men who want him dead than will fight for him.'

'Enough talk of war,' Guivret said, before taking a pull on the wine skin and passing it to the Saracen. 'You are fools if you think things can return to the way they used to be.' He belched into a fist. 'You can no sooner raise the dead.'

Beran knew that to be true, and it hurt him more than any ache in his bones or soreness in his flesh. It was a pain deeper than memory, a torment crueller even than life.

He opened one eye and looked at the boy's face, lit by a lamp's foul-smelling flame, and he saw the thoughts warring there. Damn the Saracen for telling Erbin he was the hope of Britain, when the boy should be closing his eyes and drifting away to dream of whatever boys dream of.

'Go to sleep, boy,' Beran said, hoping that he himself would fall asleep before his bladder demanded he got up again.

The boy closed his eyes, frowning with the effort of it, and Beran looked over at the young lovers. Isolde lay still in her furs, asleep already perhaps, while Tristan lay down behind her and put an arm around her.

'Would you fight for me, Beran?' the boy asked.

Beran sighed. 'I've already fought for you, boy,' he said.

'You know what I mean,' the boy said. 'If one day I become a king. Would you fight for me then?'

Isolde gave a soft sigh and, without opening her eyes, took Tristan's hand in her own.

Another man's wife.

Beran looked away, as if by doing so he might forget their crime.

'And who is going to make you a king?' he asked the boy.

The boy scowled as he thought about this.

'Go to sleep, boy,' Beran said.

Guivret caught Palamedes' eye and gestured at the Cornubians swathed in shadow and pelts and each other. 'Can you imagine ever being so in love?' he asked the Saracen.

Palamedes smiled. 'I was in love once,' he said.

Beran swallowed the sourness in his mouth. 'How well do you know these spearmen who Meriadec has watching the horses?' he asked, knowing the answer full well but wanting to steer the conversation in a different direction.

'I don't know them,' the dwarf said, 'but I trust Meriadec.'

'She was called Halima,' Palamedes went on, eyes turned inward and to the past now. 'And this was in a faraway land.'

Wearily, Beran climbed to his feet. 'I'll keep an eye on them,' he said, taking his spear from where he had leant it in the corner of the room.

'No one will steal my horses, Beran,' the Little King assured him.

Beran threw his cloak around himself and pinned it at his left shoulder. 'A deal is a deal,' he said, and stepped out into the night.

Next morning, Beran woke to find himself alone. No, not alone, he realized as he sat up and looked around. The boy was sitting against the wall, looking at him.

'You were talking in your sleep,' the boy said.

Golden light shafted into that place through several holes in the roof where the Roman tiles had slid away, promising a bright, late summer day. Beran scrubbed his eyes and face, and tugged on his beard to wake himself up. He had spent half the night watching the horses beyond the south-east wall.

'I don't talk in my sleep,' he said.

The boy tilted his head. 'How would you know? You don't have a wife to tell you.'

Beran considered this. 'I have slept beneath the stars next to other men more times than I can remember, boy. I would know. You think they wouldn't have told me if I was prattling like an old woman when they were trying to get to sleep?'

The boy shrugged. Just sat there looking at him.

Beran sighed. 'Well? What was I saying?'

The boy shrugged again and picked up a piece of straw and traced it across the flagstone floor. 'I couldn't tell. You were saying words . . .' he frowned, 'but also not words.'

Beran reached out and picked up the wine skin but it was empty. He cursed. 'Where is everyone?' Motes of dust floated in a lance of dawn light.

'Guivret and Palamedes have gone to find Rivanon,' the boy said. 'Isolde and Tristan went to look around the fort. Tristan said this could be the last day they spend in Britain.'

'Not if there's no wind or it's coming up from the south,' Beran muttered.

The boy was playing with a beetle, trying to tempt the glossy black insect onto the end of the dry stalk. 'I'll miss them,' he said. 'When they go to Benoic with Guivret.' The beetle clambered onto the piece of straw, and the boy looked pleased with himself. 'I wonder what they're doing.'

'Why didn't you go with them?' Beran asked, rolling his left shoulder to ease the stiffness there. He could feel the bones grinding in the joint.

The boy shrugged. 'They asked if I wanted to.'

'And?' Wincing, Beran got to his feet and began to fold his blankets.

The boy didn't answer, and so Beran stopped what he was doing and looked at him. 'You thought you'd sooner stay here and listen to me talking in my sleep?' he asked, though he knew that wasn't it. Not really.

The boy's lips pressed together. Not a smile but something else. Its opposite. It seemed he wanted to say something but also didn't want to.

'Don't think about it, boy,' Beran said. 'It was brave, what you did. I don't know any other boy your age who would have done it. But it's in the past now.'

The boy narrowed his eyes. 'You don't know any other boys.'

'True.' Beran raised a hand in admission of this. 'Still, you have a warrior's heart. You proved that to all of us, not least that Saxon. But *I* killed him, understand? You stuck him with that spear, and you did it as well as I could have, but he would have survived it.' Beran doubted that were true, but he also doubted that the boy wanted to think of himself as a killer. Not at ten summers old. 'I killed that Saxon before he could kill us,' he said. 'You need to know that. And then you need to not think about it any more.'

The boy nodded, and Beran knew he had been right to think that the previous day's butchery had been tugging at the boy's mind like a fish on a line. And perhaps that line went deeper still, to the forest in Caer Colun, and the killing of his mother. Now, the boy was pulling that line back up when he should have left it alone.

'You're safe here.' Beran gestured at the sturdy stone walls around them. 'There are two hundred spearmen guarding this fort, and plenty of merchants and sailors besides who would pick up a blade and stick it in a Saxon if need be. You won't have to do that yourself. Not again. Not until you're a grown man.'

The boy was holding the piece of straw in front of his face, intently watching the beetle crawl along it until it got to the end and froze, clinging on. Somewhere in the fort beyond the flint walls of the old garrison quarters, a blacksmith's hammer rang against iron in a steady rhythm. Nearer, two dogs were taking it in turns to bark, and a woman was calling for her child.

Beran watched the young prince, wondering if the boy would live long enough to become a man. There were many who wanted him dead, who even now worked to that end. Others who wanted the boy to become a lord of war, itself an ambition which few men outlived.

'Let's look around,' he said. 'Look out to sea. Feel the salt air on our faces.'

'Have you been on a ship before?' the boy asked, gently putting the straw and its passenger down. 'A real ship, on the sea,' he said, standing and smoothing his tunic and trews.

Beran chuckled. 'Yes, I've been on a real ship, on the sea,' he said, opening the door and stepping into the day. 'I lived in Gaul as a young man. I didn't walk there, boy.'

They both stood a moment, squinting in the bright light and watching the inhabitants of Portus Adurni going about their business. The place thrummed with life, and Beran was not sure that he wanted to be a part of it. But the boy did. It was written on his face as he stood there taking it in: a man and girl walking past, hefting sacks bulging with loaves of fresh bread, judging by the smell drifting to Beran, making his mouth water. A farmer leading a cow along a narrow thoroughfare between rows of workshops, waving a hazel switch at the attending cloud of flies. Over by a grain store, three children play-fighting with sticks, while a cat stalked beneath the store's wooden steps. Two spearmen leaving another of the barrack rooms, holding red-painted shields and talking and laughing easily. A knot of women by a cloth-maker's workshop, clucking over tables of red and blue yarn and hanging hanks of dyed wool and garments of every colour. An old woman carrying three fish strung through the gills in one hand and a pail of water in the other. A one-armed man and his boy pulling a creaking cart full of horse dung that steamed in the dawn.

'It reminds me of home.' The boy turned to look at Beran, and there were tears in his eyes.

'Well, it won't last,' Beran said. 'Even walls as high and strong as these. The Saxons will take it, just like they took Caer Colun.' He looked up at a swirl of gulls shrieking and crying as they tumbled and churned, as though they saw Portus Adurni's fate on the horizon and sought in vain to warn its people. *The Saxons are coming,* they cried. *The Saxons are coming.* But none below paid them any heed as they set to the day's tasks.

'Palamedes does not think as you do,' the boy said. 'He believes there is still hope. That if the kings of Britain unite as they once did, we could throw the Saxons back into the sea.'

Beran *hoom*ed deep in his throat. 'It *was* a dream. Once. But even that dream has been forgotten,' he said. 'We can't go back to how things were before. The dwarf was right. We can never go back.' He took a deep breath. 'Not now.'

Guivret and Palamedes were walking towards them, threading their way amongst another dozen spearmen who had come down from their posts along the wall after their night watch and were heading for their beds.

'But Palamedes—'

'If Palamedes has such a strong belief that some warrior will rise like . . . cream in the pail, to lead the spearmen of Dumnonia and Cynwidion, Elmet and Caer Lerion, then why has he been hiding for years in the ruins of Caer Lundein, brawling with men for his bread and ale? Why hasn't he been looking for this warlord in order to pledge his sword to him? Why hasn't he been killing Saxons?'

The boy looked away. He did not have an answer to this. Of course he didn't. And Beran silently cursed his own coldness, that callus which had hardened his soul across the years and which he knew made him poor company.

Damn you, Beran. He's just a boy.

And yet, wasn't it more cruel to fill the boy's head with dreams of a future that could never be?

'Awake at last, I see,' Guivret said to Beran as he and Palamedes approached, the Saracen nodding respectfully at the boy, as though he were a grown man, a fellow warrior, perhaps. The boy nodded back.

'Where are the lovers?' the dwarf asked, glancing around.

Beran lifted his chin. 'Out there somewhere, paying a bard to sing of their escape from a cruel king.'

Guivret narrowed his eyes. 'Are you jealous, Beran?' he asked. 'The girl is too young for you.'

Beran did not dignify that with an answer. 'When is the next ship going to Tintagel?' he asked.

Guivret grimaced. 'Rivanon is not here. She sailed to Noviomagus three days ago.' He glanced at Palamedes. 'I am thinking there is more money in olive oil than in horses.' Then he looked back at Beran. 'She and the *Osprey* are expected back on the next favourable wind, but it's likely that same wind will carry you and the boy on to Tintagel.'

'And you?' Beran asked.

Guivret shrugged his squat shoulders. 'The man who commands here, a grizzled old goat by the name of Viamundus, is expecting a ship full of pigs from Armorica any day now. I've no doubt that Rivanon will see to it that my horses are aboard when it sails south again, though it might cost me the dapple grey.'

'Until then, we wait,' Palamedes said. He was watching the western gate, which four guards were opening for a farmer leading an ox and cart piled high with golden sheaves of barley. 'And we keep our eyes open.'

The boy looked up at Beran. 'Can we look around?' he asked, his hands clasped together as though clinging to the hope lest Beran take it from him and dash it against Portus Adurni's flint rubble walls. 'I'll stay close, you have my word.'

Beran looked along the via pretoria, thronged now with traders and spearmen, horses and other beasts of burden. He did not want to step into the cauldron of that place, was loath to be seen by so many folk. But then, perhaps the hive-like busyness of the fort was to his advantage. He and the boy would be just another two bees in the swarm. No one would pay them any mind. Besides, they could hardly sit in the dark of the old barrack building until the *Osprey* returned.

'We can look around,' he said. 'But first, we find the latrines.'

A Song for the Bards

'THERE ARE NO SNAKES in Ireland,' Gawain said, laughing. 'Least none that'll bite your snow-white arse. No poison of any sort, not here. They say anything from this land will serve as a remedy *against* poison.'

Arthur squatted in the lee of the rock, sweating and gritting his teeth and feeling like his insides were being cast out of him.

'I heard of a man in Cornubia who was bitten by an adder,' Gawain went on from the other side of the rock. 'He had an Irish slave, so he cut off a hank of the man's hair and drank it down in his mead and the swelling waned before he set down his cup.'

Arthur moaned and cursed, and Gawain laughed again, a full, rich sound that defied his young years. 'Though I daresay you are poisoning the ground of Ireland even now,' he said. 'I would whistle to drown out the sound, but that wouldn't do it. Thunder wouldn't do it! Gods, Arthur! I'll be surprised if the Irish can't hear your arsehole blowing like a war horn in a puddle.'

'I told you that wine last night was bad.' Arthur thought his bowels must be empty by now, but he did not move yet, just in case.

'If it was the wine, then why aren't my guts sour too?' Gawain asked.

Arthur did not reply to that. He was too busy. The muscles in his stomach clenched again and a long, liquid gurgling sound came from it. He braced, looking up at the swath of grey sky between the copper crowns of ancient beech trees. The air itself was moist, a fine, misty rain seeking through the canopy to mix with the sweat on his face. He wondered if he was dying. Perhaps it would be a mercy.

'Gods, but will you hurry up?' Gawain asked. 'If we do not catch up with the others soon, they'll beat the bastards without us. Worse still, they'll think we were too afraid to fight. They'll call us cowards.' He chuckled. 'Well, they'll call you a coward. They know I'm just doing what I was told and not letting you out of my sight.'

'Believe me, you want me out of your sight like this,' Arthur murmured.

He cleaned himself with the elm leaves he had gathered in the dawn, then stood unsteadily, feeling weak and as sick as he had ever felt after too much ale. He took up his spear and shield and found Gawain leaning against a birch, looking off in the direction the rest of the raiding party had gone when he had told Gawain he needed to stop and drop his trews.

'We'll be fine, Arthur,' Gawain said. 'I'll look after you.' He was younger than Arthur by a handful of years, yet he spoke as though he had fought a dozen battles. It annoyed Arthur, this arrogance, though he had to admit that he was comforted by it too. There was something about Gawain that made him seem invulnerable, as solid as the rock behind which Arthur had just emptied his bowels. It was a confidence which Arthur wondered if he would ever feel himself.

'I'm ready,' he said, lifting his spear to arm sweat from his forehead.

'Good,' Gawain said. 'If we run, we might catch them up.'

They set off, loping amongst the trees, breathing easily even with the burden of their iron helmets, their armour of hardened leather, and beneath that their thick woollen tunics, and with their limewood shields and swords and long spears. They were young and strong, and under Cadwain's fierce eye Arthur had hardened like wood over a flame. Had worked with shield, spear and sword until his arms were corded with muscle and his shoulders were broad and powerful. He had thought Lord Ector worked him rigorously and taught him well, but he had never known pain or discomfort or humiliation like that which he experienced under Cadwain's cruel tutelage. The man had been harsh as winter that whole summer, and Arthur had bled and ached, smouldered and despised. And yet now, as he ran towards battle, he regretted none of the misery of the last months. He would call upon it all, because it might keep him alive.

'You stay with me, Arthur,' Gawain said. 'Just as we practised.'

Arthur leapt over some rotting deadfall and landed and ran on without missing a step. 'I didn't come all the way to Ireland to be killed by a Gael over a handful of slaves,' he said, his slung shield bouncing against his back. 'Much to the disappointment of my father, I'd wager.'

'Lord Uther needs you alive and you know it,' Gawain said, eyes sifting the woods either side as he ran. 'And they're not slaves. They're my people.'

The woods were thinning now, and Arthur caught the scent of woodsmoke on the damp air, which meant they were nearing a habitation or camp and so must be careful. 'They're slaves now,' he said, and Gawain did not reply but Arthur felt the ire coming off the young man like heat, for he burned to avenge his people.

The Gaels had come to Lyonesse in five currachs, perhaps four men to a boat, leaving room for the ten unfortunates they had carried off with them in the dawn, black sails pushing them back across the sea, north to their base in Dyfed, then back across to Ireland.

'Late in the season for a raid,' Cadwain had said, when King Lot had called a war council at the news. Arthur recalled the farmer who had ridden to the king's fort and dismounted his pony with eyes full of tears and a tale of killing that needed to be told.

'One last raid before winter.' King Lot's words were heavy with sadness and loss. 'They knew we would not expect it. Knew we would not set out after them with winter fast approaching.'

'Then they will not expect us,' Gawain had said, looking from his father the king to Cadwain. 'They will be bedding down with their cattle and waiting for winter, but they will get *us*.'

As King Lot's honoured guest, Arthur had been invited to join the gathering around the king's high seat, but he had known it was not his place to speak.

'No, Gawain. I won't risk it.' The king sat tall in his chair, the torc of twisted silver at his neck glinting now and then with the reflected flame, for the hearth fire was roaring. 'We'll go in the spring. We'll swear vengeance by the light of the Beltane fire and we'll pay the Gaels back in blood.'

But here they were, as the first ash leaves tumbled around them, and the birches flickered a mottled green and yellow-gold, and the sweet, damp, earthy scent of decay mocked the memory of summer like a hawk hanging dead in a blackthorn briar.

Even as he ran to play his part in the killing, Arthur smiled to think of how Gawain had got his own way, persuading his king and father to send Cadwain with a small war band to kill Gaels even after King Lot had said he would not. Gawain had talked of honour and the rewards of courage. Of a king's duty to his people and of a warrior's obligation to fight for those who could not fight for themselves. He had spoken well, and Arthur had seen the pride in King Lot's fierce eye, and in the end Arthur himself had been unable to hold his own tongue any longer. When the scales in the king's mind seemed to be teetering, Arthur all but begged to be allowed to prove himself a grateful and loyal friend of Lyonesse in the name of his father, Lord Uther of Tintagel and warrior of Dumnonia, and in his own name too. King Lot had given him a solemn nod, and in that moment Arthur saw the scales tip, as though one of the weighing dishes were already filled with Irish blood.

Cadwain, the king's champion, saw it too and grinned like a fiend, and then the king called for his priest, a man named Varlan, to slit a bull's throat and seek the favour of Macha the Crow, to whom his forefathers had made sacrifice long before the gilded eagles came to Britain.

'There,' Arthur said now, pointing his spear, for up ahead a knot of Lyonesse men stood amongst the trees. Five of them, passing around a skin full of ale while they waited where the birch, elm and ash thinned and the woodland gave way to heathland that shivered pale purple under the grey sky.

'Cadwain told us to stay here until you caught up,' a short, red-faced man named Gwenvael said, gripping a spear that looked too long for him. A good warrior to have beside you in a fight, was Gwenvael, so Gawain had told Arthur when it had been decided which thirty men Cadwain would take to Ireland. 'I thought you might have gone back to the boat, Arthur ap Uther,' the man said with a smile that suggested he was only half joking.

'Something I ate last night.' Arthur pressed a hand against his tender stomach. Now that he was standing still again, the sweating dizziness came upon him, as if he had outrun it only for it to catch him up. He could see dark spots floating in his vision and tried to blink them away.

'Missing the king's table, eh?' said Briec, another experienced warrior, taking a pull on the ale skin before passing it to Gawain.

Gwenvael stepped towards Arthur and reached out to grip him by his shoulder. 'You're not the first young blood to get the shits before a fight,' he said, then lifted his chin in Briec's direction. 'In his first shieldwall, my cousin there shat on the boots of the man behind him.'

'Ah, I just did that because he was an arse,' Briec said, at which the others chuckled.

'We'll keep you alive, Arthur,' Gwenvael said, stepping back and turning to look out across the heath. 'Because if we don't, our king will hang us from a tree by our balls.'

'Look there.' Gawain was holding out his spear, the blade pointing across the peaks and valleys. They watched a hawk through the mizzle, soaring eastward above the crest of a distant hill. It rolled away into the north, the underside of its wings flashing white against the slate grey sky. Then, without warning, the bird folded its wings and dropped like a stone, stooping to take a red grouse amongst the heather.

A warrior named Herenc gave a soft whistle.

'A good omen,' Briec said, which got some murmurs of agreement from the others.

'That hawk is us, Arthur,' Gawain said, grinning as he slapped Arthur's shoulder.

Arthur nodded, hoping his friend was right.

'Let's see if we can catch up with the others,' Gwenvael said. 'If they wet their spears without us because Arthur was shitting like an old dog, we'll never hear the end of it.'

They broke cover, striding out onto the heath, spear blades as grey as the day, then started up a gentle slope through gorse and heather which shivered in the autumn breeze like the muscles in Arthur's thighs and like the heart in his chest beneath the boiled-leather armour, padded wool tunic, flesh and bone.

Because he was going to make war. And he was afraid.

They loped along a spine of high ground as thunder pealed through the darkening sky in the west like the sound of iron-rimmed cart wheels rolling along a Roman road. They did not speak now, but moved with the fluid ease of shadow across ground, their shields thumping against their backs, spears gripped in their right hands and their sword scabbards in their left to keep from tripping over them. Arthur imagined this was what it felt to be a wolf amongst a pack. To be predators on the hunt, thrilling at the anticipation of blood.

Gwenvael had not liked moving along the ridges, for it made them conspicuous against the skyline, but the day was unnaturally dark, and rain hung in the air like a thin veil, and better to run on solid ground than on the slopes below, which were soft and boggy and treacherous.

The foam-fringed ocean and the safety of their vessel were far behind them now, but Arthur did not concern himself with that. They had come to kill Gaels, as many as they could, then vanish again like a sea mist rolling back across the breakers.

Keep your shield up and your head down, Arthur told himself. *Kill a man, if you can. Then get away alive and unhurt. That is all. No more than that.*

They climbed as if into the cloud itself, their beards laced with beads of water that shone like jewels when a shaft of sickly yellow late autumn sunlight fell upon the heath, warming Arthur's face for a moment. Then they descended over rocky knolls, down the damp sides of a misty valley, breathing hard now but still strong, still eager.

On through coarse bracken that was turning from gold to brown and lay across the shoulder of the land like a pelt, bristling in the chill breeze.

Then Gwenvael led them over a stony ridge and they stopped to catch their breath and stood looking down into the valley pass, wiping rain from their eyes and huffing hot breath into cold hands.

'No,' Gawain said, the first of them to speak. 'No.'

They all saw what he saw.

'They must have seen us long before we came ashore,' Herenc suggested, touching his iron sword pommel to ward off the ill luck of it, though it was surely too late for that now. At Gwenvael's gesture they crouched or went down on one knee so as to be less likely seen up there on the brow of the hill.

'Gods help them,' someone muttered. For there in the valley below were Cadwain and two dozen men of Lyonesse, standing in a line facing east, their shields overlapping, their dun-coloured cloaks and grey helmets and grey spear blades as dismal-looking as the day. An arrow flight from their countrymen were the Gaels, perhaps sixty of them, armed with spears, axes and bows, arranged not in a shieldwall like the Lyonesse men but massed in a loose host and taunting their enemy with ululating cries and crude gestures. There was a druid amongst them, the sight of whom chilled Arthur's blood. Dressed in a long black robe and holding his staff aloft, it seemed the druid was invoking the gods or perhaps casting spells, either to protect his own people or to doom those men of Lyonesse.

'There,' Briec said, pointing to a hill below and to the east of where they stood overlooking the pass. There, more Gaels were gathering, sliding off the backs of their stout ponies and arming themselves.

'Men from another tribe,' Herenc guessed.

'I count eighteen,' Briec said.

'And there,' said Gawain, pointing his spear across the valley. Still more men were making their way down the far slope, moving through the bracken like a breeze. It took Arthur's eyes a moment to fix on individual warriors, but now he saw them, could pick them out amongst the dense gold and russet stands.

'It will be a slaughter,' a big, scarred man named Ewen said.

'What do we do?' Briec was looking at Gwenvael, who had yet to speak.

'If we go down there, we're dead,' Gwenvael said.

Gawain turned to him, bristling, his knuckles white around his spear shaft. 'What are you saying, Gwenvael? We can't leave them. I won't.'

Gwenvael turned his head and spat. 'They're already dead,' he said. 'Open your eyes, lad. You ever seen so many Irishmen?' He swept a hand across the valley. 'And more are coming. Even if Cadwain bloods them good. If he beats their first attack, and their second . . .' He cursed under his breath. 'More Gaels will come. They'll come from every village within a day's ride.' He turned his gaze back to his countrymen in their pitiful shieldwall below. 'Arawn's eyes, but the High King of Ireland, Lugaid mac Lóegairi, could be here by dawn. Come to watch the slaughter.'

'Don't forget they have a druid,' Briec said. Some touched iron then, because all men knew what that meant. A druid could fill a man's belly with rats that would gnaw their way out, leaving the victim to squirm in his own bloody ruin. A druid could shrivel your manhood to the size of a maggot and call the crows to come pecking. A druid could speak to the old gods of Britain and damn a man's soul, or turn his blood to pus, or kill a child in his woman's womb.

'It's a trap,' Ewen muttered. 'They let Cadwain come into this valley, knowing they could butcher him there.'

Gawain shook his head. 'I'll not leave them to die.'

Gwenvael turned hard eyes on him. 'And I'll not let my prince throw his life away,' he said. 'Nor will I get *him* killed,' he added, nodding at Arthur. 'His uncle is High King of Britain. If Arthur dies here, King Ambrosius and Lord Uther will likely send a thousand spearmen against Lyonesse and your father.'

Gawain gritted his teeth and stood. 'It is not your decision to make,' he told Gwenvael. 'You cannot stop me or any man here from going down there to stand with our brothers.'

Gwenvael knew Gawain, knew that the only way he could stop him was by violence, and he was not prepared to fight his prince. 'How would you get to them?' he asked, pointing his spear to their left and the precipitous drop between two rocky bluffs. Then he gestured to their right. 'From here you'd have to take that route down,' he went on, 'meaning you'd have to get through those Irishmen to take your place beside Cadwain.' He shook his head. 'No man here doubts your courage,' he told Gawain, 'but you must see that there is nothing we can do.'

Gawain stood and planted the butt of his spear in the soft ground. 'We can fight. The Gaels don't want to die any more than we do, so we blood them. We kill as many as we can, and maybe they turn around and go home, knowing that we will do the same.'

In the valley below, the largest group of Gaels was now moving towards Cadwain's shieldwall, some of their warriors running ahead of the rest to hurl spears or whir their slings, cracking stones against that rampart of Lyonesse men, trying to draw them out of formation.

The druid had found a boulder to stand on, better wherefrom to cast his incantations above the heads of his own folk and exhort the gods to his murderous purpose. He was sweeping his staff about his head, his words lost in the clamour of a hundred Irishmen baying for blood.

For now, though, Cadwain's men were standing firm.

'We won't even get close,' Briec countered. 'They are my brothers, and I am no coward. But I have a family. A wife and two girls.' He took off his helmet and ran a hand through his dark, matted hair, his face twisted in anguish at the choice before him. 'How does it serve them, me getting my guts cut out here on some ill-fated raid?'

'I don't want to die in this land, either.' Herenc was looking from man to man. 'But how will we face our king and kin if we turn our backs on those men down there to save our own skins?'

'Better to live and fight for our king another day, than have our heads put on spikes by some druid,' Briec said.

'I have an idea,' Arthur said.

'Gawain's right,' Ewen said. 'If we kill enough of them, the others might lose heart. I've seen it happen before.'

'I said, I have an idea,' Arthur put in, but the others were arguing amongst themselves now and no one seemed to hear him.

'There is honour, and there is stupidity,' Briec said, and would have said more but Gawain put up his hand to stop him. His own eyes were on Arthur now. Narrowed eyes. Curious eyes.

'Let's hear it, Arthur,' he said, as the others stopped talking and looked at Arthur. And so Arthur told them.

They moved fast along their side of the ridge, staying low, only now and then crawling up through the bracken to look down. Arthur led the way, with Gawain behind him and Gwenvael next. They could hear screams now from the valley below, and the roars of men encouraging their spear-brothers, and the thump of blades on shields, and the metallic percussion of spearheads striking shield bosses.

As he picked his way down the slope between rocks and furze, Arthur realized he no longer felt afraid. His guts were not sour. His heart thumped in his chest and his blood gushed in his ears but he felt no fear. Gawain was right. *This is how the hawk feels before a kill, before it stoops and takes some creature which is unequal to it. Some prey.*

He led those six men around a bluff where rock broke through the amber bracken and purple moor grass, then on through a patch of green gorse that drew beads of blood from his hands and stabbed through the wool of his trews. When he came to the jagged crag which he had picked out from his earlier vantage point, he stopped and gestured with his spear, and they all crouched low with him.

He looked around at Gawain, for of them all, Gawain was the one who Arthur needed to know was with him. Gawain knew it, too, and he gave Arthur a sharp nod that said there was no going back now.

They had made their way eastward to where Briec had seen a war band of Gaels dismounting their ponies before descending into the pass to join the main host. Those ponies now stood hobbled, for there were no trees or other means of tethering them thereabouts. Two men had been left to guard the ponies, and they stood up on the rise, watching the battle below, oblivious of the men stalking slowly towards them.

Gwenvael went forward, gesturing at Herenc to go with him, those two being the most experienced fighters, but Gawain took hold of Gwenvael's shoulder and shook his head, then pointed at himself and Arthur. Arthur nodded, and they unslung their shields and laid them in the blond grass, and together he and Gawain covered the twenty strides with no more sound than the grey cloud roving above the hills and valleys. Yet something alerted one of the men, some instinct, and he turned, and Arthur looked into his creased and weather-beaten face as he thrust his spear into the man's belly with all the strength in his shoulders and arms and the core of his body. He saw the shock in the man's eyes, and something else too; a look of pleading, as if the man were silently begging him to pull the spear out, to undo what could not be undone.

'Arthur!' Gawain growled, breaking the spell. Arthur saw that Gawain's man was already down, and so he rammed the spear deeper still, then pushed the haft down and burrowed upwards with the blade, and he heard the ripping of the man's innards and the last breath hiss from his bloody, open mouth. Then he hauled the spear out, and the Irishman's eyes rolled back in his head and his legs buckled and he fell dead amongst the ferns.

'Here,' Gwenvael said, approaching from behind to hand Arthur his shield. The others were already busy undoing the ropes from around the forelegs of each pony.

'This is the worst idea I've ever heard,' Gawain said, though he was grinning as he climbed onto the back of a shaggy grey pony and made sure his shield was slung tightly against his back.

'We stay together,' Arthur told them, mounting a bright-eyed dun mare which snorted at him, so he stroked her neck and flattered her with praise for her thick mane and stout little legs. 'We ride fast and hard and we do not stop until we reach Cadwain,' he said.

He couched his spear across the pony's neck and dug in his heels, walking the animal up the slope and past the body of the man he had killed, and the others went with him.

'Least I'm going to die beside my prince and the nephew of the High King.' Briec was fighting to control his pony, which did not seem to like the Lyonesse man at all. 'So maybe I'll get a mention when the bards sing of it.'

'No bard will sing of you,' Gwenvael said, looking as uncomfortable on his mount as Briec did. 'It would be like adding a scrap of rancid gristle to the stew.'

The others laughed too loudly at this, as if in defiance of the moment, as if they knew it might be the last time they ever laughed.

Arthur looked down into the valley. Cadwain's shieldwall still held. There were two men down, their bodies having being pulled back behind the line, but before that shieldwall lay a dozen Gaels, unmoving in the grass.

'They're working themselves up to charge again,' Gawain said, sitting his pony on Arthur's right. But it was worse than that, Arthur saw, because the Gaels from the north, instead of joining the main body, were working their way around the left flank of Cadwain's wall. Arthur could see what would happen. His eye for the battle was an owl's eye for the woodland litter. Seeing the threat to his left, Cadwain would draw his left flank back like a bow, to prevent the Irish getting in behind him. But that would take spearmen from his front, weakening the main shieldwall against a frontal attack. The Irish would test Cadwain's left, then hit the centre hard. They would throw themselves at the Lyonesse men like a storm-driven wave, and swamp them. It would be over in the time it takes to bring a good edge back to a new blade.

'Ready?' Arthur asked his men. They weren't his men, of course. He was not their leader. Was not even a man of Lyonesse. And yet they looked to him now and nodded, their jaws set and their eyes gleaming beneath the rims of their helmets, and to Arthur they looked like the famed warriors of some fireside tale.

'Arthur,' Gawain said, leaning out of the saddle and reaching out with his left hand. Arthur leant towards him and they gripped each other by the forearm. 'I'm with you, brother.'

Arthur nodded, remembering a snowy day when he was a boy. Seventy-eight men and horses. Helmets and spear blades and tunics of iron rings, and their leader, sitting proud in the saddle, haughty with past victories and cloaked in the colour of old blood. The last equites Romani.

'For Britain,' Arthur said, loud enough for them all to hear. He did not know why he said it. Gawain frowned, for what was Britain but a disparate land of warring kingdoms, a land stumbling in the dark since the torch of Rome had guttered and gone out? But then Gawain gave a savage grin.

'For Britain,' he said.

Arthur walked his pony forward, over the brow of the ridge, and the others went with him, and the riderless ponies went too, in the way of a wild herd.

Arthur recalled Cadwain telling him that the Irish did not fight in shieldwalls but as individual warriors, as though each was a champion of his people and eager to prove it in single combat. Which they could not do now, because the Lyonesse men would not be drawn out of their rampart of wood and iron. So the Gaels were posturing just out of spear reach, some of them darting in now and then to throw a spear, or seek an opening with a sword thrust, or loose an arrow at a man's face or at his unprotected legs.

'Stay away from the druid,' Gwenvael warned in between growling curses at his pony, which was tossing its shaggy head and no doubt wondering where its master was and why he had let this outlander on its back. 'If the Gaels don't kill me, Cadwain will for bringing Prince Gawain and Arthur into that mess down there.'

'Cadwain is too busy killing Irishmen to worry about you, Gwenvael,' Gawain said.

King Lot's champion had bent his left flank back on itself, as Arthur had known he must, and he now stood there himself, thrusting his spear at a knot of warriors who had singled him out, each of them eager to claim the honour of taking his head back to their village.

'We're ready,' Herenc said, for they had all mastered their mounts now and arranged their war gear as best they could for being on horseback.

Arthur started down the slope and did not look left and right to see if the others were with him. He knew they were, and he felt proud of them.

'Steady,' he told them, leaning back in the saddle, persuading his pony to shorten and collect her stride. Some of the others were also fighting to keep their ponies from rushing down, whilst Gawain's pony, and Briec's, and that of a young spearman named Bledri, were moving as slowly as honey off a spoon, carefully picking their way over the ground.

'Well, they've seen us,' Gawain said, for some of the men at the rear of the Irish war host were looking over their shoulders, though none had turned fully around.

'They think we're Gaels,' Arthur said, as the slope became less steep and the ponies broke into a trot. 'But let us show them who we are!' he called. And now he did not try to hold the animal back, but let her run, keeping his knees and thighs relaxed and wrapping his legs around her, and telling her to show them all how fine she was.

Gawain and the others were yelling too, thrilling to the madness of what they were doing, and now some of the Irishmen were turning to face them. Across the distance, Arthur could see the surprise in their faces as they tried to understand how their enemies were behind them and on Irish ponies too.

Galloping now, his shield thumping against his back, his spear, which lay across the pony in front of the saddle, bouncing against her back, Arthur glanced to his right and saw Gawain, his face a rictus of violent glee. Looked to his left and saw Herenc lifting his spear to the iron sky and calling on Belatucadrus, the Fair Shining One, the lover of battle.

The men of Lyonesse had assumed an arrowhead formation, or else the tip of a sword, with Arthur at the point, while the riderless ponies galloped alongside, their hooves drumming the soft earth, their snorts given to the white mare Eiocha, who had been born of sea-foam at the beginning of all things. And some of the Gaels were lifting their shields, or bracing, or trying to move out of the path of what was coming.

Time was measured in heartbeats and hoofbeats and in each rasping breath between his dry lips. *Damn you, Father, can you see me now?* his mind growled as, bouncing in the saddle, the wind dragging tears from his eyes, he lifted his own spear and held it out, and now he was amongst the enemy and the clamour was deafening.

He rode a man down, hearing his terrible scream, then struck another, and another, the crack of bones filling the sky, and he rode on. Men were hit one after the other, thrown left and right like the frothing sea before a ship's bow, and the stout pony did not stop but cantered on, and Arthur braced, keeping his arm strong as the spear blade ripped open a man's neck, spraying bright crimson in the fine rain of that grey day.

'Kill them!' he bellowed, seeing Gawain bury his spear in a man's chest, haul his sword free and swing it, and charge on.

They had broken free of those Gaels who had turned to face them, and cantered on across the heath, now facing the main body of Irish warriors, and Arthur knew he had led those six men to their deaths. He could not see Cadwain's shieldwall beyond the mass of Irishmen, and even if his brave pony gave her all, she could not get through so many. Surely not even a trained and leather-armoured warhorse from the time of Magnus Maximus could have ridden into such a horde and survived.

He kicked back with his heels and whipped the reins and the pony cantered on, her brawny legs eating up the ground, and a spear streaked past Arthur's right cheek, so that he felt the closeness of it. A warrior ran at him and cast his own spear, and Arthur leant back in the saddle and saw the shaft pass over him like a raven in flight.

He brought himself back up and saw the man just in time to thrust his spear down, burying it in the Irishman's chest and letting go and riding on, reaching across and pulling his sword from its scabbard.

He was screaming now. Lost in the depravity of it. Blood-drunk and wild, and he saw the Gaels' black-robed druid on his boulder, pointing his staff at Arthur, his warping mouth working some foul mischief that Arthur could never know in the battle din of the day.

Arthur rode on, towards that druid, and men threw themselves out of his path, the riders and the riderless ponies passing amongst those Irishmen like a breeze through heather. And then Arthur could see nothing but the druid, and the man was grinning at him, for a druid has no fear of a warrior, even on the battlefield. But then Arthur saw that grin fade in the druid's eyes before the man could wipe it from his mouth. It scarce had time to disappear entirely before Arthur had scythed his sword and taken off the druid's head and ridden past that rock.

At that moment, all sound was gone from the world and he rode on in silence through that valley, looking over his shoulder to see the headless druid still standing, blood spurting from the stump of his neck.

When he turned back, he saw the enemy host part before him, saw the stark horror in their faces, their mouths hanging open, their eyes round as shields.

'Ride!' Gawain bellowed. 'Get to Cadwain!'

They drove their ponies on and it seemed no Irishman wanted to fight them now. Instead, all backed away, holding shields and spears out wide, and in silence too, as though the gods themselves had taken their tongues.

Cadwain's shieldwall fragmented to allow the riders and the ponies without riders through, and Arthur pulled up, looking around to see who was with him. His heart leapt to see that Gawain was there, his sword dripping blood, and Herenc was with him, his eyes wide and wild. Gwenvael was not there but his pony was.

'I saw Ewen fall,' Herenc said.

'Briec?' Gawain called, wheeling his mount as he looked for the man.

'Here!' Briec was trotting his pony between two Lyonesse men.

Bledri was gone too, but his pony had run on with the rest, meaning that of the seven, four had made it.

'Grab a mount,' Cadwain roared. 'The smaller men share.'

Arthur looked back at the Gaels. He could see they were gathered thickest around the boulder where their druid had stood, and a shiver ran through his blood.

'What are they doing?' Herenc asked. 'Why aren't they attacking?'

'Because Arthur killed their druid,' Cadwain said, mounting a sturdy pony and making sure his scabbarded sword was out of the way. 'And they're waiting to see what the gods will do about it.'

Arthur knew Cadwain was right. He could feel men's eyes on him, even as they climbed onto the backs of those Irish ponies. They did not know whether Arthur had saved them or cursed them, for no one killed a druid. The druids spoke for the gods and, regardless of tribe, were free to wander the Dark Isles without fear of man.

'What have you done, lad?' a gnarled oak of a warrior named Gwencalon asked him, holding a pony by the reins whilst pressing his other hand to a wound in his shoulder.

'He's given you a chance to see your woman again, Gwencalon,' Gawain told the man, still breathing hard from the fight. 'Now get on that pony before the Gaels wake from their nightmare.'

Arthur looked up at the sky. It was no darker than it had been. His heart was thumping in his chest, hot and strong. Perhaps the gods would curse him for what he had done, but for now he was alive, and so were most of the men of Lyonesse, who had thought they would never see another dawn. He had led those six men into battle and they had followed him. Had fought with him.

'You did it, Arthur.' Gawain's teeth were all the whiter for the blood spatter across his face.

'It's not done yet.' Arthur was looking back at the Gaels. They were no longer silent, but arguing amongst themselves, or jeering at the Lyonesse men, or calling on the gods to intervene for Arthur's violation of unspoken laws. Some were running forward and hurling spears, those shafts striking the ground between the milling ponies and riders. Stones from slings were whirring in amongst them, tonking off helmets and cracking into shields. One Lyonesse man fell dead from the pony he had just climbed onto, a pebble lodged in his eye socket. Others amongst the Gaels were working themselves into a frenzy, all but salivating at the prospect of tearing the outlanders apart in vengeance.

'We ride!' Cadwain called, lifting his voice above the roar coming from the Irish; a sound that was building like a wave rolling up a stony beach. Arthur looked around and saw that everyone was mounted now, with some ponies carrying two men, and the dead lying where they had fallen, for there was no means of carrying them off. Those men's heads would adorn pikes by the time the sun set.

'We ride for the sea and we don't stop!' Cadwain called.

The men wheeled their mounts almost as one, away from the mass of baying Irish, and on for the sea.

'Anyone would think we had conquered the Irish and had Lugaid mac Lóegairi's head to show for it,' Cadwain rumbled, before lifting his cup and drenching his innards with King Lot's finest ale. 'We lost good men in Ireland.'

Arthur did not know most of the lords of Lyonesse gathered in their king's hall, nor had he seen many feasts to rival that which was laid out before them this night. The tables piled high with the bounty of the harvest and the flesh of those animals which might have survived a little deeper into winter were it not for the arrival of the king's honoured guest.

Merlin sat beside King Lot, the two of them deep in conversation and sharing wine at the table nearest to the hearth and the jumping flames which lit their faces and danced in the druid's eyes. Arthur had yet to speak with Merlin, who had arrived on the neap tide as darkness fell, and so did not know the reason for his visit, though he was sure all would become clear soon enough.

'In the meantime, let's eat and drink,' Gawain had said, when he and Arthur had heard that Uther's ship, *Dragon Fire*, had brought the druid across a spume-flecked sea from the mainland. 'For in my experience, nothing good comes from having a druid around.' He arched a brow. 'Unless you have a toothache.'

In contrast to the lavish and abundant tables, and to the king's joyous mood for the return of his son and of so many brave warriors of Lyonesse, was the music, which Arthur blamed in part for Cadwain's grim air. Queen Anna herself was playing the harp, her long, skilful fingers seeming to float across the strings, drawing a sad melody from the instrument and scattering it through her husband's hall like dead petals from a summer long gone.

'By rights we should be there now,' Cadwain said, holding out his cup, 'back in that damned valley.' A servant stepped out of the shadows and filled the cup from a heavy-looking jug. 'Our headless bodies being pecked by the crows,' King Lot's champion went on, shaking his head.

Arthur and Gawain knew better than to interrupt the man, and so they waited for his next words as a gathering wind moaned in the night outside and found its way in through unseen gaps in the thatch to swirl the hearth smoke around, making people cough.

'Ah, to the good men we left behind,' the warrior said, raising his voice above the hum of the hall. Gawain and Arthur lifted their own cups, as did any who had heard Cadwain's acknowledgement of the lost.

'And to Arthur,' Gawain said, looking at Arthur over the rim of his cup. His nose was crooked now, Arthur noticed, the remnants of crusted blood still in his moustaches. 'For if he had not made us late to the fight because of having the shits, we'd all be dead now instead of drinking this.'

Cadwain's broken teeth showed in the red nest of his beard. 'That ride to the coast, with half the Gaels in Ireland screaming after us . . .' He shook his head. 'That will haunt me all my days.'

'As it should,' Arthur said, grinning, 'for if there was ever a man not born to sit a horse, it is you, Cadwain.'

The warrior grimaced, causing the terrible scar that ran down his right cheek to twist horribly. 'I'll get my own back on you tomorrow on the training field, when you're sobbing because you can't take your ale and your skull is splitting.'

Gawain banged his cup against Arthur's. 'Tomorrow is another day,' he said, and they both grinned in spite of Cadwain's grim expression, then drank deeply before calling for the servant to refill their cups.

There was pottage of goose, and salted mutton, roasted swine and great hunks of tender beef served with a sauce of ale and honey and cooked apples. There were fresh golden loaves of bread, and pungent slabs of cheese, and dishes of sweet jam made with honey and the flesh of rose hips. There were platters of purple plums and beech nuts, hazelnuts, and the sweet chestnuts which the Romans had brought to the Dark Isles, and there were jugs and skins of wine and ale enough to drown in. And even Cadwain seemed in better spirits by the time the dishes and platters were half empty and the king called for silence in his hall so that he could raise his own cup to Merlin and thank the druid for honouring Lyonesse with a visit.

'When I was a boy, my father would speak of a prophecy which foretold that Lyonesse would sink beneath the waves,' King Lot said, looking at Merlin beside him, 'but here we are still, these many years later, and hosting a druid, too.' He smiled, and he looked the kindly ruler and proud man he was by the light of the fire and before his people, who were enjoying the fruits of their labours ahead of the coming winter.

'What is more,' the king went on, 'it is hard to put much store in such ominous portending when the gods have blessed us with the return of so many sons of Lyonesse from their adventures across the sea.'

Men and women lifted their voices in cheering then, drowning out the keening of the wind in the night beyond the hall, though Arthur saw some with tears glistening in their eyes for their sons, husbands or brothers who would never come home.

Beside the king, Merlin smiled, a mischief glinting in his eyes which Arthur recognized well. 'I have heard of your great victory over the spearmen of Corcaigh, lord king,' he said. 'Even now there are bards in Britain who sing of it.'

Cadwain nearly choked on his ale at that, and some turned to look at him, though he had the sense to hold his tongue.

'Do not be modest, Cadwain.' Merlin's voice carried across the hall. 'For did you not slaughter the Gaels by the dozen, you and your brave champions of Lyonesse? I heard that the men of Ireland fell before you . . .' he lifted his cup towards the hall door '. . . like leaves from that alder out there.' The folk standing between the king's table and his champion parted, so that Arthur, Gawain and Cadwain found themselves in the druid's line of sight and under the scrutiny of his penetrating gaze.

Cadwain's face flushed beneath his red beard. 'We did the best we could, lord,' he said. 'And we showed the Irishmen what men of Lyonesse can do.' He coughed and frowned, squirming under Merlin's eye and looking more ill at ease even than in that Irish valley when his shieldwall had been about to buckle. 'But it was Arthur here who brought us the victory.' With that, both he and Gawain took a step back from Arthur, who felt the firelight from the hearth fall fully upon him, though the heat of that was nothing compared with the intensity of the druid's glare and that of everyone else under King Lot's roof.

'Is that so?' Merlin lifted an eyebrow. 'Our own Arthur.' He ran a hand through his short hair, raising it in messy spikes. 'Arthur ap Uther ap Constantine ap Tahalais,' he said, the hint of a smile tugging at the corner of his mouth. 'Am I to believe young Arthur has earned his keep, my lord king? If so, I am pleased, though not as pleased as Lord Uther will be when I tell him.'

'Arthur.' King Lot extended his arm, inviting Arthur to speak. 'Tell Merlin how you slaughtered our enemies.'

It was an invitation Arthur could hardly refuse. He looked at Gawain, who showed him his palms as if to say his friend was on his own now.

'Come, Arthur!' the king called, sweeping his arm through the hall smoke and causing the oil lamps on his table to gutter. 'A victory feast is no place for modesty. Let us hear your account of it.'

Arthur swallowed. His mouth and lips were dry despite the ale. He cleared his throat and straightened. 'I came late to the valley,' he said, 'which afforded me the time to make a plan. I—'

'You came late, Arthur?' Merlin interrupted. 'Why in the name of Arawn were you late? Were you not with fearless Cadwain and the other brave spearmen of Lyonesse?' The druid lifted one eyebrow, and Arthur knew that the man was playing with him. He would have wagered his sword that Merlin had already heard the story of it from some spearman or fishwife before he passed the threshold of King Lot's hall.

'I—' Arthur began.

'He had the shits, lord,' Gawain interrupted. 'From the ship's wine.'

Arthur shot him a sour look, as a low rumble of suppressed laughter competed with the sound of the wind around the place. 'Now you help?' he hissed. Gawain grinned. Arthur turned back to face the king's table. 'We came to a hillside above the valley where Cadwain had built his shieldwall in the face of an overwhelming force. We saw that some of the Gaels had come to that place on ponies.' He heard Cadwain mutter something filthy. 'And I saw that there might be a way to hurt the enemy.'

'Yes, yes, you have always had a thing for the Romans and their horse warriors.' Merlin lifted his cup and leant over towards King Lot beside him. 'They used Gauls and Thracians mostly, of course,' he said, then sipped his wine. 'And there were Hannibal's Numidians,' he added, 'and the murderous horse archers of the Parthian Empire.' King Lot's face said he knew nothing about any of this, and Merlin sighed and looked back at Arthur. 'You are no bard, Arthur.' He gestured with his cup at those gathered in the hall. 'You are sending these good people to sleep with this tale of yours.'

'I did not ask to tell it.' Arthur felt his hackles rise.

'Then I shall tell it,' King Lot announced, and with that he stood, and his people cheered or hammered the tables with their fists because the old spear wound in his right leg, which had never healed properly, would not stop their beloved lord from spinning his yarn.

The king smiled, raising his palms for them to be silent, and the noise subsided until there was only the sound of the hearth fire crackling, and the crunching of a hound gnawing a knuckle of bone beneath one of the tables, and the occasional cough in the room, and the moaning of the wind without. 'Arthur and six brave men rode down into the valley,' the king said. 'They would not be stopped, but galloped on . . . like foaming white breakers across the grey sea. Arthur led from the front, spearing men, laying about him like Belatucadrus himself, sowing death amongst the Gaels.'

Men and women cheered, and Arthur felt the heat in his face and on the back of his neck. He looked to the door and for a heartbeat considered walking out of the hall, but he knew that would cause the king no little offence. Instead, he stood there trying not to frown.

'On they rode, these brave sons of Lyonesse and their fearless leader, Arthur ap Uther, reaping the lives of our enemies, and no man could stand before them.' King Lot took up a wine jug from the table. 'They broke through the Gaels,' he said, swinging the jug and smashing it into two cups on the table, knocking them off into the floor rushes. Another cheer rose to the thatch. 'And they joined with Cadwain and those other bold spearmen, who had held their ground all the day and sent scores of Irish to Annwn and its lord, Arawn.'

The king was adding honey to the brew, in the way of all bards, and everyone knew it. None seemed to mind but for Arthur himself, and perhaps Cadwain, who Arthur saw had found a bench to sit on and was busy pouring ale into the grimace of his mouth. The rest of the folk were eating out of their king's hand, as Lot went on to tell of how Arthur led the survivors back to the ship, fighting for their lives every step, and by the end of his tale he'd had to raise his voice to be heard over the clamour of those in that hall who had needed to hear a tale of courage and champions, that they might forget the bitter truth of it: that the Irish had stolen three men, four women and two children of Lyonesse and carried them back across the sea. And then had chased out King Lot's war band which had meant to avenge his people.

'Thank the gods for Arthur!' a warrior shouted.

'Arthur, lord of the ponies!' another man yelled, which got some laughs.

Then someone started chanting his name, and the others joined in.

'Arthur! Arthur! Arthur!' they yelled in unison.

While Arthur stood there like a lone tree around which a storm was raging, he looked across the smoky hall at Merlin. The druid was leaning forward, pulling his short beard between his finger and thumb and watching Arthur, a grin on his face.

'Arthur! Arthur! Arthur!'

He couldn't take it any more, and so he turned and pushed his way through the crowded hall towards the door, people still calling his name and grinning in his face and thumping his arms, shoulders and back as he passed them.

Then he was outside, breathing the clean air and watching the dark shapes of leafless trees moving in the wind.

The hall door clumped open and shut. Arthur did not need to turn round to know who had come out after him.

'I think the King of Lyonesse would sooner have been a bard,' Merlin said, coming to stand beside him and looking up at a rent in the cloud. The moon poured pale light through that gash, turning the sea to molten silver an arrow's flight from where they stood listening to the merriment within. Neither the wind, nor the roar of the breakers, nor the seethe and rattle of the waves sweeping over the shingle could smother the sound of laughter and singing now rising to the rafters of the king's hall.

'He's a good man,' Arthur said. 'He treats me like a son.' He knew that barb was misaimed at Merlin, but his father was not here and the druid was.

'You are a fool, Arthur,' Merlin said. 'To risk your life for those thick-skulled idiots in there. What if you had been killed? If some strutting young Irishman had sheathed his blade in your belly . . . what of our plans then?'

'What plans?' Arthur asked.

Merlin was stroking his right palm with two fingers of his left hand, tracing the triskele of conjoined spirals that had been etched into the skin and then the wound rubbed with some green dye so that it would remain there as long as his body endured.

The druid made a low sound in his throat. 'I am afraid, Arthur.' He nodded. 'Yes, afraid.'

Arthur looked at him. He had never seen Merlin afraid, nor would he believe the man capable of feeling fear. 'You, afraid?' he said. 'Of what?'

Merlin turned to face him now, and his face belied the joyous clamour seeping through the walls and thatch of the hall. Arthur had half expected some quip, or another insult perhaps, but now he saw a different Merlin, and this one chilled his blood.

'Do you know what you've done, Arthur?' the druid asked. There was fire in his eyes. 'I suppose you feel like a young hero, bringing King Lot's spearmen home to him when their heads should be on spikes in some dung-heap village? I expect you wish your father could see you now? That Uther's ears could be crammed with the voices of those men in there raising their cups in your honour?'

Arthur said nothing to this. He would not admit it but neither could he deny it, for it was true. He had even thought of his father as he rode down that hill towards the Gaels, imagining what Uther might think if he could see him then.

'I spend my life preparing for war,' he said. 'What would you have me do when the spears are flying and men are looking to me to lead them?'

Merlin's lips twisted, so that Arthur saw his teeth in the moonlight. 'You killed a druid, Arthur.' He seemed to shudder. 'Just saying it sickens me.'

Arthur felt the words like a thin blade piercing his guts. 'That is how we won,' he said.

'Won?' Merlin raised his bearded chin.

'How we survived,' Arthur corrected himself. No one would say that the Lyonesse men had won anything other than their own lives.

'No man may kill a druid.' Merlin's eyes held Arthur's like polished brass rivets. 'It is forbidden. Even in a battle a druid is safe. He may walk the field and no man can touch him. He may dance dryshod over the corpses themselves, or wade in blood, knowing that the enemy's spearmen cannot harm him. But you! What do you do?' He shook his head as if he still could not quite believe it. Then he said in a quiet voice, 'You took a druid's head off his shoulders.'

The rent in the cloud had healed now, so that the world was cast in darkness. Arthur felt some cold portent in it. 'The Irish druid was cursing us,' he said. 'Cursing me.' He swallowed. 'Had I not killed him, I would be dead or worse.'

'The man's name was Fionnbhárr,' Merlin said. 'An arrogant fool, though not without power. I once saw him produce a two-headed goat from an enormous cauldron.' He frowned at the memory. 'Arthur,' he said, his bushy brows lifting, 'your offence against the gods is more grave than any I have seen or heard of. Truth is, I don't know if I can protect you.' He reached out and put a hand on Arthur's shoulder. 'Yet years ago I gave your father my word that I would do what I could for you, and so I will. But, Arthur, you must let me guide you. If you are not to be cursed by the gods of Britain themselves, if you are not to suffer their torments and miseries all your life, you *must* listen to me.'

Arthur felt as if a great weight were settling upon him as he waited for Merlin to continue, and a cold wind blew off the sea like a reminder that the season had turned.

'As I said, Fionnbhárr was a talented druid,' Merlin went on, 'but I do not think I am being too conceited when I say that I am closer to the gods than he ever was. If there is a way to shield you from the gods' wrath, I am the only man alive who can find it. If you are to become beloved of Balor and Cernunnos, Arawn and Manannán, rather than endure the scourge of their contempt, it will be because *I* have shown you the way.' He lifted his other hand, the one with the triskele on the palm, as green as a vein, and held it up. 'Do you understand, Arthur ap Uther?'

Arthur nodded. 'I understand,' he said. For he feared to be cursed, as any man alive feared it, and Merlin was the only person in Britain who might have the power and the will to avert such a fate.

'Good,' Merlin said. 'You must never talk of what you did. Never!' He inclined his head. 'I will see to it that these men and women of Lyonesse never so much as whisper it in the night. It will be as if it never happened. Let them talk not of Arthur the druid-killer, but of Arthur the warrior, who charged upon his brave steed into the fight.' His lip curled beneath his dark moustaches. 'But you are mine now, Arthur. Don't ever forget that.' With that he stepped back and breathed deeply and nodded. 'Together we will sing the old songs of Britain and all her gods will hear us.'

'Is that why you came?' Arthur asked. 'To bind me to you?'

Merlin almost smiled. 'To protect you, Arthur,' he corrected. 'But no, that is not why I came. I'm here to take you back across the sea, to Tintagel.'

Arthur shook his head, confused. 'I have not been here a year,' he said. 'There is still much I can learn from Cadwain.'

Merlin grunted. 'Like how to be a fool and lead men into a trap in Ireland?' he asked, then his face hardened again. 'I came because your uncle the High King, the sword of Britain these last ten years, is dead. Uther will be proclaimed king at Samhain. You need to be there.'

'Ambrosius is dead?' Arthur's mind conjured an image of his uncle, squat and well-built and haughty-looking with his crooked nose and long drooping moustaches. The kind of man whom one expected to outlast even Dumnonia's ancient burial mounds and the wind and sea-blasted rocks of that kingdom's southern coast. 'How?' he asked.

Merlin clenched a fist and thrust it against his own chest. 'An assassin's blade,' he said.

'Who?' Arthur asked. 'Who did it?'

Merlin shrugged. 'Caer Gloui? Cynwidion? Or perhaps King Donnabhan of Ebrauc past the Wall sent the man to do it? Your uncle was High King but he was not short of enemies.' He pulled his beard through a fist, smoothing it. 'I asked the killer, of course, but he would not answer, perhaps on account of the king's men having hacked him into half a dozen soggy pieces. A little late, I think you'll agree, but you know what warriors are like when they've got their swords in their hands.' He sighed and looked out across the dark sea. 'I will dream to the gods and perhaps they will tell me.'

Arthur shivered to think that his uncle was no longer in the world but had passed into the hereafter. Into Arawn's realm. 'Why do I need to be there?' he asked. 'My father will become High King. What has it to do with me?'

Merlin scowled. 'Did Fionnbhárr blow a rat into your skull to gnaw at your brains? You're his son, Arthur!'

Arthur felt the frown on his own face. 'I will have to ask King Lot's permission.'

Merlin wafted that away. 'I have already told him. We leave with the tide. Come, I'm getting cold,' he said, turning and walking back towards the hall door. 'Oh, and that oaf Gawain is coming with us,' he added over his shoulder. 'Seems you have made an impression on him.'

'Merlin,' Arthur said. 'What about the . . . other thing?'

The druid stopped before the threshold, his hand on the door. 'Morgaine is well,' he said without looking back at Arthur. 'The birth went hard for her, yet she lives.'

Arthur felt breathless, not as from running or training with spear and shield, but as though there were suddenly no air in the world to draw on. 'And the child?' he asked in a low voice, hardly daring the words.

Merlin looked up, beyond the eaves and to the night sky, where the swift-running cloud was hazed silver by the unseen moon. 'Come, Arthur,' he said. 'The folk of Lyonesse want to see their hero.'

Arthur imagined a night such as this was, and an infant wrapped in swathing bands. In the eye of his mind he saw a man's hands shoving lake stones in amongst the tightly wound cloth, saw the little bundle sinking down and down in the dark water, as if he too were descending with it. Saw it nestle in the swaying reed-beds. He thought he heard Morgaine screaming, but it was just the wind in the trees.

'Arthur,' Merlin said, breaking the spell, then the druid walked into the noise and the golden light flooding out of King Lot's hall.

And so Arthur followed him.

12

A New Pendragon

'How did you know where the latrines were?' the boy asked him. They had sat side by side on the bench in the stinking dark, as the legionaries of Rome had done before them, and afterwards cleaned themselves with sea sponges and rainwater. Now, they stood outside that foul-smelling place, breathing the sea air, as gulls shrieked above and the day grew warmer.

Beran pointed to where the via pretoria, leading from the main land gate on the west to the sea gate on the east, converged with the fort's other main road. 'See how the ground slopes?' he asked. 'Just a little, but enough so that any rainwater from the roofs and roads flows down here and carries the shit away.' He thumped the butt of his spear against the paved road. 'They always built the latrines on the low ground.'

The boy looked impressed, surprised even, that Beran should have such knowledge of the Roman way of doing things. 'And I've been here before,' Beran admitted, almost smiling. 'Just the once, and a long time ago.' He was staring up at one of the great stone bastions over-looking the harbour, wondering what the spearmen in his father's day must have thought when they looked out from that tower to see ships brimming with Saxon warriors prowling along the southern coast like wolves seeking ingress to the fold. Would those spearmen have fought so hard had they known that more and more Saxons would cross the Morimaru and sail south in search of silver, slaves and land? Would his father have fought so hard? *Would I?* he thought.

'So what's that?' the boy asked, hauling Beran back to the here of it. The boy was pointing at the grand-looking flint, limestone, and red brick building beside the latrines. From somewhere beyond the pitched roof of clay tiles, smoke drifted up to smear the blushing sky.

'That, boy, is the bathhouse.'

The boy pressed his hands against his cheeks, his mouth hanging open. It was an expression that both amused and surprised Beran. 'You have Roman baths in Caer Colun,' he said.

The boy shook his head. 'The fires have not been lit since before I was born. My mother told me that a druid came to my father. His name was Merlin.' He eyed Beran. 'You must have heard of him?'

Beran took a breath. 'Yes, I've heard of him.'

The boy nodded. 'Merlin the druid pleaded with my father to pull down the bathhouse and the statue to Minerva. He said that those . . . symbols of Rome were an offence to the gods of Britain.'

Constantine had worn Roman armour and shaved his face. The man had been as Roman as a man could be in the Dark Isles without the legions and the towns and the great villas to remind people of the glories of the empire. He had carried himself with the arrogance of a man clinging to the past as the world around him broke apart. He had worn Rome like the red cloak around his shoulders. And perhaps some Roman god had remembered him, even if he *had* offended the gods of Britain, Beran thought now, for Constantine lived a long life and fought many battles and won more than he lost.

'Constantine pulled down the bathhouse?' Beran asked the boy, thinking that not even Merlin could have persuaded the man to do such a thing.

'No,' the boy said. 'But the fires beneath were never lit again. For all my life, the bathhouse has been where we store grain.'

'Well, this one is still in use by the looks,' Beran said.

'Can we go in?' The boy crinkled his nose at Beran. 'You smell bad.'

Beran cocked an eyebrow. 'You don't smell like meadowsweet your-self, boy.'

The boy smiled like a hunter who knew his prey had taken the bait. 'So let's go and wash,' he said. 'When was the last time you washed?'

Beran couldn't remember and said so. 'But you don't just walk in. And I don't have the money.'

The boy eyed him, lips pursed.

'Don't give me that look,' Beran said, though he was already fishing in the scrip on his belt for coins. 'Hmmm . . . I suppose these belong to you, anyway.' He held up two of the silver siliquae which he had taken from the chest that he'd pulled from the carriage in which the boy and his mother had been fleeing Caer Colun. 'The rest of it will still be safely hidden where we left it,' he added, feeling suddenly guilty.

'Is that enough?' The boy nodded at the coins which had vanished into Beran's closed fist.

The *clump* of a door drew Beran's eye and he saw a clean-shaven, bare-chested man stumble out of a timber and thatch building which leant up against the bathhouse, wincing at the morning light and pulling his tunic over his head.

'It's enough,' he told the boy, as two women with dark-painted eyes and tousled hair came out after the man, watching with conspiratorial amusement him make his unsteady progress along the street.

'Ready?' Beran asked the boy. The boy nodded, and so they went up to the bathhouse entrance, where an enormous woman with red cheeks, hard eyes and strong shoulders sat on a bench in the shade, picking the flesh from a mackerel on a plate on the bench beside her. A short spearman with a neat, grey beard leant in the entrance, looking bored, though the day had only just begun.

'Not him,' the woman said without even looking up.

'He's older than he looks,' Beran said.

Now the woman lifted her eyes to them, regarding Beran first, then the boy. 'Still makes him no more'n eleven or twelve.'

Beran curled his lip. 'The boy needs to bathe. He stinks.'

She looked Beran up and down. 'He's not the only one,' she said, lifting a hand to point at the gulls screaming above. 'Those mews followed you here.'

Beran saw the spearman grin at that, before pushing a hazelnut into his mouth and flicking the shell halves away with his thumb.

'I can pay,' Beran said.

The big woman shook her head. 'If I let you in, I'll lose customers.' She put some flint in her eyes now. 'And I don't know you. Never seen you before.' She gestured vaguely towards the south-east. 'Bathe in the sea. Won't cost you anything.'

'We want to bathe here,' Beran said.

At this the spearman made a fist, cracking a nut against the others in his grip. But he did not speak. Clearly he was used to the big woman dealing with troublemakers without the need for him to do anything beyond making them aware of his presence.

'One word from me and your day will end worse than it started.' The woman gestured up at the wall and the half-dozen sentries stationed there, some looking out, others looking into the fort, their spear blades glinting now and then in the sunlight. 'You and the boy'll be dragged up there and thrown over the wall. Tide's out, so you won't drown.' She turned to the spearman behind her. 'Though, there was that mouthy shit from Lindisware. Mud got him. Swallowed him whole.'

'Crabs had him in the end,' the spearman said, chewing.

Beran stepped forward and dropped the two coins onto the woman's plate of food. As silver as the mackerel's scales, those Roman coins, but if the woman was surprised, she hid it well.

'You're a stubborn old bear, aren't you?' the woman said.

The guard of the baths must have decided it was time to earn his keep, because he came forward, spear raised. Beran strode to meet him, bringing up his own shaft and sweeping it across to knock the other man's spear aside before reversing his spear and punching the butt end into the man's forehead, dropping him amongst the litter of hazelnut shells on the ground.

He turned back to the woman, who picked up a piece of the mackerel's flesh between finger and thumb and popped it into her mouth. Beran noted that the silver coins had vanished from the plate.

'I have Saxon blood on me that I want to wash off,' he told her. 'And the boy here has never seen a Roman bath, so I'm going to show him one.'

The two women at the threshold of the timber hut were coming, but the big woman raised a hand and shook her head, so they retreated again. Then she wiped her fingers on the front of her overdress and waved her hand towards the bathhouse entrance. 'Take your time,' she said. Then she smiled at the boy. 'And make sure you clean behind those ears.'

'Are you going to stand there all day?' Beran sat back and put his arms out either side, resting them on the edge of the bath, his heart racing at the shock of the heat on his skin.

'What does it feel like?' The boy was standing on the side, shrouded in the vapour which filled the place almost to the roof, so that with his pale, naked body, unmarked and so thin that Beran could have counted his bones, he looked like an ill-fated spirit lost in the veil between the dead and the living.

'Like I'm being cooked alive.' Beran could feel his blood rising up through his flesh as if seeking release. Could feel his face flushing and the skin of his scalp already beginning to prickle with sweat.

'I don't want to,' the boy said.

'Get in,' Beran said.

The boy shook his head. 'No.' He was staring at the water, his teeth gritted, his hands cupped over his groin.

Beran looked to his left. Through the thick fog he could make out two men by the bath steps, submerged up to their necks and talking in low voices. To his right, two more men and a woman were splashing and cavorting, like children in a stream on a hot summer's day. From the looks of it, this end of the bath had once been open to the sky, but someone had covered the opening with timbers, no doubt seeking to keep out the worst of the winter weather. But that meant that the rising vapour could not escape.

'Get in,' Beran hissed, but still the boy just stood there, and so Beran pushed off from the side and waded through the water towards him. 'There's every chance we're going to get dragged out of here before I've even soaked my beard,' he growled. 'So get in, before I pull you in by your feet.'

'He shouldn't be in here,' one of the men by the steps said.

'And we watched you,' the other one said. 'You didn't clean yourself with oil. See the water there! You're making it foul.'

Beran looked up at the rising mist and breathed a curse, then turned and waded towards the two men, teeth clenched, his blood gushing in his ears.

'We ... we mean no offence,' one of the men said, as both backed away through water that shimmered with a gloss of oil.

'Please,' the other man said, stumbling, finding his feet again, his neat brown beard glistening, his hair plastered back from a wide forehead.

Beran made three more strides, then stopped and raised a hand, vapour rising from his arm like smoke, his outstretched finger dripping. 'Talk to me again and see what happens,' he said, glaring at each man in turn. They had the soft, untried bodies of merchants, these two, and he could see their eyes roving across the many pale and puckered scars that criss-crossed his shoulders, torso and upper thighs. These scars had always put Beran in mind of the Saxons' runes, those twig-like inscriptions that you found on stones and wood and even on the blades of their swords, only these scars told the story of his own life. They spoke of battle and blood, of pain and of his refusal to yield, and these men knew that he was a wolf and they were sheep, and so they showed Beran their unscathed hands and turned and climbed out of the bath, their white arses vanishing like roe-deer tails in morning mist.

Even so, Beran was beginning to think the whole thing had been a bad idea, and when he turned back to peer through the rising fog, he could not see the boy. His stomach tightened.

'Here, I'm here,' the boy said, and Beran breathed again because the boy was in the water, only his head visible above its surface.

'Well?' Beran said. 'What does it feel like?'

The boy's eyes were as round as the two silver siliquae it had cost them to get into the place. His mouth rounder still. 'It's so hot!'

Beran laughed in spite of himself. 'That's the idea,' he said, lowering himself until the water covered his shoulders. A woman's giggle echoed off the walls.

'We should tell the others,' the boy said, looking to the steps as though he was considering getting out and running naked through Portus Adurni to find them. 'Isolde would like this very much, I think.'

'Let's not worry about them now,' Beran said. 'This cost us, so let's just enjoy it.'

'I want to stay in here all day.' The boy rolled onto his back and looked up at the mist-hung ceiling as he floated. 'My father should not have closed the baths.'

'Druids can be persuasive,' Beran muttered. He ran a hand through his hair and closed his eyes and gave his body to the water. Now he could feel his heartbeat slowing. Could feel the warmth reaching deeper and deeper into his flesh, dissolving the pains in his muscles and bones. 'I had forgotten how good this feels,' he said.

A gasp came from the mist where the woman and her two companions were. Then the sound of lapping water, then another gasp. Beran saw the boy look over, but the three were mostly veiled in the warm floating fog, though Beran caught a glimpse of slender pale shoulders and glossy slick of wet hair, and a man's back, dark with moss-like fuzz.

'Boy,' Beran said under his breath.

A man grunted and the woman gave a small cry.

Beran flicked water at him with the back of his hand. 'Boy,' he said again. 'Want to see what's through there?' He pointed to an archway leading to another area of the bathhouse, the wall plaster painted faded green like the mantle of a standing pool in summer. The boy's gaze yet lingered on the place in the bath, a spear's length away, from which those noises came, and Beran caught sight of the writhing knot of limbs and flesh, and he cursed this day.

He could have asked the three to stop enjoying themselves, but that would almost certainly end in violence, and Beran was just getting comfortable, enjoying the softening of his body, the loosening of his sinews and the deadening of a dozen aches. Besides, he did not relish the thought of fighting two men while he himself was naked. But neither did the boy need to witness what was happening just a few feet away. It would only lead to him asking Beran questions, and Beran was too tired for all that.

'Well?' he asked the boy. 'Shall we try the other bath?'

The boy nodded and they pushed themselves to the side and climbed out, steaming like a cauldron in coals, and moved silently through the fog, which was even more dense in the next room, though Beran could make out the design of the black and white mosaic beneath their feet: figures riding on horse-like creatures, except instead of hind legs, these mounts had the curling tails of some strange sea beast.

They lowered themselves onto the side of the bath and slipped into the water, and the boy gasped because it was even hotter than the previous bath. But it seemed they were alone and so Beran found the stone ledge beneath and sat back, resting his head against the smooth, cool marble and closing his eyes. When was the last time he had felt no pain in his body? He could not remember. It did not matter now, and so he let himself be borne off on the hot, alleviant pleasure of it, like a downy feather carried on a late summer breeze. Or, like a tired old man drifting from the world, memory and regret, love and loss fading until it was but a distant cuckoo call, the faintest echo of a long life easing into silent, eternal blackness.

Sleep now.

It was the boy that woke him, hissing in his ear, a sound like a wet log seething in the hearth. Slowly – unnaturally slowly it seemed to Beran – he was hauled back to himself to see the boy's face a beard's bristle from his own.

'A man is drowning someone,' the boy whispered, his eyes bright, his fingers digging into Beran's forearm.

'What?' Beran heard the sound of water being disturbed, then it was gone and all he could hear was the boy breathing. 'Where?'

The boy pointed towards the other end of the bath. Beran could see nothing but the thick cloud hanging in the place. 'Do something,' the boy said.

Beran shook his head. 'Nothing to do with us,' he said in a voice barely above a whisper.

'Please!' the boy hissed.

'Why should I get involved?' Beran said.

'Someone's dying, Beran. Please! We have to do something.'

A loud splash then. Droplets of water struck the surface nearby, followed by a loud gasping breath, then another splash, then silence.

'Beran!' the boy grabbed his arm again and Beran felt the sting of fingernails gouging his flesh.

Beran sighed and shook his head. 'Stay here,' he said, and now he was moving through the water, and as he got closer, he saw the back of the man who was doing the killing. He had his right arm crooked around the other's neck and had driven his own weight down so that the other man's head was underwater, his hand clutching at his attacker, his back arching as he struggled in vain to rise. But that struggle – the gush and occasional splash of water, the laboured breathing of the killer and the muted, subaqueous screams of the drowning man – covered the sound of Beran's own movement through the pool. He threw out his left arm, wrapping it around the killer's neck whilst putting his right hand on the back of his head and pushing it forward.

'Let him go,' Beran said through gritted teeth. He was using all of his strength to squeeze his arm against the sides of the man's neck, though he did not know if that would be enough, because he was old, and this man was half his age and his physique was that of a warrior. 'Let go,' Beran said again, and now the man let go of the other, instead trying to grab hold of Beran's arm around his neck. He lifted a leg and pushed against the side of the bath and drove backwards through the water, but Beran held on, even when his own back struck the stone of the other side and the breath was driven out of him.

Looking past the back of the man's head, he saw the other man leaning against the side, coughing and choking but alive. Saw the silver hammer pendant strung around his neck and the scars on his forearms, and the not fully healed wound on the back of his left shoulder.

The Saxon climbed out of the pool, still spluttering, and vanished in the rising fog, leaving Beran cursing himself for a fool because he no longer owned the strength to win this fight. His arm was trembling around the man's neck, his muscle failing, and the man had got some fingers of his right hand up underneath, between his own throat and Beran's arm, so that he was able to draw enough breath to live. And Beran did not know if it was his own strength ebbing or the other man's strength growing, but he did know that he could not hold on much longer.

You're going to die helping a Saxon, he heard his old friend say. *Now there's a song for the bards.*

Then he heard a muffled *splosh* and he saw the Saxon striding through the water and the mist towards him, and he held on around the man's neck because that was all he could do. The Saxon stood before him, his face a rictus of fury, and then the man in Beran's grip was bucking against Beran's body and there was blood in the water, blooming in a red cloud. Beran saw the muscle in the Saxon's right shoulder swelling and contracting as he punched into the other man's stomach and side again and again. And now the man against him went limp, his hands falling away from Beran's arm, his life fleeing his body.

'Enough.' Beran let go of the dead man and stepped away. He saw a dark slick in the water now and knew the man's bowels had let go too. The stink came soon after.

The Saxon took hold of the dead man and half lifted him and pushed him away into the cloying fog, then pushed his scramasax this way and that through the water to clean it. He nodded at Beran, who stood his ground in case the Saxon should come at him next.

'Who are you, and who was he?' Beran asked in the man's own tongue, gesturing at the corpse floating face down nearby.

'Uffa,' the Saxon said, pressing a clenched fist against his powerful chest. His neck was red, already bruising where the other man had held him underwater.

'A Saxon!' the boy said, standing naked on the side of the bath. He had fetched Beran's spear and now gripped it across his little body.

The Saxon looked from the boy to Beran, then at the floating corpse. He spat at it. 'Bealdwulf,' he said through a warped mouth. 'My . . . brother.'

Beran knew some Saxon, had gathered words across the long years, but he did not know if the Saxon meant that the other man was a spear-brother or his brother by birth. He supposed it didn't much matter now.

'Why was he trying to kill you?' Beran asked, piecing the strange words together as best he could.

The Saxon pulled his long moustaches and beard through a fist and lifted his chin and spoke, and when he had finished speaking, Beran had gathered enough of the meaning of it.

'This man is of the South Saxons,' he told the boy. 'And that one turning the water red wanted what he had. Wanted his woman, his furs, his land.'

The boy still gripped the spear as though he intended to use it. 'But how are they here, in the fort?'

Beran shrugged, watching the Saxon, who was watching him. 'He told me they slip over the walls now and then to come and use the baths. I think they have an arrangement with some of the local men, who lower a rope and turn a blind eye. And I imagine they make it worthwhile for that woman outside, too.'

The Saxon studied Beran as he spoke, his pale eyes at once distrustful and curious. His nose was aquiline and his beard, even wet, was the colour of dry sand. He was handsome and haughty-looking, and he recognized in Beran, in his scars and in the knots of his gnarled body, a fellow warrior and an enemy. The living embodiment of the violent struggle in which the Saxon people had partaken since the keels of the first boats had ground upon the shores of Britain.

'He must think the baths are a marvel,' the boy said.

'Worth risking his life for,' Beran agreed.

'We should go.' The boy was looking around now, as though expecting someone else to appear in the fog. The floating corpse might not be seen for a while, with the mist so thick in that place, but no one would fail to notice the water in this bath was red, and there was a foul smell in the air.

The Saxon held out his right hand, his gaze riveted to Beran's own eyes. Beran's mind told him not to trust the man. *Look to the blade in his other hand*, it warned, *for he will sheathe it in your ribs the moment you take his hand.*

'He's thanking you,' the boy said, 'for saving his life.'

'I wouldn't have done it had I known,' Beran said. 'Any luck, they would've killed each other.' Still, he put out his hand and gripped the Saxon's, neither of them speaking again, though both knowing that they were no more friends than the wolf is with the bear. Then Beran climbed out of that red water and he and the boy left the Saxon standing there, gripping his hammer amulet in one hand, the scramasax in the other, and mumbling to Thunor and Woden, those Saxon gods, as though they were in that place with him. And perhaps they were.

The *Osprey* did not swoop so much as waddle into port at dusk the next day, taking on water even as her crew bailed with the relentless rhythm of a fevered heart. As news of her approach spread through Portus Adurni, crowds had gathered on the foreshore and walls to watch the vessel, some invoking gods for luck, some placing wagers on the ship's fate, others just watching quietly, wondering if they were about to witness the doom of that ship and her crew. In the event, she docked safely, without loss of cargo or man, and most of those standing in the dusk cheered, and the boy cheered with them, and Beran did not tell him that most of the joy was doubtless for the saving of the *Osprey*'s cargo, the wine and olive oil, rather than for the lives of her sailors.

The thought had made Beran hungry as he and the boy stood in the street watching folk running off to the wharf to greet the ship and learn what had befallen her. Beran had known he would hear the story soon enough.

'A Saxon ship came on us like a wolf when we rounded the headland out of Noviomagus,' Rivanon now explained to Guivret, her eyes bright with the memory of it. She was a small woman, barely taller than the boy, and her skin was leathery from a life spent facing the sea winds. 'They sat too low in the water compared to us, and could not come aboard easily, so they tried to hole us.'

Beran and Palamedes looked at each other with surprise. 'You had no spearmen aboard?' Beran asked.

'A dozen good men,' Rivanon said, glancing from Beran to Guivret as though expecting the Little King to explain who these others were and why they were questioning her abilities or wisdom or both. 'We threw spears and clay pots and barrels down on them,' Rivanon said, 'but they made a rampart of shields to protect their axemen, and we couldn't stop them.' She picked up her cup and drank through bared teeth, her expression pained as though she could still hear the Saxons' axes biting into her ship's hull.

'Thank the gods you came safely home,' Guivret said, lifting his own cup towards the merchant.

The woman scoffed at that. 'The gods had nothing to do with it,' she said. 'Thank the Saxons' thirst. I gave them three amphorae of wine and a barrel of ale to leave my ship alone.'

All agreed it was a price worth paying, then Rivanon tilted her head back, lifted her brows and eyed the Little King suspiciously. 'But you didn't come here to listen to my troubles.'

Guivret dipped his head and turned his palms uppermost to acknowledge the truth of that. 'There is always business to be done,' he admitted, then gestured at Beran and the boy. 'I have come to ask if you will take my friends here to Tintagel. I will pay the usual price, of course.'

Again, Rivanon looked at Beran, then she smiled at the boy, who smiled back. 'The *Osprey* needs repair. It will take four or five days, by which time we may have lost the wind.'

'But you'll take us?' Beran asked. 'When you can?'

She nodded. 'I'll take you. I have a jar of the best garum for the Lord of the Heights. He will be pleased to see me.' Then she turned her weathered face to Guivret. 'I hear you have horses in the south paddock.'

Guivret and Palamedes exchanged a look, no doubt wondering how Rivanon already knew about the horses, though she had only been back in Portus Adurni half a day. Of all the creases in her sun-browned face, the lines at the corners of her eyes when she smiled were the deepest then.

'I need them all,' the dwarf said, guardedly. 'I am taking them to Benoic.'

Rivanon pursed her lips. 'Viamundus has said you can use his ship?' she asked.

Guivret frowned. The little man could see where this was leading. 'You know he doesn't like me. I was hoping you could persuade the old bastard,' he said. 'For the sake of our friendship.'

Rivanon nodded. 'For the sake of our friendship,' she agreed. 'And for a good-natured mare. I have just the buyer in mind.'

Guivret muttered a curse. 'You haven't changed,' he said, extending his hand. 'Throw in two skins of your Roman wine and you can choose any horse in the paddock.'

Rivanon's eyebrows lifted at that and she shook his hand. 'You have a deal, Little King,' she said, looking half pleased, as though she believed she might have won the richer part of the deal with the dwarf, but half suspicious too, as if she knew better than to think she had triumphed so easily.

Beran looked at Palamedes, seeing a smile tug at the corners of the Saracen's mouth, because Rivanon did not know that Guivret's finest horses were not in the paddock but stabled not a spear-throw from where they now stood.

'I will fetch you when it is time,' the merchant said, nodding to Guivret, Palamedes and Beran in turn. 'Now I need to find new strakes to patch up the *Osprey*.'

They said their goodbyes and had just stepped out into the bright day when Rivanon called after Guivret, asking to speak with him for a moment alone.

'I'll see you back at the barracks,' the dwarf told Beran and Palamedes, who went on without him into the busy street, the boy looking up at the gulls wheeling and shrieking in a blue sky.

'I think they like each other very much,' the boy said, grinning.

Palamedes looked at Beran and they both laughed.

They spent the next days enjoying the relative comfort which Portus Adurni provided, immersed in the ebb and flow of that fort which the Romans had built to guard Britannia's southern shore and which still stood as safe harbour for vessels plying the coast or ploughing the Dividing Sea.

The weather remained kind, the summer clinging on even as the days drew in, and folk ventured into the woods to gather elderberries, sloes and rose hips before badger and fox took them all, and huge flocks of swallows lined up along Portus Adurni's southern wall before flying through the veil to vanish until spring.

The boy was eager to show Tristan and Isolde the Roman baths, and Guivret, seeing the boy's excitement and the young lovers' dubious fascination, bought the Cornubians entry, to clean themselves in the Roman way with warm oil, and after, bathe in the hot waters. When they emerged from the bathhouse, Tristan and Isolde looked to Beran's eyes even younger than before. Their skin was clear, their hair glistened as though they had been anointed in some secret rites, their eyes were round and their smiles broad, and they talked of the wonder of it all the rest of the day.

That night, Tristan said there had been no talk of the killing that had taken place in the baths only days previously, though that came as no surprise to Beran, for doubtless the woman who ran the place did not want Viamundus, the commander of Portus Adurni, to know that she had been allowing Saxons to use the baths. 'The guard has a lump the size of an egg,' Tristan went on, touching his own forehead as he knelt to spread his furs and blankets across the old barrack's reed-strewn floor.

'You must have hit him very hard, Beran,' Isolde chided Beran, frowning at him.

'There would have been little point otherwise,' Beran muttered.

'He said it should have cost us more to bathe because they changed the water and we would never have cleaner,' Tristan said, making himself comfortable.

'Thank the gods they did change it,' Isolde said, folding a cloak for a pillow and putting it beside the one she had already made for Tristan.

'You can thank Beran for that,' Palamedes said, carrying a bench over to the open door and setting it down. The sun had set some time earlier, so the streets and thoroughfares were no longer busy and the fort was falling into darkness.

'I would have stayed out of it but for the boy.' Beran placed an oil lamp on a stool and sat down with his back against the wall, his knees drawn up.

The boy had gone with Guivret to the stables to check on his horses. At first Beran had forbidden him to go, but Isolde had sided with the boy, saying he needed a little freedom from Beran now and again. 'He has a habit of drawing me into things that would be better left alone,' Beran said, and not for the first time he wondered what he was doing in that place with the boy and the dwarf and the two runaway lovers hunted by a king. And yet, he felt uneasy having let the boy out of his sight, even for a short while.

'Perhaps that is because you can see what the boy might be, given the chance,' Palamedes said. He was sitting by the open door, looking into the gathering night, and Beran wondered if the Saracen too was waiting for Guivret to bring the boy safely back. 'He has a good heart and he is brave. And he is the son of a king.' He scratched amongst his beard. 'Men will follow him,' he said. 'Like you follow him, Beran.'

Beran was watching a mouse scrabble across the rushes as he kneaded the swollen knuckles of his right hand, gritting his teeth at the sweet pain of it. 'I'm not following the boy,' he said. 'He's following me . . . like a stink.'

The Saracen grunted. 'Tell yourself that if it makes you feel better,' he said. 'But you see what he could be. *Who* he could be, for Britain. Another Pendragon.'

'If you thought that, then why are you waiting for passage across the sea to Benoic? Why sell your sword to the Little King for silver and ale, if you truly believed you could give it freely for Britain and it would make a difference?'

Palamedes did not give him an answer, but Tristan said, 'What if the boy doesn't want to be a leader? What if he just wants to be free?'

It was not hard to see why Tristan would propose such an idea, and Beran saw him reach out to Isolde lying beside him and take her hand in his.

'You call this freedom?' Palamedes asked. 'Being crammed in between these Roman walls like fish in a trap?' The Saracen was using the tip of his knife to dig out the dirt from under his fingernails, as though Tristan and Isolde's bathing had shamed him into cleaning himself. He had, Beran noticed, trimmed his beard, so that even he looked younger. Everyone looked young to Beran. 'There is no freedom while the Saxons stalk the land,' Palamedes went on, 'and you all know it. Beran knows this better than anyone, don't you, Beran?'

They looked at one another through the dark, Beran warning the Saracen with his eyes to say no more, then Palamedes looked back out at the night where copper blooms of light from sentry fires shimmered against the deepening dark.

'The Saxons are lords of Britain now,' Beran murmured, preparing his furs again, though he had no intention of lying down to sleep until Guivret and the boy returned. But then Palamedes said he could see them coming along the via pretoria, the dwarf's bow-legged gait unmistakable even in the gloom, the two of them laughing like old friends.

Beran let out a long, relieved breath, then lay back and closed his eyes before the boy came through the door.

He was awakened by a hand on his shoulder, shaking him. Once, he would have jumped up, sword in hand and steeled for sudden violence. Now, it took him an age to rouse himself from slumber, so that it crossed his mind that one of these nights he lay down to sleep, he might simply never wake.

'Wha—?'

'Shhh,' someone hissed. Tristan. 'It's Isolde,' the young man whispered, his eyes fearful by the weak light of the oil lamp which he had reignited and which now sat on a mat of woven rushes beside Isolde. 'She's unwell. I think it's the child.'

'It's too soon for the birth,' Beran said, scrubbing his face with a hand and stretching his eyes wide, trying to come back to the world.

'I know, but there's some blood,' Tristan hissed.

Beran looked over at Isolde, who was lying back, her hands on her stomach and an expression of fear and shame in her eyes. There was something else Beran recognized in her face. She had the look of a prey animal, her wide eyes like those of a deer when it knows it is surrounded by hounds and there is nowhere left to run.

'What do you think I can do about it?' Beran murmured, glancing around the room. The others were dark shapes snoring in their furs.

'You're old.' Tristan shrugged. 'You must have seen such things before.'

'Spent my life killing Saxons, not gossiping with wise women and mothers,' Beran said.

'Please, Beran,' Isolde said through teeth clenched against the pain of whatever was ailing her. 'Do something.'

Beran looked from Isolde to the man she loved, seeing the desperation in them both. What did they expect from him? Besides, they had brought all this upon themselves. They had betrayed their lord and king, and now Isolde had another man's child in her belly, and perhaps the pain and the blood was the gods punishing them for the offence against the man who had loved and lost them both.

Beran grunted. *There are no gods in Britain*, he thought. *At least, no gods who concern themselves with the trials of a king of Britain and two young lovers.*

'Can you move?' he asked Isolde. She nodded.

'You'll help?' Tristan asked him, relief flooding his face.

'I told you, there's nothing I can do for her,' Beran said. 'But there may be someone who knows what to do.'

Together, he and Tristan helped Isolde to her feet, careful not to wake the others, for Isolde did not want to worry the boy, then they went into the night and the dark streets of Portus Adurni. Neither questioned Beran about where he was taking them, and nor was their progress along the via pretoria hampered by the groups of spearmen patrolling the fort, though now and then they had to stop, Isolde doubled over in such pain that tears stood in her eyes, and in Tristan's too at seeing her thus.

'Here we are,' Beran said when they came to the wooden dwelling built against the east side of the bathhouse. He hammered his fist on the door, whilst Tristan stood holding Isolde in the shadows behind him, and when the door opened, Beran heard the man growl a curse even before he recognized the bathhouse guard.

'What do *you* want?' the guard asked, bringing his spear up so that the blade wavered between himself and Beran.

'I want to speak with the woman who runs this place.' Even in the gloom Beran could see the swelling on the man's forehead. 'I have no quarrel with you.'

'No quarrel?' the guard said. 'You might have cracked my skull!' He lifted the spear higher. 'I ought to gut you here and now.'

'You could try.' Beran was glaring at the man, daring him to fight, hoping he would, truth be told. But no, the man did not have the courage in him. Beran could read that the way druids had once read the flights of birds or the entrails of beasts.

'Beran, please,' Tristan behind him said in a low voice. 'Please. She's in pain.'

'Fetch the woman I paid so generously four days ago,' Beran told the guard. Flame glow suddenly illuminated the dark interior and by its light Beran saw one of the whores from the other day, then she was gone.

'Leave,' the guard said. 'Berc'hed is sleeping and has no wish to see you.' He jerked the spear. 'Away from here, or I'll send for the night watch.' With that the man shut the door on them and barred it, leaving the three of them standing in the street as a sea gust swirled smoke from a sentry fire around them.

'What now?' Tristan asked.

Beran did not know, though he wished he had used the other end of the spear on the man.

He strode forward to thump on the door again, but heard the locking bar being drawn and so stepped back as the door opened and Berc'hed stood there, pulling a comb through her grey hair which was loose across her shoulders now.

'Last time I saw you, I had to drain the baths,' she griped. 'Do you know how long that takes? And to heat up all that water again?'

Beran ignored that. 'We need your help.'

'And why would I help you?' she asked, but she was not looking at Beran now. Rather she was looking round him to the young man and woman in the shadows behind. 'How far along are you, child?' she asked Isolde.

Beran stepped aside, letting the two women see each other.

'Three moons,' Isolde answered. 'But something is wrong.'

Berc'hed looked back to Beran. 'You killed one of my best customers,' she accused him.

Beran shook his head. 'Not me,' he said, which was true enough. 'But what do you expect, if you let Saxons use the baths?'

Berc'hed seemed to consider this as she studied Beran the way a smith might appraise a sword for defects, or the way Guivret might weigh up the virtues and faults in a horse.

'Bring them inside,' she said.

The dwelling was partitioned by wattle walls, and Berc'hed had Isolde lie on a bed of skins by a fire in the largest room while she examined her, placing her hands on Isolde's belly and, with tender care, pressing hereabouts and asking her where she felt the pain most. Three other women attended Berc'hed, being those who worked for her in that place and in the bathhouse next door, and they were gentle and kind in spite of their trade, one fetching Isolde a drink of warm wine with spices and honey, another burning rosemary in a dish and urging Isolde to breathe of the fragrant smoke for she said it would help calm her.

They fussed around Isolde, telling her that she was beautiful, that they envied her for her golden hair and fair complexion and for her handsome husband who loved her, and even for the unborn child in her belly which would, they all agreed, be beautiful to behold, be it a girl or a boy.

'We are not married,' Isolde said, smiling even through the pain.

'Being not married never made love less,' Berc'hed muttered, 'no more'n being married made love greater.'

'Still, we shall be married,' Isolde told her. 'And we shall love this child,' she added, sharing such a look of hope and fear with Tristan as made the eldest of the three whores kiss her on her head.

'If there is anything at all good about this world, that'll be so, dear girl,' the woman said.

Then, telling them that Tristan's dread-filled face and restless agitation were not helping Isolde one bit, Berc'hed ordered Beran to take the young man away, which Beran was glad to do, and so they sat in another room, each with a cup of sour wine and neither having any words worth the saying, until a young woman came in from the night and took one look at Tristan and asked if he wanted to spend the rest of it with her, for a price of course.

'We are not here . . . for that,' Tristan stammered in reply, his cheeks flushing red by the light of a foul-smelling fish-oil lamp, so that any other time Beran might have smiled at his discomfort. As it was, he sipped at the wine and idly watched the young woman rebraiding her long brown hair and blushing her cheeks in readiness for the next man with silver in his purse to knock on the door, while Tristan wrung his hands and clutched the back of his neck and paced the floor.

'Told you about the lump on that man's head,' Tristan said distantly, half looking for distractions.

'He's in the wrong line of work,' Beran said. Berc'hed had sent the guard back to his bed, which was probably for the best. 'Take a breath, lad. I've seen men your age look less afraid before their first shieldwall. I'd wager Berc'hed has seen this more times than she can count.'

Tristan stopped pacing and turned and stared at Beran in the gloom. 'Have you ever loved anyone so much that it's like a pain?' he asked. 'Here?' He struck his palm against his own chest.

Beran swallowed. 'I have.'

This seemed to catch Tristan off guard, as though he had not expected it. 'Who was she?' he asked.

Beran shook his head. He felt the young woman's eyes turn to rest on him too, but he looked at the rushlight rather than at either of them. Its sooty flame trailed up in a black tendril, like the malevolent spirit of some serpent questing where it was not wanted. There was a roaring in his head. He fought to quell it. He did not want it all to come gushing in on him, and yet he had her face in his mind now, and part of him wanted to cling to that, wanted her shade to stay a little longer.

'She was . . .' He stopped. His throat was tight, pressing in on itself as though trying to deny the words the air they needed to live. He took a breath and held it and let it go. 'She was my queen,' he said. He lifted a hand, wiping away a tear with a swollen knuckle. 'My . . . queen.'

There was silence then, but for the murmur of the women's voices through the wattle wall and the small hiss of the burning reed which was failing to dispel the darkness in that place. And for a while Beran lowered the shield which he had carried over his heart so many years, and allowed the ghosts of the past to thrust their unseen blades into him. More than that, he welcomed them, savouring the pain and torment of it. *This is what will kill me*, he thought. *This agony. And that is good. That is how it should be.*

'I'm sorry, Beran,' Tristan said.

Beran opened his eyes and through the blur of tears he saw the young man's face, unlined by age, unworn by the tragedy of life and the loss of all that made it sweet to draw breath. There was hope in Tristan's eyes still, and for a moment Beran saw what Tristan saw: a future with Isolde. A child whom they adored. A life lived beyond the blights of famine and war and disease. That is what the young man saw, and Beran could not resent him for it.

'I hope you have it all,' Beran said. And he meant it. Had never said truer words. 'I hope you and Isolde live as free as birds.'

Tristan stepped forward and Beran stood and they embraced each other, Beran feeling the man's heart beating fiercely against his own chest.

'Thank you, Beran,' Tristan said. They drew apart and then they turned to see Berc'hed standing in the shadow beyond the lamp glow's reach.

'She is healthy and strong,' she told Tristan, drying her hands on a piece of linen. 'Her hips could be wider, but they'll serve when the time comes.'

Tristan let out a great breath, leaning his head back and closing his eyes.

'The pains are not unusual after three moons,' Berc'hed went on, 'but I have given her hedge-garlic seed bruised and boiled in wine. That will help a little, but if you can find any of the tall yellow flower which the Romans call agrimonia and the Saxons call stickwort, you can crush it and make a draught with ale and it will take away her pain when it comes on.'

'And the child?' Beran asked.

Berc'hed smiled. 'Growing, as is their way,' she said, looking from Tristan to Beran, perhaps wondering who Beran was to the girl. 'She is a fortunate young woman to have the love of two good men.'

Beran felt dazed still. Haunted still, as though the ghosts of the past had not fully passed back through the veil but lingered yet in the dark corners, watching him.

'Thank you, Berc'hed, for your help,' he said.

'Tell us what we owe,' Tristan said, gesturing at Beran. 'My friend will pay.'

Beran eyed Tristan from beneath an arched brow. 'Yes, it's not as though you are rich and she a queen,' he mumbled, taking the purse from his belt.

'I want no payment,' Berc'hed said, holding up a big hand. 'You helped my friend that day in the baths. Uffa told me what happened.' She sighed. 'Bealdwulf was a jealous man.'

'You count Saxons amongst your friends?' Beran asked her.

She put her hands on her ample hips and inclined her head. 'You have lived long enough to know that the world is a tangled briar,' she told him. 'I daresay you've a few thorns in your own past, Beran ap whoever.'

Beran half smiled by way of admission, as Isolde came in, still arranging her clothes as Tristan went to her and folded his arms around her, she nestling into him, though her eyes met Beran's in silent thanks.

Berc'hed took them to the door and they said their goodbyes, stepping out onto the cobbled street. Beran looked to the sky above Portus Adurni's eastern wall, where night was retreating before the dawn. A lone gull flew seaward through the gloom, squealing as it went, so that Beran wondered if that was *her*, his once-love returning to the hereafter, for had she not used to journey in the bodies of birds and other creatures? And perhaps it was her fate to do so for ever.

'Keep her close until it's time,' Berc'hed called, and Beran knew she had aimed that at him as much as at Tristan, who was walking with his arm around Isolde. 'And look after that boy, Beran.'

'I will,' Beran called back, looking up at the dark sky in the wake of that lone gull's cry.

But the bird was lost to him now.

13

Damn the High King

THE STABLE DOOR FLEW open and in came Gawain, along with the rain and the sea wind which had been gusting across the heights of Tintagel for three days and nights. The horses skittered and snorted, and Arthur looked up from the milking stool he sat upon, bowl of pottage in one hand, spoon in the other.

Gawain loomed at the threshold as ill-portended as the day itself. 'There you are! I've been looking for you,' he said. The wind, swirling straw around, was fierce enough to rattle two chains which hung over a thickly cobwebbed and bird-dropping-bespattered beam beside an ox halter and an ancient, threadbare cloak.

'Here I am,' Arthur said, gesturing with the spoon at their dim surroundings. The four mares and two foals, which had seemed agitated by Gawain's intrusion into their sanctuary, were returning to their feed buckets again. 'Enjoying some peace,' Arthur said, then frowned. 'Well, I was, anyway.'

Gawain looked around the dark interior and up at the rafters, frowning at the old swallow nests of cup-shaped mud, and the thin patches in the thatch where rain was dripping through. Clearly, he wondered what Arthur was doing hiding in a stable, but he did not ask. 'You need to go ... somewhere else,' he said, stepping into the stable now and pushing the door closed on the weather, though one last gust threw rain into the place before the door thumped shut.

Those three days of fierce gales blowing in off the grey sea had left Tintagel battered, such that folk were starting to wonder if the gods disapproved of Lord Uther's accession to the throne of Dumnonia and the title of High King of Britain.

'Go where? What are you talking about?' Arthur asked.

Gawain palmed rain off his face and beard and swept his long hair back. 'There's a red-haired woman looking for you.' He sniffed and wiped his nose on the back of his hand. 'She's mad, Arthur.' He looked more afraid than he had in Ireland when two hundred screaming Gaels were chasing them back to the sea. 'When one of the servants told her I was your friend, she spat at me, then screamed a mouthful of curses at you as if you were standing right there. Said she's going to cut off your stones and slit your throat.'

Arthur put down the spoon, his appetite having fled like a skiff before the wind. 'Idiot,' he said to Gawain, who was squeezing his impressive beard with a fist that filled then dripped with water.

'Eh?' Gawain looked taken aback. 'What have I done?'

'Chances are she followed you here.' Arthur was already standing from the stool.

Gawain shook his head. 'There's no chance of that in this storm.'

Then the stable door opened and the mares spooked again, one snorting and tossing her head, another gnashing her teeth and pawing at the ground.

Morgaine did not stand in the doorway as Gawain had, but rather she flew at Arthur, as though she were the storm herself, and he found himself rooted to the spot, so that suddenly she was on him and the two of them fell together into the dust and grain and old straw and horse muck.

'I'll kill you, Arthur!' she screamed, and he saw the glint of a blade down near his groin and he squirmed backwards, at the same time reaching out to try to grab the hand holding that knife. 'You knew!' she yelled. 'You knew they were going to kill my son!'

'No!' He hauled his head back because she was trying to bite him, her mouth a snarl of vengeful teeth. 'No, it was to be left to the gods!' he blurted, taking hold of her right hand and wrenching the knife from its grasp and casting it into the straw. But this only made Morgaine wilder still, and she went at him like a falcon with deadly talons, clawing at his face.

'Liar!' she screeched. 'You knew! You're a devil!' He felt her fingernails gouge the skin of his left temple and rip down his cheek. 'I hate you!'

Then her weight upon him was gone, and so Arthur took his chance and scrambled back against the barn wall, glaring up at Morgaine, who shrieked like a fox in a trap. Gawain had hold of her, his brawny arms binding her so that she could not break free.

'Enough!' Gawain told her, pulling her backwards and away from Arthur, who felt like he had just been thrown from a horse and trampled on. 'Enough now!' Gawain said. 'No more, you mad bitch!'

'Get off me!' Morgaine screamed at him. 'Who are you to lay hands on me?' She was bucking in his arms, vicious as a sea storm, but try as she might she could not break his hold. She struggled and fought, but soon her strength was ebbing, her anger receding, and even the steel in her eyes dulled a little.

'He is our child!' she told Arthur, staring at him through tears of rage and frustration, ignoring the man holding her. 'Our child.'

Arthur's heart seemed to freeze in his chest. Then it was pounding again. 'What do you mean, *is* our child?' he asked, climbing to his feet, gesturing at Gawain to lessen his hold on Morgaine lest she be starved of breath.

Gawain obliged, his own expression curious now.

Arthur held up a hand, entreating Morgaine for a moment to gather himself before hearing more. He swallowed. 'The child lives?' he asked.

Morgaine eyed him through the wild tendrils of her fiery hair. 'He's alive,' she said. 'But you will not see him. You will not touch him.'

'I wouldn't hurt him,' Arthur said, offended, but it was in her eyes that she did not believe him.

'Let her go, Gawain,' Arthur said.

Gawain frowned and did not lessen his grip on her.

Arthur inclined his head. 'Do it,' he told his friend.

And so Gawain slowly let go of her. 'Easy now,' he breathed in a low voice, as one might use to a horse just broken yet still suspicious, and he stepped back, giving the young woman space.

To Arthur's relief, she did not fly at him again, but stood with her shoulders slumped and all her strength spent. Yet hatred still writhed in her pale face, like maggots squirming beneath the skin. 'He will never know that he is your blood,' she hissed. 'You are a monster like your father.' She lifted a hand and Arthur saw his blood on her fingernails. 'I curse you, Arthur ap Uther,' she said. 'In the name of the Morrigán, I curse you.'

He had no words now and so he said nothing.

Then Morgaine spat at him and turned and walked out of the stable, leaving the door swinging in the wind, and the rain hissing in the thatch, and Arthur and Gawain staring at one another like men newly come from a battle.

'I told you she was mad,' Gawain said.

'She has every right to be.' His heart still galloping, Arthur went over to a bright chestnut mare and began stroking her neck. 'Every right,' he said again. The mare shivered and nickered softly at his touch.

Gawain frowned. 'I wouldn't know about that. But I do know you shouldn't be in here.' He gestured towards the open stable door and Lord Uther's great timber-built hall on the wind-flayed plateau of Tintagel. 'People are asking where you are. They expect you to be present. Doubtless Lord Uther expects it too.'

Arthur put his lips to the mare's neck and kissed her. 'Haven't they finished yet?' he asked, wishing he could saddle the mare and ride out into the storm and forget about all of it. The lords and kings of Britain had been acclaiming Lord Uther since noon and Arthur had slipped away because he would rather the company of horses and the rough comfort of the stable than linger amongst those men thronging around his father's high seat, giving flattery and seeking favour.

'It will go on until dark, as well you know,' Gawain said.

Arthur straightened and put a hand to his cheek, which burned like fire from the scratches which Morgaine had given him. His fingers and palm came away bloody.

'Here.' Gawain produced a scrap of cloth from somewhere about his person and handed it to Arthur. 'Your father becomes High King today, Arthur. Which means *you* are heir to that high seat. Let us go and remind people of that.'

Arthur pressed the cloth to his face and held it there. 'Thank you,' he said, meaning for saving him from Morgaine and her tooth-and-nail fury.

Gawain nodded and smiled. 'She's a wild, red-haired beauty,' he admitted, grinning like a fiend, 'but I'd sooner go back across the sea to Ireland and piss in King Lugaid mac Lóegairi's ale before upsetting her again.'

'I'd sooner go back to Ireland than into that hall,' Arthur said, looking out across the wind-whipped tufts of bristling grass, above which a pair of tiny redwings swirled like autumn leaves, their *seep, seep* carrying on the wind.

But Arthur was Uther's son, and Uther was being acclaimed the High King of Britain, and so Arthur went to see it done.

Uther's hall, which had once belonged to another man, was heaving with the kings and queens, warlords and champions and princes and bards of Britain. They had come from a dozen kingdoms near and far, from Bernaccia and Ebrauc in the north, to Cornubia in the south, and even from several kingdoms across the Dividing Sea. Most had come to pay their respects, some to sue for peace, some to entreat the new High King to help them in their own wars, and others perhaps to weigh Uther in the scales against his brother Ambrosius, that they might determine what sort of man the new High King was, and thus might know how far they could test him. Like a man drawing a new bow to see how far it would bend.

Each had brought Uther a gift. Einion ap Mor, King of Northern Britain, brought him an ancient war chariot which had been used in battle against the Romans to the glory of Taranis and the war gods of these Dark Isles. Prince Cynfelyn of Cynwidion brought Uther a pair of white bulls. King Meirchion Gul of Rheged brought a cauldron made of gold. Menadoc, King of Cornubia, came bearing a beautiful leather saddle and halter, and a great boar spear which, he said, could only be wielded by a warrior of Uther's stature. From Cyngen Glodrydd, King of Powys, a sword sharp enough to cut the air, which men whispered was a threat as much as a gift, for raiders from Powys regularly wet their spears in Dumnonia, and some said Ambrosius, before he was murdered, had been muttering of war. From the Lady Nimue of Karrek, a dozen pots of salves and herbal tinctures, and bushels of dried herbs, and jars of remedies against all manner of ills, for her knowledge of herblore was famous in Britain and she wished Uther a long life and the strength to 'hold the coming dark'.

Arthur had purposefully missed the acclamation and ancient rites conducted by Merlin, and the oaths of fealty and the assurances of peace from those other kings and lords. He had missed most of the feasting, too, preferring to be alone in the stable with the mares, so when he came into King Uther's hall, it was as the mead was flowing and the tales were spilling from the mouths of bards, and some of the wiser kings were already saying their farewells and preparing to leave lest a sour look or drunken word lead to war between kingdoms.

'You look like you've been fighting with a polecat,' Gawain told Arthur as they pushed their way in amongst the crowd. 'A drink will dull the sting of it.'

'It will take more than a drink,' Arthur muttered, thinking of the infant who had somehow survived Uther's intentions. The guilt sat like a stone in Arthur's throat, so that he suspected it would take a barrel of ale to wash it down.

'Look,' someone hissed.

'Arthur,' someone else whispered, as he and Gawain forced their way towards Uther's table.

'See, it's Arthur.'

'Arthur's here!'

He heard his name on people's lips, but he avoided their eyes. Then someone grabbed his arm and he turned to look into Merlin's face.

'Where have you been, Arthur?' The druid's eyes flicked to the livid furrows on his head and cheek. 'Ah, so she found you, then?' He frowned. 'Well, never mind about all that now. Come and pay your respects to your father. In case it has escaped your notice, he has just been acclaimed High King. It was quite the moment, if I say so myself.'

'There he is!' a voice boomed, and the crowd parted to reveal King Uther glaring at Arthur from his bench at the high table. Hearth smoke hazed the air between them, and the hum in the hall faded like a wave dying on the shore, the crackling of the fire now the only sound. 'My son has decided to join us at last,' the new High King said, holding both arms out over the table, which was strewn with silver dishes and bowls and picked-at bones like a battlefield littered with the armour and corpses of the slain. 'We are honoured that you found the time, Arthur,' the king bellowed. 'Where have you been, boy?'

All eyes were on Arthur. He felt the weight of them like so much rain-soaked cloth. 'I've been seeing to the Queen's horses,' he said, catching the eye of his mother, who was sitting beside the King, a cup in her hand, her eyes warning Arthur against upsetting his father. Everyone knew it was too late for that.

'Ha!' Uther pointed a ringed finger at Arthur. 'You mean you've been rolling in the straw with some young mare,' he said. 'Whoever it was has left her mark on you by the looks.'

Arthur felt Gawain thrust a cup into his hand. 'Do it, Arthur,' he murmured.

Arthur gritted his teeth and lifted the cup high in the smoky air for all to see. 'I raise my cup in your honour, lord king,' he announced. 'My sword is yours.'

Uther frowned, and then his drunken eyes widened and his lips spread and then he began to laugh, holding his long beard in a fist and slamming his other hand down on the table, knocking over an empty cup and rattling the silverware. Some others in the hall half-heartedly echoed their lord's laughter, though not many. 'Your sword?' Uther bawled. 'I heard you and the *brave* men of Lyonesse were chased back to the coast by a pack of Gaels.' This got some genuine laughter, and Arthur felt Gawain beside him bristle.

'Lord king, Arthur fought bravely in Ireland by all accounts.' This from Merlin, who sought to smother these embers before they burst into flame. 'King Lot himself praised Arthur for his actions.'

'Did he? And where is King Lot?' Uther swept an arm through the fug. 'I thought he would be here today.'

Everyone knew that King Lot's old wound made it all but impossible to manage the climb to Uther's hall, nestled as it was like an eyrie, two hundred and fifty feet above a sea that hurled itself with relentless fury against the foot of the cliffs. There had been murmurs of amazement that King Meirchion of Rheged, whom men called Meirchion the Lean, had made it, for he was impossibly fat.

Gawain stepped forward. 'My father the king's old wound prevents him being here, lord, as everyone in this hall knows.' Gawain held his arms wide. That his hackles were up was obvious to anyone with eyes or ears. 'Nevertheless, he sent me with generous gifts to honour you,' he told Uther. 'Again, as everyone here knows.'

Uther batted Gawain's words aside with a hand, whilst picking up his cup and drinking deeply and dragging a hand across his beard and moustaches.

Merlin caught Arthur's eye and in that look warned him against saying more. Then Uther stood and lifted his cup. 'I drink to my brother,' he roared. 'Ambrosius, a true warrior and a great king!'

'Ambrosius!' men and women called in reply, raising their own cups in honour of the last High King, and the tension was broken then, as though a knife had cut the plucked string of a lyre, killing the last humming note.

'Uther, High King of Britain!' one man yelled.

'Uther! Uther! Uther!' they called in one voice.

'We've done our bit,' Arthur said to Gawain, who nodded and turned his shoulder as though to carve them a route back to the hall door.

'My lord king!' a voice called, as the tributes to the murdered king and his successor faded away. Arthur turned back as folk moved aside, revealing a short man with a narrow face and bright copper hair and beard. 'I have a question, lord king,' this richly dressed man said. A king himself by the looks.

A flutter of whispers rose to the roof beams, and Arthur looked from the copper-haired man to Merlin. 'Einion ap Mor, King of Ebrauc,' Merlin muttered in answer to his unspoken question. 'Nothing good will come of this, mark my words, Arthur.'

Uther extended a hand in the man's direction. 'Speak, King Einion,' he said.

Einion nodded respectfully, then took another step forward into the space the other lords had made for him. He glanced left and right, meeting other men's eyes for a heartbeat here, a heartbeat there. Then he looked back to Uther and lifted his chin. 'We have all gathered to acclaim you this day and see you made High King before the gods and according to the ancient laws. I have honoured you with a gift far beyond the worth of its weight in silver, for it is a sacred treasure of Britain. I do this because I know a warrior when I see one.' With that, he looked around again. 'Believe me,' he told the gathering, 'Britain will need a warrior in the time ahead. We will bury old grievances. Put aside our many differences. We will bring our spears to your banner, High King, for the darkness is coming and you will hold the flame.'

Arthur knew that his father was no fool, that Uther would not be blindsided by this flattery, though he also suspected idle flattery to be beyond a man like Einion, who more or less ruled in northern Britain.

'If there is something you want from me, King Einion,' Uther said, eyeing the man suspiciously, 'I will hear it in the morning along with a score of other petitions.'

'No petition, Uther.' King Einion shook his head. 'As I said, I and these other kings acknowledge your accession. We have pledged our spearmen to the dragon banner, should the need arise. What we want to know is, who do you name as your successor? If you fall in battle or if you are taken by disease . . .' He turned his hands, palms uppermost. 'Or, may the gods forbid it, should the assassin's blade strike again.' He glanced around the hall again. 'At such times, chaos can reign if there is no strong hand to keep a grip on the land and the dragon-carved throne of Dumnonia.'

Gawain looked at Arthur, who answered his look with the merest of shrugs. Then Merlin was in Arthur's ear, and Arthur caught the sweet, musky scent of burnt herbs on the druid's black gown: sage and mugwort. And the smoke of burnt juniper. 'Be gracious now, Arthur, whatever is said.'

'I shall not tempt Arawn by preparing for my death on the day of my acclamation,' Uther said.

'Your brother named no heir,' King Einion said, 'and it might have—'

'Because my brother knew it would be me,' Uther interrupted.

Einion nodded. 'Perhaps,' he admitted, 'but it might have sparked war had his son, Prince Constantine, been stronger. More ambitious. He is, after all, Ambrosius's first-born son.'

Eyes turned towards Prince Constantine then, whose clean-shaven face was unreadable through the smoke.

Uther straightened his back. 'Prince Constantine, do you believe I have robbed you of the right to rule?'

Arthur saw his cousin's eyes flick to King Einion, quick as an adder's tongue tasting the air, then settle back on King Uther. 'No, lord king,' he said. 'You are the warlord of Dumnonia, the spear and shield of Britain. You have my loyalty.'

This was well said, Arthur had to admit, and Uther looked back to King Einion and turned his hands out as if to say *there you have it*.

'Still, High King,' Einion said. 'We would know under whose banner our spearmen will fight in the event of your death.' With that, he held out a hand towards Prince Constantine. 'Will it be Constantine, who has pledged his loyalty before all of us here today?' He turned and gestured with his other hand at Arthur. 'Or, do you name your own son, Prince Arthur, recently returned from Lyonesse where he has earned some small fame fighting the Gaels?'

A snarl curled beneath the High King's long moustaches. 'Why do you push me on this, Einion?' he asked, lifting his cup towards Constantine, then swinging it across, wine sloshing over the rim, until it was raised in Arthur's direction. 'Neither of these pups has shown themselves worthy to be named my successor. Time will tell what kind of men they are. Their actions will show us all how much of their fathers' blood fills their veins.'

This raised whispers and murmurs in the hall, but Uther had not finished yet. He stood, and he loomed in that place, looking every inch the warrior king raised above all other kings in these Dark Isles.

'When the time comes, I may name one of you who are here in my hall this day. Or one of my brave spearmen. Or I may slaughter these white bulls from Cynwidion and ask Merlin to read their entrails and tell me whom I should choose, for he alone in Britain can make sense of the vagaries of the gods.' He threw the cup into the hearth, the remaining liquid sizzling in the flames, and some of the women in the hall gasped. 'I will make my decision when *I* choose to make it, and no man will squeeze it from me like milk from the teat.' The silver cup in the flames sat blazing brightly for a moment, then dulled like a dying eye and turned black. 'But I will not speak of it more. Not today.'

Arthur heard his name spoken in whispers again, and Constantine's too, and he burned with humiliation, for everyone under the High King's roof knew that he and his cousin had been openly slighted, if not insulted.

'Drink!' Uther bellowed. Lifting another cup, newly filled by a slave. 'Drink and make merry, in the name of the gods and your High King!'

The kings and lords of Britain cheered and raised Uther's name to the ancient, worm-holed roof beams.

'Pay it no mind, Arthur,' Merlin said. 'Your father is in his cups, as any king would be on such a day as this. I will talk to him.' He squeezed Arthur's shoulder and leant in close. 'Come in the morning, when he's pledging spearmen and silver to these beggars here in this hall. You'll find him in more generous mood then, if a little ale-tired.'

Arthur was watching his father, who was laughing and drinking with Deroch, King of Caer Gwinntguic, as the clamour once again filled the hall and someone started playing a drumbeat that sounded to Arthur like two horses at the gallop. He wondered if his father had been laughing and drinking thus when he had ordered some nameless man to take Morgaine's infant child – *his own child* – and drown it in a lake.

'You'll come?' Merlin asked. 'In the morning?'

Arthur did not answer him. A servant squeezed past them, carrying a wine jug in each hand, and Gawain stopped the man and relieved him of both.

'Come on, Arthur,' Gawain said. 'You were right. There's no reason to be here.'

Arthur nodded and he and Gawain pushed their way through the hall, past the most powerful men in Britain, and now hardly one of them paid Arthur any heed at all.

'How many more?' the High King growled, as a clerk who was clutching an armful of rolled parchments dropped one of them and stooped to recover it, only to spill more of these scrolls amongst the muddy rushes. He took up one scroll in particular and stood, handing it to Merlin. 'From King Gruffyd ap Gwrgan of Glywyssing, lord king,' the clerk said, for all the seals had been cracked, so that the man could sift through the petitions and only trouble his lord with the most important ones. Today, at least.

Merlin read, then looked at Uther, who was sitting beside the leaping hearth fire in his dragon-carved throne. 'He wants cattle. Thirty head. Heifers and steers. Says men of Dyfed stole two score over the summer and that he cannot send spearmen to your banner if he cannot rear strong lads because there is not enough meat for them.'

'Fuck him,' Uther said. He wore a heavy torc of twisted silver in which reflected flame played, turning the silver to red gold. 'Tell Gruffyd to keep a better watch on his cows.'

Merlin glanced at Arthur, who stood waiting beyond the reach of the fire's warmth, then frowned in Uther's direction. 'If you do not show generosity, Gruffyd will make war against Dyfed,' the druid said. 'And then neither kingdom will have any spearmen left to send us.'

Uther considered this, then sighed. 'Send him fifteen heifers and a bull. Gruffyd can make his own cows.'

Merlin smiled at that. 'That is . . . reasonable,' he said, accepting the next scroll from the clerk. The druid's face darkened as he read the petition. 'Queen Kanna of Rhegin sends her compliments. She would have been here for your accession but dares not bring so much as one spearman west and thus rob her people of a warrior. Since the death of her husband the king, who was killed fighting the Saxons, she has spent day and night looking to the survival of her kingdom.'

Merlin lifted his eyes to Uther, who was watching the flames as he listened. 'She begs you to send a war band,' he said. 'Forty men if you can spare them. She writes that six more keels have beached on the southern shore since the last Beltane fires. Her people have been driven north. More and more Saxon wolves are overwintering. She fears Rhegin cannot hold, and that her people will be scattered like leaves to the storm.'

Uther made a gruff sound in his throat as Queen Kanna's words settled in his mind. 'This will require three score spearmen. All killers. I will lead them myself.' He nodded, his lip curled as though he could already smell the iron tang of slaughter and hear the coarse clamour of ravens fighting over corpses. 'See if we can't thin these wolf packs.' He smiled grimly. 'Turn the Rhegin sea red and send some of their ships home crew-light.'

Merlin clearly thought this a fine idea, for his own eyes had caught alight, too. 'A show of strength so soon after your acclamation will help settle the other kings,' he agreed.

'Father?' Arthur said.

'Wait,' Uther said, holding up a hand.

'I would speak with you, Father,' Arthur continued. He had already waited through five petitions. Was he supposed to linger in the shadows like a slave leashed to its master's voice?

'I said, wait,' Uther snapped. 'Watch. Learn what it is to be a king.'

Arthur clamped his teeth together, throwing blades with his eyes, his hands knotting at his sides.

'Won't be long now, Arthur,' Merlin said, reading another parchment. 'Ah, King Syagrius. Still fighting the Franks in the forests of Gallia, just like his father before him. Still clinging to the last rump Roman state in northern Gaul. I'd wager that man will outlast the western Roman Empire itself.'

'And I suppose he wants me to send him Dumnonian spearmen to die in his forests? Good men, to be hacked down by Frankish axes.'

'Three score spearmen and ten strong horses which he will train for war and use in the Roman way.' Merlin looked at Uther. 'That is his request. He hopes that you will honour the agreements which

Ambrosius ever honoured while he lived.' One of the druid's brows lifted. 'And he hopes you enjoy the three score amphorae of wine which he sent as a gift on the day of your investiture.'

'A generous gift,' Uther admitted. 'But I cannot give him what he wants. Dumnonia is the beating heart and I must keep it strong.'

Merlin thought about this, pulling on his beard. 'We have horses, though,' he said. 'They are of no use to us in war. Send a score to Syagrius, thirty if we can find them, and they will be more valuable to him than even your spearmen.'

Now it was Uther's turn to weigh it up. 'And that will hold with the terms he and my brother observed?'

Merlin nodded. 'I believe it will. The king's envoy is hereabouts. I spoke with him last night. He means to sail home as soon as the wind is favourable, but if you were to send him back to Syagrius with the horses aboard, I suspect that would keep the king happy killing Franks for another season or three.'

'They'll bleed me dry,' Uther said to no one in particular. Then Merlin caught his eye, drawing his attention back to Arthur beyond the flames.

The king's fierce gaze raked over Arthur like a fire iron over coals, and Arthur felt the heat of enmity in his own blood.

'Well?' Uther said.

'You insulted me, Father,' Arthur said.

Uther grimaced. 'And you wait until now to tell me? Where have you been, sobbing into your mother's breast?' He sat back in the dragon-carved throne and folded arms that gleamed with warrior rings. 'If I thought a man had dishonoured me before the kings of Britain, I would have taken his head from his shoulders before laying my own head down for the night.'

Arthur bit his lip. Exhaled. 'I do not think Dumnonia would survive the deaths of two High Kings within a moon of each other.'

Uther liked that, from the look of the smile warping his lips. 'Not without a strong leader to keep everyone in their place,' he said. 'And that is what this kingdom will need when I am gone. We all know it, Einion included.' He swept an arm through the air. 'But I wasn't going to dance to his tune last night. Not on the night of my accession.' He grunted. 'Besides, whoever I'd have named, Einion would be in his ear from then on, promising him women and silver, swords, wine, grain . . . Yes, Einion would shape him like a lump of clay. Then, one morning whilst having a piss, I'd look down to see an assassin's knife in my ribs and hear Einion declaring himself High King and Dumnonia his hearth hound.'

Arthur saw the sense in this, though it did not excuse the insult. Nor Uther's lifelong neglect of him. Nor the attempted drowning of an infant boy.

'Am I to be acknowledged?' Arthur asked. 'As your heir? As a prince of the blood? As a warrior of Dumnonia?'

Uther sat forward, gripping the arms of his throne. 'Are you?' he asked. 'You tell me, Arthur.'

A heavy silence hung in the hall then, until Merlin broke it with a cough.

'We have more petitions to get through, Uther.' He held up a scroll. 'There is one here from—'

'Enough!' Uther stood from his chair and snatched the petition out of Merlin's hands and tore it in two, tossing the pieces aside. 'Enough begging for one day,' he said.

Merlin glanced at Arthur. 'The Fisher King will not be getting his Dumnonian oak, then,' he said.

Arthur ignored him, his glare still boring into Uther. 'You would have murdered my son,' he said.

'I would have spared you humiliation and the gods' retribution,' Uther countered. He pointed at Arthur. 'You yourself did nothing to stop it. I told you I would clean up your mess. You could have opposed me on it. You could have hidden the child or warned its mother, but you did nothing. Just like you did nothing last evening when you believed yourself insulted.'

'I despise you,' Arthur said.

Uther nodded. 'Good. Good, Arthur. Do not hide it like a knife beneath the cloak. Be a man.' He held his arms wide, the bulk of him bronzed by the hearth fire. 'Come at me, boy. Fight me!'

Merlin held up his right hand towards Arthur, whilst looking at his king. 'No, Uther,' he said. 'I cannot have this.'

'Leave us, druid,' Uther said without looking at Merlin. He lifted his arm and fluttered his fingers and thumb together. 'Go and whisper to the gods and leave us to fight like men.'

Arthur shook his head. 'I will not fight you, Father,' he said. He had told Uther that he hated him, and that had felt good, like the lancing of an angry boil. It was enough for now.

'Then, what will you do, my son?' the king asked, the challenge clear in his words.

Arthur held his eye. 'I will fight,' he said, 'but not here. And not for you.'

With that, he turned and strode past the rippling hearth flame and out of Uther's hall. He went into the grey day to find the envoy of King Syagrius, last Roman general in northern Gaul. Because Arthur would be on that man's ship with twenty good horses or more as soon as the wind blew kindly. He would go to Gaul and fight the Franks and make his name. Damn Dumnonia. And damn its High King.

The *Osprey* did not carry Beran and the boy west along the coast to Tintagel when they had hoped, for its repair was taking longer than expected.

'A few more days,' Rivanon told them when they went to see her a second time. 'The damage was worse than we thought, and our smith is making an iron brace to strengthen the new timbers.'

Nor would Viamundus's ship, *Minerva*, bear the Little King and his horses and Isolde and Tristan across the Dividing Sea to Benoic, because the commander of Portus Adurni was trying to settle a dispute between merchants.

'A cloth-seller from Bro-Dreger has twelve bales in *Minerva's* hold,' Rivanon explained. 'But he will not let them be brought ashore until the buyer pays the price that he says was agreed last spring.'

'There will be no room for my horses until the ship is unloaded,' Guivret muttered.

Rivanon shrugged. 'You know how these things are. I will fetch you the moment Viamundus resolves the matter,' she said.

And so there had been nothing to do but wait within the walls of the fort, watching craftsmen at work, or talking with traders, or looking out across the iron sea. Until at last, one fair dawn, when Portus Adurni was bustling beneath a weak autumn sun, and gulls wheeled and tumbled in a chill wind that whispered of winter, a messenger from Rivanon found Beran and the boy on the wall overlooking the harbour and told them that *Minerva* was ready for Guivret's horses.

They went first to the stables, where they found Palamedes and the Little King already preparing to leave, the Saracen feeding the black stallion grain from his own hand while the dwarf settled his account with Meriadec, whose stables these were.

'A fine day to be at sea,' Beran said, as Meriadec left with his coin and they loaded the horses, Guivret passing Beran each saddle, because the Little King could not reach the animals' backs himself.

'It's not too late to change your mind, Beran,' he said. 'The boy will be safe with us far from here.'

Beran shook his head. 'We all have our path,' he replied, securing Isolde's rolled-up furs to the saddle and watching the boy, who was saying goodbye to each of the horses in turn, whispering in their ears and stroking their necks.

Tristan and Isolde came soon after, both thrumming with excitement at starting a new life together in Armorica. 'I was beginning to think we would grow old here inside these walls,' Tristan said, looking up at the gulls careening above one of the Roman-built towers as though he envied the birds their freedom. He shared a smile with Isolde, who had wrapped her arms around the boy and now tickled him, making him giggle.

'Our son or daughter . . .' Isolde grinned, 'I think daughter . . . will not live trapped like some poor animal in a pen. She will visit the markets with her mother and hunt with her father in the woods.'

'It sounds like a good life,' the boy said, as though trying to imagine it for himself.

Beran knew of another girl who had lived wild and unfettered, roaming the Avalon marshes, stalking amongst the reeds and withies, a predator in the low-lying mists, for she had hunted Saxons as much as water fowl.

'But I wish you weren't going,' the boy said to Isolde, looking up into her eyes.

'I know, my brave boy.' Isolde buried a kiss amongst his messy hair. 'But we have no choice if we want to be free.' Again, she looked at Tristan, who gave the slightest nod, like a seal upon an agreement which had long been written in tears and blood and in oaths proclaimed by beating hearts.

Beran saw Guivret watching them, his expression grave, and it seemed to Beran that the dwarf was sad at the prospect of leaving the boy. Or maybe something else troubled the Little King. Nerves perhaps, at leaving Britain and all but starting again in Benoic. Whatever it was, it showed in the two vertical furrows between his eyes. And in his twisting of the ring on his forefinger whenever his hands were not busy with some other task, such as now, as he went and stood with his back to them all, looking out from the stable, the wind rippling his beard as it would soon ripple *Minerva*'s sail.

'Save the gloomy farewells for later,' the dwarf said over his shoulder. 'We've work to do.' And with that, he set off along the cobbled road, expecting the others to lead the horses after.

Palamedes looked at Beran. 'We'll get these aboard and settled first,' he said, patting a mare's flank, 'before Rivanon sees them and realizes she could have done better out of their arrangement.'

'Nobody gets the better of the dwarf,' Beran said, leading the stallion by his reins and wishing he had the silver on him to buy the animal from Guivret, though he supposed even if he had, he would then have to pay for the stallion's passage aboard Rivanon's ship, and for whichever horse the boy rode also.

No, he did not need such a fine horse, not any more, for all that in that moment he recalled some part of last night's dream. Three score horses or more, galloping across hard ground. Whinnies and grunts, hot breath and hooves drumming so that thunder rolled as if within the earth itself. He remembered no more of the dream, but that part echoed in his mind, and Beran wondered if this was some trick of old age. The mind reaching back, trying to grasp the past to distract an old man in his last days. Like a sleight of hand making it easier for death to creep up on him.

No need to creep, he thought. *I am nearly ready. And I am not afraid. But first let me keep my word to the boy. That is all I ask.*

So they led the horses through the busy streets towards the sea gate, each of them immersed in their own thoughts, taking in the sights, sounds and smells of Portus Adurni a final time before their little group split apart. And somewhere beyond the veil, in Anwnn, where old age and disease held no sway, the lord of the Otherworld kingdom was preparing a table of abundant delights.

14

The Lovers

BERAN LED THE STALLION up the boarding planks and onto *Minerva* himself, for he knew even the proudest and noblest horse could be reduced to teeth-gnashing, eye-rolling fear by the prospect of boarding a ship swaying and dipping with the movement of the sea. The wind was getting up, too, and Beran had never known a horse that liked the wind.

'Easy, boy. There now, all is well,' he soothed, stroking the stallion's glossy black neck where the jagged veins pulsed beneath the skin. 'This is nothing to you. A brave boy like you. Don't let the others think you're afraid.' And the stallion tossed his great head and nickered softly, his nostrils flaring with the salt tang of the sea, and the pine-tarred rigging, the rotten stink of the dank bilgewater, and the horse fat which waterproofed the sail and helped it hold the wind. Smells that tugged at Beran's memory, recalling his own journey across the Dividing Sea. Long ago now.

'I hope you find a worthy friend in Benoic,' he told the horse. 'Someone who will feed you well and brush your coat, and let you gallop when the spirit is in you.' Then he put his forehead against the beast's muzzle. 'Be brave, but don't be too proud, you hear? There's a good boy.'

Seeing the stallion aboard and calmly eating out of Beran's hand, the other four horses followed without complaint, Palamedes and Tristan leading them up the planks, all making what haste they could, for they still had to fetch the remaining horses from the paddock and stow them before the ebb tide.

Guivret, Isolde and the boy watched from the timber wharf where old fishermen sat mending nets and a crew unloaded their pre-dawn catch, and some of the fort folk had gathered, drawn by the decisive commotion of a ship preparing to set sail on a fine, wind-blown day.

Viamundus himself was there to oversee the loading of his ship, and he bellowed orders at the men hefting bales of wool and heavy crates of tin ingots from the mines of Cornubia, and even five slaves from the markets on the Liffey: three women and two men who would likely live out the remainder of their lives far from home and loved ones, toiling for some lord in Armorica.

It was the commander of Portus Adurni, standing there giving orders like some general on the battlefield, that caused the first knot of uneasiness to draw tight in Beran's stomach as he crossed the boarding ramp back onto the wharf. His duty to the stallion discharged now, his eyes and ears and senses were his own again. And something wasn't right.

'Palamedes,' he called out to the Saracen, who was crossing the planks behind him, leaving Tristan aboard to settle the grey mare.

Palamedes followed Beran's line of sight with his own, his gaze coming to rest on Viamundus, who had been joined by Rivanon the merchant now, the two of them discussing weighty matters by the looks.

'Let me guess,' the Saracen said. 'You are thinking, why is he wearing mail to the loading of a ship?'

It was not so easy to see beneath his great cloak, which Viamundus wore gathered around himself against the chill wind, but Palamedes had spied it: the sea grey of ringmail at the fort commander's neck.

'And there, see?' Beran nodded at a knot of six Portus Adurni spearmen standing by the huts that served as storehouses for goods coming and going by sea.

'There are always a few down here when there's a ship in harbour,' Palamedes said.

Beran nodded. 'Look again,' he said. 'Do those men look bored to you?' Then he swept an arm out, drawing the Saracen's gaze along the various clusters of folk on the wharf going about their business. 'There's no danger here. Nothing for them to do. Bored spearmen sit down. They play dice. Talk to pretty girls.' He looked back to the garrison men. 'They don't stand like that.'

'Maybe they are waiting for him to leave,' Palamedes suggested, nodding at Viamundus.

'Maybe,' Beran said. 'But I think they are waiting for something to happen.'

Beran turned around and looked up at the south wall and tower, where there were usually a half-dozen more spearmen stationed. There were at least twelve up there now and, so far as Beran could see, most of them held not spears but bows.

'Beran.' Palamedes drew his attention to a man walking towards them from the sea gate. A short man with a neat grey beard. No discoloured lump on his forehead now, but Beran recognized the man as the guard who worked for Berc'hed. His face was all clenched jaw and hate-filled eyes as he came up to them, managing a respectful nod to Palamedes before turning to Beran, his cheeks flushing with humiliation.

'Berc'hed sent me,' he said, 'else I wouldn't be here.'

'Go on,' Beran said.

The man's teeth dragged at his bottom lip as he hesitated, as though even now he was thinking of saying nothing after all, but simply turning around and going back the way he had come. He sighed. 'Berc'hed said to tell you to take the girl and go. The one with child.' He jerked his neat beard in Isolde's direction. 'They are coming for her.'

'Who is coming?' Beran asked.

'Blue cloaks. Cornubians,' Berc'hed's man said. 'You must go now. Hide if you can.' He looked over his shoulder back towards the sea gate. 'I tell you, they're coming. They were right behind me.'

Beran's stomach sank like an anchor stone dropped overboard into the depths. He turned and looked at Isolde, who was holding hands with the boy, the two of them walking along the wharf together, the sea wind in their hair.

'What do we do?' Palamedes said, as Berc'hed's man turned and walked back towards the fort, his task discharged.

Beran's mind reeled. He looked across the wharf, where Guivret stood with their belongings, which included their spears. Then he saw the dwarf nod at someone, and he followed the little man's eye line and saw Rivanon. Having given Guivret some sort of signal, the merchant looked back towards the fort's sea gate, and so too did Beran, and what he saw then set his heartbeat thrashing in his ears like waves breaking on rocks.

'Tristan!' Beran yelled, turning back to *Minerva*. Palamedes was already running towards Isolde and the boy.

Tristan hurried across the boarding ramp, and Beran saw the young man's eyes widen as they took in the sight. Spearmen striding out of the sea gate towards the wharf. Towards them. A score at least, with blue cloaks and shields painted with rays of yellow ochre and red so that they looked like suns.

'No!' Tristan called. 'No, it can't be!'

But it was, and at the head of these Cornubian spearmen was a man in a cloak of lighter blue than the others, and that cloak was fastened at his left shoulder by a silver brooch whose pin was as long as a knife. He wore a long tunic of mail, the rings polished and gleaming in the autumn sun, and at his hip was scabbarded a sword whose hilt glittered with gold and garnets. And Beran knew that they were looking at King Mark, lord of Cornubia, uncle of Tristan and husband of Isolde.

'Put it down!' a man shouted. Beran realized he had drawn his own sword, and he turned to see the six Portus Adurni spearmen coming towards them arrayed in a crescent formation, spears levelled.

'Put it down, now!' one of them demanded.

Tristan was running, but more of Viamundus's men had appeared from somewhere – one of the storehouses, Beran guessed – and they now blocked Tristan's way to Isolde, who stood there holding the boy tight to her breast, their faces ashen but their eyes bright.

'Won't tell you again, old man,' the one leading the garrison men said, jerking his spear to the side in a gesture to show Beran what he should do with his sword.

Beran looked across the wharf, past folk running this way and that as they hurried to be somewhere else. He saw Palamedes put himself in front of Isolde and the boy, his spear threatening Viamundus's men, and he knew that the Saracen would give his life here and now in protection of her. As Beran would himself.

'You deaf, old man?' Beran heard all right, but he was looking at Guivret, who must have sensed his glare because he looked back at Beran.

And his expression told Beran everything.

'I'll kill you,' Beran muttered, and though the Little King could not hear the words, he felt the ire across the distance. Perhaps he felt ashamed, too, for his eyes fell from Beran's, like a hand above a flame unable to bear the heat any longer.

'They're just here for the girl and the young man from Cornubia,'

Viamundus bellowed, throwing his cloak back to free his sword arm as he strode over to meet King Mark, his booted feet clumping on the timber boards.

The six spearmen had edged closer to Beran now, so that he could have reached out and touched their spear blades with his sword. 'You'll die if you don't put down that blade,' the leader of the garrison men said.

There were some bowmen amongst the blue-cloaks, and four of them had arrows nocked and aimed at the boy and Isolde, so Palamedes was left with no choice but to back off, though he bristled and strained against his own good sense, to be let off the leash and to kill.

'You heard Viamundus,' the garrison man told Beran. 'This isn't about you. This is King Mark's business. Just sheathe that sword before someone spills blood that needn't be spilled.'

Something struck Beran in the back of his head, and he stumbled forward, and then they were on him, two men holding his sword arm, two his free arm, the one behind who had hit him with the butt of his spear now throwing his arms around Beran and binding him, while their leader brought his spear blade up to Beran's throat.

'Don't hurt him!' This from Rivanon who, along with Guivret, was remonstrating with Viamundus now, demanding he not renege on their agreement, whatever that agreement was. Beran watched through the swarm of black motes blurring his vision, as Tristan was hauled in front of King Mark.

'What have they to do with you, eh?' the man holding a spear to Beran's throat asked, but Beran ignored him. He was watching King Mark, whom he saw properly now for the first time. The King of Cornubia was richly dressed, and he looked every inch a king, but his face was a mask of anguish. His eyes were sunken and red, the skin beneath them swollen and dark. His beard, brown though shot with grey, was unkempt, and the skin of his lips was ragged and bloody, as were the quicks of his fingers which he held pressed to those lips now as he looked not at Tristan before him, but at Isolde, whom his blue-cloaked men were trying to separate from the boy.

He loves her. He loves her but he knows that she is not his. That she does not love him as she loves another. Beran felt that he knew the King of Cornubia then. Knew him heart and soul. He was broken, like a spear snapped in battle, only it was no battle that had ruined this man.

'Please!' Isolde screamed as the blue-cloaks finally got a grip of the boy and hauled him away, though he kicked and fought savagely.

'Don't hurt the boy!' Guivret yelled, and some of the blue-cloaks laughed at him, for they saw only a dwarf and not the Little King.

'Please, lord, the boy has nothing to do with this,' Tristan said, and King Mark flapped a hand at his spearmen. They let go of the boy, who ran into Palamedes' open arms.

'I've got you, boy,' the Saracen said. 'They won't touch you again.'

'I'm sorry, Uncle,' Tristan said, and with that he dropped to his knees before his king, his face turned up to the man, tears standing in his eyes. 'I love her,' he said, his eyes finding Isolde's for a heartbeat before he looked back to the king. 'I love her and she loves me.' He swallowed, his hands clenching and unclenching, like things trying to breathe.

A hush had fallen across those on the wharf, and across the fort as a whole, or so it seemed, as though every ear in Portus Adurni strained to hear the words being spoken. And yet the King of Cornubia did not speak. The tide lapped at the rocks and timbers, and *Minerva* and the *Osprey* creaked at their moorings, and gulls shrieked overhead. But King Mark said nothing.

'Uncle, please,' Tristan implored, his handsome face drained of blood as he held his king's gaze, desperate for the man to say something. 'We did not mean for any of this to happen. We tried to stop it. Isolde would not see me. She would not countenance my being at court.' He shook his head. 'But I could not be away from her. I would rather have died.'

King Mark just stared down at him with those tired, washed-out eyes.

'Do not blame her, lord, for she meant no dishonour. I swear it. I am to blame for all of it. It was I who pursued Isolde, for I could not take a breath without her.' He pressed a hand against his chest. 'There was no air in my lungs when we were apart. She is my—'

King Mark raised a hand as if to stop Tristan's next words, as though forcing a bung into a flask.

But Tristan defied him even then. 'She is my life,' he said, his eyes now on Isolde, whose fair cheeks glistened with tears. Then he looked at the king. 'She is my life,' he said again, in a quiet but firm voice, and then he bowed his head like a penitent awaiting some final judgement.

'Let them be, lord king,' Beran called. 'There is nothing you can do to stop what is already done.'

King Mark turned his head and regarded Beran with the unseeing eyes of a man full of wine or ale, or a warrior grievously wounded, which, in truth, he was.

'She was never yours.' Beran's throat wanted to strangle the words, but the words would not stay unsaid. 'Never yours, lord king,' he said.

'Shut your mouth, old man,' the leader of the garrison men snarled, reversing his spear and ramming the butt end into Beran's stomach, driving the breath out to leave him gasping and bent double, arms still in the grip of Viamundus's men.

King Mark held his gaze on Beran a moment longer, perhaps wondering who this man was, then he turned back to Tristan, tilting his head on one side as he regarded the young man whom he had hunted across Britain and who now knelt before him, his slave and yet also his master.

Beran watched this king through the blur of his own tears. Watched this ruined vessel and felt the man's pain as his own, and all the lonely years fell away from Beran, and it was as though he was looking at himself.

'It's all right, Tristan,' King Mark said, holding out his hands. 'Stand, nephew.'

Tristan lifted up his eyes, then his head.

'It's all right,' the king said again. 'Come, Tristan. You know you have always been like a son to me.'

Tristan glanced at Isolde, who shook her head at him, the sea breeze whipping her golden hair across her face, yet slowly Tristan stood, stiffly, hands clenched, his eyes full of suspicion but of hope too as he looked at the king. And the king smiled, his arms still outstretched.

'It's all right,' King Mark said again, and Tristan stepped into his open arms, slowly bringing his own arms up to return the embrace, his hands clutching his uncle's sky-blue cloak.

'I'm sorry, lord king,' Tristan said. 'Please forgive me.'

Beran saw the king's lips moving against the young man's crow-black hair, though he could not hear the words which the king spoke. Then he saw King Mark's right hand fall to his belt and draw a knife, and Beran cried out – too late – as the king punched the blade into Tristan's side. The young man's hands twisted in the snarl of that blue cloak, and the king pulled the knife out before driving it home again, and Beran fought against the men holding him, but he could not break free.

'No!' Beran yelled. 'No!' The knife came out bloody, then burrowed deep once more, and Tristan's legs buckled but he clung on still, and the king clung on, and his blue-cloaked warriors just stood there and watched it.

Isolde was screaming, and the horses aboard Minerva shrieked as if in echo, as if they sensed her pain. Then King Mark simply stepped back, and Tristan fell to his knees once again.

'Tristan!' Isolde wailed, ripping a hank of golden hair from her scalp as she staggered towards her love, her eyes wild and the sinews in her neck straining.

The king nodded to one of his archers, and the man raised his bow in Isolde's direction, and then the king turned his face away, for he could not watch.

Beran was rage itself, bellowing like a bull, spittle flying and hanging in his beard as he fought against the strong arms binding him, but he could not break free, and the archer loosed.

'No!' he roared as the arrow streaked, and Isolde jerked and looked down and saw the goose-feathered shaft sticking out of her belly.

Three more archers stepped forward and drew and loosed, just as Isolde lifted her head again, their arrows thumping into her body, two into her chest, the third burying itself in her right shoulder. Her eyes were wide and terrible as she stumbled forward, somehow still on her feet, towards Tristan, and now came a low rumble from the warriors gathered in that place, for none liked to see this abhorrent thing, and they cursed under their breath or looked away, or muttered that it was ill-doing.

The boy was screaming but Palamedes held him tight. Guivret stood with his hands pressed to his mouth, shaking his head as though to rid himself of a foul dream, as Isolde's will failed her now and she fell to her knees, two spear lengths from the man she loved.

'Gods,' Beran moaned, his own strength gone now, drained like the blood of those young lovers seeping through gaps between the wharf timbers, his body like a dead weight hanging from the spearmen holding him. But he watched. He could not turn his face away, as King Mark had done, and he saw Tristan, who lay curled around his own pain and ruin, lift his eyes to Isolde. He saw the young man grimace, blood frothing at his teeth with each breath, and summon from somewhere the will to defy the shadow of Arawn which was even now bearing his spirit through the veil. He dragged himself along, through the dark pool of his own hot blood, as Isolde knelt a moment longer, the fletchings of those cruel arrows bristling in the breeze. One knee forward, two knees forward, and then she fell on her side, feet pushing for purchase, her left arm reaching through the grit and dirt until, with arms outstretched, their fingers and palms met and clasped and they laid down their heads, their last weakening heartbeats felt in the fading throb of the other's hand.

And so they slipped from this world into Anwnn's realm together, lovers still. Young, still.

King Mark wept then. He went over to the bodies of his wife and his nephew and he fell down beside them, burying his face in Isolde's hair. The King of Cornubia wept bitter tears amongst her golden hair, and his warriors, not knowing what to do, just stood around, talking in low voices with the Portus Adurni spearmen, waiting for their king's orders.

The garrison men let Beran go, and he found that his legs were weak, and so he sank to the timbers and sat for a while, watching the broken king and feeling the air on the open wounds of his own past.

'I didn't know,' Guivret said, and Beran looked up, blinking his tear-brimmed eyes to see the Little King standing there, one hand raised, the other on the hilt of his Saxon long knife, as though he suspected he might need to defend himself. But Beran was weak with grief, and from struggling in vain against Viamundus's men, and there had already been too much blood that autumn day. 'I just thought King Mark would take them back to Cornubia.' The dwarf was pale and frowning, and angry too, in the way that all traders are who feel that they have been duped.

'You sold them out.' Beran despised the man then. 'You treacherous bastard.'

'I had no choice, Beran,' Guivret said. 'Viamundus knows about the boy. There was a cloth merchant here not long after we arrived. The man recognized the boy from Caer Colun. He told Viamundus, who told Rivanon.' He looked over at the merchant, who was standing with the commander of the fort, and his eyes were sharp with malice. 'She told me that she would not be able to make Viamundus keep the secret, that his intention was to imprison the prince and send word to Lord Cyndaf in Caer Celemion.'

'Cyndaf is an eel.' Beran spat. He had known Cyndaf in another life and his memory of the man still sat in his mind like curdled milk. 'He'd as soon sell the boy to Queen Morgana as keep him safe.'

Guivret shook his head. 'I knew that if word got out about the boy, his life would be measured in days.'

Beran understood now. 'So you gave him Tristan and Isolde instead. And he and your friend have kept us here while they sent word to King Mark, feigning problems with their ships, giving him time to get here.'

The Little King denied none of it. 'I couldn't give them the boy.' His eyes held Beran's eyes. Then he raised both his hands. 'I never thought King Mark would do this. I swear it, Beran.' He inclined his head then, as one about to dare words which might bite. 'But it was only a matter of time for those two.' He half turned his head in the direction of the dead lovers and the king who had murdered and now mourned them. 'That man would have hunted them to the end of the world. You know it, Beran.'

Beran did know it. Still, he said, 'They might have made it. They had a chance.'

The dwarf sighed. 'It was them or you and the boy. And I've known you a long time. Known the boy long enough. Long enough to know he's important.'

Beran said nothing to that. He remembered a thin dawn long ago. And *her*. Chained to a stake. Their eyes in each other. Talons snarled in talons. Roots entwined in roots. The wind-whipped firebrand in his own hand, then the crackle of the first flames questing amongst dry straw and wicker, and tendrils of foul yellow smoke. He remembered *him*, coming for her, galloping on a black horse, his bronze scale armour shining like the sun, his helmet trailing a long white plume. A lord of war. Chaos and blood then, like some dark ritual sealing the lovers' matrimony.

He had watched them ride away together, a wound that this Cornubian king would never suffer now, though Beran did not envy the man.

The blood which King Mark had spilled this day, as young and vibrant as it had been, was as poison now, and it would be the king's death.

Beran stood, and two or three of the blue-cloaks watched him, gripping their spears a little tighter, but he had no fight left in him. No anger, either. Just misery, dark and fetid as the water trapped in *Minerva*'s bilge. The spearmen seemed to recognize this and so they turned away.

'They're taking them back to Cornubia,' Palamedes said. Beran turned, as if in a daze, and saw the Saracen and the boy standing there. The boy's eyes were raw with tears, his breathing was ragged, and he was trembling.

'The baby, Beran,' the boy said with stuttering voice.

'I know.' Beran went to the boy and put his arms around him, at which the boy's tears came again. 'I know,' Beran said again, not knowing what else to say. He saw that King Mark had gathered himself now, and stood looking up at the sky while his men set about moving the bodies.

'Come, Palamedes,' Guivret said softly, 'the captain won't wait, and we still have to fetch the other horses.'

'Did you know?' Beran asked the Saracen.

Palamedes frowned. 'Did I know what?'

Still holding the boy close, Beran dipped his head to indicate Guivret. 'That he had sold them out to Rivanon and that bastard Viamundus?'

Palamedes looked at the dwarf with such an expression of disgust as told Beran what he needed to know.

'It was them or the boy,' Guivret explained to Palamedes now, but he spoke with weary resignation, as though the whole thing was well beyond the defence of reason. 'I could not have known King Mark would do this.' He firmed his jaw, his beard jutting. 'But the boy is more important. We all know it.'

The boy pulled away from Beran and turned to face the dwarf. 'I don't want it, any of it,' he said, arming tears and snot from his face. 'I don't want to be important. I want them to be alive.'

'I'm sorry,' the Little King said, and Beran realized this was the first time he'd ever heard the word pass Guivret's lips.

But the boy would not meet his eye, instead looking down at the wharf timbers and through the gaps between them, where the sea churned with a suck and plunge.

'Will you help me with the horses, Erbin,' Beran said, keeping his voice low so that no one else would hear the boy's name. It was the first time he had called the boy by it, and the boy looked up at him, his eyes acknowledging the fact. 'They'll be afraid, but they like you,' Beran added.

'And we need the help,' Palamedes said.

The boy nodded, and the four of them set about fetching the remaining ten horses from the paddock, leaving the chestnut mare which Rivanon had chosen as payment for helping to persuade Viamundus to grant Guivret and his horses passage aboard *Minerva*.

They spoke little as they completed this last task, the absence of Isolde and Tristan a weight which each of them carried. Then, when it was done and all the animals were aboard, and *Minerva* was ready to set sail, Guivret approached Beran and the boy. He came warily, like a man who fears getting too close to a fire.

'I'm sorry, Prince Erbin,' he said.

The boy turned his face away. He still would not look at the man.

'Beran?' Guivret said. He looked tired. Resigned.

Beran shook his head. 'If I ever see you again, I will kill you for what you have done.'

Guivret's mouth began to shape some reply, but he chose to leave whatever it was unspoken, merely shaking his head as one who knows there is nothing more to be said or done. Then he turned and walked back towards *Minerva*.

But, after his little legs had carried him twelve paces, he stopped and turned back to them once more. 'Come, Palamedes,' he said, avoiding Beran's eye.

The Saracen shook his head. 'No, lord. I am going to stay. I am going to help Beran get the boy to Camelot.'

Guivret's shoulders slumped. He threw a hand out towards Palamedes. 'But what will I do without you?' he asked.

'You are the Little King,' Palamedes said, as though that was all that needed saying.

Guivret shook his head, muttering into his beard, and turned and walked away.

'You're coming with us?' the boy asked Palamedes, as one who dares not fully believe what he has heard.

The Saracen gave a sad smile. 'If you will have me,' he said, then swept an arm towards the boy. 'You are the future of Britain. Beran must think it, too, or else he would not still be standing here.'

'I told you.' Beran folded his arms. 'Said I would take him to Camelot. What happens after is not my concern.'

Palamedes gave a placating nod, though he sent Beran a look which held secrets.

They watched *Minerva* slip her moorings and turn her bows into the harbour, her sail snapping loudly as it filled with the early autumn breeze, her captain aiming for the narrow channel beyond which the open sea waited.

'We need to leave,' Palamedes said, before the ship was a good arrow's flight from shore. 'I don't trust Viamundus not to come for the boy. Or Rivanon not to sell his whereabouts to whoever she thinks would pay well.'

'You want to walk across Saxon land?' Beran asked him.

The Saracen's brows drew together. 'You think we should wait for the *Osprey*?'

Beran did not know what he thought. He looked to the place where the young lovers had died. A black and grey dog stood there now, licking at a pool of congealed blood. Of Tristan and Isolde there was no other sign; they might never have been in this place, nor any place that would remember them. Their lives measured in a season's turn. Their illicit love nothing but a breath of wind passing through the crown of an autumn beech, briefly stirring the golden leaves.

King Mark and his blue-cloaked spearmen had gone, that broken king following the sun westward, back to his kingdom of sorrow. The folk of Portus Adurni were going about their business as usual, and perhaps the day seemed like any other now.

But Beran was not the same. The past swirled all around him, and in him, like the seabed, whipped up by storm-driven waves, clouding the water, so that the world was opaque.

'Beran?' someone said.

He had the notion that he might be dreaming. Perhaps he was sitting in the shade of a tree even now, waiting for death. And his mind had conjured Tristan and Isolde from some old tale. A trick of a dying mind, like a bard singing the old familiar tune but changing the people in the story. Showing Beran what might have been. A ruse to make him drag up what should have remained submerged.

'Beran, what is it?'

Or, if it were not some apparition, and he really was standing here on the southern shore now, then surely it was the old gods of Britain tormenting him, punishing him one last time for all his failures. Making good on the curse promised long ago.

He startled. The Saracen's hand was on his shoulder. 'Beran, you don't look well.'

'I'm breathing, aren't I?' Beran said.

Palamedes grimaced and glanced at the boy, who returned his furrowed brow.

'We'll give it two days,' Palamedes said. 'If the *Osprey* sets sail, we'll be on it. If not, we'll risk the journey on foot.'

Beran felt a breeze on his right cheek and turned his head. He saw a crow there, standing on his shoulder, head twitching, watching him. He could see the ghost of himself in its dark, glossy eye. He shivered. Hadn't Isolde said that the Morrigán perched on Beran's shoulder, foretelling of doom? Hungering for violent death. The goddess was greedy for it. Well, she must be satiated by this day's serving, he thought. *That is why I am living still.*

'Beran,' Palamedes said.

'You know I will give you more death,' he told the crow.

'Beran!' the boy said.

Beran looked at him, then felt another gust in his beard and turned back to the crow, thinking to watch it flap up into the sky, its wing tips spread like fingers as it clawed up and up.

But the bird was gone.

'You should have left with the dwarf,' he told the boy. 'There's only death if you stay with me.' He turned and walked away from the sea, back towards the gate. He would find wine or ale, or both. He would drink until he forgot, and then he would sleep.

'The boy, Beran,' Palamedes called after him. 'We need to keep him close. We need to stay on our guard.'

Beran kept walking. Wine and a dreamless sleep. It wasn't so much to ask.

*

He made his way along the via pretoria like a squall-caught ship floundering across the Dividing Sea, maintaining some approximation of a heading but heeling from side to side and taking on water. Now and then he lifted the flask to his mouth and drank, though he could no longer taste the wine, nor ensure that it ran down his throat rather than amongst his beard.

At one point he staggered over to the side of the street and bent and vomited into the gutter. After, he stood and rinsed his mouth with wine and spat into the wind which moaned through the fort, flattening hissing sentry fires and scattering smoke.

'Damn you,' he snarled, glaring into the shadows, then looking up at the fast-moving cloud. He hoped the Little King's ship had been blown onto rocks and sunk. Then he thought of the horses and cursed again, for they did not deserve such a fate.

He stumbled on. A patrol of half a dozen garrison men emerged from the gloom ahead, coming along the street towards him, but he did not change course. *Whoresons can go round*, he thought vaguely, almost careening into them, so that they stopped, more amused than wary.

'No one on the streets at night without good reason,' the oldest-looking one said.

'If you're looking for Saxons, try the bathhouse,' Beran slurred.

'It's him, from earlier,' a spearman said, recognizing Beran. 'The one it took us all to hold.'

'Try it again now.' Beran fumbled for his sword but could barely grasp the hilt.

'Mad old bastard,' another man muttered, 'stinks of puke.'

'Let him be,' the leader said. 'Old bear's just drowning memories, that's all.' He gestured at his companions to walk on. 'Get to your bed,' he told Beran. 'You know as well as I do, what's done is done, and there's no changing it.' He watched the others' backs a moment as they continued along the road, then he looked back at Beran, who was swaying where he stood. 'Men like us have seen too much to sleep well, I know it. But we're still here, aren't we? And there's plenty's not.'

With that he followed the others, and Beran went on his way, lifting the flask to his lips only to realize it was empty. He cast it aside and peered through the dark, recognizing the old barracks ahead, and surprised himself by getting to the door without falling sideways into the gutter.

He tried the handle and found the door unbarred, so stepped inside, into the pitch dark, knocking over a stool and banging his shin. He muttered something foul and was tempted to wake Palamedes and scold him for not leaving a reed lamp burning for him to see by.

He stopped and turned his left ear towards the deeper dark. Tried to still his breath. Something was not right, but he could not fasten his mind on what, as he stood there swaying like a ship's mast in a swell.

He looked over to where they had all slept on the rush mats, where now only the three of them would sleep, and he saw the shapes of the Saracen and the boy lying there, though he did not think that he could hear them breathing.

'Boy?' he said, plenty loud enough.

He sensed someone behind him and he turned and saw the bone-white hilt of a knife before it cracked against his temple. He reeled, throwing up a hand to defend against the man who had stepped out of the shadows and struck him.

'Good to see you again, Beran,' Nabor said, pointing the knife at him blade first this time. Then a fist came out of the dark, glancing off Beran's chin, and from his left a booted foot, driven into his stomach, robbing him of breath. He knew that to go down could mean his death, but the wine had made traitors of his legs and his knees gave way.

'The boy,' Beran said, looking up at Nabor for a heartbeat before a foot between his shoulder blades thrust him forward onto the floor. Then they were kicking and stamping, and he did not fight, did not try to squirm away from the onslaught, like some submissive, beaten animal.

It was strange, he thought, how even as they rained their blows upon him, on his head, his ribs, his thighs, his back, he was more aware of their ragged breaths and their grunts as they worked, than of any pain. He felt himself drifting away. He sensed a deeper darkness closing in on him and he welcomed it.

'Balor's arse,' Beran groaned. 'Why am I alive?' He pushed himself into a sitting position against the ancient, moss-cloaked stump of a hazel, watching Nabor poke at the campfire with a stick, sending sparks crackling up into the night air.

'You sound disappointed.' Nabor was watching the embers weave up towards the canopies of oak and ash above them.

Beran answered that with a gruff, guttural sound from his throat as he tried to find a more comfortable position. He had not escaped the pain after all, not that he had expected to. Every part of his body hurt. At least one of his ribs was broken, his nose had been broken again, and the vision in his left eye was reduced to a narrow slit, the flesh around it puffy and hot, so that he imagined it to be swelling like the Saracen's had after his fight in the temple chamber at Caer Lundein. He suspected that if he lived long enough to bathe in a stream again, and look down at his naked body, he would see a patchwork of bruises as green as the moss on the stump behind him.

But he was alive and hadn't thought to be.

'Why didn't you finish the job?' he asked Nabor, who looked up at him, easing his legs out of the squat to sit back against an ash. Beran saw the others now too. Yann and Stenes, Dyfnwal and Konan and other men he had fought beside. Killed beside. A couple sat by the fire, another two were snoring in their furs, while the rest stood nearby, on watch or talking in low voices.

But he could not see Palamedes or the boy, and their absence twisted his guts with cold hands.

'That day you betrayed me and my men,' Nabor said, 'you also took a share of the prize from that pretty Roman carriage.'

'And you didn't?' Beran asked, thinking of the chest brimming with bronze, silver and gold coin, the necklaces set with green emeralds, jet and amber, the torcs of twisted silver and the finger rings shining with precious stones. The treasures of a doomed people, which he had hidden and which, to his small amusement, Nabor had clearly not discovered.

Nabor's lip pulled back from his teeth. 'Having failed to kill the boy, I thought it would be unwise to upset Queen Morgana further,' he said. 'That old crone can see inside a man's skull.' He put two fingers to his own eyes, then pointed them at Beran. 'She's a damned witch, Beran. I'd wager she can weigh a man's thoughts and count the silver in them.' He shrugged. 'I saw a few spilled coins in that carriage and thought to myself, old Beran likely stashed a handful or two somewhere, like a squirrel burying acorns for later.' He smiled, the gaps where teeth used to be as dark as the night. 'So, I will take your share, Beran, after we've given her the boy.'

The thief must have seen the relief in Beran's face. 'Oh, he's alive, Beran,' Nabor went on. 'The Saracen too.'

'No one else was going to lug you all the way from Portus Adurni,' Dyfnwal remarked, placing a hazelnut on a flat stone and bringing the pommel of his knife down on it.

Nabor looked off into the dark woods. 'Gone for a piss, I think.' He turned his gaze back to Beran. 'So, I need you breathing a little longer, old man, whether you like it or not.'

Beran heard someone coming through the trees and turned his pain-ridden torso as much as he could so that his good eye could see. It was Palamedes and the boy, being led back to the fire by another of Nabor's men. Their hands were tied but they looked unhurt. Beran's heart kicked in his chest to see the boy alive, though when the boy saw Beran, he looked away and would not meet his eye again as he and the Saracen sat down on the other side of the fire.

'Guess I won't need you to carry him now,' Nabor told Palamedes, shooting the Saracen a sour grin.

Palamedes nodded at Beran, who nodded back.

'Why is the boy alive?' Beran asked Nabor.

'What's he to you, you old snake?' Stenes rumbled, running his Saxon long knife along a whetstone, just as he had been doing the night before they had ambushed Queen Brendana and her son, Prince Erbin, and slaughtered those fleeing from Caer Colun and King Cynric's Saxons.

Nabor threw his stick into the fire. 'So many questions, Beran. I preferred it when you were lying there senseless as a log. But, since you ask ...' He scratched his bearded cheek and looked up as the wind stirred the heavy boughs above, causing one to creak ominously. 'The queen wanted him dead before. Now she wants him alive. Don't ask me why.' He spread his arms wide. 'You know how it is. We do the job and we take the money. That's it.' He frowned. 'What I want to know is, why did you betray us? Did you plan to sell the boy to someone else? Or claim the witch's silver for yourself? Tell her we were dead, then disappear with the reward before we turned up?' He leant his head back against the tree trunk and eyed Beran with suspicion. 'Because I can't think why else you would kill Red Tooth and Hygwydd and Blandigan.'

He flapped a hand. 'Donan, I understand. That arse rag was never meant to grow old. All the brains of a shit bucket, that boy.'

'I didn't kill Blandigan,' Beran said.

Nabor shrugged again, as if it made no difference.

'Let the boy go, Nabor,' Beran said. 'You know who he is?'

'I know,' Nabor said.

'Then you know why Morgana can't let him live. Because since King Cerdic died and the Saxons turned on her, she knows her only way back to power is to put Melehan on Uther's high seat.' He turned his good eye onto the boy. 'The boy threatens that ambition. She knows he is the rightful heir. He's the grandson of Ambrosius Aurelius.'

'Such things are far above the likes of you and me, Beran.' Nabor shrugged. 'What does it matter to us whose arse polishes some throne in Dumnonia? Camelot will be gone soon enough anyway, along with anyone foolish enough to stand in the shieldwall against Cynric.' He lifted a hand to his unkempt beard and raked fingers through it, teasing at the knots. 'There's no stopping the Saxons now. That's a dream that died long ago.'

'No,' Palamedes said. All eyes looked to the Saracen then. 'Prince Erbin can unite the kingdoms. Like Arthur did,' he said, his gaze weighing on Beran.

'He's just a boy,' Nabor said.

'Maybe Queen Morgana is right,' Dyfnwal said, cracking another shell and putting the nut in his mouth. 'Maybe Prince Melehan has a better chance of raising the war banners. Better than any other. Better than some boy from a kingdom of ash.'

Beran shook his head. 'Morgana sided with the Saxons once. The kings of Britain will not trust her again.'

'Not my business,' Nabor said. 'And I'd never have thought it was yours.' He turned to Palamedes. 'Nor yours, you Saracen devil.' He shook his head. 'You could be in Armorica now, drinking wine with that arrogant little bastard. Instead, you've thrown in with this miserable old turd and a boy who'll be food for the crows two days from now.' He glowered at Palamedes. 'Join us. You're a good fighter. The gods know I've won many a wager thanks to you. Black skin of yours puts the fear of Belatucadrus in men's bellies. That's useful to me.'

'I follow him.' Palamedes nodded at the boy beside him.

'Then you're a dead man, too,' Stenes said without looking up from his work on the scramasax.

But Nabor held up a hand. 'We'll see,' he said. 'When we've delivered the boy to Queen Morgana, I'll ask you again, Saracen.' His lip curled. 'I don't think you'll want to follow where he's going.'

No one spoke for a long time then. They watched the fire and listened to the wind in the trees and the scrape of iron against stone. Somewhere to the south, an owl screeched.

Beran half wished he had some strong wine to numb the many pains, some throbbing, some aching, others feeling like fire in his flesh. But it was nothing less than he deserved. He knew that. He had failed the boy. As, truth be told, he had known he would. The boy was not the first to have misplaced his hope in Beran.

But he would be the last.

'Boy,' Beran said.

But the boy would not look at him.

'Boy, I'm sorry. I should have been there.'

The boy turned his head away, as though he was looking at something in the darkness between the trunks of oak and ash.

'I'm sorry,' Beran said again.

'It's too late for all that, Beran,' Nabor said.

And perhaps it was.

15

Warlord

A BIG WARRIOR WITH TWO braids of reddish hair had pulled the strap from his own shield and tied Arthur's wrists with it, and now Arthur strained against the binding, his right shoulder screaming in its joint, until his efforts earned him a dig in the ribs with a spear butt and another in his back.

A Frank growled at him in words he did not understand, though he understood the man's meaning well enough, and they pushed him on through the darkening forest, leaving the remnants of Prince Aegidius's cataphracts lying where they had died, a scattering of ruined bodies amongst the forest litter.

He looked back and saw them butchering his mare, the animal shrieking and snorting as they hacked at its limbs with their feared franciscas, gouts of blood flying from the edges of those short axes. He felt the mare's suffering like a blade in his own heart, though he knew that death was a mercy now. She had snapped her right foreleg in some creature's burrow amongst the roots of a tree, and he had been catapulted from the saddle, landing hard enough to rattle his bones and knock the wits out of his head.

How many riders had broken from the main force, following the prince as he galloped headlong after the fleeing enemy? A score, perhaps? Arthur did not know, but he had known it was madness.

It was coming back to him now as his head cleared and the pain in his shoulder and ribs sharpened his mind again. He could picture it, the way an eagle must view the world and its people as it soared high above.

The Franks had fled the field, scattering in the wake of King Syagrius's charge like sparks flying from the blow of the forge hammer, but Prince Aegidius had seen the enemy's leader, King Childeric, running for the safety of the trees, his silver-decorated helmet and richly dressed household warriors marking him amidst the chaos. And so the prince had peeled off from the main thrust and spurred his grey stallion after the Frankish king, his scale armour and lance blade glinting in the late afternoon sun. And Arthur had followed him.

A madness of the soul. A fever of blood in spate.

It would be dark soon. It was already dark in the forest, where shadows reigned and sound deceived the ear, being scattered amongst the tall trunks, or being masked by the rustle of leaves, the sway of bough, the creak of stem. And this forest being mostly unknown to him, a strange place, heavy with unusual, unidentified scents and the ghosts of an unfamiliar people.

He thought he could hear the distant roar of battle still, out there beyond the forest, like the faint murmur of the sea breaking on rocks.

Somewhere nearby, a raven croaked, its hoarse voice carrying amongst the trees. There would be a feast of flesh for the bird this day, Arthur thought, his muscles still thrumming with the thrill of the battle, like wing beats in his flesh and blood. His ears still thumping with the drumbeat of a hundred warhorses' hooves on sun-parched earth.

They had pushed the enemy back, reclaimed lost land. A victory for King Syagrius, though it would not feel like one to the king, knowing that his son lay pale and sightless in the forest barely an arrow-shot from his own hall on the banks of the Liger.

Arthur looked up as he walked, spying patches of red sky between the tall pines. A blood dusk. He wondered if the gods had been watching the battle and, if so, which gods they were, for they said that the Christ had grown powerful in this land, and that the old gods were fading like morning mist.

One of the warriors barked at him to stop and so he did. He did not know why they had chosen this spot. Perhaps because there was more sky above them here, where an old pine had died and another had fallen.

Other men had already taken his helmet, spear and sword. Had pulled him out of his mail shirt, so that he had felt vulnerable and defenceless in nothing but his tunic and trews, like some creature of the tideline prised from its shell. And yet they had not killed him as they had killed his mare and those six or seven of his companions who had not died outright amongst the trees when the Franks had turned on their pursuers and fallen like a darkness upon them. These two older warriors, war-warped and grizzled men both, had claimed him for themselves, and the others had not defied them.

Could it be these men did not honour the Christian god like their axe-brothers, but rather sought the favour of some lord of battle, a god of war? Perhaps they meant to cut his throat and give their invocations to the sky before returning to their village and their kinfolk with tales of courage and loss, and of armoured men on armoured horses setting the earth itself to tremble.

Arthur's mouth was dry, his breathing fast and shallow. There was no give at all in the strap binding his wrists, the leather digging into his flesh so that the skin there was white as bone.

He looked up again and wondered what the druid would say if he could see him then. Something about proving Uther right by getting himself killed before he had achieved anything worthy of a tale from a cheap bard. He smiled at the thought in spite of himself.

He saw a squirrel scrabbling up the bare, brown branches of a pine, and wondered if Merlin was here in a way, watching him through the eyes of that creature. For such spirit-journeying was not beyond the druid's abilities, or so he claimed.

One of the Franks leant his spear against a tree and opened the scrip at his waist, pulling out a small carving of a bull, while the other warrior kept the point of his spear pressed against Arthur's spine at the base of his neck.

'I am gods-cursed,' Arthur told them. 'For killing a druid.'

The spear blade stayed where it was against his neck, and nor did the other man, with the little bull in one hand, show any understanding or interest, and so Arthur did not feel he risked Merlin's fury for speaking of it. 'I tell you this because I do not think your gods, whoever they are, will thank you for cutting my throat in their name.'

The older of the two warriors, his dark beard sprinkled with snow, had pulled his francisca from his belt, so that he held the short axe in one hand, the carved bull in the other. It looked snug in the big man's hand, that axe, its blade sharp enough to cut the veil between this life and the next.

And now he was walking towards Arthur, his boots crunching on dry pine needles, his intention as red as the sky.

The warrior behind Arthur moved the spear blade down, so that it now rested in the middle of his back.

Now. Do it now.

Arthur rolled around the spear blade, knocked the shaft aside with his right elbow and kicked the warrior between the legs. Then he was running, jumping deadfall and weaving between the pines. He felt the thrown francisca cut the air beside his left ear before it thunked into a trunk two spear lengths ahead, and a heartbeat later he was cutting his bonds on the part of that wicked sharp blade not buried in the wood.

The leather strap fell away and he yanked the axe from the pine tree and turned, twisting out of the path of a spear thrust before scything the francisca backhanded, opening the Frank's throat in a spray of blood. The man crumpled to the ground, his ruined neck bubbling with gore, and Arthur took up the dying man's spear and faced the other warrior then, who was pale and grimacing, reeling still from the injury to his stones. Yet the Frank steeled himself and squared his shoulders and came.

Arthur held the spear in his left hand, in his right the francisca, feeling strange with its heavy head and curving haft.

'I told you, your gods don't want me,' Arthur said, and the Frank jabbed with his spear. But Arthur was too fast. He parried the blade into the earth, then stepped in with his right foot and swung the short axe into the man's neck. He felt the man's hot blood hit his face like a slap.

For a heartbeat he looked down at the man, whose lifeblood was pooling impossibly fast, too fast even for the dry ground to drink it. Then he turned and ran.

Someone saw him and yelled to warn the other Franks, but Arthur was light in only tunic and trews, and he was young and fast, and he weaved amongst the pines as agile as a sparhawk in flight.

He glimpsed a blur of movement ahead, two Franks racing to cut him off, then one of them appeared amongst the trees ahead, bellowing a challenge, and Arthur did not stop but threw the francisca, the short axe turning end over end before embedding itself in the man's chest with a crack of splitting bone.

The second warrior emerged and hurled his own francisca, which spun amongst the trees, whirring past Arthur like a fleeing spirit, and the Frank hauled at his sword, scrabbling to draw it from its scabbard, eyes round with fear as Arthur speared him in the belly and ran on.

He was near the edge of the forest now, close to where they had butchered his horse and where the last light of the day yet lingered, a slack tide of gold at the margins. There were Franks everywhere, looting the dead, or treating the wounded, or standing in knots of four or five as they passed around flasks and relived the day. They were calling out to one another in that twilight of shadows, for they had heard the clash of arms and the shouts, and they did not know who was fighting who in the darkling.

Arthur ran towards the forest fringe and the ebbing day, his heart pumping, his stride seeming impossibly fast in that gathering gloom, as though he meant to outrun the darkness itself, as though he knew that more than his own life depended on him making it out of that forest.

A warrior saw him and hurled a spear but Arthur did not slow. Then it seemed as if the forest itself turned against him, the trees pointing out the intruder amongst them, for there were warriors coming for him from every direction, baying like hounds, wild for the thrill of the chase.

Franciscas flew, one of them cutting Arthur's right arm as it spun on, another hitting the forest floor ahead of him and bouncing and slicing the flesh of his left thigh, but he did not slow. He leapt over a streamlet, ducked a low branch, crashed through leafy boughs, then broke from the trees and ran on. Through sun-scorched grass, disturbing ground-nesting birds which scattered in a flap of wings; little wraiths fleeing in the gloaming.

He glanced over his shoulder and saw some three score warriors pouring from the forest, some of them casting aside helmets and shields to take up the chase less encumbered.

They howled as they pursued him, and had he the breath in his lungs he would have laughed, for they had failed to kill him when they had the chance, and now he knew that they never would.

Thunder then, rolling towards him over the brow of the hill to the north. Thunder not in the sky but in the earth, and then there were horses, war horses in shaffrons and breastplates of boiled and polished leather, spilling down the shoulder of the slope like a dark cloak. The warriors on their backs were clothed in iron ringmail or bronze scale armour, red horsehair plumes flowing from their helmets, long spears couched under their arms or held diagonally across their saddles in front.

King Syagrius himself led them, a lord of war riding on Cloud, his white horse. They came in a formation like the broad blade of a spear, and Syagrius was its tip, his polished helmet holding the last light of the day, his red cloak billowing behind him. At his right shoulder rode Gawain, stiff and ungainly in the saddle, yet spurring ahead of even the king when he recognized Arthur running across that sun-faded meadow.

'Arthur!' Gawain roared, grinning like a fiend, his mount throwing up dust as he reined in, the animal wheeling round and round because it had not wanted to stop, and now the others were cantering past, like a river around a rock, except for the king, who pulled up on Cloud, the stallion snorting, its mouth flecking at the bit, eyes bulging and wild.

Gawain wrested back control of his beast and extended an arm down to Arthur, who took it and swung himself up behind the big man.

'I was beginning to think you had given up on me,' Arthur said, thumping Gawain's shoulder and hauling breath into his scalding lungs. The equites were chasing the Franks back to the tree line, the first of them already spearing men in the back as they fled.

'I can see you've been making friends,' Gawain said over his shoulder. Arthur tasted blood on his lips then. He lifted a hand to his face and it came away slick and red, and he looked down at himself and realized he was sheeted in blood. His right arm burned like fire. So too his left thigh, where the short axe had bounced up and struck him.

'Arthur,' King Syagrius said, his eyes hard and cold beneath the rim of that shining helmet. 'Where is Prince Aegidius?'

Arthur hardened his mind against the pain that was announcing itself in his body. 'Lord king,' he greeted Syagrius, wishing he did not have to be the one to say what the man already knew. 'The prince is dead.'

King Syagrius looked down the slope towards the forest, his jaw firm and his eyes showing nothing of the pain he felt. For a moment it seemed he might ride Cloud in amongst the trees and sow death amongst the Franks, even if it must be his last ride. And if he chose that course, Arthur would go with him.

'Aegidius fought his way through a dozen men, lord,' Arthur said, 'trying to cut his way to King Childeric. That was the last I saw of him. My own horse fell.'

The king closed his eyes for a moment, perhaps imagining his son's last moments in this life.

'He was always a brave fool,' King Syagrius said, then he turned those fierce eyes onto Arthur. 'Thank you, Arthur, for riding with him. For being a fool and following him.'

Arthur swallowed, tasting copper and salt. 'I will avenge him, lord,' he said. 'I will make the Franks pay in blood.'

And he would.

He saw her as he and Gawain rode in through the gates behind King Syagrius, the rest of the equites following in column, hunched, tired and saddle-sore from the day, some wounded, others dazed from the loss of friends or kin.

Wearing a dress the same green as the trees in the pine wood where he had nearly died, she was standing by the well near the king's hall, watching the riders file in, her arms wrapped around herself against the cool evening air. And Arthur could not take his eyes off her.

'Aye, she's a beauty,' Gawain said, sensing the object of Arthur's attentions, perhaps caught in the same enchantment himself.

'Who is she?' Arthur asked.

The young woman's eyes had been darkened as though with soot, but for the eyelids, which were as green as copper ore. And her lips were red. She was pale-skinned and thin but she did not look frail or weak, and there was something defiant about the set of her face, something proud in the high cheekbones and full lips. No, something wild.

'She's the daughter of a Lord Leodegan,' Gawain said. 'He's a Christian, so I've heard.'

They had almost drawn level with the young woman now, and Arthur's breath caught in his chest when her eyes met his. Then he saw her mouth tighten and something like revulsion flash across her face, and he remembered that his own face was covered in the blood of other men, and he felt ashamed and looked away.

'What's she doing here?' he breathed in Gawain's ear. They had passed her now and so he twisted in the saddle, looking back at her, though she was half turned away from him, running her eyes along the rest of the column of riders, seemingly looking for someone.

Arthur drank in the sight of her, her raven hair braided and coiled and set in place with silver pins. The silver thread which hemmed her long dress. The coiled serpent of silver around her right arm, the red garnets of its baleful eyes glaring after Arthur like a challenge.

'She was betrothed to Prince Aegidius.' Gawain shrugged. 'An alliance with Leodegan would have brought two hundred spearmen. More. Albeit those men would be Christians too, I should imagine, so who knows what kind of fighters that makes them?' He grunted. 'Mind you, many of the Franks are Christians, and they fight well enough. Apart from the ones who made a mess of killing you.'

Arthur did not reply. He was still staring over his shoulder, the muscles in his right side cramping from twisting to look over the horse's rump. There would be no alliance now, with Aegidius bloodless and stiffening and never to see another dawn.

Never to see *her* face again, Arthur thought, which was a thing worse than death, he realized.

'How are your wounds?' Gawain asked. 'Will you live?'

Arthur had forgotten about the cuts in his arm and leg, and the savage jarring of his shoulder where he had landed on it when his horse had thrown him. 'Do you know her name?' he asked Gawain.

Gawain snorted. 'Forget about her, Arthur,' he said, shaking his head in amusement. 'She'll be part of some other plan, if not this one. Daughters of lords like Leodegan have to play their part, same as any spearman, horse, or stablehand. Same as us. Besides, you scared her half to death just now.'

'She didn't look scared,' Arthur said.

'Even so, Leodegan will weave another web for his daughter, and I daresay King Uther and Igraine will be weaving plans for you.'

'So you don't know her name?' Arthur said.

'I don't,' Gawain said. 'Heard it mentioned in the hall some nights back, but it's flown now. Might have remembered had I known she looked like that.'

They rode to the long line of stables, where grooms were waiting to care for those fine horses, to help remove their shaffrons and breastplates, to feed and water them, to brush the day off them and treat any wounds with salves and charms and healing words.

They dismounted and Gawain stroked his horse and put his face against her muzzle, thanking her for her bravery and for bringing him safely back. Then, as the stablehand led her away, he told the boy to give her an extra portion of barley, for she had carried Arthur too. He turned to look at Arthur, at the cut in the arm of his tunic which was soaked with blood, and his bloody trews, and his face a mask of red and death. It was no wonder the flies were clouding around him as much as they were bothering the horses.

Gawain shook his head. 'Next time I'll come and get you sooner,' he said. 'Better still, next time wait for me before you go riding into a forest full of Franks.'

'I will,' Arthur said, wincing because the various pains in his body were very much making themselves known to him now. The cut in his thigh was the worst of them, sore enough that it felt like a flame being held against his skin. He was aware, too, of the spilled blood from that wound squelching in his boot.

'Ah, I remember now.' Gawain lifted his chin as he handed Arthur a spear to use as a staff, for they would have to walk the rest of the way back to the king's hall, where servants would be waiting with jugs and bowls of warm water and mint for the equites to clean themselves. 'Guinevere,' Gawain said. 'Her name's Guinevere.'

Arthur tried the name in his mouth, speaking it too quietly for Gawain to hear. 'Guinevere,' he whispered again. It tasted as sweet as mead.

King Syagrius's foot soldiers returned soon after. Darkness had fallen and Adecavus was lit by a waxing moon, and they poured in through the gates, these Roman warriors, to where loved ones were waiting by fires and tents, ready with food and ale and whatever comforts they could provide.

The king had given over his hall to the wounded, and they lay in rows on furs and skins spread with hay to soak up the blood, as the womenfolk of that place tended to them, making them drink strong mead or wine to numb their pains, or stitching up wounds after bathing them with vinegar, or holding the hands of the dying.

While Arthur washed his hands and face, and slaked his thirst with ale, Gawain went off to find them a jug of good wine before the king's supply ran dry. He was gone so long that Arthur imagined his friend must have fallen into a barrel and was drinking himself out of it. Or else he had come across Aemiliana, the king's daughter, and the two of them had snuck off together to find a quiet corner away from prying eyes.

And so Arthur limped amongst the tents and red-cloaked warriors, the fires and folk of this Roman enclave on the banks of the great

Liger river, back to the stables. Men nodded in respect or called out a greeting, for he had forged a name for himself among these people and they were glad to fight beside him.

He remembered how in awe of Syagrius's stables he had been when he first laid eyes on them, some eight years ago, for they were not like those at Tintagel or King Lot's stables at Lyonesse. He had learnt that here, in Gaul, horses were bred for size, strength and speed and trained for battle, and Arthur had thought they were treated perhaps better than any horse in Britain. Having heard tell of it as a boy, he had seen for himself King Syagrius's love of war horses, had been amazed to find that the stables themselves were as long as Syagrius's hall, with stalls running the full length, usually two horses to each stall, and so he had not expected to be alone now.

Grooms and stablehands went about their tasks, some of Arthur's fellow cataphracts overseeing this work, still in bloody mail, muscles still trembling with the ebbing battle thrill, because they cared so much about their mounts and found it hard to be parted from them after sharing the bloody carnage of the day. As for himself, Arthur felt he owed it to his other horse, a dun mare called Lomblanda, to tell her what had happened to her stall companion.

'I am sorry,' he said, stroking the mare's flank with one hand, the other pressed against the thick muscle of her neck. 'She ran well all the day, and did not balk even when I took her in amongst the trees.' The horse whickered softly, as though she understood, her breath sweet with the scent of summer hay. 'It was not the enemy that brought her down, but the uneven ground,' he said. 'I should not have taken her into the forest, but I could not leave the prince and those other brave men to face the enemy alone.'

He promised Lomblanda he would not make the same mistake again, and she tossed her head and whinnied, and Arthur was sure this was her way of saying goodbye to her friend. Then he sat down in the straw with a bone needle and some linen thread which he had pulled from an old saddle, and took off his tunic and set about stitching the cut in his right arm.

Earlier, he had washed away the dark, crusted blood. Now, fresh blood welled beneath his fingers, running in rivulets down his arm as he pierced the flesh and pushed the needle in, teeth clenched against the pain.

Lomblanda snorted and whickered again.

'I know,' he said, not looking up from the task. 'But it looks worse than it is.'

Then he realized the animal was not sympathizing with him but rather telling him that someone had come.

'Do you want to die of wound rot?' said a voice.

He looked up and there she was, standing at the threshold of the stall, holding a jug by its base and handle. She wore a wolf skin around her shoulders now, so that in that dark green dress she looked like a queen of the forest and its beasts.

'Why go to the trouble of escaping from the Franks if you are going to kill yourself with a filthy needle and thread?' she asked him, looking disapprovingly at the wound in his arm.

'Lady Guinevere,' he said, staring. After a moment he closed his mouth lest he catch the moth which was fluttering around the horn lantern on a stool beside him.

He wanted to stand, knowing this was the daughter of Lord Leodegan, but he was mid stitch and bleeding. Added to which, the sight of her had put more fear in his belly than the two Frankish warriors who had intended to murder him in honour of some god of bulls.

'I'm Arthur.'

'I know who you are.' She stood with her head leaning slightly to one side. 'Arthur ap Uther. What is the son of the High King of Britain doing here? Other than riding his horse into a forest and breaking its leg on a tree root?'

'It was a hole,' he said, disliking that she had brought his poor mare into this. 'I came to Adecavus to learn about war. Syagrius is the last Roman king in Gaul.' He looked at the moth which was hurling itself against the lantern.

'Then it seems you have more to learn,' she observed.

He looked back at his wounded arm. 'It was my duty to protect the prince.'

She made a humming sound. 'Then you failed, Arthur.'

This stung him and he swung his eyes up to meet hers. 'Prince Aegidius should have known better than to leave the main body of horsemen,' he said.

She glowered, and he felt ashamed. 'I did not mean that,' he said. 'I am sorry, my lady. I know that you and Aegidius were to wed. I have fought beside him many times. He was a great soldier and a brave man.'

She lifted her chin and studied him for a moment, before gesturing at his arm. 'Do you want me to do that?' She half turned her face back to the stall door. 'Your friend with the broken nose saw me treating a spearman. He asked me to come here. He said you cared more about your horse than yourself, so I should make sure you are looking after those wounds.'

Arthur looked at the cut in his arm. 'This, this is nothing.'

'And your leg?' she asked. 'Were you just going to order it to stop bleeding?'

He saw that the left leg of his trews was almost completely soaked in blood, then he looked at her again. She was so lovely it hurt his eyes. He nodded. 'I would be grateful. Thank you, my lady.'

She came over and set the jug down, then picked up the horn lantern and told him to hold it, while she sat on the stool. He watched her in silence as she untied a drawstring bag from her belt and took out two clay pots and set them on the ground beside her. Then she took his arm in her hands and examined the wound, her dark eyebrows drawing together.

'I think you know more about battle than about healing, Arthur ap Uther,' she said, taking up the jug and pouring wine and vinegar over the open flesh to wash it clean.

He hissed at the sting of it, teeth clamped together as she put the jug down and took hold of the first thread which he had stitched, and pulled it from the meat, drawing forth another trickle of bright blood.

Then she took the first pot, and with a slender finger scooped out a mash made of herbs and the petals of summer flowers. Arthur smelled lavender, yarrow and sage as she gently pressed this poultice into the torn flesh.

'Closer,' she said, meaning the lamp, and so he brought it nearer the wound and by its light he studied her face.

Gods, she is beautiful!

'I didn't really know him. The prince,' she went on, without looking up from her work. 'We met once, briefly. South of the river. My father and the king went to hunt boar, leaving Aegidius and me alone.' Her lips pursed. 'So that the prince could look me over before agreeing to the match.'

Arthur tried to imagine that first meeting between them. 'I am sure it went well,' he said.

One of her eyebrows arched. 'My father was happy with the arrangement. He is wealthy enough, but seeks reputation. Half his spearmen and a daughter in return for an alliance with a great king.' She shrugged.

'And you?' Arthur watched as from her linen purse she produced a curved copper needle. 'Were you happy with it?'

She frowned as she began unpicking the silk thread on the neckline of her dress.

'I think I would have been a young widow,' she said, bit by bit drawing the thread free of the linen, that strange needle seeming alive in her nimble fingers.

A young widow or an unhappy wife, Arthur thought, picturing some of the many young women of Adecavus and beyond with whom he had seen Prince Aegidius over the years. He could not really imagine the prince married.

'The wedding was to be at the next full moon.'

'So soon?' Arthur felt a stab of something like jealousy at that. He wondered why Aegidius had said nothing of it.

'It was to be a surprise to all but a few,' Guinevere said. 'My father did not want the other lords of Britain to know of his alliance with the king.'

She had freed a good length of that silken thread and now she soaked it in the wine and vinegar before threading it through the eye of the copper needle. 'My father will come with tin and silver, wool and baskets and hunting dogs. A rich dowry. But he will find that I have disappointed him yet again.'

Arthur was taken aback to hear this. 'It was not your fault that Prince Aegidius died. Why would your father blame you?'

Guinevere's teeth dragged at her bottom lip as she considered the question. 'My father is a Christian. He surrounds himself with priests who despise the old ways. They would see the gods of Britain driven out.' She tutted. 'Hold still,' she said. He held still. 'Ready?'

He nodded, and she pierced his flesh with the needle and made the first suture. He barely felt it.

'What has that to do with you?' he asked her.

She frowned, then lifted her eyes to meet his. 'My father and his priests are afraid of me, Arthur.'

For a moment he thought she was joking, but then it was clear she was not.

'Why?' he asked her.

She pulled the needle out, drawing the thread with it. 'Because men are always afraid of that which they cannot understand. And that which they cannot tame.'

For a moment he wondered how wild this young woman was, and what she could do to cause her father and his Christian priests such consternation. Then he realized what she had meant and he almost recoiled, but stopped himself, knowing it would make him as bad as those priests in her father's court. As bad as her father.

'They cannot see what I can see,' she said. 'And it frightens them.'

'You have the sight?' he asked her.

Again she tilted her head slightly to one side as she regarded him, as though to study his reaction to what she was telling him. As though that reaction would tell *her* all she needed to know about him.

'The gods show me things that others cannot see. Sometimes, they allow me to . . . journey. I can run through the bracken with the deer.' She ran her eyes up a timber joist to the roof. 'Tumble and fly in the dusk with the rooks,' she said.

Arthur frowned. 'Only a druid can do such things. Can weave together his own spirit with that of some creature. A bird or a stag . . . or a bear.'

'Some druids, perhaps,' she said. 'I have journeyed with Merlin. When I was young.'

He was surprised to know that she had met Merlin. Surprised that Merlin had never mentioned Guinevere to him. But then, why would he? It must have been many years ago, and the druid spent his life roaming the Dark Isles, and the man was a tangled nest of secrets.

'I don't know why I'm telling you this, Arthur.' She smiled then, but there was sadness in it. 'At least I took your mind off it.' She let go of his arm and leant back to examine her work, for, to his surprise, she had finished. The wound was neatly yet loosely sewn with the silk thread from her own dress, and Arthur felt as though she had somehow bound him to her, too.

'I have not drawn the flesh tight because we will need to wash the poultice out later.' She laid a hand on the skin next to the wound, and he felt a thrill run through him. 'If it becomes hot and inflamed, we will open it again and flood it with vinegar.'

He was barely listening.

'What will happen to you now?' he asked, as she picked up the other pot from the hay-blanketed ground. Honey in this one, he guessed.

'I don't know,' she said. 'My father is coming for a wedding, but instead will see a balefire and a funerary feast.' She dipped her finger into the pot and smeared a thin layer of honey over the sutured wound. 'He will not be expecting to take me back to Dumnonia with him.'

And nor did Arthur want her to go. He could smell the sage which she had chewed to sweeten her breath. He watched her lips as she spoke, and his loins stirred, his soul too.

'Perhaps you will find reason to stay awhile,' he suggested.

She sat back and appraised her work. 'Perhaps,' she said.

He lowered his arm. 'Thank you, Guinevere.'

'Will you return to Britain?' she asked him. 'Surely your father will have use for a lord of war. Britain is beset by Saxons, like a stag by wolves.' She fixed him with those blue, green eyes. 'Yes, I had heard of you before today. You are Arthur, the lord of horses. Killer of Franks.'

He felt his cheeks flush, but he didn't know why. Was she teasing him?

'Syagrius is my king,' he said. 'I fight for him. But . . . yes, I may one day return to Britain. If I do, it will be to lead cataphracts in battle. To drive the Saxons back into the sea from whence they came.'

She smiled that sad smile again. 'I believe you, Arthur.' She was holding his gaze, so that he felt she was looking into his very thoughts. Hearing her say his name was wonderful.

'Now take off your trews,' she said.

His stomach rolled and he leant back in surprise, and he knew she had seen the sudden fear in his face.

'The wound in your leg, Arthur,' she said. 'I can't treat it if I can't see it.'

He felt like a fool, but he did as she said and removed the ruined trews.

And somewhere across the Dividing Sea a druid was dreaming to the gods, and the gods were listening.

16

Caer Caradog

THEY TRAVELLED NORTH-WEST UNTIL dawn, then lay low in a coppice of grey willow while two of Nabor's men scouted ahead. At midday those men returned with tales of Saxon war bands roaming the lowlands and dry valleys and stalking the woods. Nabor would not risk a fight, and so they waited in that sallow wood until dusk before setting out again, and even then avoided open ground or ridges of higher ground on which they might stand out against the sunset.

They walked north through the night, skirting the eastern fringes of Dumnonia, the darkness around them whirring with bats and restless with the nocturnal exertions of fox and deer, owl and wolf, badger and boar. It was hard going for Beran, his muscles and bones raw with pain and tired with age. But his former companions were always there to encourage him on. A dig in the ribs with a spear butt here, a punch in the back of the head there. At one point, a man named Manguy grabbed him from behind and put a blade to his throat.

'I should cut you from ear to ear, you old bastard,' he snarled, his fetid breath hot against Beran's cheek. 'Blandigan was my friend, and you murdered him.' He pressed the edge of the blade hard enough to draw blood. 'He'd want me to do it,' Manguy said. 'You know he would.'

'Then do it,' Beran said. He could feel blood running down his neck, pooling in the hollow of his collarbone.

'Let him go, Manguy,' Stenes said, pushing the man on so that he had to release Beran from his grip. 'You kill him now and we'll never find what he owes us.'

'Aye, and there'll be ale and meat waiting for us at Caer Caradog,' Nabor said over his shoulder. 'Plenty of time for killing Beran after,' he added, grinning sourly at the thought. 'And when it comes to it, we'll all get our turn.'

'I wouldn't want Red Tooth waiting for me in the afterlife,' Yann put in, and some of the others murmured in agreement.

Beran walked on, glad that it was night, so that at least he was not plagued by flies coming to feed on the blood crusting on his face and neck. They would come soon enough, for the new day was a pale line between the eastern hills and the night sky.

He knew what that day would bring, and in spite of himself he shivered. Even after all the battles and fights, all the pain and misery, the loss and the regret across the years, the thought of the queen dried his mouth and put something cold and slithering in his guts.

Morgaine once. Morgana now. Queen Morgana because she had married the Saxon warlord King Cerdic, who had swept across the land in a wave of blood and death and conquest. But old Cerdic was dead now, lying in his burial mound with his ship and his sword, his spears and his hunting dogs. His son, Cynric, was now the Saxon power in the land, and other Saxon chieftains paid tribute to him, but Cynric despised Morgana and so the old queen had all but retreated from the world, respected enough by the Saxons that they let her live, feared by the British who did not have the strength to fight her. Beran knew all this, even though he had himself withdrawn from the world and affairs of Britain. He knew too that Nabor and the others would never see the treasure which he had hidden amongst furze and brambles beside a rotting beech in the woods near Caer Colun. They could not know that Beran would never take them there. They could not know that to Morgana, seeing Beran would be like seeing a dead man's shade take flesh again. First, there would be surprise. Blood-freezing shock. Then Morgana's hatred would boil back up and she would kill him.

At dawn, when the mist cleared from the river valley, they could see the great earthworks of the old hill fort rising from the land. It sat on a westward-facing rock spur, the river valleys either side providing the ancients with a natural defensive position around which to create their ramparts of banks and ditches.

'You see that, boy?' Palamedes asked Prince Erbin, his eyes on the palisade of wooden stakes crowning the summit. 'That is why the Saxons have let Queen Morgana live. Because it would cost them too many lives to take it.'

The boy was pale and tired-looking. He must have been afraid, though he was doing his best to hide it.

'Is it true that Queen Morgana is a witch?' he asked Palamedes.

The boy would still not speak to Beran, would barely look at him, but that was fine by Beran. He did not need that face reminding him that he had given his word and it had meant nothing.

'I don't know what she is,' the Saracen said, still looking up at the place. 'But if I get the chance, I will kill her.'

Being the last days of summer, the river was running low and they found a fording place thick with pink hemp agrimony, where cattle came to drink and where they could cross using spears as staffs. Soon after that, they saw riders descending the track leading from Caer Caradog's west gate.

'Here they come,' Nabor said. 'They don't get the boy until they've paid. Understand?'

His men grunted their approval.

Beran looked up at the old fort. He saw rooks fly up from the south palisade, scattering noisily into the blue sky, as though fleeing from death.

Well, death is coming, Beran thought. He could feel it like the ache in his wrists and knees before rain. Death was coming, and the Morrigán was perched on its shoulder, stabbing at her own black feathers with her beak.

Death had arrived already at Caer Caradog. The track leading to the west gate was lined with severed heads mounted on stakes driven into the ground. There were scores of them, some little more than skulls with scraps of leathery skin and wisps of lank hair flapping in the breeze, others more recently set in place, crawling with flies, their eye sockets spilling maggots and the mounting poles dribbled with blood.

One stake had been lashed crossways to another, so that it resembled the cross worshipped by the Christians, and the head mounted on this one had the tonsure of a priest, its sightless eyes turned upwards in their sockets as though looking to heaven.

'Let's not stay here longer than we have to,' Konan said, watching a dog stand on its hind legs to lick fresh blood from a stake. The eyes on that freshly severed head must have seen the previous day's sunrise. The mouth eaten and drunk, the lips kissed a wife or child.

'Coming here is a mistake,' Beran said.

'Shut your ale hole.' Manguy jabbed his spear butt at Beran's head, as Morgana's men, crow-painted shields slung across their backs, led them through the gates beneath a two-tiered wooden platform from which spearmen leant to get a good look at them.

'There he is,' one of these men said, 'Constantine's boy. Don't look much, does he?' He hawked and spat a wad of phlegm which missed the boy, but hit Yann, who barked an insult up at the guard, causing the other Caer Caradog men to laugh.

'What have you seen out there?' another crow-shield called down at them. 'Word is the Saxons are coming west. Thousands of 'em.'

'So? We don't need to piss in our trews now,' his companion squawked, jabbing his spear in the boy's direction. 'Not now the little Roman is here. King Cynric will take one look at him and run back to the sea. Bastard'll swim back to Saxonland.'

The crow-shields laughed, and Beran growled at the boy to pay the fools no mind, as they entered Caer Caradog beneath a pale midday sun.

Other folk flocked to them, following the band through the fort like gulls behind a fishing boat, though they were more interested in Palamedes than the prince from the ashes of Caer Colun, few of them having seen a man with such dark skin before. They dared not come too close to him, though now and then a boy or girl would dart in and touch him, then run away crowing of their little triumph.

'Leave him alone!' the boy yelled at them, trying to put himself in front of Palamedes, protecting the big man with his own body.

'It's all right, my prince,' Palamedes told him, touching the boy's shoulder with his bound hands. 'I'm used to it.'

But the boy was angry on his behalf, even though he had his own reasons to be fearful, coming before the queen who had ordered the murder of his mother and of him too. 'They wouldn't do it if they knew you once rode with Arthur,' the boy said, at which Palamedes smiled.

'No, they would scatter flowers at my feet and the bards would sing of me,' he said, glancing at Beran. 'Palamedes, the black butcher of Saxons.'

'More likely they would put our heads on stakes with the others,' Beran said, noticing that the folk of Caer Caradog did not seem well fed or prosperous. Many looked ill, their cheeks hollow, eyes bulging. This place was like Portus Adurni, in that it was cut off from the rest of Britain, but that shore fort could be resupplied by sea, whereas Caer Caradog was surrounded by enemies, both British and Saxon, and its people were suffering.

They came at last to the queen's hall, which was not as impressive as Beran had expected. There were human and animal skulls mounted above the door, no doubt meant to intimidate visitors, and on the door itself had been nailed the flayed skin of a man. A Saxon, judging by the silver hammer amulet of Thunor hanging beside it.

All meant, perhaps, to draw the eye from the thatch, which was old and green with moss, and the timbers that were rotting where rain had exposed the grain, and here and there the charcoal-black scars of fires.

At the base of the wall, the earth itself had built up over years, as though the hill was claiming the building, so that damp from the ground was rising up those timbers.

But there was something else about the place too. It was a place out of time, enduring long after it should have been nothing more than a stain in the soil. Beran felt it because he knew what it was to be here still, alive beneath the sky when he should have been gone.

They were told to wait while a spearman led Nabor inside. The mercenary stopped at the threshold and turned and pointed at the boy. 'No one gets close to him,' he told his men, who made a ring of flesh and spears around Beran, Palamedes and the boy.

Standing beside Beran, Palamedes lifted his chin towards the hall door above which those macabre trophies hung. 'You ready for this?' he asked.

Beran grunted. 'I could live a hundred years and not be ready.'

The Saracen grimaced. 'So, how long has it been?'

Beran thought about it. 'More than forty,' he said.

Palamedes whistled softly.

Feeling the boy's eyes boring into him, Beran turned to him. He knew what was coming.

'You know Queen Morgana?' the boy asked.

Beran raised an eyebrow at the boy. 'So, you're talking to me now?'

The boy frowned as though he'd been tricked.

'I used to know her, yes,' Beran went on. 'When we were both young.' His mind reached back and back, to a night of hoar frost and stinging snow, warm furs and even warmer flesh. 'Young and stupid,' he added.

The next question he was not expecting, and it struck him harder than anything Nabor's men had dealt him.

'Is Queen Morgana going to kill me?' The boy stood tall, his chin lifted defiantly, though his young eyes glistened with unbidden tears.

Beran and Palamedes exchanged a look, the Saracen giving an almost imperceptible shake of his head.

'No, boy,' Beran said. 'I think she's changed her mind about that.' He lifted his bound hands towards Stenes and Dyfnwal. 'If she still wanted you dead, one of these stinking whoresons would have done it by now.'

Nabor's men paid this insult no mind, but the boy was biting the inside of his cheek, his face betraying his doubt.

Beran knew the boy did not trust him any more, and he didn't blame him. He also knew that the likely reason why Nabor hadn't already cut the boy's throat was because Morgana wanted to see it done with her own eyes so that there could be no doubt. She would see a blade drawn across the boy's pale throat, or plunged into his brave heart, so that her own grandson could claim his right to sit on the high seat of Dumnonia. Melehan ap Mordred ap Arthur ap Uther, hope of a people and High King of Britain.

'They want to see you, boy.' Nabor was standing in the doorway. 'All three of you.' He gestured at Stenes to bring them in.

'You are a prince. Remember that,' Palamedes told the boy as they passed beneath those old skulls into the queen's hall.

'Being a prince is what's going to get him killed,' Beran groused into his beard, too quietly for the boy to hear.

The hall was dimly lit and foul-smelling. Beran saw the boy jerk his head back and grimace at the stench that hit them: rotting wood and cat urine and rancid tallow, but most of all it was the pungent, suffocating odour of dead things.

'Welcome to Caer Caradog, Erbin ap Constantine ap Ambrosius,' said a man sitting in a lord's oaken-carved high seat. As soon as Beran laid eyes on him, his guts twisted and his breath snagged in his throat. Even in the gloom, he knew that lean, contemptuous face. The upward tilt of the chin, and the hitched upper lip, like a fixed sneer. The cruel eyes: though Beran had never seen them before, he knew them, because they had once belonged to another.

Beside this man sat a woman in a matching chair. Dark-haired, pale, thin and beautiful, she wore a look of such sadness as could darken even this dark, foul-feeling hall.

A score of spearmen lingered wraith-like in the lamp-lit shadow behind, their eyes on the newcomers like weevils burrowing in wood.

'Do you know who I am, Prince Erbin?' the man asked, the boy's title sliding out of that spiteful mouth like something venomous.

The boy shook his head.

'You are Prince Melehan,' Beran said, stomach sick to be standing here in front of the son of Mordred, whom Beran had last seen on the bloody field at Camlan. 'Traitor and son of a traitor.' With those words he felt the ache of the old wound in his shoulder, where Mordred's blade had bitten into his flesh, as he had thrust his own blade deep into Mordred's chest.

Melehan turned to glare at Beran. 'From what I have heard, it is you who are the traitor, old man,' he said, 'for did you not kill your friends and take the boy for yourself?' He glanced at Nabor, then rested his gaze on Beran again. 'What I don't understand, knowing Nabor here, is why you are standing in my grandmother's hall and not rotting in a ditch somewhere.' He turned to the woman with the ash bud lips, whom Beran guessed must be the Lady Triamour, Melehan's sister, but she was watching the boy and the boy alone. 'Makes me wonder if this boy was not the only . . . prize which the old man took from under the nose of our friends here.'

Nabor brought both hands in front and rested them on the hilt of the scramasax slung there, ostensibly affecting a casual stance, though the warning was clear enough to every warrior in that hall.

'Beran used to work for me, Prince Melehan,' Nabor said. 'That makes him mine to do with as I choose. Your only concern is the boy, and seeing to it that I am paid what I am owed.'

'Aren't you an insolent hound?' Melehan said, his mouth twisted in a smile as cold as his eyes.

Nabor's men's hackles rose, and the crow-shields of Caer Caradog straightened and gripped their spears a little tighter, looking at each other and at Melehan, in case he should order them to kill Nabor and his men.

Melehan raised a hand. 'Of course,' he said, 'we care nothing for the old man and this Saracen.' He smiled. 'You have done well, Nabor.'

'How old are you, Prince Erbin?'This from the pale, thin woman in the other oaken chair. Her first words since they had entered the place.

The boy looked at her but held his tongue.

'I mean you no harm, Prince Erbin,' she said, then she blinked slowly and almost smiled. 'I shall go first, if you like? I am Triamour, the queen's granddaughter. You have a noble face and good shoulders, I see. But you are a little thin. Are you hungry?'

The boy shook his head. Still his tongue would not stir.

'So,'Triamour went on. 'You must be eleven? Twelve?'

The boy lifted his chin. 'I am thirteen,' he said.

Lady Triamour knew it for a lie, but she pursed her lips and widened her eyes. 'Almost a man,' she said.

'I am Prince of Caer Colun and a lord of Britain,' the boy said, his tongue loosened now. 'You have no authority to keep me here.' He took a step forward. 'I demand that you let us go.'

This was well said and everyone knew it. Beran looked at Palamedes, knowing the Saracen felt the same pride he did in this boy who stood there like a king amongst traitors, thieves and killers.

'You are a brave young man,' Lady Triamour said. 'If there were more like you, perhaps Britain would not be lost.'

'Britain would be strong now, had my grandson not been butchered by that rabid dog Galahad ap Lancelot.'The voice was the grating rasp of a carrion bird and it came from the gloom at the back of the hall, where an ancient and faded tapestry hung damp and limp. It was not the voice that Beran remembered, but he knew, just as everyone did, who had spoken.

'My grandsons should be Pendragons, to whom the other kings and lords of Britain bend the knee,' Morgana said, emerging from the shadows like old blood seeping from beneath a scab. She was withered and bent, swathed and cowled in black, and she moved with the help of two gnarled sticks. 'Instead, one is long dead, and the other sits here like a cockerel on a hill of horse shit.'

Melehan's lip twitched at that, but he said nothing as the queen made her slow and difficult way to stand in between the twin high seats and her two remaining grandchildren.

'Grandmother.' Melehan dipped his head respectfully. Lady Triamour stood and stepped away from her chair, ceding it to the queen, who shuffled to it and handed her sticks to a waiting spearman and perched there, hunched over, so that her lank hair hung like a veil over her bowed head.

Beran had heard stories over the years, of how Queen Morgana had become the living embodiment of the Morrigán. Of her cruelty towards her enemies, and of her enduring ambitions for Melehan, for whom she would spill a sea of blood if it would make him High King of the Dark Isles like his great-grandfather Uther Pendragon. But in Beran's mind she had still been young and red-haired, strong and fiercely beautiful. Now, she was a bent and shrunken crone, and yet she was a queen.

'Let me see the boy,' she said, for it seemed she could not lift her head, or else her eyesight had gone the way of her good looks.

One of her crow-shields came forward and grabbed the boy's arm and hauled him across the packed earth floor, stopping some three feet from the queen.

It seemed to take a considerable effort, but Morgana pushed her swollen, crow's claw hands down on the arms of the chair and raised her head just enough to turn those jaundiced eyes on the boy.

The guard shoved him forward, closer still to the old woman.

A phlegmy rattle escaped her throat.

'As I promised,' Nabor said. 'Prince Erbin ap Constantine.'

Morgana hissed in Nabor's direction, then reached out, taking the boy's chin between the gnarled talons of finger and thumb.

'You look like your father, boy,' she said. 'I knew him. The fool who thought he was a Roman general.'

'My father was a great warrior,' the boy said, but his voice was small now, as though being so close to the woman who had ordered his mother's murder – and his own, too – had leached the courage from him.

'Pah!' Morgana pushed the boy's chin away. 'He was an arrogant swine. A fool whose abilities did not match his ambition.' She coughed, and the boy recoiled, though stood his ground. 'The Roman general's line ends with you, boy. Leaving my grandson as the last scion of the House of the High Kings.'

Melehan straightened a little in his chair, his gaze passing from man to man in that hall, as though he dared any to dispute the queen's statement. To Beran he looked like a man who knew he would never step out of his grandfather's shadow to cast his own.

'What about the Lady Iselle at Camelot?' the boy asked.

Melehan's eyes swung round to him. Clearly, he had not expected the only refutal to come from that young mouth.

'King Cynric is moving against Camelot even now,' Melehan said. 'Three thousand Saxon spears, maybe more. It cannot hold.' He glanced at his sister. 'Besides, there is no proof that the Lady Iselle is Arthur's daughter.' His lip was hitched, revealing his teeth.

'The Lady of Camelot is an imposter,' Triamour said. 'And her husband is nothing but the son of a traitor.'

'Lancelot was no traitor!' Beran heard himself say.

All eyes in that hall turned on him then.

'Lancelot was the slayer of Saxons,' he said. 'The killer of our enemies and the lord of war. He was . . . my friend.'

Morgana hissed again as she lifted her ear towards the voice which had filled her hall. Slowly, horribly slowly, her head came up, eyes glaring from between the grey strands of her thinning hair.

'Who said that?' The queen's voice was the *kraah* of a crow. She was pushing herself up from the chair, back onto her feet, grimacing with the effort of trying to straighten her bent back.

'His name is Beran,' Nabor said. 'He is the reason the boy is alive.' The mercenary was frowning, as though confused by Queen Morgana's reaction, for she seemed suddenly feral, somehow reinvested of some former strength.

'I know that voice,' the queen said, as the guard handed her the hazel sticks.

'He is mine,' Nabor said, 'and will leave Caer Caradog with me. The Saracen too.'

'Saracen?' Morgana sneered, lifting her chin as though smelling the air.

She was coming towards Beran, planting each stick in turn onto the earthen floor, which had been strewn with old ashes from the hearth to soak up the damp.

'I know that voice,' she rasped again. 'I know it, I know it.'

Beran took a step backwards but felt Stenes's spear shaft against his shoulder blades.

'It cannot be.' Morgana was close enough to Beran now that he could smell her sourness and see the spittle on her chin. Once, her hair had been so thick she had braided it into ropes which could have moored a ship, but now Beran could see her speckled scalp through the fine, grey strands.

'No,' she said. 'The gods would not give me this now. Why would they, after making me suffer so?' She brought a hand and the stick it held up to her mouth, as though to stop her own words lest they spill too far to be reeled back in.

'Do what you want with the boy, my queen, but Beran is mine,' Nabor said.

She half turned, pointing a finger at him. 'Another word from you and I'll feed your tongue to my birds.'

Nabor gritted his teeth, sending Melehan a warning with his eyes, to which the prince raised a placating hand and returned a look that said: *Just wait. All will be well.*

Morgana shuffled a step closer to Beran. He had thought himself old and weakened, as creaky as a storm-savaged willow, but Morgana was unrecognizable. She was not much older than he, but disease, or perhaps hate, had eaten away at her over the years. In truth, he knew he had played no small part in her transformation from the proud and noble young woman he had once known, to this crow-like creature before him, and this only sickened him the more.

'Light,' she said, her head on one side as she peered up into Beran's face.

One of her men picked up a sooty tallow lamp and brought it over to Beran, lifting it to cast its light over his face, and by that feeble, rancid-smelling flame he saw in Morgana's eyes the very moment when she knew for certain who was standing before her.

'No,' the queen said in a quiet voice. She staggered backwards on her sticks, as though from intense heat. 'No,' she said again, shaking her head. 'No, no, no . . .'

'Grandmother?' Prince Melehan had half risen from his chair.

Morgana let one of her sticks fall to the floor, then the crow's claw hand was fumbling amongst the black linen and wool of her clothes.

'Grandmother,' Melehan said again, reaching out. He stopped short of laying a hand on her shoulder, yet she turned and hissed at him, and he backed off, arms raised.

She had found what she sought: a knife with a blade no longer than Beran's middle finger, and not polished but forge black except for a sliver glinting along its edge in which the lamplight played.

'No,' Nabor said, 'don't touch him, don't you do it!'

She came at Beran on her other stick, jabbing it against the floor, then he felt that blade against his windpipe and her frail body against his own.

'You!' Her foul breath was like spiders' legs on his cheek, though he did not pull away. Rather, he lifted his chin and readied himself for the bite of that blade.

'We had an agreement, Prince Melehan!' Nabor called behind him.

'How can it be?' Morgana's face pressed against Beran's, her voice the soft sibilance of air escaping a bloated corpse through a slit in the belly. 'How are you here when my son is not?'

'Prince Melehan!' Nabor roared. 'I need Beran alive!'

Beran hoped she would slice hard and deep, for he did not want to die flapping and spluttering on his own blood in front of the boy. But he feared Morgana would lack the strength, and so he would help her. The moment the blade cut, he would lift his bound hands and pull the blade into his throat. Then it would be over.

'Our son,' she whispered. 'Do you remember?'

He wanted to tell her that it was all so long ago. He wanted to say that if he could go back and reroute the whole poisoned stream of it, he would.

But he said nothing, because he knew that his words would mean nothing to Morgana now.

'I do not forgive you,' the queen seethed in his ear. 'Know that I have never forgiven you.'

'Grandmother,' Melehan said, daring to put a hand on Morgana's shoulder now. She spun, lashing out with the knife, so that only Melehan's reactions saved him from having his own throat ripped open or his face sliced into. But Morgana's momentum overtook her and she stumbled and threw out the hand gripping her remaining stick, which slipped on the ash-strewn floor, and she fell headlong after it.

A gasp went up from the crow-shields and even from Nabor's men, as Lady Triamour snarled at Melehan to get back while she helped their grandmother, the Queen of Caer Caradog and once Queen of Camelot, who now lay in the dirt.

'Get them out of here!' Melehan ordered the crow-shields, gesturing at Beran, Palamedes and the boy. 'Lock them up and have them guarded. No one goes in or out.'

Having helped the queen to her feet, Lady Triamour now escorted her back to the oaken chair, her arms around the trembling old woman as they made their slow way through the lamplit murk.

Morgana was muttering under her breath, which had men touching the iron of their spear blades, buckles or helmets to ward off ill luck in case their queen was weaving some dark spell, some curse as thick with malice as a dead rat with maggots.

'What about us?' Nabor exclaimed. His men were ready for violence. Beran could feel it in that place, as he lifted his arms to dab blood from his neck with the back of a hand.

'We will honour the terms, Nabor,' Melehan assured him. 'The queen must rest. I will have food and ale sent to you and your men, and you shall have a place to sleep. Tomorrow, you will have your silver.'

Nabor glanced at Stenes, neither man seeming happy with this arrangement, but what choice did they have?

'Move.' A crow-shield shoved Beran in the shoulder, and they followed the Saracen and the boy back out of the hall.

'Don't you die on me, old man,' Nabor said as Beran walked past him. 'Not until I've got what you owe me.'

In his mind, Beran saw Nabor standing on the muddy bank of the Tamesis holding Emmeline's severed head by her hair.

'I won't die until I've killed you,' he said.

The mercenary grinned at that. 'That's the Beran I know,' he said.

Beran followed the boy out and into fresher air he had not thought he would breathe again.

Beran had been on the very edge of sleep when he felt the cool water against his temple and running into his beard. He opened his eyes to see the boy on his knees in front of him, dabbing at the cut with a scrap of cloth.

'Leave it alone, boy, I've worse pains than that.'

The boy picked up the flask and held the cloth against its neck and tipped it to wet it again.

'I might as well start somewhere,' he said, pressing it against the wound, and this time Beran winced. He knew the butt of Stenes's spear had gouged a furrow in the thin flesh, and truth be told it *was* sore.

Still, he pulled away, laying his head back against the wall of the grain store into which they had been thrown. 'I'd sooner sleep,' he said, closing his eyes.

'The boy is just trying to help,' Palamedes said.

'He can help by letting me sleep,' Beran said.

There was a long silence then, but for the sound of an owl screeching somewhere in the night beyond Caer Caradog's walls. And nearer, the muffled voices of men drinking the night away. Nabor's men most likely, Beran thought, being sure not to waste a drop of the queen's hospitality.

'Why did Queen Morgana want to kill you?' the boy asked.

Beran sighed. 'I told you, we knew each other long ago. She was called Morgaine then. King Uther killed her father and took her home as his own. She was treated unkindly.' He felt a stab of shame. 'I played my part in that.'

The boy sat back, thinking.

It was dark in the grain store, for they had been given no lamp, but in the deeper dark behind his closed eyelids, Beran saw terrible things. He saw a cowled man rowing a boat out onto the lake, a squirming sack between his feet. The man's jaw clamped tight as he steeled himself against the infant's muffled cries.

Beran opened his eyes and looked into the boy's. 'I treated her unkindly.'

'None of us can change the past, Beran,' Palamedes said. 'We have all done bad things.' A deep sound rose in his throat. 'Well, maybe not the boy here, but only because he hasn't lived long enough.'

'I've done bad things.' The boy looked away. By the starlight that found a way in through the gaps between the old timbers, Beran saw the glisten of tears in the boy's eyes. 'I didn't save my mother. I didn't protect her.'

'Listen to me, boy,' Beran said. 'There was nothing you could have done that day. Your father, the great warrior, could not have saved her had he been there.'

The boy sniffed and dragged tears away with the back of his tied hands. 'I'm sorry,' he said, bringing those eyes back up to Beran. 'You are only here because of me. Because you tried to help me.' He turned to Palamedes. 'You too, Palamedes. I'm sorry.'

'No, Prince Erbin. You don't owe apologies to me.'

'Listen to me, boy.' Beran felt anger rising in his stomach. 'None of this is your fault. None of it. You couldn't help being born a prince. You can't stop the High King's blood running in your veins.'

The boy considered this. 'But Morgana can,' he said, with an understanding far beyond his years, and it hurt Beran to see it. The boy seemed so much older now than when first they met. Those eyes, which had reminded Beran so much of a man he had once hated, were now the boy's and his alone.

'They will kill me tomorrow,' the boy said. 'Queen Morgana had me brought here so she could watch me die.'

Beran shook his head.

The boy nodded. 'I know it, Beran. And when you have taken Nabor to that coin chest in the forest, he will kill you too.' He turned to Palamedes. 'And you, brave Palamedes, unless you side with them.' He nodded again. 'You must give up on me and side with Nabor.'

A stifling silence spread amongst them then, binding each to his own thoughts as tightly as the rope binding Beran's wrists, and against which he pulled now in vain.

'No,' the Saracen said eventually. Beran ceased his struggle, he and the boy both looking at Palamedes through the gloom. 'No, I do not believe we are lost.' The Saracen frowned, as though searching for his next words. 'I was not born in this land. Your gods are not my gods.' He looked at the darkness around them. 'But I feel them, even here, I feel them.'

Beran could not feel the gods, just his cuts and his aches and his many deeper, unseen wounds, the wounds of his soul, which had opened anew and spilled fresh blood since the day he had met the boy. Yet, he was grateful to the Saracen anyway, for trying to comfort the boy when Beran himself had been unable, or perhaps unwilling, to find the words.

'I have known this man a long time,' Palamedes said, looking at Beran. 'And where he goes, the gods of Britain are.' His teeth showed white against his thick beard. 'Maybe because they mean to punish him for ever.' He shrugged. 'Or maybe for some other reason. Some better reason.' He smiled weakly. 'I hope it is that.'

The boy was looking at Beran with different eyes, it seemed, as though he was trying to understand why the gods of Britain would be interested in such a man. Beran might have wondered the same, but of all the things he had forgotten in the years, the druid warning him he would be cursed by the gods was not one of them.

'Who are you, Beran?' the boy asked.

'Who I am and who I was are different things, boy,' Beran said.

The boy frowned. 'Then, who were you? Who were you when you knew Morgana, and when you fought beside Palamedes?' He forced a smile onto his young face. 'Who were you when you could ride as I saw you ride that day the Saxons came to take the Little King's horses?'

Beran nodded. That was the right question. And perhaps he owed it to the boy to give him an honest answer. Perhaps he owed it to himself to remember, to draw the blade from his heart in one savage pull, rather than bit by bit with each memory or vision that drew him back and back and down into the tangled roots of things.

'I think you know,' Beran said, fixing the boy with his unblinking gaze. 'I think you know who I was. When your father and I were young and Saxon keels roared up the strand each spring and we couldn't tell the Beltane fires from burning villages.'

The boy's lips stirred, as if he knew what he should say, had formed the name in his mouth but dared not speak it. He swallowed. 'But you died,' he said, lifting his clenched hands to his mouth. 'You died after the great battle at Camlan.'

Beran did not deny it.

The boy was wide-eyed. 'The bards sing of it. You were carried from the field and died of your wounds.' He shook his head slowly. 'But . . . you didn't die.'

'I had my reasons to keep breathing,' Beran said. He thought of *her*, lying in his hut amongst the marsh reeds, though her mind had flown and was trapped in some . . . other place. The slow turn of the years in that lonely, haunted den.

The boy sat back, still staring.

'I'm not the man I once was, boy,' Beran said, glancing at Palamedes. 'He'll tell you that.'

Palamedes dipped his head at the boy. 'But *you* could be the man he once was, Prince Erbin.'

The boy turned back to Beran and opened his mouth, but only whispered. 'Arthur.' It was the sigh of a summer breeze through tall grass. The shiver of oak leaves. The swaying ears of barley before the harvest. The breath of a fire newly caught. 'Arthur. The Never King.'

For a long moment, no one spoke, as though they all knew that those last words needed time to settle, like snow falling on a black winter's night.

Then Palamedes lifted his tied hands. 'Beran,' he said. The Saracen had turned an ear towards the door. From beyond that door they heard a muffled cry and grunt, and the sound of something hitting the ground. Then nothing. No, not nothing. Laboured breathing. Beran sensed whoever was on the other side of that door. He felt them listening too, as though they waited to see if the distant hum of those drinking in Morgana's hall continued uninterrupted.

He lifted his chin, silently telling the boy to get up. Palamedes was already moving, putting himself between the door and the boy.

The door was unbarred and opened, and a warrior with a face scarred by fire stood there, the knife in his hand dripping blood onto the grain-covered floor. He did not speak, but gestured with the blade for them to get out.

'Who are you?' Beran asked.

The warrior pointed the knife at Beran. 'Out,' he said, the raw, ruined skin of his hairless face shining in the starlight.

Beran lifted his bound hands and pushed the boy further back into the dark place. 'No,' he said.

Then a woman's voice told the fire-scarred warrior to make way, and so he stepped back, and Lady Triamour came into the grain store, the russet pelt around her shoulders bristling in the breeze.

'We're leaving. Now,' she said.

'Why would we go with you?' Beran asked her.

Lady Triamour looked at Beran with those sorrowful eyes of hers. 'My grandmother will kill the prince to clear the way for my brother.' She looked from Beran to the boy. 'Prince Erbin. The queen has sworn a blood oath to kill you. Tomorrow, she will take you to the highest part of Caer Caradog so that everyone can see. Then she will have your head cut off and mounted for the crows and ravens to peck.'

'Enough,' Beran said.

She looked back to him. 'I offer Prince Erbin life.'

'Why?' Beran saw that there were more warriors waiting outside, peering nervously into the night.

'Because my brother is not fit to rule. Had Ambrosius lived, I would have supported him. Not Melehan.' She looked from Palamedes to

Beran. 'The kings and spearmen of Britain will not follow my brother.' She gave the boy a sad smile. 'You and I shall marry, Prince Erbin. Together, we will forge a new line of kings . . . or queens.'

'You can't marry the boy,' Palamedes told her, his expression incredulous.

She turned to him, lifting a slender hand to tuck a wisp of dark hair behind her ear. 'Why not?' she said. 'My grandmother is dying. My brother is weak. But the Pendragon fire is within me, Saracen. Imagine what Prince Erbin and I can achieve together. We will raise war banners across Britain. We will take back what was lost.'

'I don't want to marry you,' the boy said, edging away from her.

Lady Triamour's full brows arched above blue eyes the shape of little spear blades. 'Am I not beautiful, Prince Erbin?' she asked the boy.

He frowned. 'Yes,' he admitted. And she was. 'But you are too old for me.'

She almost laughed at that. 'Let us worry about that another day, Prince Erbin. When we are far away from here.'

'How will we get away?' Beran asked.

Lady Triamour glanced behind her. 'My brother's men are preparing to murder Nabor and his companions while they are too drunk to stand. He means to make you lead him to the treasure you took from Prince Erbin's carriage.' Again, she looked at the boy, only now she stepped forward and put a hand against his face, running a thumb across his cheek. 'But that treasure is yours, my prince, and will buy us spearmen. Better men than Nabor ap Nabor.'

'We need to go, my lady,' the fire-scarred man said.

'Cut us loose.' Beran lifted his hands. 'We can fight if it comes to it.'

'Not a chance, old man,' the scarred warrior said.

Another warrior appeared at the threshold. 'It's happening, my lady. Prince Melehan's men are going for Nabor.'

Lady Triamour nodded and went to the boy and gripped him by the arms. 'Will you come with me, Prince Erbin?' she asked. 'I have friends nearby. They will help us.'

The boy looked to Beran, who nodded, then to Palamedes.

'I told you the gods were still here,' Palamedes said.

Then, surrounded by six spearmen who were loyal to Triamour, and led by the lady herself, they fled into the night.

17

Marsh Harriers

THE HALL OF KING Syagrius, the last Roman general in northern Gaul, shone as brightly as the proud eagles under which that shrinking empire had once marched to conquer distant lands and peoples. A hundred beeswax candles lit the draught-stirred smoke of sweet incense. Two hundred honoured guests stood in linens and fine-spun wool of every colour, cloaks pinned with brooches that gleamed in the flame glow, necks adorned with silver and amber, garnet and gold. The women wore their hair pinned with silver or tied with silk, and had made more of lips, cheekbones and eyes with false shadows and salves and all the secrets of their art. The men had washed and combed their beards and put on their cleanest, most embroidered tunics, and they stood tall in that place with the fragile pride of unaccustomed comeliness.

From this assembly there rose a hum of indistinguishable voices, growing in fervour and intensity, like the burble of a mountain stream in the spring thaw. And in amongst this thrum of tongues could be heard a lyre, its strings pouring a mead of sweet sound like some libation, or like sunbeams amongst breeze-flickered leaves dancing on the woodland floor.

It was a golden day. As bright inside that oaken hall as without, where summer had returned as if the gods themselves gave the day as their own marriage gift to the young couple.

Arthur stood on the dais where the king's own chair usually sat, though it now lingered in shadow at the back of the hall, just a thing of wood on a day of gold.

'I've seen men dead a week with more colour in their cheeks than you, Arthur,' Gawain beside him said, his own beard combed and run through with beeswax, though not entirely tamed. 'You look like a boy afraid of the dark on Samhain eve.'

'You wait until it's your turn,' Arthur said, holding a smile on his bloodless lips for the benefit of all the eyes in that hall resting upon him. 'I'll be sure to be just as unhelpful when you're the one standing here about to speak the words.'

Gawain slapped him on the back. 'Enjoy it, man!' He grinned. 'Look at this lot.' He spoke from the corner of that smile. 'There are lords here from Armorica, Aquitaine, Burgundy. See that scarred old boar next to Leodegan? That's Lord Balsant of Benoic.' He dipped his head in another direction. 'And that man with the stag brooch is Claudas of the Wasteland. Everyone is here.'

'Not everyone,' Arthur said.

He had not expected his father to come. In truth, he was glad that Uther had not accepted King Syagrius's invitation to cross the Dividing Sea and share in the three days of joyous celebration. Even so, Arthur could not help but feel his father's absence like the slow twisting in the guts after some bad meat.

'He would only sour the mood,' Gawain said. 'And besides, he sent Merlin.'

They both looked at the druid now. Robed in white rather than his usual black, Merlin was moving through the hall like a tendril of smoke, going from lord to lord and king to king, complimenting them, paying his respects and garnering what news he could about affairs in their lands.

'It's a great honour to have a druid at your wedding,' Gawain said.

Arthur hitched an eyebrow. 'You know as well as I do why Merlin came,' he said, for really, of course, the druid was weighing those men in the scales of his mind, measuring them against his sacred druid's staff. He was sifting those kings and lords like grain, gathering the wheat for the future and leaving the chaff for fire or fodder, or whatever unremarkable fates the gods had designed for them.

'No,' Gawain said. 'He's here for you, Arthur. Anyone can see how he loves you. You are the golden one in his eyes.' The grin on Gawain's lips made creases in the sun-browned skin beside his eyes. There was no jealousy in Gawain, for all that he was himself a prince. He had thrown in his lot with Arthur for better or worse, and Arthur would not have wanted any other man beside him now, for all Gawain's teasing.

He slapped Arthur on the shoulder again. 'You are the hope of Britain, Arthur. Yet here you are, all but trembling with fear over a woman.'

The hope of Britain? Had he any blood in his face, Arthur might have flushed at that. He had not set foot in Britain for eight years, nor raised a sword in defence of Dumnonia. In truth, he felt more like the son of Syagrius than of Uther, and now he would marry Guinevere in the stead of Prince Aegidius, whose bones littered some forest floor on the banks of the Liger.

Guinevere. What a prize had he won. He barely knew her, and yet she intoxicated him like the finest wine. She had set his blood trembling in his veins from the first moment he had seen her, and his blood trembled still.

'Here we go,' Gawain said, under his breath.

The Roman priest whom the king had brought to Adecavus approached, and Arthur nodded respectfully. A priest of Jupiter, so Arthur had been told, the man wore a toga like those seen on the frescoes on ancient lime plaster walls inside the villas that still stood in Gaul. As well as Merlin, there were two solemn-looking Christian priests present, for the Romans had long worshipped Christ, though men like Syagrius seemed content to accommodate as many gods as might aid him in his wars.

'Are you ready, Arthur?' the Roman priest asked. He wore a close-fitting white wool cap on top of which sat a bronze disc, and from that disc, surrounded by a lock of wool, protruded a pointed piece of olive wood. The whole assemblage was held in place by two strings tied beneath his grey-stubbled chin, and though Arthur did not know what any of it signified, he felt the weight of the moment too keenly not to be in some awe of the man, and so he nodded again, his tongue stuck to the dry river bed of his mouth.

He looked up, expecting to see Guinevere at any moment, but instead he caught Lord Ector's eye. Ector smiled warmly, and Arthur tightened his lips and swallowed. *There* was another man who was more a father to him than Uther ever was, and just the sight of him swelled the lump already crowding Arthur's throat.

Then the hum of voices drained to silence, leaving only the music of the lyre, which stumbled for a heartbeat as the player herself looked up to see the woman now standing at the threshold of the king's hall.

Guinevere. Arthur's heart kicked in his chest. He felt Gawain beside him straighten, heard the sharp intake of his friend's breath, as he heard his own pulse crashing in his ears and felt his own stomach rise and fall, like the suck and plunge of the sea in some tide-swirled cove.

Gawain stepped back, leaving Arthur alone on the dais. The lyre player's fingers resumed their skilful wandering across the strings, the melody and the moment drawing tears from many a lady's eye in that place, and Guinevere took that as her cue to start her progress along the channel which had opened up for her and Lord Leodegan, who had come to walk beside her.

Guinevere's hair and face were covered by a veil the colour of flame, but the rest of her was white. A hemless tunic of the lightest and finest wool, woven by her own hands on a warp-weighted loom and drawn in at her waist by a white woollen belt. One of her ladies had fastened that belt with a Hercules knot, and it was for Arthur's hands alone to untie that knot, when all the words had been spoken and they two were all that was in the world.

That bridal dress, as light as sea-foam, clung to her flesh at bosom and hip, and hung almost to the floor, affording only a glimpse now and then of her white-slippered feet, and she seemed to glide across that hall like a swan across the still surface of a lake.

And Arthur could not take his eyes from her.

She came and stood beside him, and she did not turn her face to him but looked at the priest standing before them both, and Arthur knew he must do the same, yet he would rather have defied the gods than look away from Guinevere.

The priest was speaking now, welcoming everyone, thanking them for coming to Adecavus to witness the joining of hands of Arthur ap Uther and Guinevere, daughter of Lord Leodegan. He said something about the lamb that was to be sacrificed to appease the gods and draw their attention to proceedings. He spoke on and on, but to Arthur the priest's words were as the bleating of a sheep. For he was held spellbound by the young woman standing beside him. It was as if everything else had faded to darkness and only the moon of her remained. And then Guinevere lifted that flaming veil and Arthur saw her face, and his breath caught in his throat.

Now she looked at him, and he saw fear in her eyes but also strength, and he smiled with his own eyes, trying to reassure her. And then he pursed his lips and the stuck breath escaped softly between them, and Guinevere smiled because she saw that he was afraid too.

Her eyes were dark with kohl and green with malachite, and her lips were red, and her hair was braided into six locks tied with white silken ribbons and pinned up on her head. Resting high against her forehead, she wore a crown of woven herbs and flowers: rosemary and marjoram, verbena and lilies and late-blooming roses. A symbol of her fertility.

Arthur fancied he could smell the woodsy, pine and evergreen scent of that rosemary in her hair, but he could not be sure, for the air was already thick with incense rising on scented tongues of smoke to the rafters and to the gods beyond, whispering to them of the marriage of Arthur and Guinevere.

Arthur and Guinevere.

'Give me your hands,' the priest of Jupiter said. Arthur took Guinevere's hand in his own and lifted it, and from within his robes the priest produced a ribbon of red silk and with it bound their hands together, and so were they bound together until death. Arthur looked at that ribbon and knew he would have his warriors tie a ribbon of that sort to their spear shafts beneath the blades, and that henceforth he would wear a red plume into battle so that every friend and foe would know that he fought for Guinevere.

The priest asked Arthur to speak his vows to Guinevere, and he said the words in a voice so clear and true that even the beetles high up in the thatch of that hall would know his promise. Then it was Guinevere's turn. Her eyes never leaving his, she drew a long breath. Held it. Released it haltingly, like wine stuttering from a flask. Then she spoke the words, and Arthur watched her mouth, beguiled by it. And when he drew his eyes back up to hers, he saw that they glistened with tears.

The priest declared that it was done, and then King Syagrius himself raised his voice like the lord of war that he was.

'My son, Arthur!' he roared, and Arthur saw many a warrior in that hall cuff tears from their bearded cheeks at that, for they had fought beside Prince Aegidius, whom the king had lost. But they had fought beside Arthur, too, and he had proved himself to them in the bloody storm of battle, and they loved him.

'And Guinevere!' yelled the king. 'May their love endure until the forests fall and the great river runs dry.'

'Arthur and Guinevere!' the men and women in that hall called out in one voice. 'Arthur and Guinevere!' The beams shook with the thunder of it. Arthur's heart galloped in his chest, and he felt Guinevere's hand tremble in his own. 'Arthur and Guinevere!'

Arthur ran his eyes across the assembly before them, nodding and smiling at men he knew, accepting with modest grace the goodwill of those he did not. His gaze was drawn to the other white-robed figure in the king's hall. He smiled at Merlin, expecting the druid to return the gesture, but Merlin simply stood there, looking at him, his hands resting on the top of his staff, which was planted on the floor amongst the newly cut rushes. The druid's head was cocked slightly to one side, his eyes narrow, his brow heavy. Then Arthur realized that Merlin was not looking at him but at Guinevere, and so he turned and looked at his wife.

There were twin tears rolling down her cheeks.

'My son!' King Syagrius bellowed, hoisting his cup, cutting a swathe through the smoky air. 'Arthur!'

Arthur lifted his and Guinevere's hands, which were still bound by that red ribbon. He lifted them high for all to see, and he smiled.

But in the meat of his heart, something ached. And whatever it was, he knew Merlin felt it too.

They saw fires in the night and knew that King Cynric had loosed his Saxon wolves in Dumnonia. Whole rounds were aflame, their palisades and spearmen having failed to protect their people. Individual steadings poured fire into the sky, thatch and timber, wattle and daub burning into night's dark cloth, so that a copper glow lay above the land, spreading into the west.

There was one such copper bloom to the north, above the forested hills, and the boy asked if Beran thought that the Saxons had burned Camelot.

Beran shook his head. 'Camelot will not fall so easily,' he said, though he did not know if that were true, and he watched the sky with veiled worry as they walked.

They were following an old drovers' track beside a stream which glistened under the moon, ten figures moving fast and wraith-like through the night.

'You must wish you were at Camelot now, with your daughter,' the boy said in a quiet voice so that none but Beran would hear. 'Instead of being with the son of the man you hated.'

Beran heard the rasp of steel and flint in those words and knew the boy was challenging him to insult his dead father. Of course the boy was angry. He had learnt that Arthur, the great battle lord of whom the bards sang, was just a tired old man who wanted no part of the songs of Britain. But that was the truth of it. He had given Britain his best years. More, he had given his soul. Or rather, he had lost it. Either way, he had nothing left to give. Not any more.

'Your father and I were enemies for a time,' he said. 'But we came to respect each other.' He thought a moment. 'Well, I respected him, anyway. Constantine visited me after I vanished from the world. I asked him to never speak of my being alive. He kept his word.' He saw something splosh into the stream just a few feet ahead. An otter, perhaps. 'I was grateful to him for that.'

The fire-scarred warrior, whose name was Gwennec, turned to those following and pointed his spear into the dark. 'We cross the stream there,' he said, the rest of them filing past as Gwennec looked back to the south, to Caer Caradog looming against the night sky.

Beran had travelled far enough with the boy that he could feel the frown on Erbin's face even if he could not see it.

'But how can you turn your back on it all?' the boy asked him as they came to a place where someone had laid timbers across three boulders in the shallowest part of the stream. 'Don't you want to help Lady Iselle and the people of Camelot?' He crossed nimbly, arms outstretched, Lady Triamour herself having cut his bonds, warning him that if he ran the Saxons would have him. Then he turned to watch Beran and Palamedes cross, Beran taking his time because he did not want to walk the rest of the way with wet feet.

'I barely know the lady,' Beran said, glad to get to the other side without incident. 'She has her people. Doesn't need me.'

They walked on and Beran looked back to make sure they were not being followed by Queen Morgana's crow-shields. Melehan might know by now that his prisoners had flown. Then again, as Palamedes had said, the prince might have found that he had underestimated Nabor ap Nabor and his men, for they were killers every one of them.

'They say Lord Galahad is a great warrior.' The boy swung an imaginary sword at a ghost in the gloom. 'Do you think he is better than Lancelot?'

Beran ignored this.

The boy put another foe down and sheathed his invisible sword and came closer to Beran, glancing at the nearest of Lady Triamour's spearmen to make sure he would not be overheard. 'Were you as good as Lancelot?' he asked.

'Enough questions, boy,' Beran said.

'You can't blame the boy for being curious,' Palamedes said. 'He has heard the stories all his life. Since he was old enough to sit up with the bards, he has drunk the wine of it.' He lifted his bound hands towards Beran. 'But now he can eat the grapes straight from the vine.'

'He'll get no grapes from me,' Beran muttered. He looked to the east because the breeze carried the scent of smoke. 'This is no time for old stories. What good did any of it do? All the blood. The years of fighting, for what?' He looked up at a swath of low cloud shredding into the west and suffused with flamelight.

He did not need to say more. Everyone could see what was happening. Dumnonia was a great stag, and the Saxons were wolves trying to bring it down, biting its legs, haunches and belly, hanging off it, draining it of lifeblood. Camelot was the stag's heart, and once the wolves sank their teeth into that, Dumnonia would die.

But the boy would not die. Beran had been given another chance to keep his word. He had stood face to face with the woman who despised him above all others. She had held a blade to his throat and yet he lived still. He had been at the mercy of the Morrigán and had been sure that all his sins had led to that moment, as though at last a death horrible enough to fit him had come. And yet he had survived. Somehow, the fates had intervened in the guise of the strange woman whom they followed in the night. Triamour.

Beran watched the boy now as they walked. The little legs, the narrow shoulders. The nape of his neck, pale and vulnerable against the dark. His hands, clenched into small knots because he was afraid, even if he wasn't showing it. Just a boy trying to live, Beran thought. Yet others saw him as a piece on a gaming board.

Maybe the boy is the reason I'm still here.

'Beran.' Palamedes came up beside him, scattering his thoughts. The whites of the Saracen's eyes were bright in the dark. 'If the chance comes, we need to run.' He glanced over his shoulder at the three men who amounted to a rearguard, then up ahead, where Lady Triamour walked using a spear as a staff, her hair flying loose on the night breeze. 'She's mad, Beran.'

'I know,' Beran said.

'And what do you think Morgana will do when she learns of this? I'll wager she already knows, and that every crow-shield in Caer Cara-dog is flying into the night after us.' Palamedes' expression said he knew very well what would happen. There would be men on foot and men on horses, and hunting dogs too, sniffing after Triamour and her few loyal men. Beran knew they would be lucky if they stayed ahead of their pursuers until dawn. He knew the chances were that Morgana had already promised her gods that their heads would be on stakes or mounted above the door of her hall by sunset of the next day.

He looked at the boy, who was talking with one of Triamour's spearmen, keeping pace with the man, who could not have been more than twenty summers old.

'Whatever happens, we protect the boy,' Beran said.

Palamedes nodded. 'Whatever happens,' he agreed.

They pushed their way through thick ferns, careful on the undulating ground lest they twist a knee or an ankle, then ascended a rise and came down into an oak wood that reminded Beran of the druid. Merlin had used to spend whole nights in such woods, dreaming to the spirits of the land and the gods of the sky.

Protect the boy, Arthur. He could almost hear Merlin's voice in his head as they shouldered through the shrub layer of hazel. Above them, an owl took flight, clattering up through the foliage. *Protect the boy.*

'I will,' Beran said under his breath.

For, even with smoke on the air and fire in the heavens, with King Cynric's Saxons loose in the land, their long knives spilling blood into the soil of Dumnonia, he, Beran, Arthur . . . the king who never was, yet lived and breathed. And so maybe the gods were not so very far away.

By dawn there was a veil of grey cloud hanging over the wet meadows and ditches and low hills of Dumnonia, and a fine rain misting the air, and the pungent smell of burnt villages lingered in that mist like the memory of a sad tale.

Gwennec had pushed them hard and they had not stopped to rest or drink, for they all knew that Queen Morgana and Prince Melehan would have men tracking them northward.

Just before sunrise, they had heard a dog's incessant barking and feared that it was one of Melehan's hunting hounds picking up their trail. But it could just as easily have been a dog warning its folk of Saxons prowling the kestrel-haunted fields or setting light to the palisades.

'Where are these friends of yours?' Beran asked Lady Triamour, when at last they stopped so that she and Gwennec and the others could argue over whether or not they were going the right way.

'Close, I think,' Triamour said, shivering and pale in the dawn chill, as they looked out from atop a grassy hummock, mizzle blurring the world and glistening on faces and beading on Triamour's dark hair and the men's beards.

'There's a reed-bed that way.' Gwennec was pointing to the north-west. 'No way through without boats.' He swept his thick-shafted spear to the north. 'So, we take that trail there and skirt to the east of the reeds. There's a wood thick with heron nests. Hundreds of them.'

'That's where our friends will be waiting, Prince Erbin,' Triamour said, trying to reassure him with that heartsick smile of hers. She pulled the fox pelt tighter around herself and fixed it in place with a silver brooch whose long pin gleamed in the weak light.

They were all damp, cold, hungry, but Beran thought the lady looked frail out here, far from roof and hearth. The boy, too, looked fragile and tired, and Beran hoped that the little pools of shadow under his eyes did not portend some sickness.

'What if they're not there?' said the young spearman who had made a friend in the boy. Beran had seen him looking over his shoulder more than most in the night. He had the look of a man who had yet to wet his spear in a fight, and Beran thought it more than likely that he had chosen to follow the lady for no better reason than because he thought her beautiful.

'I have known these men we are meeting half my life, Addaf,' Triamour said, as though that were answer enough.

The young spearman nodded, readjusting the crow-daubed shield on his back, his cheeks flushing and with no beard to hide it. They had come to an area of willow scrub and wet grassland. Egrets and herons drifted silently through the grey above, and Beran felt and smelled the landscape around him like an old familiar cloak. He had lived beneath this wide sky. Had lingered amongst the reed-beds and scrub, the ditches and the open water like a mist.

'Let's move,' Gwennec said.

'Look, Beran.' The boy was pointing into the grey sky to the north.

'I see it,' Beran said. A marsh harrier was hunting over the reed-beds, holding its black-tipped wings in a V-shape as it searched for frog or mouse, moorhen or coot. 'I have seen two of them lock talons in the air and tumble down, then break free to wheel and rise again. In spring, before the female lays her eggs.'

For a moment, they both watched that bird, Beran remembering how he and Guinevere had for a time locked their own talons together and revelled in one another, in the glorious days before winter came. They had tumbled down and down, too, only he had never broken free.

'Come on, boy,' he said, and they followed the others into the marsh.

'I have a bad feeling about this,' Palamedes said, his gaze sifting through the oaks around them, searching for the cause of his unease. The wood was as Gwennec had described, the trees thick with old heron nests, more than could be counted. But the warrior had said nothing about how still it was in this wood. The nests were old, ancient some of them, and long abandoned. And the air seemed unmoving, as though the place itself were holding its breath, the oaks standing watchful. Waiting. No stirring of the green canopies above. No creak of bough or snap of twig. No skittering of a squirrel up some ladder of coarse bark, or rustle of hedgehog in the litter of the last autumn's fallen leaves.

'Too quiet,' Palamedes muttered, drinking from the flask which Addaf had given the boy.

Beran had not felt it before now. His right knee was hurting and his wrists were swollen with the damp dawn, which wasn't helped by the rope biting into the puffy flesh. But the Saracen was younger by ten or more years and he had felt it. To him it was as perceptible as milk souring in the pail.

Beran and Palamedes sat with their backs against a fallen tree which was cloaked in green moss, its earth-clogged roots upended and seeming to hang there, frozen in time.

'Do you think the lady's friends will come?' the boy asked him. He was on his knees, prising a piece of rotten bark off that deadfall to see what was underneath.

The Saracen shook his head. 'I think they are already here, Prince Erbin.'

Addaf overheard that. He started looking around, and Beran saw him thumb the iron strap end of his sword belt to ward off ill luck.

Lady Triamour stood alone beside a tree swathed in lichen, her arms wrapped around herself, her teeth worrying at her bottom lip as she watched the woods. She was afraid that her friends would not come, Beran realized, and she put him in mind of a spooked roe deer that has caught the hunter's scent. And yet he knew there must be an edge of steel in Triamour. It had taken courage to betray her brother the prince and her grandmother the queen. It took ambition to see herself and Prince Erbin ruling Dumnonia and uniting the battle lords and kings of Britain as they had not been united since the bloody fray at Camlan so many years before.

'She is my granddaughter,' Beran said, the truth of that like a knotted ball of twine in his thoughts.

Palamedes grimaced. 'She is Mordred's daughter.' As though that was all that needed saying.

'I don't want to marry her,' the boy said. He had discovered a hoard of ants, beetles and wriggling white larvae and was studying them with a boy's endless fascination.

'They're here,' hissed the spearman named Girec, and all eyes looked to the north-east, Lady Triamour's men picking up their shields and hefting their spears just in case.

'Stay with the prince,' Gwennec ordered Addaf, his fire-scarred face making it impossible to know if he was grinning or growling.

'Beran.' Palamedes' voice had a steel edge to it.

'I know,' Beran replied.

Because the warriors coming through the trees towards them, breaking the heavy stillness of the oak wood, had rune-painted shields and silver hammer amulets, and each carried a scramasax slung from his sword belt. Many had fair hair, braided to keep it from hampering vision in battle, and a few carried long-hafted axes like the one Beran had taken from big Blandigan, who had taken it from a Saxon just like the one now walking ahead of the rest. Still more warriors hung back amongst the trees.

'Lady Triamour,' this leader of the Saxons greeted the lady before nodding respectfully at Gwennec, who went forward and clasped the Saxon's hand and greeted him.

'Gwennec,' the fair-haired Saxon replied, then leant back and lifted his chin to indicate the Caer Caradog man's scarred face. 'Still no beard, I see.' His own beard was braided into a rope, which jutted stiffly from his chin, tied off with a leather thong.

'Those days are behind me, Beorhtwulf,' Gwennec said, 'but the women like me better now that there is nothing hiding my handsome face.'

The Saxon laughed, and his men, of which there were two score, came forward, moving with the confidence of a war band tempered in fire and quenched in blood. Behind them came other men leading horses.

'I knew you would come, Beorhtwulf.' Lady Triamour dipped her head.

The man threw a hand back towards those of his warriors waiting with the horses. 'Cynric's men are everywhere,' he warned, the words good, the accent iron-heavy. 'The king has raised his war banners around the great hill. Camelot.' He spoke the name like a curse, which it might as well have been, for the Saxon blood that had watered the ground in sight of that ancient fortification. The warrior smiled at Triamour. 'We had to be . . . careful,' he said.

Triamour nodded, favouring those closest to Beorhtwulf with a glance, so that at least three of them looked into those sad but beautiful eyes for a heartbeat or two. 'The courage of you and your men will be rewarded,' she said, and the leader of the Saxons nodded.

He was wolf-lean and dangerous-looking, this Beorhtwulf, and he looked past Lady Triamour with hungry eyes. 'You have the prince?' he asked, though he had already seen the boy. He had shared a look of amused satisfaction with one of his men, who stood with his arms folded over a broad chest, his great axe hooked over his shoulder so that it hung there, the long haft reaching down to his knee.

Lady Triamour looked off into the woods. 'My brother will be close. We must take Prince Erbin north, to Caer Gloui. Lord Gweltaz is waiting. He has sworn to support us if Camelot falls.'

Beorhtwulf turned his face and spat into the leaf litter. 'Camelot will fall,' he said, then gave his bull-shouldered companion a look. 'Cynric is too strong.' He shrugged at Triamour. 'So *I* will take the boy to him.'

Swords whispered from scabbard throats and the Saxons fell on Lady Triamour's men.

Gwennec turned on Beorhtwulf, spear raised. 'No!' he bellowed, 'No!' but he was silenced when the big Saxon buried his axe head in Gwennec's back.

'Run, boy,' Beran said, desperately trying to pull a hand free of his bindings. But the boy did not run. He fell on his knees by Beran, his fingers worrying at the knots, though his head was turning this way and that, eyes full of the horror of that slaughter. 'I said, run!' Beran snarled.

The boy returned his attention to the task, working at the knot. His little fingers were not strong enough.

'I can't, Beran!' he said through gritted teeth. 'I can't do it!' All around them, blades bit and men shrieked.

Beran shoved the boy back. 'There's no time, just go!'

The boy looked to his right, his gaze settling on the body of one of Triamour's men who lay throat-cut, his spear beside him in the litter. He scrambled across the ground.

'No time, boy!' Beran was watching another of Triamour's men being forced back by three Saxons. He was sweeping his spear this way and that, holding them at bay, but another Saxon came up behind him and clamped an arm around his head and punched a scramasax into the small of his back.

'Go, Prince Erbin!' Palamedes called, but the boy was crawling back to them with the dead man's spear, his eyes bulging and his face spattered with someone's blood. Gripping the spear just beneath the blade, he sawed at the rope around Beran's wrists.

'Damn fool,' Beran growled at the boy.

Over the boy's shoulder he saw Lady Triamour just standing there, pale and forlorn and strangely calm in the midst of that slaughter. He hoped against hope that she would run, too, but he knew it was impossible, just as Triamour herself knew it.

'Get away, Prince Erbin!' Addaf shouted, taking a sword blow on his shield, while another Saxon ran a spear in between his ribs. 'Run!' the young man said again, blood spraying from his lips. Another spear blade burst from his chest, and his legs gave way.

And then it was done.

Beorhtwulf told the bull-shouldered warrior to grab the boy, but the boy sensed the big man behind him and he spun, coming up with the spear blade pointing at the Saxon's chest.

The big warrior grabbed the shaft and pulled it from the boy's grasp, and took a fistful of the boy's tunic and pulled him into his chest, where he clamped his arms around him.

'Stop wriggling, little fish,' the man said, grinning.

Triamour's loyal men were dead, the Saxons already scavenging their bodies, pulling from them finger rings and arm rings, knives and amulets and anything of worth. One man was chopping fingers off with his longsax, the better to get the rings off them later.

The lady herself was surrounded, as though by wolves, and it was clear that they hungered to taste her. Beorhtwulf himself most of all, by the carnal look in his eyes and the drool glistening at his lips.

She looked over at the boy, the inner corners of her eyebrows raised, her lips almost pursed, so that one might believe she had been waiting for this moment, as though some druid had prophesied to the sad little girl the death of the woman she would become.

'No!' Beran yelled, straining against his bonds, trying to rise. 'Don't touch her! Leave her alone!'

Beorhtwulf shared some foul joke with another warrior as he moved towards Lady Triamour, but she stepped backwards, pulling the long silver pin from the brooch fastening the fox pelt at her breast. That wicked sharp pin gleamed in her hand for a heartbeat before she took the point with her other hand and guided it to her right eye and thrust it in, screaming as its momentum stopped and blood spilled in rivulets down her hands and her pale face.

'No!' the boy screamed.

The Saxons bellowed and Beorhtwulf lunged for her, but before he could reach her Triamour hammered the long pin with the heel of her hand and it must have been deep in her brain now, and Beran felt a moan of anguish escape his throat as the lady dropped to the ground, dead.

'Gods,' Palamedes muttered into his beard.

'Listen to me, boy,' Beran called to the boy, who was still trapped in the big Saxon's embrace. 'I need you to be brave now, whatever happens.'

The boy's expression was one of unfathomable misery, yet he nodded and firmed his jaw, and it broke Beran's heart to see his courage.

Beran nodded. 'Good boy,' he said, though he felt a storm raging in his own broken soul, swirling pieces of the past and the present around. Even after everything he had seen in his long life, he knew he could not watch the boy die now. He could not endure that, and though he knew it made him a coward, he hoped they would kill him first, so that he did not have to see them kill the boy.

More Saxons were threading between the trees, bringing their horses into that place of death, talking amongst themselves in their guttural tongue and taking but little notice of the slain littering the ground.

The big warrior pushed the boy to where Beorhtwulf stood, the leader having left Lady Triamour where she lay. Then Beorhtwulf barked a mouthful of orders and more than a score of Saxons mounted, Beorhtwulf himself pushing the boy up into the saddle of his own horse before climbing up behind him.

Beran and Palamedes were on their feet now, surrounded by warriors who did not know what to do with them, and for a moment Beran and the boy held each other with their eyes, Beran muttering a curse at any god that might have ears to hear.

Then Beorhtwulf kicked back his heels and rode off through the woods, his wolves following after.

Beran watched Beorhtwulf and the boy until they were swallowed by the forest. Then he turned to Palamedes, of whom the Saxons seemed in awe, for they crowded around him. Two were all teeth, threatening him with spears. Another was holding an iron hammer amulet towards the Saracen, as though the thing might have some power over him.

'We'll drink together in the next life, Palamedes,' Beran said.

The Saracen gritted his teeth and nodded, and he gave Beran a look that said that however death came upon them now, they would hold their honour close and die as well as any man could.

Beran glared at the Saxon whose spear blade was closest, that blade dark and crusted with iron rot. 'Some day, other keels will come,' he told the Saxon in the man's own tongue. 'Men will come and kill your sons and take the land which you have taken from us.'

The Saxon, whose eyes were red-rimmed, the left one weeping a yellow crust onto his cheek, hawked, dragging phlegm up his throat, and spat it at Beran's feet.

'That is the way of it,' he said.

And maybe it was, Beran supposed. He had lived a long time, long enough to have many regrets. But now, as he stood there waiting for death from a rusty blade, the only failure that really hurt, that squirmed in his belly like a living worm in a pile of bones, was the boy. He wished he could have helped the boy. Wished he could have kept him safe.

My life for his. I would have made that bargain happily. Now, the boy was gone.

Everything was gone.

He saw Merlin in his mind, the druid wandering in whatever green woods and flower-filled meadows were to be found in Arawn's realm. *I am coming, my old friend.*

'Do it, Saxon,' he said. Beside him, Palamedes was knocking spear blades aside with his bound wrists and lurching forward, growling and laughing to see how the Saxons were afraid of him, though he was unarmed and had not even the use of his hands.

'Kill me, Saxon,' Beran said, 'before I change my mind.'

The Saxon with the weeping eye exchanged a look with the two men either side, all of them taking their spears in a thrusting grip and bracing to punch the blades into Beran's stomach and chest.

The pain would be fierce, all-consuming. But the release would be exquisite.

A command rang out, like a smith's hammer striking an anvil.

'Do it,' Beran told Weeping-Eye, but the man did not lunge with that rusty spear. Nor did the others make the kill, instead pulling their spears back and turning their heads to see who had come. That same voice gave another command, and the Saxons planted their spear butts on the ground, their blades accusing the canopy of an ancient oak that had grown from an acorn long before the first Saxon ships were spotted prowling the shallows of Britain's southern shore. Before even the Romans had come, carrying their gilded eagles into the shadow-filled forests of these Dark Isles.

'What now?' Palamedes asked. If anything, he looked disappointed, as though he had steeled himself for the moment when sharp steel would rip into his flesh, when blood would gush in the ruin of it, and their lives of many years would be measured in fading heartbeats and shallowing breaths. Now, death had been interrupted, and so they would have to work themselves up to it all over again.

The Saxons surrounding them, and those others nearby, were

turning to acknowledge a man striding amongst them, his sword pointed at Beran and Palamedes. And no wonder the eyes of the men gathered in that place were drawn to him like cold hands to a hearth. His helmet was a thing of terrible beauty. Shining with little panels of polished tinned copper alloy, it comprised a neck guard, cheek pieces and a mask, so that the warrior's face was hidden. His neck was adorned with a torc of twisted gold, the hem of his under-tunic was thick with golden thread, and the shoulder clasps of his leather tunic, which he wore over a coat of mail, were gold inlaid with red garnets.

'I feel better knowing we'll be sent to our ancestors by a king,' Palamedes said.

'Cynric is at Camelot with his whole wolf pack,' Beran said. 'The gods know who this is.'

The gleaming warrior barked at the lower men to stand aside, and he came to stand before Beran, still pointing his sword, so that another step would have seen it slide into Beran's throat.

'Are you going to use that pretty sword, or just wave it around?' Beran asked him. He wanted the whole thing over with. He did not dare ask himself if *she* would be waiting for him beyond the veil. He knew the answer. She was not his. Had never been his.

The warrior lowered the sword, sheathing it in a scabbard whose straps were studded with garnets matching those on his shoulder clasps. Up close now, Beran could see that the panels on that magnificent helmet depicted scenes of warriors fighting with sword and spear, and serpents entwined around each other, and a mounted warrior trampling a fallen enemy. The face-mask itself boasted thick eyebrows of copper inlaid with silver wire, a nose and a moustache, but despite its richness and craftsmanship, and the overall effect of that helmet, Beran's eyes were drawn to the eyes looking out from the holes in the mask.

'I know you,' he said.

The Saxon lifted his hands and removed that shining helmet, and suddenly the effect of that austere iron and copper visage was broken by the smiling face beneath.

'Balor's breath.' Beran took in that face, which he had last seen in Portus Adurni. 'Uffa.'

The warrior dipped his head, some of his sweaty, sand-coloured hair falling across his face. Beran thought back to the blood in the water and the killing of a man in the bathhouse.

'I . . . meet with you . . . again,' the Saxon managed, trying the words like an unfamiliar drink. The smile suited his handsome face, making him look less arrogant than the last time they had met. He drew his scramasax and gestured for Beran to lift his hands, so Beran did, and the Saxon sawed through the rope bindings.

'And my friend.' Beran nodded at Palamedes, who lifted his hands. A moment later he was also free, rubbing life back into his wrists and rolling his cramping shoulders.

'Thank you, Uffa,' Beran said.

The Saxon looked at the litter of dead men who had been stripped of anything of value or use, but his eyes lingered on the body of Lady Triamour, which no man had touched. His lip curled to see her lying there, her hands gnarled into claws by her pale face, her ruined eye pooled with dark blood. Flies buzzed around that terrible little well, and other creatures too would come to feed in the gloaming, when the men here now were gone.

The Saxon warlord turned back to Beran and lifted both hands towards him and lifted his voice too, so that every Saxon still lingering in that oak wood could hear. He spoke in his own tongue, but Beran got the marrow of it.

'Does he know?' Palamedes asked him, while the Saxon spoke to his people in a voice that must have carried across row benches in the teeth of the sea wind, and across field and plain where shieldwalls stood. 'Is he telling them who you are?'

Beran shook his head. 'He's telling them that I saved his life. That if not for me, that dog's arsehole Bealdwulf would be leading them now, getting them killed, making widows of their women. Making their sons and daughters fatherless.'

Palamedes scratched his silvering beard, his eyes wide. 'You saved this Saxon's life. Now, he gives us ours.'

Beran looked off in the direction Beorhtwulf had gone. 'I only did it because the boy asked me to.' He clenched his teeth. 'Damn the boy.'

The Saracen nodded. 'We are alive because of him. What game do the gods play?'

Uffa finished addressing his people, and they showed their respect – for him or for Beran, it was impossible to know – by thumping spear staves or the hilts of their long knives against their shields in a low, rolling thunder which filled that shady place.

But Beran cared nothing for it. He was thinking only of the boy. Was thinking that whatever breath he yet had in his body, however many beats yet lay stored in his old heart, they must be expended for the boy and only the boy. If it were not already too late.

The Saxon warlord raised his left hand to silence the beating of shields, and with his right he offered that beautiful, shining helmet to Beran.

'No.' Beran would not take it. Did not want it.

'Yours,' Uffa told him.

Beran shook his head. 'No.'

'It's a gift,' Palamedes said. 'You will shame him in front of his men if you refuse.'

Uffa dipped his head and frowned, as if to confirm that Palamedes had the right of it, and so Beran put out his own hand and took the helmet, weighing the heft of it.

'It is beautiful, Lord Uffa,' he admitted, looking down at the helmet and a silver panel that showed a warrior leaping. Or dancing, perhaps. He remembered another gift then, a pair of bronze greaves to protect a warrior's legs from foot to knee, shaped to show the curve and swell of calf muscle. Over the knee of each piece, the image of a hawk, all beak and glaring eye and bristling feathers. He'd had the greaves made for his friend, a fitting reward for all Lancelot's victories, so he had told him. But that had not been the truth of it. He'd had Tinas the smith craft those beautiful greaves to sweeten the bitter draught of sending Lancelot away across the sea to fight in another king's war. And Lancelot had gone. The loyal friend that he was.

'I have never seen its like. Thank you, Lord Uffa,' he said, and Uffa called out to his men and they took up the thumping of shields once again, as Beran traced a finger over the panel of the dancing warrior, remembering how Lancelot had seemed to dance in the midst of battle, such was his poise and his skill as his blades sang, reaping lives, felling his enemies like a wind amongst autumn leaves. He had been the best of them.

'We must go,' he told the Saxon, looking into his eyes. 'Both of us,' he added, gesturing at Palamedes. 'They took the boy.' He pointed at the part of the forest in which he had last seen the boy sitting that horse in front of Beorhtwulf.

The smile on Uffa's face turned to ash. 'Too late for the boy.'

Beran's stomach tensed. 'Your spear-brother, Beorhtwulf, is taking the boy to King Cynric, yes?'

Uffa turned his head and asked a question of Weeping-Eye, who conversed with the warrior beside him before gnarring a reply to Uffa.

Uffa turned back to Beran and nodded. 'Beorhtwulf give boy to Cynric. We go to Camelot,' he said, sweeping an arm across the men taking their ease in that ancient oak wood. 'Many chieftains. Many spears.' He pointed in the opposite direction to that in which Beran had pointed. 'You go there.'

'No.' Beran lifted the masked helmet. 'We follow the boy.'

Those Saxons who understood Beran's words scoffed, or shook their heads, or in some other way showed what they thought. Uffa himself gripped the hilt of the scramasax hanging from his belt.

'I kill you now,' he said, nodding. 'Better.' He smiled darkly. 'Quick.'

'We have to try,' Beran said. 'I promised the boy I would protect him.'

'He's just a boy,' Palamedes said.

Uffa's brows lifted above that aquiline nose, as he eyed the Saracen, twisting the end of his beard between finger and thumb. He knew well enough who the boy was and why he was important. Likely he knew by now that the boy could grow to become a leader behind whom the kings and warriors of Britain might one day stand, a great forest of spears to spread from Bernaccia in the north to Dumnonia in the south, pushing Uffa's people back towards the sea.

'Boy will die,' Uffa said, then took his hand from his beard and pointed at Palamedes and then Beran. 'You both will die.' Then he shrugged and turned and barked a slew of orders, and soon thereafter a warrior came forward leading two horses.

Thinking that their lord had gone too far with his generosity, some of the Saxons growled their disapproval, though Weeping-Eye was not one of them, Beran noticed.

Uffa ignored the protests. He was the biggest wolf in that pack and he was confident that none would challenge him over this. Besides, they had other things on their minds, those Saxons, for they were going to war.

Holding Beran under his proud gaze, Uffa clenched a fist and pressed it against his own chest. 'Today, friends,' he said. 'Tomorrow . . .' He dipped his head and turned his palms over, leaving the rest unsaid. His men had fallen silent again, though still they looked on with the pale eyes of their fathers and grandfathers and of those first brave men who had crossed the Morimaru lusting for silver and land.

'Thank you, Uffa,' Beran said, thinking how strange it was that here was a man with whom he could have been friends had things been different.

'Merlin would have something to say about all this,' Palamedes observed as they mounted those horses and Beran tied the helmet by its strap to the saddle horn. Then they tugged the reins, turning into the west.

'Some riddle like tangled twine with no beginning or end.' Beran patted his little mare's flaxen coat. He glanced up, looking for some busy, keen-eyed thing, a bird or squirrel perhaps, which he could fancy was a living vessel through which the old druid yet kept watch on the doings of men. But he saw nothing moving, nothing living amongst those gnarled and furrowed boughs, and dark, abandoned nests.

'Don't go to Camelot, Lord Uffa,' Beran said. 'Its warriors are favoured by the gods of Britain. Your men will die on that hill.'

Uffa smiled with his teeth. Even without his beautiful, glimmering helmet, he looked like a hero from a tale told by a scop, like a man favoured by the gods of his own land. And maybe this *was* his land now.

'You and me, we drink together in Woden's hall,' Uffa said.

Beran held the man's eye a moment, then nodded and gave the mare his heel.

18

The Return of Arthur

THEY CAME TO CAMELOT under a waning crescent moon glimpsed
now and then beyond a mass of westward-driven cloud. It was a
night of shadow and flame, for the Saxons were the lords of Dumnonia. They had flocked to this place like crows to a ploughed field: a
score of chieftains and a half-dozen lesser kings, leading war bands of
oathsworn men to whom they owed silver, meat and mead in return
for sword, shield, spear and courage.

Often these wolf packs fought each other, for land or plunder or
reputation, but at this season's turn they had smelled blood on the air
and put aside their petty quarrels to fight for King Cynric.

That golden Saxon, that son of Cerdic and lord of war, had promised them the destruction of Camelot, and they had imbibed that
promise until they were drunk on it, for with that legendary bastion
against the Saxon tide destroyed, Dumnonia would fall like ripe fruit.
And perhaps it would not then be long before all the kings and men
and women of these Dark Isles would have no choice but to accept
their Saxon overlords and forget themselves, like children unable to
recall the dreams that used to race their hearts as they lay in their
beds.

Now, Beran and Palamedes stood on a ridge of high ground to the
south-east of the great hill fort, and Beran's mind was besieged by
memories.

'They will not believe their eyes when they see you come out of the
night,' Palamedes said, his own recollections of the place no doubt
bright enough yet to cast off night's shroud and reveal themselves in a
score of golden summers and Beltane fires, in victory feasts and the

songs of bright-eyed bards. When hope still swelled men's hearts and spearmen stood tall and thick as fields of wheat.

'They have more important things to deal with than an old man coming back from the dead,' Beran said. The Saracen did not deny it.

Camelot rose above that rich and fertile farmland, its sentry fires casting a bronze glow onto the underside of that cloud which was now releasing its cargo of fine rain into the night. Below the stone walls and tiered ramparts, and surrounding Camelot on all sides, the Saxons' campfires flickered like myriad embers spread across the undulating land. Enough flame perhaps to dry this rain before it soaked into the earth.

'And anyway, how are we going to get through?' Beran asked.

Palamedes scratched his beard as he considered the challenge facing them. 'I'll admit you look more like a Saxon than I.'

Beran pulled his cloak in around his neck against the rain and pressed his left thumb into the knuckles of his right hand. He felt so tired. He wondered where the boy was now. He wished he could send him some sign. For the first time in his life, Beran wished he possessed some measure of the talent that Guinevere had owned, and Merlin, for then he would cast his spirit into some night creature, an owl perhaps, or fox, or badger. He would find the boy and somehow the boy would know. *I am coming, boy,* Beran wanted to tell him. *You are not alone.*

But Beran had never possessed the talent. In truth he had never understood it. His only talent had been for war. *Now you're just an old man. What do you think you can do for the boy?*

Palamedes swiped rain off his face and turned to Beran. He looked ashen and gaunt. Bone-tired. 'We cannot fool them into thinking we're Saxons. We cannot get past so many without being seen, but we cannot fight without weapons.' His eyes were flint shards in which tiny distant fires burned. 'What is the plan, Arthur?'

The name took him aback. He felt the weight of it like so much mail. Like an anchor stone pulling him down into the past. He thought of Merlin and wished his old friend were alive, for the druid would know what to do.

He turned and looked at the gnarled and windswept shape of an ancient hawthorn, knowing that such trees were said to stand at the threshold of the Otherworld. That tree must have stood like a sentinel in this place since before the first Saxon keels ground upon the shingle shore. How many springtimes had folk gathered the white-blossomed branches of just such a hawthorn and taken them into homes and halls to ensure the beauty of the coming year and to sweeten the air with that scent so evocative of the carnal act?

There was no blossom now. Soon that tree would be bare, its branches skeletal and hoary with frost. For now, though, the tangled crown atop that knotted and fissured trunk would provide shelter from the rain, and that would do.

'I'm tired, Palamedes,' he said. 'I need to sleep.'

He would wrap his cloak around him and lie down beneath that hawthorn and shut his eyes. Just for a while. Shut his eyes and remember. Let it all come back. All that once was. All that could never now be.

'I will wake you, Arthur,' Palamedes said, turning back to gaze upon the hill fort of Camelot once more. 'Do not think that I won't.'

'Do what you must,' he replied, walking towards that old tree.

He could already hear voices in the breathy sigh of the rain. They stayed with him, those voices, those unseen ghosts, until he drifted away.

'Arthur. Wake up, Arthur.'

The voice seems far away. He wants to ignore it. To stay in the past. But he knows he cannot stay.

'Arthur, wake up. You need to see this.'

The voice is one thing, the strong hand gripping his shoulder, shaking him, is another. There is no ignoring that. 'I'm awake,' he growls, opening his eyes to see Palamedes. The Saracen is squatting beside him in a way that Arthur's own knees would never now allow. 'Have I even been asleep?' he asks, though he knows that he has, for the ghosts of his dreams linger all around still. And somewhere nearby, a thrush pours its liquid song into the dark, singing for a mate before it is light enough to search for food.

'Look around, Arthur,' the Saracen says, his own eyes wide and glimmered with awe. 'How is it possible?'

Arthur sits up, expecting the familiar ache, the stiffness in his joints, the burn of a bladder straining. But he feels none of it. Perhaps his body is numb. He blinks to vanquish the sleep and the faces from his eyes, and he peers into the pre-dawn dark, and for a moment he does not believe what he sees.

'At first I thought it was smoke,' Palamedes says. 'From all the fires.

Then I feared they were burning Camelot.' Arthur turns his face to the north-west, though he cannot see Camelot now. Palamedes shakes his head. 'But it is no smoke.'

It is mist. Arthur has known it in this part of the world. Has seen the mist lying thin as a grey veil over the green pastures. Has known it as thick as a fur, clinging to the willows and golden reeds, or rising from the dark waters into the wide and boundless skies. It can seem like a living thing, this fog, and Arthur wonders now about the hawthorn beneath whose wind-shaped foliage he had slept. Has he crossed over to the Otherworld? Is he now in Anwnn? It would explain the voices and the faces, the spirits of old friends and spear-brothers with whom he shared the night.

No. Palamedes is no ghost. His grey-bearded face still wears the worries of this world. His eyes still hold his fears for the boy. 'This is the gods' doing,' the Saracen says, touching the iron strap end of his belt to ward off evil.

Arthur reaches into the neck of his tunic and touches the silver ring strung there.

Perhaps this is *the gods' doing.*

'Come,' he says, climbing to his feet. Nearby, the horses lift their heads from cropping the damp grass. They too seem to eye with distrust the mist closing in, as if it is some predator creeping upon them. But Arthur's flaxen mare nickers softly, comforted by his touch, and together he and Palamedes mount and urge their horses down the slope, and the mist swallows them.

They do not speak now. They ride slowly, letting the horses choose their own way down the limestone ridge, sitting still in their saddles, hips loose to allow their seat bones to follow the movement of the horses. Down into the valley, where the fog hangs heavier still, as thick as pottage stew because of the smoke from so many Saxon peat fires. And soon they find themselves amongst those campfires, whose light stains the mist, so that it seems a score of jaundiced eyes watch their slow progress from beyond the veil.

He sees the dark shapes of figures around those fires. Hears their low voices. Hears their words, which had once claimed nothing but those possessions which they brought here, but now encompass the flowers and birds, forests and streams, while all that once was fades with the passing of those who had known them by another name.

He does not need his eyes to know the way. His blood is in this land, soaked into the earth beneath the mare's hooves, and all the years cannot now separate them.

They pass so close to a knot of Saxons that one of those spearmen reaches out and strokes Arthur's mare, running his hand from her ear, down her neck to the shoulder. The animal snorts and walks on, and for a moment Arthur looks into the eyes of that Saxon. Then the man is gone, fading into the mist.

How many fires have they passed? How many warriors, huddling in the dark, waiting for dawn?

Riding beside him, close enough that Arthur could almost touch him, Palamedes turns his face, his night-haunted eyes asking Arthur how this could be. But Arthur does not know how. He slips a hand into the linen bag tied to his saddle horn, pressing his fingers against Uffa's magnificent helmet, feeling the iron crest and hoping that whatever spell this is, it will last a little longer yet.

Then they come onto rising ground and he knows they are at the foot of the great fog-wreathed hill upon which Camelot sits like a sentinel guarding Dumnonia and the eastern frontier. Still, no one challenges them, neither Saxon nor Briton. Still, they do not speak, but ride slowly up that steep hill, following a shallow, bramble- and furze-tangled track. Up and up they go, cloaked in reverence and awe, like pilgrims coming upon holy ground, or like men of a secret cult recalling some arcane initiation of a lifetime ago.

Arthur sees movement up ahead. A horseman, coming down the slope towards them, the mist parting before him, rolling aside like white spume before the bow of some vessel. Arthur recognizes the way the man sits his sturdy-looking pony, his back straight, the arrogant tilt of his chin.

No.

His stomach twists. It cannot be. He feels the old ache in his shoulder, where a blade had ripped into flesh and split bone. A blade thrust by the young man now coming towards him as if returning from the dead.

Mordred. My son.

Arthur wants to call out to him, but he knows that Mordred cannot see him. The young man's eyes look straight ahead. His thoughts belong to another time, another place.

'My son,' Arthur whispers as they pass each other and he looks into

Mordred's pale face. He wants to tell him that he is sorry. But Mordred rides on, the four severed human heads tied by their long fair hair to his saddle horns gently swinging. And then he is gone.

The hill is very steep here. Arthur leans forward, his cheek brushing his mare's sweet-smelling neck as she picks her careful way up a stony gully in the second rampart. It is so narrow here that Palamedes rides behind him, his own mount as sure-footed as Arthur's, the soft scuff of the animals' hooves the only sound.

Arthur thinks he can smell the rich soil which was turned over when the ramparts were dug. When hope was ripe and folk sweated to reclaim this hill from the bones of their ancestors who had stood in this very place against the soldiers of Rome. He can almost reach out and touch those golden days. But some movement catches his eye and he looks along the ditch and sees Lancelot there.

My friend. My brother.

Lancelot is digging, thrusting down with his spade again and again, and it brings tears to Arthur's eyes to see him so young and so strong. The two of them had once raced to the summit of this hill. They had been fierce as hawks then. They had been lords of war.

How their brotherhood had soured, and with it the world.

Arthur cannot bear to watch his old friend toiling there, digging Camelot's defences, building their shared dream, and so he looks away. And he and Palamedes come up over the fourth rampart, and there he sees a ghost who almost stills his old heart.

Guinevere wears a dress of green silk and a wolf's pelt around her shoulders. Her hair is braided and coiled and set with silver pins. Her face is marble white, her eyes are dark. And she is the most beautiful creature he has ever seen.

'My love,' he says in a voice as old as the whisper of the breeze through barley.

He looks to Palamedes, for surely the Saracen can see Guinevere too. How can she be a ghost?

How can she be gone when I am still here?

But Palamedes cannot see her. He is leaning forward in the saddle, scanning the horizon as they come up to the plateau, where the mist is thinner, drifting in tendrils before the wooden palisade and walls of dressed stone.

And so Arthur turns to look at Guinevere one last time, but she is not there.

The door clumps shut behind him. For a long while he stands in the shadows, beyond the slow play of light licking at the dark. The fire is dying, yet flames still leap now and then, briefly pushing the darkness away, then succumbing to it once more.

He presses his palm against one of the great posts supporting the roof, remembering how he had helped build this hall, smoothing timbers, one hand guiding the adze on its swing, pushing it upwards and then pulling it downwards, over and over until the sweat stung his eyes and his back filled with fire, and he felt a kind of peace which was more precious to him than gold.

This had been his hall once. *Their* hall.

He looks up at the soot-blackened beams and the old thatch, thinking of all the smoke that has risen from the hearth, all the voices too, the stories and the hopes, the secrets and the fears. For a moment he can hear those voices, all of them at once, like the murmur of the sea, and he closes his eyes and lets it wash over him.

'You took your time, Arthur.'

That voice. It cuts through the hum inside his head. It is from another time. It is the cold ash from a long-extinguished fire. And yet . . . it is as familiar as the touch of his own hand.

He opens his eyes, looks over at the three empty oaken chairs before the hearth. No, one of them is not empty after all. The one turned slightly away from the door and facing what flame still dances in the hearth. A gnarled staff leans against that chair. And is that the shadow-masked outline of a face?

'Well, are you going to stand there gawping all night? Or do you expect me to dance my way over there with a cup of wine and a piece of cheese? If so, you'll be waiting a long time, Arthur ap Uther.'

Arthur shakes his head as if to rid himself of this ghost. He looks around for Palamedes, then remembers that the Saracen went off with the guard who had shown them to Lord Galahad's and Lady Iselle's hall. *Their* hall now.

He goes to take a step, then stops himself. 'Can it be you, Merlin?' he asks into the dark.

Silence then, but for the quiet flap of flame and something scratching amongst the dry floor reeds. It *is* in his head, then. And yet . . .

He edges forward. He sees that there is a dog sleeping by one of the oaken chairs, its head resting on its outstretched forelegs. An old hound, grey as storm cloud, dreaming of its hunting days.

'Who were you expecting, you old fool?' the druid says.

Arthur scoffs. 'Old fool? That is rich, coming from you. How can you be alive still? You were old when I was into my first beard.'

'I wasn't old, Arthur, but you were always a fool.'

Arthur walks along the hall's central aisle, knowing each of the twelve paces from door to hearth, recalling how he had paced out the length himself, measuring it against his memory of Uther's hall.

Now, the druid stands, the claws of his hands clutching at the chair's arms as he pushes himself to his feet, grimacing with effort and with habit. He takes up his staff and turns to face Arthur, and the hearth flames flicker in his eyes.

'I told them to expect you,' he says, lifting a frail arm towards the darkened door. 'I said, watch for Arthur, for he will come.'

'Merlin.' The name escapes his lips like a breath. 'I thought you were dead.'

The druid sighs. 'People do so enjoy telling me that they thought I was dead. It is not flattering, Arthur.' He arches a brow. 'Mind you, I expect you're going to hear a lot of that yourself.'

For a moment, Arthur just stands there, drinking in the sight of that face. His old friend. The druid's hair and brows are white, his cheeks are sunken and shadow-pooled. He is as thin as smoke. But he is alive, and Arthur can feel his heart swelling.

'It has been so long, Merlin.'

Merlin's lips tighten. His eyes gleam in the firelight. The watery eyes of an old man, perhaps. Or perhaps not. 'What dreams we had, Arthur,' he says. 'We would have remade Britain, you and I. The gods talked to me back then. I dreamt to them and they answered in their way.'

Arthur is about to ask if the gods talk to him still, to ask Merlin if he sent the mist which allowed them to slip through the Saxon lines like shades, for hadn't Merlin performed such a feat of magic for Uther long, long ago? But he hears the latch of the door and the squeak of its hinges.

'Oh, you're in the dung heap now, Arthur.' Merlin's thin lips pull back from his few remaining teeth.

Arthur turns and sees a figure looming in the open doorway. He cannot see the man's face, but he does not need to see it to know him.

'I thought they were talking out of their arses,' Gawain says. 'It can't be Arthur, I told them. No, Arthur turned his back on us years ago. Left us to fight the wars he started. Vanished into the marsh like some restless spirit at dawn after Samhain.'

'Gawain . . . I . . .'

'No!' Gawain takes four strides and stops. He is still beyond the bloom of light cast by those fitful, dying flames, but he lifts a hand and points a finger at Arthur. 'You left us. You have no voice here, Arthur.' It is as if Gawain fears to come closer, though Arthur had never known his friend to fear anything.

'I was . . . broken,' Arthur says. He takes a step towards Gawain. He wants to throw his arms around his old friend, to hold him tight as though that will close the gap between them, as though it will stitch the wound. But he is afraid to. They are not the same men they were. How can they be? 'I was broken, Gawain. You know that I was.'

Gawain is old now, too, his hair all but gone and his beard stained by wine. His shoulders are rounded where once he had stood square like the iron-studded oak door at his back. 'I know that you died many years ago,' Gawain says. His hands are clenched into fists at his sides. 'You died in the marsh.' He shakes his head. 'I don't know the man standing before me now.'

'Tell me, what difference would it have made had I stayed?' Arthur asks him. 'What could I have done, brother?'

Now Gawain strides towards him, pointing that accusing finger again. It might as well be a blade, such is the hate behind it. The bitterness.

'You could have fought!' Gawain says, spittle lacing his beard. He stands within arm's reach now, his lip curled as though Arthur stinks of death. 'You could have fought, Arthur.' He throws his arms wide. 'Like we did. Like your daughter did.'

There it is. The knife in his belly.

I had no fight left in me, thinks Arthur. *Not then.*

'Damn you, Arthur,' Gawain snarls, and the old hound lying by the fire lifts its head warily, looking at Gawain with red-rimmed eyes before settling down again. 'You could have led us still. Spearmen would have come . . . for you. Instead, you slipped away. Like a coward.'

Arthur feels his own hands tighten, feels violence rising in his blood, craving release. 'Careful, Gawain,' he warns. 'I loved you as a brother, but I will not hear more.'

'Enough!' Merlin hobbles over and puts himself between them, swinging his eyes from one to the other. 'Fools, both of you. As stubborn as each other.' He lifts his druid's staff, as Arthur has seen him do a thousand times. 'There are Saxons enough to fight out there, without you going at each other like two old boars.' He reaches out and pulls a loose thread from the shoulder of Gawain's cloak and holds it up to the old warrior's face, hand trembling. 'The past cannot be unpicked, you dolt,' he says, casting the thread aside.

He is so old and bent, so worn by years and burdened by the absence of all that might have been, that Arthur wonders what magic has kept the druid's heart thumping in his breast. What spirit rides in the old man yet?

'Arthur is here now,' Merlin says, then he winces as though in pain, and coughs, and coughs, and Arthur reaches out, offering his support, but Merlin bats his hand away, and well he might, for he has survived until now without Arthur's help.

The coughing subdued for the present, he looks up at Arthur, a crooked staff trying to straighten itself. 'Perhaps I am a fool too,' he says, 'but what if the gods have brought Arthur back to us now?' Teeth bared with the effort, he looks up at the dark thatch and the sickly smoke hanging above the roof beams. 'It may be that only the ghosts of the gods of Britain linger here still. But what if they yet possess . . .' he pinches a thumb and forefinger together, '. . . a sliver of power? What if they themselves remember the dream of Britain, like I do?' He turns his gaze on Gawain, and for all his seeming frailty there is still fire in those rheumy eyes. 'Could it be that they have conspired to bring Arthur back to us? To return him to Camelot?'

Gawain shakes his head, but before he can say what he thinks of such things, Arthur says, 'The gods have nothing to do with it. I am too old for dreams, Merlin.'

'And yet you dream every night, don't you?' the druid says.

Arthur says nothing to that. Merlin shakes his head. 'You have never understood your part in all this. That was my burden. Yours was to fight. To kill.' He presses a skeletal hand to his chest. 'To give our people heart, Arthur, and make them think that they could win.'

'We could never win,' Gawain says. 'I see that now. And Arthur being here cannot change that.'

The door is flung open, drawing the fading hearth flames. Arthur wonders who has come now. How many more knives to be sheathed in his heart? There is one he knows of certainly.

'Best if you say nothing,' Gawain rumbles at him under his breath.

For warriors are spilling into the hall, cloaked in conversation of Saxon chieftains and the size of their war bands, of food and water, arrows and grain. They are grizzled, tired-looking men in dirty mail and damp cloaks, helmets tucked under their arms, and they have not noticed Arthur standing in the ebbing glow.

And now in come the warrior Lord and Lady of Camelot, both in long tunics of scale armour whose weight Arthur can feel from where he stands.

She has changed much, and seeing her now is a blow to his stomach, driving the breath from him.

My daughter.

Iselle is not the same girl he had last seen at his hidden steading in the marshes of Avalon. She is careworn and austere, her mouth tight and her brow heavy, and yet he can see Guinevere in her. There is no doubting that. Can see himself too. And that is all he has given her.

And now she looks up, as if some voice has whispered in her ear, telling her who is standing there with Merlin and Gawain. She stops dead, even as the others in the party continue walking towards the hearth.

'I still say we can hold,' a black-bearded warrior says, leading the others towards the fire.

The Lady of Camelot is staring at Arthur. Her jaw is clenched like a fist.

'If we can break them once on our ramparts, they will begin to slink off after easier prey,' the black-bearded warrior says, just a few feet away now.

'They don't need to attack,' the tall man at his shoulder says. 'They just need to wait for us to starve.'

Arthur and Iselle are tethered to each other across the copper-licked gloom of the hall, and Arthur will not be the one to break the bind of their eyes.

To think that they are now under the same roof, breathing the same air.

'What is it?' Galahad has stopped now too, and turns back to Iselle to see what's wrong. To ask what ghost has slipped through the veil to haunt her.

And now the black-bearded warrior reaches the fire and he looks up and sees Arthur, as do the others. As does Galahad.

'For any who don't know . . .' Merlin's voice stills all others as he lifts his staff towards Arthur, '. . . this man is Arthur ap Uther. Whom men called Lord of Battle.'

Silence now, but for the soft sputtering of flame. Mouths hang open. Eyes bulge. Men's hands creep towards iron pommels or strap ends, even though their other hands cradle iron helmets.

'Arthur,' the man with the black beard whispers, staring.

But Arthur is still looking at Iselle, wondering at all the lost years, gazing in awe at the woman his daughter has become.

'You have all heard the songs,' Merlin says. His voice trembles, as does the hand he holds aloft, finger pointing at the smoky gloom. 'The bards sing that in our darkest days, when we need him most, Arthur shall come again.' He lowers his arm, placing both hands on the apple-sized knob of his hazel staff.

'Lord Artorius,' another says in an outward breath. This warrior's cheeks are pockmarked, his beard thin and wispy. 'How can it be?'

Galahad pushes his way through the knot of warriors and stands before Arthur. Gods, but he is so like Lancelot that it hurts to look at him.

'Lord Arthur,' Galahad says, extending his hand and dipping his chin in a gesture of respect which Arthur knows he does not deserve. They grip each other by the forearm, the young man's unblinking gaze as heavy as ringmail. Over his shoulder and the heads of the other men, Arthur sees that Palamedes is there too. 'You look well, Arthur,' Galahad says.

'He looks old,' Gawain puts in, sharing a look of mutual respect with the Saracen, the two of them acknowledging shared fights, fires and ale of years ago.

'Why have you come?' Galahad asks Arthur. He does not ask *how* he has come.

'This man cannot be Arthur,' one of the other warriors says. He is young, but battle-scarred, his face grimy with ingrained soot. 'Arthur died after the great battle at Camlan.'

'No.' They turn to the voice. Palamedes stands in shadow, but his presence defies the gloom. 'This man is Arthur ap Uther. I know because I rode with him at Camlan. I was there when we broke the Saxons and those spearmen of the traitor Mordred.'

'That was a long time ago,' Arthur says.

'Maybe Samhain has come early,' Gawain says, standing apart and throwing logs one by one into the fire. 'But this *is* the man who broke the Saxons at Camlan. I was there too, when the world held its breath.'

'I did not break the Saxons,' Arthur says. 'That was Lancelot.' Arthur holds Galahad's eye as he says that, and the young man's lips tighten, his brow darkens. Galahad bears his own burdens, Arthur knows.

'We will not waste breath talking of the past,' the Lady of Camelot says. Her first words to them all, and all eyes turn to her. 'Cunedda, do we have any proof of who the boy is?' There is a calm authority in her voice, and even the men's shock at Arthur's presence there subsides, their attention turning to the lady to whom they owe fealty.

Cunedda scratches his black beard and shakes his head. 'Could be any whelp taken from any village in Dumnonia.'

'What boy?' Arthur asks Iselle.

'This is not your concern,' Iselle tells him, her eyes saying more than her tongue.

Still, to these other men, Arthur's name has been the meat and mead of fireside tales since they were old enough to listen, and they look to him again now, and Arthur knows what it must feel like to be some spirit returned to the world on Samhain or dug out of some ancient burial mound.

Cunedda dips his head to Arthur. 'King Cynric sent a message, lord,' he says. 'He claims to have Prince Erbin—'

'King Constantine's son,' another warrior puts in.

'Arthur has no authority here,' Lady Iselle says. 'You do not answer to him.' She turns to Gawain. 'Take him from my hall, Gawain.'

Gawain glances at Galahad, who nods to second the lady's command.

Gawain takes a step towards Arthur. 'Best come with me, Arthur,' Gawain says. The others look on in mute disbelief.

'It's true,' Arthur says. 'The boy is Constantine's son.'

'And how would you know anything about that?' Gawain asks. Now, even Iselle's venom is cut with curiosity; she steps through the knot of men to get closer to Arthur, her hand resting on the hilt of the sword at her left hip.

'Palamedes and I have been travelling with the boy,' Arthur says, and some heads turn towards the Saracen.

Palamedes nods. 'Prince Erbin is a brave young man. A credit to his father the late king.' He looks at Arthur, crestfallen. Ashamed even. 'Cynric's men took him from us.'

'I found him the day they burned Caer Colun,' Arthur says. 'We were bringing him here.'

'We failed,' Palamedes says. His gaze seems unformed, foggy like the world beyond the timber walls, as though he is looking inward at the events of the last weeks, weighing their efforts and finding them wanting.

'Damn them,' Cunedda rumbles into his beard.

'Why were you bringing the prince here?' Galahad asks Arthur.

Arthur tries to remember why. He shrugs. 'The boy thought you would help him.'

'And what did you think?' Iselle asks him. She says it like an accusation.

She is so proud, and yet still wild. He remembers how she had seemed like a she-wolf roaming the marshes, hunting Saxons. Haunting them. Killing them with her bow. He wonders how she has taken to this new life, as a leader of spearmen. As a queen in all but name, yet cooped up behind a palisade on top of this hill.

'I gave my word I would help him,' he tells her. 'I would have walked him up to the south gate and then I would have turned round and walked away.'

The lady nods, the lines of her jaw showing beneath the skin. 'You are good at walking away, Arthur,' she says. Not *Father*. But then, he has never been a father to her.

'Come now, Arthur.' Merlin leans his staff towards him. 'The boy is Constantine's son. You know what that means.'

Arthur gives a slight shake of his head. 'It means nothing to me.'

'His grandfather was High King Ambrosius,' one of the other men says, looking from face to face. The new fuel in the hearth has taken the flame now, casting them all in red and bronze and chasing away the darkness. 'The boy could have a claim to the high seat of Dumnonia. Who would challenge him? No one has more right.' He glances at Arthur. 'Well, except Lord Arthur.' He acknowledges Arthur with an open hand.

'The prince has the makings of a warrior,' Palamedes says. 'I saw him kill a Saxon with my own eyes. I believe men would fight for him.'

'And with Arthur at his side,' Merlin puts in, adding his own fuel to the flame of it, 'we could raise a thousand spears. More. Men would come from Powys and Rheged, from Caer Lerion and Caer Gloui and Cornubia. We could raise an army the likes of which hasn't been seen since Camlan.'

Gawain grunts. 'The kings won't send their spearmen. They've no fight left in them. Not any more.'

'He's right,' Galahad agrees. 'We've tried. We lit the beacons. We sent riders. No one has come.'

Some of the others mutter their opinions of the lords and kings of Britain.

'With respect, Lord Galahad,' the druid interrupts them, pulling his white beard through a talon-like hand to smooth it. 'They won't come for you because you are the son of a traitor. The son of the man who betrayed Arthur.'

Arthur recoils inwardly from his words. He knows now, more than ever, the real truth of it. But Galahad makes no effort to deny it.

'And they won't come for Lady Iselle,' Merlin goes on, 'because they are fools and will not be led in war by a woman.' He sighs. 'Even though it was a warrior queen who led our people against the Romans. Who slaughtered the invaders in their thousands.'

'Have I not killed enough Saxons?' Iselle asks them all. 'I have proved myself the equal of any man.'

Cunedda and the others nod and grunt in affirmation.

'You have done more than that, my lady.' Galahad lifts his chest. He is proud of her, and it tugs at Arthur's heart to see it, for his own loss, yes, and because he doesn't know his own daughter, but also because he is thankful that Galahad and Iselle have each other. 'It was King Constantine who poisoned them against you,' Lancelot's son says.

More rumbles of accord.

'None of it matters.' Cunedda looks from Galahad to Iselle. 'Cynric's message was clear. We must abandon Camelot, or he will burn the prince before the gates.'

Arthur catches Palamedes' eye, his guts clenching with fear for the boy. He looks at Cunedda. 'When?'

Cunedda lifts a hand to swipe a trickle of sweat from his forehead. 'Midday tomorrow.'

'Three times he has ordered us to cede this hill,' Gawain says. 'Three times we have told him to come and take it.'

'He didn't have the prince then,' Galahad says.

'A man on the gate said he heard them chopping wood,' Cunedda says. 'Can't see with this fog but . . . could be they're building a pyre.'

Arthur's teeth ache from biting down on his anger. What is he doing here when the boy is out there somewhere? Alone and afraid. Watching the Saxons pile up wood, preparing to burn him alive.

'If we leave this hill at dawn, Cynric will give us safe passage west.' The words squeeze themselves out from between Cunedda's teeth, as though he almost dare not say them, or else is ashamed to.

Iselle is biting at her bottom lip. 'If we give them Camelot, Dumnonia is lost,' she says.

'But if the boy lives, there is hope,' Merlin counters.

'Hope?' Gawain almost laughs. 'You know better than anyone that the Saxons will burn him or cut his throat anyway. Cynric is no fool. I've met him. He knows that the son of Constantine is valuable to us. He won't let him live. He can't.'

'Camelot is more important than one boy, no matter who he is,' Galahad says. 'And even if we gave it up, who here thinks Cynric would let three hundred spearmen walk away when he has more than twice that number slathering at the mouth to slaughter us?'

Arthur can feel Palamedes watching him. Waiting for him. 'Arthur,' the Saracen says, 'we can't abandon the boy.'

'And I will not abandon Camelot,' Iselle says.

They argue amongst themselves then. Merlin and Palamedes are talking of Prince Erbin, son of King Constantine, grandson of High King Ambrosius, future king of Dumnonia and, perhaps, even the new Pendragon. They speak of him as a talisman, like the sword Excalibur, which Arthur once wielded in battle after battle and which united the kings and warlords of the land. So will Prince Erbin draw men to his banner, they say.

Iselle and Cunedda speak for Camelot, maintaining that this ancient fortress is more than a hill of limestone and turf, more than a defensive bulwark against the ever-advancing Saxon tide. They say that Camelot is a flame burning in the creeping night, and that so long as it burns, so long as men and women of Britain stand upon its earthen ramparts, hope remains.

Gawain is leaving them to it. He stands with his back against a roof post, drinking ale while the others debate.

No one speaks for the boy. No one speaks just for him.

As the others talk, Arthur watches the fire lick at the white bark of the birch logs. There is much he regrets. So much. He cannot change any of it now. But the boy has brought none of this upon himself. He has not made the mistakes Arthur has made. He is just a boy.

'Arthur.' It is Galahad who breaks the spell of the fire, bringing Arthur back. He even sounds like Lancelot. 'What do you say?' He lifts a hand to still every other tongue in the room, even Merlin's. 'What should we do?'

That Galahad would hear his mind on it, after everything. The pain of that is like damp in his bones. He looks at Iselle, expecting her to forbid him to speak, but she does not. She stands with her arms crossed over her mailed breast, her chin lifted. Still wary. Still angry. But she would hear him too.

'You cannot give them Camelot,' he says. 'Once lost, it may never be recovered.'

Some murmurs of agreement at that.

He holds Galahad's eye, as though through him he will make a vow to Lancelot. 'But I will not forsake the boy,' he says. 'On my life, I will not.'

'Are you mad, Lord Arthur?' Cunedda asks.

'They will cut you down the moment you walk out of the gates,' the pockmarked man says.

Galahad shakes his head, his gaze hardening. The vein in his temple seems to throb beneath the skin, just as with Lancelot when he was angry. 'Have you come here to find your death, Arthur? Would you throw your life away so cheaply, after everything?'

Iselle is just watching him. She knows better.

'No, Galahad.' This from Merlin. His old lips are curled at the corners. 'If the gods wanted Arthur to be being a fool in Anwnn, he could have sweated to death from a fever, or fallen from the cliffs at Tintagel, or shat himself inside out after some bad fish, or had his skull staved in by one of his beloved horses.' He sweeps the staff through the air. 'He might even have had his belly opened by a Saxon blade.' He is grinning now, his last three or four teeth clinging to his gums like limpets to worn rock. 'No, our lord of war did not come here to throw his life away in the name of some boy, like a man hoping to wipe clean his slate.' He lifts his face to Gawain, who is refilling his cup from a jug. His moustaches are wet with ale. 'Do we still have Lord Arthur's banner, Gawain?' the druid asks.

Gawain drags a hand across his lips. 'I'll wager it's full of holes and home to a nest of mice ... but yes. We have it.'

'And Arthur's pretty fish-scale armour?' Merlin asks.

Gawain nods. 'And his sword.'

Merlin says nothing for a moment, just stands with his eyes closed, his face turned up to the roof beams, hands gripping his druid's staff. No one speaks, for they know better than to interrupt him. When he opens his eyes, they are riveted to Iselle. 'Tell me, lady, would your warriors follow Arthur, slayer of Saxons and lord of battle, in one last fight?'

'You'd have us leave the safety of the walls?' Cunedda exclaims. He glares at Iselle. 'You would abandon these ramparts and take the fight out there?'

Iselle ignores him. She is not looking at Merlin, but at Arthur.

'Yes,' she says. 'My warriors would follow him.'

Arthur dips his head at her, and she does the same, her lips pinched, her eyes still defiant. He does not know this woman, this daughter of his lost love, Guinevere, but in that moment perhaps they understand each other, and that is more than he could have hoped for.

Merlin nods, then looks at Gawain. 'Will you, Gawain, son of King Lot of Lyonesse, fight at Arthur's shoulder, as you have so many times before?'

Arthur tears his gaze from Iselle and looks at this man, this prince who gave up a kingdom for him.

'Aye,' Gawain says, locking eyes with him the way stags will bind antlers during the rut. 'I'll kill Saxons for him.' He is all challenge and pride, hurt and memory. 'I always believed in you, Arthur. I followed you from the moment we met. I would've died for you and your dream of Britain a score of times.' He grunts. 'So if you've got it in you to ride again, to remind us what it was all for ... then I'll ride with you.'

Arthur can barely breathe. His vision is blurred, yet he can see the glistening of Gawain's eyes by the flamelight, before his old brother-in-arms looks away.

Merlin makes a gruff sound in his throat. 'Lady,' he says, leaning his staff towards her. 'Will you yourself take up arms and follow Arthur out of the gates of Camelot? Will you soak the earth with Saxon blood?'

Iselle breathes deeply. She turns to face Merlin, the firelight dancing in the bronze scales of her armour. She says, 'I will.'

The druid nods. He does not need to ask Galahad, for he is Lancelot's son.

Arthur looks at Iselle. He is more proud of her than he has the right to be.

'Lady,' he says. He squares his shoulders. Feels the old thrill like an echo from the past. A quiver in his chest. A slight tremble in the blood. 'The songs say I will come again.' He lifts his chin. 'Here I am.'

19

The Horse Lords

TIME ITSELF SEEMS CHANGED. It is no longer night, yet dawn has not come. The day is as yet unmade, like a skein of wool hung on a loom. A thin rain hazes the air, and the mist lingers still, stealing through the world as though reluctant to slink back to the dykes and marshes. It gives the faces and buildings around him the intangible, unformed quality of dreams.

The stallion upon whose strong back he sits belongs to Galahad. It is called Malo, in honour, so the younger warrior told Arthur, of a stallion which his father had loved as a boy.

'You must ride Malo,' he had said, introducing Arthur and the proud beast at the stables. He had grinned then. 'He is brave and fast and he hates Saxons.'

'Thank you, Galahad,' Arthur had said, letting Malo smell his hand and his face.

'I'm honoured, lord,' Galahad said. And no more words were needed after that.

Now, Galahad is mounted behind him on a white mare, dressed in Lancelot's scale coat and wearing Lancelot's helmet with its white plume, so that Arthur feels as if Lancelot's shade will be riding with him; their enemies should pray to their gods to help them now.

Gawain is mounted too, a thick-shafted spear resting diagonally across his saddle and his stallion's neck, and beside him is Palamedes on an angry dun mare, his face grim beneath a silver-chased helmet. Behind Palamedes is Parcefal ap Bliocadran, his long white hair tied back, his white beard rope jutting from his raw-boned, sunken-eyed face. He is old, and Arthur never thought to lay eyes on him again in this life. But when the old warrior had come to the lady's hall at news of his return, and he and Arthur saw each other in the flamelight, tears had sprung in Parcefal's eyes and he had felt no shame at them.

'I knew this day would come, lord,' he said in a breaking voice, trying to stand straight, though his back was twisted like an old roof beam.

'You were the truest of us, Parcefal,' Arthur said. 'Will you ride with me one last time, old friend?'

The flame glow had danced on Parcefal's face, so that by some ephemeral illusion were revealed glimpses of the young man he had once been. 'Aye,' he had said, thumbing a tear from his cheek. 'To the green fields of Anwnn, lord.'

With Parcefal now are nine more horse warriors. They are resplendent in mail and shining helmets from whose crowns plumes of red horsehair hang damp in the pre-dawn drizzle. These men are stiff with pride and sharp with honour. Old men all, they are the last of the horse lords of Britain, called now as if by some ancient war horn to climb up into their saddles and ride into memory.

The horses are themselves armoured, in boiled leather rubbed with beeswax so that it gleams like polished oak, shaffrons covering their faces, breastplates protecting their mighty hearts. And Arthur knows that the grandsires and granddams of those horses carried his warriors into battle at Camlan.

Over a tunic of russet wool and one of leather, Arthur wears his old war gear, Galahad having kept it safe all these years, just as Arthur had kept Lancelot's armour after he fell at the great battle. The long coat of bronze scales feels heavy now, and yet so familiar. The iron greaves cling to his lower legs. The sword belt presses on his right shoulder, passing obliquely across his body down to the other belt at his waist, all of it glinting with silver scales. And the scabbard, battered and scarred but newly oiled. Empty now, though soon to be filled with iron, as a body with its own breath.

A boy waits in the dark, looking up at him with wide eyes, holding a spear in one hand, and in the other the silver and copper helmet once owned by the Saxon Uffa, its sightless eyes staring as if through the veil into the world beyond.

'The spear, boy,' Arthur says, and the boy hands it up to him, and Arthur thinks back to a snowy day when he was just a boy himself, and he had run across the white-mantled fields to watch the last charge of the equites Romani. And one of those horsemen, whose name he had not asked, had given him his bear fur.

'What's your name, boy?' Arthur says.

The boy swallows. He is nervous. 'Girflet, lord.'

Arthur nods, as though he thinks it is a good name. A strong name. He draws the long silver pin from the brooch at his right shoulder and takes off his red cloak – heavy with dampness now – and hands it down to the boy. 'Take this.'

The boy looks unsure. 'But you will need it, lord.'

He shakes his head. Presses a hand to his bronze armour. 'Would you hide such a coat of scales, boy?'

The boy grins now. 'I would not, lord,' he says, clutching that damp cloak to his chest.

'I want the Saxons to know who is killing them, Girflet,' Arthur says. He twists in his saddle to look at Gawain and Palamedes, Galahad and Parcefal and the others. He holds the sight of them all like a man holding his last breath. Looks into the eyes of these proud warriors, and they look into his, and they are all young men once more, hot-blooded and eager and foolish for the thrill of battle.

They are fourteen armoured men on armoured horses. Not enough, and yet he knows what carnage such mounted warriors can wreak. He knows the screams of fear and pain, and the splintering of bones and pummelling of flesh beneath iron-shod hooves. And in the creeping mist which still haunts the land, fourteen may seem like forty.

Behind these last of the horse lords wait the spearmen of Camelot with their lady. Two hundred and sixty-eight men, the remaining two score being spread amongst the old men, women and boys who will stay at the ramparts, spear blades pointing at the sky to fool the Saxons into thinking that steadfast warriors yet guard the walls.

'To a man they will fight like heroes for you and Lady Iselle,' Galahad had told Arthur as the spearmen gathered in the gloom and made their way down to the south gate, silent as wraiths but for their footfalls, the creak of leather or the jangle of armour and iron fittings.

Arthur had felt their eyes on him in the dark, sensed their awe and wonder, and so he had given them what they wanted. What they needed. He had polished his fish-scale coat and his greaves until they gleamed. He had combed and oiled his beard and moustaches, and straightened his back in defiance of the years he bore, and he held his head high. Wading heart-deep through the mire of memory, he had become the lord of war again. He had even taken a red plume from an old helmet and fixed it to the masked helmet which the boy now held ready for him, but *that* he had done for himself.

Wherever I fight, men will know that I fight for you.

Somewhere nearby, a crow calls in guttural clicks and rattles. He looks up and sees the bird sitting on one of the palisade timbers, stabbing at its own jagged feathers with its glossy black bill. It caws then. A gnarled, shrunken note, loud in the strange stillness.

'I am coming,' he tells the bird under his breath.

'Who are you talking to, Arthur?' It is Merlin. He was not here a heartbeat before, but now here he is, a black-robed figure in the shadows, looking up at Arthur. He holds the druid staff in one hand, the sword in the other. 'The gods, I hope,' he says, but Arthur does not reply. 'Here, Arthur.' Merlin holds the sword aloft, so that some of the warriors and folk gathered there might see it with their own eyes, then he hands it to Arthur.

For a long while, Arthur holds the sword with a reverence not entirely for show. He studies the long, straight blade, the gleaming ivory grip and the guard and spherical pommel of dark wood. The sword has been known by other names, Caliburn and Caledfwlch being two. But he knows it as Excalibur, and, even after so much time, it fits his hand perfectly, feels like part of his own body. No cheering now, even at seeing Arthur reunited with the sword that once bound the kings and warlords of the land. The warriors of Camelot must be silent. Must wait for the moment.

'I have missed you,' he tells Excalibur, like a man to a lover, then he guides the oiled and sharpened blade into the scabbard at his left hip. Now he brings a hand to his neck, slipping his fingers inside his scale coat and the leather and wool beneath, chasing the green ribbon down until he feels the ring where it rests in the notch of his collarbone. Presses the tips of finger and thumb together through the silver band, and closes his eyes, and in the stillness of the moment he feels the pulse in his own flesh.

'It's time, Arthur,' Merlin says.

Arthur pats Malo's neck, remembering his faithful mare Llamrei, who had carried him into battle so many times. He even thinks of the Little King and his horses, and wonders how they fare across the Dividing Sea.

'Ride well, Arthur,' Gawain says, a grin stealing onto his face. 'I'll try to save one or two for you to kill.'

The others smile at that, and Arthur smiles too. 'Let us give the bards one more song, Gawain,' he says. Then he looks at Palamedes and nods. Their plan – not that it's worthy of the name – is to ride straight out of the gate to the place where the Saxons are building the pyre, for the chances are that is where King Cynric himself will be, and the boy too. After that, chaos, but if Arthur knows anything, it is that the gods love chaos.

He twists the other way and looks at the spearmen, or at least those he can see in the mist, and the smoke from the sentry fires burning in defiance of the mizzled air. Two big men hold his old bear banner stretched between a pair of long boar spears, the faded cloth hanging heavily. He hopes that black bear on its red field will put fear into Saxon hearts like it used to.

A little further back is the Lady of Camelot's banner, showing a leaping wolf, black as shadow upon its field of green cloth. And beneath it stands Iselle, in bronze scales and a silver-chased helmet with a wolf tail hanging from its crown. She carries a bow, and on her belt hangs a quiver thick with white-fletched arrows.

Her men love her. Arthur can see that. They will kill for her. They will die for her. She should be queen, he thinks. But men are fools and would sooner have an unfledged boy on Dumnonia's high seat than a woman.

Merlin reaches up and grabs Arthur's forearm, and though the druid can barely stand, there is strength yet in his grasp.

'I will be with you, Arthur,' he says.

Arthur nods at the druid. 'If you have an ounce of sway left with the old gods,' he says, 'if, after all the years there is one more day that they may hear you, old man, let it be this day.'

The *clump* of beams being drawn from the heavy gates lifts Arthur's gaze. Men pull those gates open, and mist spills into Camelot like spectres of the long-dead returning home. He urges Malo forward, out of the gates, out onto the plain, the others following slowly. The faint jangle of tack, the occasional snort of a horse, and the muted scuffing of hooves on the soft earth are the only sounds, as pallid dawn creeps upon the world.

His eyes are not what they were. He looks left and right, gaze sifting the mist for Saxons. They are close. He can feel them out there. He can smell the wet wool of their cloaks, and their rancid furs, and the damp ash of their fires, and the onions simmering in their cooking pots, and he can smell the foulness of their dung.

He looks over his shoulder. The others have moved into position, fourteen armoured men on armoured horses now riding slowly in a wedge formation, with him at the point. They all know this ground, could ride it blind. Still, he feels a breath of wind on his face, and sees up ahead the mist shredding. In his mind, he hears Merlin invoking the gods with words known only to his ancient Order and so perhaps known only to Merlin himself now.

It is nearly time.

His heart thumping so vigorously that he fears it must be heard, he looks to his flanks and sees figures materializing as if from nowhere, men of flesh and bone emerging in the vapour. He opens and closes his hand on the shaft of the spear crossing the stallion's neck, its iron blade resting two feet in front of Malo's left eye.

Almost time. The gods be with us.

A Saxon shouts. Then another. They know. It is as if the air itself is changed with the enemies' realization of what is happening.

'Now!' Arthur yells. 'Now ride!'

He kicks back with his heels, and he feels Malo's great muscles bunch as the stallion leaps forward.

'Now, men of Camelot!' Gawain bellows.

'Artorius!' Parcefal gives this up like an invocation. 'Artorius!'

'For Arthur!' Galahad shouts, his white plume leaping.

They are flying now, their horses' breath trailing in tendrils. Their hooves drumming the earth, filling the ground with thunder.

'For Britain!' Arthur screams, his blood rushing, his spear hungry to kill.

'For Arthur!' the spearmen of Camelot shout, a great chorus of voices to rend the dawn. To turn Saxon guts to iced water. 'For Arthur!' they cry. Hundreds of voices, so that even the shades of any gods that yet linger in Britain must surely hear.

'For Arthur!'

*

A figure streaks out of the mist, roaring and wielding a two-handed axe, and Arthur spears him in the shoulder and is jolted back in the saddle, but clings onto the spear and pulls it free as Malo gallops on.

'For Arthur!' Gawain at his shoulder bellows, sending a Saxon spinning away in an arc of bright red blood.

Arthur bends forward, and a spear streaks past him. Another flies across his path like a swallow in the dawn, but he rides on, Malo throwing men aside with the terrible cracking of bone and shrieks of pain. Riding them down, his sharp hooves grinding Saxon flesh into soil from which the winter wheat and rye will grow.

'Kill them!' Arthur screams, thrusting the spear and ripping open a throat. 'Kill them!' His voice inside that helmet is like the fury of breakers in a sea cave.

A Saxon appears on his right, wild-eyed and screaming, and Arthur brings the spear up and over Malo's head and then down, the blade knocking the Saxon's shield flat before burying itself in his chest, but this time Arthur cannot hold on, and the spear is yanked from his grip as Malo flies into the thinning mist.

But where is the pyre? It must be close now, but he cannot see it in the fading mist.

'Whoa, Malo!' he calls, leaning back, hauling on the reins, then releasing, then pulling again, but Malo is full of the same savage joy and does not want to stop now, and it takes all Arthur's strength to master him, using one rein to spiral him down, turning him in tighter and tighter circles until at last he stops.

Arthur twists in the saddle, trying to get the lie of the land, his vision reduced to that allowed by the eye-holes in the masked helmet, as Gawain and Galahad and the others rein in around him, their mounts whinnying and tossing their armoured heads. Breath plumes in the chill morning.

'Where is it?' Palamedes growls, his mare turning in circles still, his spear blade red with gore. Behind them, the spearmen of Camelot are fighting. The thunder of shield on shield, the song of blade on blade, and shouts of rage and pain carry across the plain.

'It must be here!' Gawain says, looking left and right. His face and beard are blood-spattered.

Arthur knows that Iselle's spearmen are slaughtering their enemies now, for they have caught the Saxons by surprise. But it won't be long before the Saxon chieftains realize how few have sallied from the gates, and then they will make their numbers count.

'There!' Galahad calls over his shoulder, having walked his horse ahead of the rest. A Saxon comes screaming at them out of the mist, but Parcefal launches his spear from the saddle and it takes the Saxon in the neck and he falls.

'I see it!' Arthur calls back to Galahad. It must have been veiled by the mist before, but now there it is. A great pile of wood and reeds around a stake. Tied to the stake is the boy, and Arthur's blood boils.

A Saxon spear flies, just missing Palamedes. Another shivers through the air, but Gawain lifts his own spear and knocks it aside.

'Looks like they're ready for us,' the Saracen says. The Saxons have built a shieldwall in front of the pyre. King Cynric's hearthmen, by the looks of their iron helmets and mail tunics and fine war gear. Good warriors. The best of the Saxons.

And Arthur whispers thanks to the gods. He is already walking his horse forward. He can feel Malo's eagerness to run again, the stallion stomping its foreleg again and again, its head high, ears swivelling.

'Arthur?' Gawain says. 'The longer we wait the worse it's going to get.'

The fighting behind them is getting closer. More Saxons are being drawn from their respective camps to the battle.

But Arthur is not ready yet. He knows this moment needs time. He must breathe life into it, like a man blowing into the ball of tinder cupped in his hands.

Two big Saxons come at him from the left, but Palamedes and Galahad spur their mounts forward to cut them off, the Saracen spearing one, Galahad riding the other man down before wheeling his mare and thrusting his spear down.

Arthur walks his horse another ten feet, then stops and sits tall in the saddle, his breathing loud inside that helmet. He knows that the Saxons can see him. He feels their eyes on him as they peer over their shield rims, feet planted on ground their king has told them they will not yield. They see a lord of war, a warrior of gleaming bronze in the mist. They see other warriors who have come as if from the past. Plumed helmets and bloodied spears pointing into the sickly dawn sky, and great, muscled beasts sheathed in leather armour.

They must wonder who he is, this lord of champions, his face hidden behind that shining helmet with its warrior's face of silver and copper. Its long plume, red as blood.

He lifts his hands and removes the helmet.

'I am Arthur!' he calls. 'Lord of Battle. Protector of Britain. Son of Uther Pendragon. Killer of Saxons!'

He cannot know what effect these words have on the Saxons a spear-throw from where he sits upon Malo in this strange dawn, this unmade day, twin plumes of silver shooting from the beast's muzzle. But he sees the Saxons' heads turn to one another. He sees a man peering over the heads of others at the centre of that wall of shields, and he knows it is King Cynric himself.

'My banner flies again!' Arthur bellows across the distance. 'I have come to kill you. I am your death.' He reaches across himself and takes hold of Excalibur's ivory grip and hauls the sword free. 'I am coming for you, Cynric son of Cerdic,' he announces, pointing Excalibur at the Lord of Saxons. 'I have returned, and I shall return again!'

He lets this promise hang for a moment like the mist.

'Just give the word,' Gawain beside him growls.

Arthur half turns his head to speak over his shoulder. 'Are you with me?'

'We're with you, lord,' Galahad says, grinning.

'Always, Arthur,' Parcefal says.

Arthur nods and puts on the helmet and kicks his heels, and Malo screeches as if to the horse goddess Rhiannon and breaks into the gallop. And Arthur is young again, his sins forgotten, his failures unwritten.

Hooves strike the ground, the four-beat gait like a rolling peal of thunder, and now they are close enough for Arthur to see the fear in the eyes between helmet rim and shield, as the Saxons realize that they are about to relive a hundred nightmares sown by their scops in poem and song.

'Artorius!'

Even as Arthur levels his spear, he hears Merlin in his head. *Kill them now, Arthur*, the druid rasps. *Kill them as you were born to do.*

To their credit, the Saxons hold the line, but Arthur does not care, and Malo will not be stopped. The stallion smashes into the rampart of shields and flesh, and the Saxon wall breaks like a ship's hull on jagged rock, and the horse lords pour through the breach, stabbing down with their spears, the stallions hammering their great heads down, smashing noses and cracking skulls.

Arthur is through, then Palamedes, then Galahad. The others are wheeling their mounts, knocking men aside or flattening them like barley underfoot. They are thrusting down with their spears or hacking with swords. Arthur sees a man spear Parcefal in the side, then another Saxon drags the old man from his horse and he is lost from sight. He sees Gawain chopping down on one side, then the other. Sees another of his horse lords fall.

Blood mists the air and screams ring out in the dawn.

A Saxon warrior in a long mail coat roars a challenge at Arthur and comes at him with a boar spear, but Galahad urges his mare forward, blocking the Saxon's path, then slips from the mare's back and takes the fight to the Saxon.

Arthur dismounts and strides towards the pyre, but two Saxons block his path. The bigger of the two, a warrior with silver rings in his beard and a flat nose, comes at him looping a long-hafted axe through the air, its blade singing.

A spear streaks over Arthur's shoulder and takes the big Saxon in the chest and he drops onto his knees. Without breaking stride, or looking to see who threw the spear, Arthur scythes Excalibur through the air, taking the warrior's head from his shoulders. The headless torso pitches forward, and now Arthur faces the man he knows must be King Cynric.

'Are you really Arthur?' the Saxon asks. He is handsome and tall, the hair beneath his helmet golden like his beard, and his eyes hold the sea by which his people came to this land.

Arthur lifts the shining helmet and drops it onto the ground. 'My father was Uther, and his father was Constantine, and his father was Tahalais,' he says.

Behind him, the lady's spearmen have joined the fight against King Cynric's hearthmen. It is carnage now, as day creeps upon the world, revealing mankind's enmity and his shame.

'This land is ours,' King Cynric says. There is no give in him. There can be no negotiation. He is a man who has fought for what is his. A man who will fight to keep it.

'That is the way of things,' Arthur says, lifting Excalibur.

Cynric raises his own sword and comes at Arthur, but then

Palamedes is there. He puts himself between the Saxon king and Arthur, his mail slick with dark blood.

'Get the prince, Arthur,' the Saracen says, as his blade rings against Cynric's.

Arthur peers through the mist. There is Gawain, dismounted now, fighting as fiercely as he ever did, his face sheeted in blood. There is Galahad, in the thick of it, spinning and cutting, light on his feet, seeming to dance, almost as good as Lancelot was.

A war horn sounds. More of the lady's spearmen are coming, yelling with the terrible joy of battle. 'Camelot!' they cry, and, 'Arthur!'

He sees his bear banner, rippling now in the breeze, the beast upon it seeming alive.

The rope binding the boy to that stake offers little resistance to the desperate sawing of Excalibur's keen-edge.

'It's all right, boy. I'm here now,' he says. But the boy does not speak, just stares, eyes round as Roman denarii, and when he is free he falls limply against the stake, so that Arthur must pick him up and carry him like a babe. 'I've got you, boy,' he says, half clambering, half sliding down the rushes and loose wood of the pyre.

Palamedes is on his knees, pressing a hand against his side, blood welling between his fingers. Just feet away lies the Saxon king's headless corpse.

'Cynric is dead!' Galahad yells. He is holding Cynric's head by its golden hair, the raw stump of the neck dripping, the blue eyes clouded now. 'Cynric is dead!' Galahad roars, hoisting the head high.

'King Cynric is dead!' Gawain echoes the shout in his gruff voice, then others take it up, the news spreading through the fight like fire in dry straw, or like a stone skimmed across the surface of a lake, and there is a change in the air.

The warriors of Camelot take heart, pushing on into the press of the enemy. Here and there, the Saxons are breaking, or if not breaking, they no longer drive forward with the same ferocity. Yet, Cynric's hearthmen fight on. Perhaps those brave warriors mean to feast and drink with their lord this night in Woden's hall.

For a moment, Arthur peers into the murk. Listens to the screams and shrieks, the terrible chaos of it all. It is as though the battle itself is the fevered dream of a dying world.

'Come on, boy.' He lifts the boy up onto Malo's back, then he climbs up behind him. The fighting is close. Just two dozen paces away, men are slaughtering each other. He pulls Malo round and they ride off into the mist.

'You're alive, boy,' he says in the boy's ear, and he can smell the boy's hair and feel his warmth against his cheek. He has left the helmet, he realizes, but he does not care about that now. He wonders if the boy is grievously wounded. Or if they have taken his tongue. 'Won't let them hurt you again, boy,' he says.

They ride on, the clamour of battle receding behind them.

The boy lifts his head a little. 'You came for me.'

The voice is small, but his heart swells to hear it again. 'Of course I came for you, boy,' he says. 'You think I'd leave you? After everything?'

The boy says nothing, and soon they come to marshy ground, where Arthur slows Malo to a trot. He looks around at the formless world. There, the low shapes of sedges, ferns and moss-cloaked deadfall. There, the dark shadows of birch, alder and willow which mark the edge of the mere. He walks Malo a little further, then they stop and he dismounts and helps the boy down.

He looks back, thinking he saw something, but it is just the mist, drifting in breeze-stirred tendrils.

'They would be mad to follow here,' he tells the boy.

They have not come so far, but the battle sounds far away.

'Palamedes,' the boy says, clutching his hands and looking back the way they came.

'Nothing can kill him, boy,' Arthur assures him. 'Are you hurt?' He can see no sign of it, but he needs to be sure.

The boy shakes his head. 'You?'

Arthur grins. The battle thrill still flutters in his heart and his limbs. 'I feel young,' he says, his throat raw from yelling. He knows that later all the years will come crashing in again, and he will be struck by countless pains. When it comes, it may be too much for his old body. But for now, he is still the lord of war.

'Beran.' The voice comes from the mist. He and the boy turn towards it. 'Or is it Arthur?'

'Get behind me, boy,' Arthur growls, as Nabor ap Nabor strides out of the mist towards them, grey in a battered coat of mail, sword in hand. His face is bone white, bloodless-looking but for the discoloration of bruising around both eyes, chin and right cheek.

'I told Queen Morgana's bastards that I wasn't going to Anwnn before I'd killed old Beran,' Nabor says, broken teeth visible in the rictus of his mouth. Then he is running, and Arthur is just thinking how the gods love chaos and death when Nabor's blade rings against Excalibur.

Their swords clash three more times, then they both step back, breathing hard, Nabor's face betraying his surprise that Arthur managed to parry his attacks. But Arthur's blood still surges from the mounted charge and from the glories of the past, and this has lent him speed and strength.

Nabor points his sword at the prince. 'I should have killed you myself, boy,' he says, then he comes again, thrusts high but Arthur deflects his blade and drives off his right foot, punching Excalibur's hilt into the mercenary's face, and Nabor staggers backwards, blood spilling from his burst lips.

'Now I have a story to tell, Lord Arthur,' Nabor says through a bloody grin. When he comes again, he is fury itself, and it is all Arthur can do to meet every slash and thrust with Excalibur, their swords ringing in the dawn. But Nabor does not break off. He comes and comes, and Arthur can feel his strength ebbing now. Can feel his arms growing heavy and his legs weakening beneath him.

Nabor's blade finds a way through, scything against his left shoulder to send bronze scales flying. That sword comes again, and Arthur is too slow, and it hits his chest, the steel edge glancing down and away.

Arthur hears the boy call his name, and the sound fans the fury inside him.

You will not hurt the boy.

He stumbles forward, swings Excalibur, but Nabor blocks and lunges, the point of his blade bursting through the armour at Arthur's right shoulder and the wool beneath and then biting into the flesh beneath that. Arthur roars and throws himself at Nabor, driving him back, but Nabor breaks free and brings his sword down onto Arthur's back, staggering him. Yet Arthur refuses to fall.

'It's over, old man,' Nabor rasps.

Arthur steadies himself and turns back to face his enemy.

'No, it's not,' he says. He launches himself at Nabor again, their swords resounding in the mist, Excalibur singing one last song, but a song that will never live again on the lips of bards.

There is no way through now, not even for the sword that once brought the lords of Britain to fight beneath the bear banner at Camlan. Arthur is losing. He cannot breathe. He is suffocating. He thinks of the boy, and the boy is the last of his strength, as Nabor hammers his blade down onto Excalibur, forcing Arthur back. Forcing him down onto one knee, yet still Arthur's arm holds.

He grits his teeth. Strains with every sinew in his old body. He is Artorius, Lord of Battle. He will not yield.

'Die!' Nabor screams, bringing that blade down again and again, as if he cannot understand how this old man has the strength to check every blow.

But Arthur is the sword of Britain and he will not fail.

With an effort beyond mere flesh and blood and bone, he somehow gets his left foot beneath him again, and drives himself up, still taking blows on Excalibur, still gasping, hauling breath into scolding lungs.

But then, the unthinkable. Excalibur is gone. The blade is broken. He holds the ivory hilt, still, and a short length of blade remains, but the rest lies in the grass at his feet. It is in this moment Arthur knows it is over.

All of it is over.

Nabor seems as surprised as he. As if the mercenary feels the weight of the omen. As if he knows that Britain is lost.

And yet, Arthur breathes still, his heart beats still, and so there is hope.

I will not yield. I will never yield.

Nabor grins. Lifts his sword, its edge jagged now, where Excalibur has bitten it.

'I'm still here, boy,' Arthur gasps, turning to look into the boy's eyes, to give him at least that. Then he lifts that broken sword and invites Nabor to come.

I . . . do not . . . yield.

Nabor raises his sword and comes, and then he stops mid-stride, and stands a moment, staring at Arthur, his expression one of confusion. There is an arrow through his neck, the head and protruding shaft wet with blood, the white swan-feather fletchings quivering in the breeze.

Nabor takes one faltering step more, then falls to his knees, hands clutching at the arrow, and Arthur looks into the mist and sees Iselle on the back of a white mare, her bow in her left hand.

'Lady! They are breaking!' a disembodied voice calls from somewhere behind her. 'Now is our time!'

Arthur looks at his daughter and she looks at him, their eyes full of unspoken words. Then Iselle pulls a rein, wheeling her horse away, and she shrieks in savage joy like some bird of prey, and rides back towards the sound of battle.

When Arthur looks back to Nabor, the man is dead on the ground, those swan feathers shivering against the grass. Then Arthur feels another blow, but it is just the boy throwing himself against Arthur's body, wrapping his arms around him, his cheek pressed to the bronze scales of his armour.

'We're alive, boy,' he says. He holds the boy to him and looks around. They are alone once more. Just the two of them on the edge of the mere and, like wraiths, he thinks they could just vanish.

'Come, boy. Let's get you to Camelot. You'll be safe there.'

The boy does not answer, and they walk for a while, Arthur limping, the boy helping him, bearing some of the weight of that scale armour and the old man beneath. They do not ride Malo, for the stallion is puffing still, his flanks slick with lather. He deserves the rest, and so Arthur leads him by his reins, and they can see the old hill fort now. It rises out of the mist. While it stands, all is not lost. It cannot be.

Other things, though, lie hidden in the mist. Broken bodies. Open flesh steaming in the dawn, adding to the strange fog. Now and then the pitiful whinny of a stricken horse, a cry of pain or low moan of a dying man. Soon to be silent, all, the wrack of corpses left on the strand now the tide of battle has ebbed.

'Not long now, boy,' he says.

The boy does not speak, but he is looking up at the ramparts too, at those banks and ditches behind which fires have long burned against dark nights and in the hearts of men and women since before the Romans came to Britain. And yet, hope is a heavy thing. Arthur knows that only too well. Knows what it is to carry the hopes of others, just as the boy all but carries him now.

The boy is not the first to do so, either. Arthur knows he never bore the weight of this land and its peoples alone. There were others who shared the burden. Gawain, as loyal a friend and sword-brother as any man ever had. And Merlin, who dreamt to the gods and perhaps tried harder than any of them to remember the old ways, to bring them back and save Britain. There had been Lancelot, too, the greatest and best of them. How he had loved Lancelot, and how that love had torn him asunder.

And Guinevere. His heart. He had fought for Guinevere. Always for her.

'Soon be there,' he tells the boy, because it seems the boy is tired. Their pace has slowed. Not much, but enough to tell it. 'There'll be food. Soft furs. A fire.'

They walk a little further, then the boy stops. He pulls away. Looks up at Arthur, tears standing in his eyes. 'I don't want to go,' he says.

Arthur doesn't understand. 'They will look after you there,' he says. 'You're Prince Erbin.' He can feel blood at his shoulder. Myriad pains rising in him like storm rain in a barrel. He should keep moving while he still can. 'You are the hope of Britain, boy.'

The boy shakes his head. 'I don't want it. I don't want any of it.'

To Arthur this feels like a blow, after everything.

And yet . . .

'What *do* you want, boy?' he asks.

The boy frowns, looks at the ground, then brings his eyes back up to Arthur's. 'I want to stay with you.'

Arthur's breath catches in his chest. Did he mishear the boy? 'I cannot stay here,' he says. He lifts an arm towards the distant clamour of battle. 'I'm too old for all this.'

The boy says nothing.

Arthur inclines his head. He needs the boy to listen and listen well. 'I can't stay, boy,' he says.

'I know,' the boy says.

It dawns on Arthur then, but he almost doesn't dare allow himself the hope. He looks around again, chewing on his next words, then fixes his gaze on the boy once more.

'If you come with me, you don't get any of this,' he says, lifting his chin in the direction of that great hill fort, that beating heart of Dumnonia. 'You don't become a king. You don't lead men. You don't have everything that they would give you. Do you understand?'

The boy nods. 'We should go.' His eyes are full of hope.

Arthur cannot speak now. His throat is too tight. He blinks the tears from his own eyes, lifts a hand to scrub them from his cheeks. He takes a breath and takes the boy's hand and they go to Malo, who nickers softly, and Arthur mounts, then pulls the boy up behind him. He turns the stallion into the west, and together they head back towards the mist-wreathed birch, alder and willow. There is an old path through the mere. A secret way across the water. Perhaps he is the only man still alive who remembers it.

Epilogue

T HE DAY EBBS NOW. The sun has dwindled to a yolk of brightness
on the southern horizon, where it rests in a bed of light the yellow
of mullein petals and the red of campion. Clouds loom above me,
drifting on a chill northerly which shivers my feathers as I watch
through the interplay of light and dark the others of my kind tumble
and course for their evening roost in the far trees across the stubble
field.

I am crow.

I hop three times, then walk obliquely towards him, leaning back a
little so that I might fly away from him should he move. But he does
not move.

A rattle and caw escape my throat and I take to the air, my wing tips
spread like fingers, and I cannot stop this creature from calling out
with the joy of it. *Caa-caa. Caa-caa.* Wings beating, rowing against the
biting wind. Up and up, then jinking sideways, then momentarily still,
as a small boat on the crest of a great ocean wave, before falling, down
and down to alight on the branch of an alder in a clump beside the old
man's steading.

I will have to go soon. Back through the veil. I cannot stay with this
crow, and she must fly into that cauldron of noise in the far woods and
take her roost before nightfall. But I may hold to her a little longer yet.
I still have some small power to move where I will in this eternal
dream.

And so I watch the old man. He lies beneath a hazel which still
holds its leaves, though some are flecked with dull yellow now at the
season's turn. I watch and I ache for the old man and for the past, yet

I am happy because he has found peace at last. His eyes are closed and he lies there as still as the coming winter. No breath in him that I can see. No pain. No anguish for things done and things not done.

Arthur. I speak his name, feeling the magic in it, though the world hears only a crow's caw.

The clump of the steading door startles me, and I resist the bird's instinct to take wing. The boy emerges. He wears a bear skin around his shoulders and holds two spears and a flask, and he walks with eager step to the hazel beneath which the old man lies. And he bends and grips the man's shoulder and speaks to him in a soft voice.

The old man does not move.

The boy shakes him again, and this time the old man opens his eyes and looks at the boy and mutters something in reply.

The boy offers the old man his hand, but the man refuses it and climbs to his feet unaided. Presses his hands into the small of his back. Loosens his neck. The boy hands him the larger of the two hunting spears, then sets off towards the woods. But the old man does not follow straight away.

He looks up at me. His hand falls to the iron strap end of his belt, for he thinks I am the Morrigán. Thinks I have come for him. But I hold his eye, just as I hold this bird to the branch though she wants to be gone. And the old man lifts a hand to his chest and keeps it there, and breathes slowly out. And there are tears in his eyes now.

Caa-caa. Caa-caa. I call his name.

Arthur. Arthur.

He knows. He knows I am here. That I have come back.

It is too much now.

He smiles. Holds my eyes a moment longer. Then he turns and follows the boy.

I stay for another dozen heartbeats, but my hold on this creature has ebbed like the day, and I must go.

I call his name for the last time.

Then I leap into the sky and beat my wings for the darkness.

Author's Note

THE WRITING OF THIS book was never part of some grand plan.
Indeed, having written *Lancelot*, and then *Camelot*, I felt I needed
to step away from these stories and the process of writing them, which
I found emotionally and creatively exhausting. It was the right decision, because the experience of writing my thriller, *Where Blood Runs
Cold*, was invigorating and, well, thrilling. What a contrast it was,
writing a story set in the modern world, for the most part in one
environment (the snowy mountains), and spending almost the entire
time with just two characters.

Still, I knew it was not without risk. After eleven historical novels,
would I be able to write a contemporary story and respect the unwritten (and sometimes written) rules of the thriller? Could I write in
short sentences, disregard worldbuilding in favour of a plot-driven,
exhilarating tale, include unexpected twists, a wicked bad guy, page-
turning tension, cliff-hangers, and bring it all in at around 85,000
words (*Lancelot*, after all, was over 200,000)? And of course, would
those readers who enjoy my historical novels take a chance on my
present-day thriller? It's not for me to say in which of these things I
succeeded (although at 88,000 words, I just about got that right), and
which I failed, but I was utterly amazed when *Where Blood Runs Cold*
was made *The Times*'s Thriller of the Month and went on to win the
Wilbur Smith Adventure Writing Prize 2022. On a personal level,
that award alone was vindication for my decision to venture off-piste
and write a contemporary tale.

So, what next? Well, this is where other powers began to exert their
influence. Something was calling me back to the fractured, darkening

world of sub-Roman Britain. Turns out I had underestimated the allure of this island's greatest myth and the rewards available to someone lucky enough to be able to play with it. And now, having relished my adventure in the Norwegian mountains, I felt ready to re-immerse myself in Arthur's world. If I were to get mystical about it, I might even suspect the power of 'threeness' of playing a part. *Lancelot* and *Camelot* are of course imbued with Celtic mythology, and triadism is a recurring theme in Irish and Welsh tradition. The Morrigán, for instance, occurs in triple form, and there are other three-faced divinities. Images of sacred bulls are rendered with three horns. Ulster's warrior hero Cú Chulainn wore his hair in three braids and killed enemy warriors in groups of three. There was a tradition of killing the king in three ways, by wounding, burning, and drowning. There is the totality of time as represented in the past, present, and future. There's an acknowledgement that things happen in threes. A belief in the three realms of sky, earth, and water (or underworld), an understanding of Man's journey through birth, death, and rebirth. And on, and on. Indeed, the importance of triplism is not lost on my Merlin, who has tattooed on the palm of his right hand a triskele, a symbol comprising three conjoined spirals. The triskele has had different meanings in different cultures across the ages, but it cannot escape its association with triadism.

There is power in three, then, so how could I not write another book in my Arthurian retelling?

Furthermore, whilst a duology is a statement of intent, I think a trilogy of Arthurian Tales really stakes a claim on my little slice of the myth. And, because these books are companion novels rather than a linear series, there would be a synergy, I hoped, in adding another book.

But what kind of story would it be? Well, I left Arthur in *Camelot* a shadow-man, a broken vessel, and I felt he deserved another chance. I owed the legend, the great warrior, his shining moment. I may never have made him a king, but I could give him one last charge into glory. So, the subject of this book was never in doubt. It had to be Arthur.

Of course, *Lancelot* and *Camelot* were written in the first person, because telling the story from the narrator's point of view seemed the best way of really getting under the skin of both Lancelot and Galahad. For whatever reason, it didn't feel right to put myself in Arthur's skin, as it were, and write in the first person, though I still wanted the reader to feel as close to our hero as possible and for the story to feel intimate and focused. And so, I went for the 'limited third person' approach (as opposed to the more traditional omnipresent third person), so that we only ever see the world through Arthur's eyes. Until the epilogue, that is, when Guinevere, her spirit inhabiting a crow, slips back through the veil to cast an eye upon Arthur for the last time.

As I explained in the Author's Note in *Lancelot*, you won't find much of the traditional myth in these books, and I'm sorry if that's disappointing. One reason for this is because many stories in the myth are, frankly, strange to say the least. Apart from some implied magic, such as that relating to Guinevere's spirit journeying, and despite the elusiveness of a historical Arthur, my books are grounded in a historically rendered world: a sub-Roman Britain being inexorably overrun by incoming Saxons. It would be difficult, therefore, to include Geoffrey of Monmouth's pig-gobbling giant with his club that two men could barely lift off the ground. Or a sinful king and his sons who are magically transformed into savage boars. Or a sword-catching Lady who lives beneath the surface of a lake. Or a headless green knight. And so on.

Rather, I've had fun subverting some aspects of the legend, giving subtle nods to characters and episodes in the age-old stories with my own versions and conceivable explanations. In *Camelot*, my 'Green Knight' is a warrior with skin stained by the copper bands on his arms and at his neck, and from living in the caves of a copper mine. Gawain cuts off his head, of course. In *Lancelot*, my 'Round Table' is the stump of a once huge oak tree, around which Arthur and his most trusted warriors gather to talk of war. My 'Lady of the Lake' is a Pictish priestess who symbolically submerges Excalibur in the water (or underworld) before drawing it out again.

I could not resist inserting Tristan and Isolde into the tale, because it seemed to me that their situation, their unfortunate love triangle with King Mark at the sharp end, provided the perfect mirror through which Arthur could reflect on his own relationship with Lancelot and Guinevere. Thus, through their tragedy he might gain some objective insight and, hopefully, find some redemption for his own.

The Saracen warrior Palamedes first appears later in the legend, in the thirteenth-century French romance *Palamedes*, the *Post-Vulgate Cycle*, Thomas Malory's *Le Morte d'Arthur*, and the Prose *Tristan*. But I thought him too good a potential character not to include here. The trouble with discovering such a character late on is that I wish I'd written him into *Lancelot*. Guivret the Small, also known as the Little King, pops up in Chrétien de Troyes's *Erec* and the Welsh *Geraint*, but I have taken only his name and stature into my own tale. In fact, the role of dwarves in Arthurian literature (there are many mentions) is a subject all on its own. I won't get into that here, other than to say the theories are quite fascinating.

One thing I was pleased to do was revisit the younger Morgana (or Morgaine as she was) in the backstory timeline, because I felt it was important to give some context as to why she becomes the twisted, hate-filled figure we see in *Camelot*. Well, Uther killed her father, took her mother for his wife and her home for himself. Arthur then gets her pregnant, is openly ashamed of having done so, and stands by as Uther arranges for the infant Mordred to be rowed out upon a lake and thrown overboard. If the actress playing Morgana in a screen adaptation was to ask, 'What's my motivation?' there would be plenty to get into! Later, of course, Arthur kills Mordred and Galahad kills her son Ambrosius, so one can perhaps understand the old woman's demeanour in my stories.

Some other familiar faces, e.g., Gawain, Galahad, Iselle, do appear towards the end of *Arthur*, but it was a deliberate decision to keep them in the background. They had their time in the previous novels, and it was important for this story to be about Arthur and about the boy in whom he sees, in many ways, his younger self, burdened with the hopes and expectations of others. It was also imperative that this should be a self-contained story as much as possible. I like to think that a reader could come to this novel and enjoy it even if they hadn't previously read the other two, although I suspect the experience would be enhanced if they had.

Of course, traditionally, Arthur is never seen or heard of again following his mortal wounds received at the hands of his own son, Mordred, at the Battle of Camlan. However, it was too exciting for me to imagine that he did not die of his wounds, nor was he healed in Avalon (where I sent him to live a hermit's life in *Camelot*), there to remain until his death from old age. The question I wanted to pose is, what if Arthur had lived? What kind of man would he have become? And, more importantly, could he be tempted back to the world, to wield Excalibur one final time before slipping through the veil at last?

I particularly enjoyed having rumours of Arthur's existence circulating around Britain (no doubt spread by Merlin!), and then having Beran/Arthur return to the world after his self-imposed exile. This was my way of playing with the enduring, and very romantic part of the legend which says that in our darkest time, when we need him most, shall Arthur come again.

Despite these nuggets inspired by previous retellings, *Arthur* is almost all invention. There's little point, for me at least, in walking well-trodden ground. I've always done things my own way and, in these novels, have wandered wherever the story led, for better or worse.

But why 'Beran'? you may wonder. I chose to call the old exile Beran because of that name's association with the Old High German 'Bero', meaning 'bear'. I liked the idea that the Saxons who had crossed paths (or swords) with the hardy old warrior gave him the nickname, which was more fitting than they could have known, what with Arthur's own sigil being a bear. I have also seen the name 'Beran' linked to the verb meaning to carry, or to bear. I must stress that I'm no expert on names or etymology, but I liked the idea of giving Arthur a nickname that suited both his character and warrior stature, and also perhaps hinted at his great curse, his charge to metaphorically bear the hopes and expectations of a people. Furthermore, one commonly proposed derivation of 'Arthur' is from the Welsh for 'bear', so all in all, his nom de guerre Beran seemed a pretty good fit.

As my career has gone on, it has become increasingly important for me to find new ways of telling a tale, rather than feeling like my current work in progress is the same as the last. For this reason, I ended up going with a dual timeline for *Arthur*. The challenge here, of course, was to try to ensure that the two stories (in this case the young Arthur, and the old Beran/Arthur) were equally strong and engaging. You don't want the reader skipping sections to get to the parts which they consider the important, or best bits. The two strands must weave together to create a satisfying whole. For me, the sections set in the past helped reveal our hero's origin story and his humanity, but most of all I wanted these backstory episodes to enhance the emotional resonance of what was happening in the present-day narrative. And so, I tried to segue from one to the other in subtle ways. Perhaps those ways were too subtle at times, and those reflections were missed or felt merely nostalgic, but better that than beating the reader over the head with clumsy transitions.

Another big difference between *Arthur*, *Lancelot* and *Camelot* is the cast list and timescale over which the tale unfolds. The list of protagonists in this book is very short in comparison with the previous two. As for the timescale, *Lancelot* covers most of the eponymous hero's life, *Camelot* takes place over a period of months, or about a year, but *Arthur* spans just a few weeks. It's much smaller in scope, more intimate and self-contained. I like to think it's the Arthurian fiction equivalent of a road-trip movie.

In terms of style, when writing the first couple of chapters it felt more akin to my early Viking novels than to *Lancelot* or *Camelot*. There was a grittiness, a rawness, an edge to the violence that's to be found in those books, and I was gleefully aware of it. However, my love of a more lyrical prose style soon took hold and the writing ended up staying true to the previous novels.

So that's it for my Arthurian Tales. I'm almost certain of it. I hope that between the pages of *Lancelot*, *Camelot*, and now *Arthur*, you have been transported, entertained and, at times, possibly even moved. There is something about the passing of time and the ending of things, the decline of what was once strong and golden and glorious (or at least the memory of which seems so) that has always resonated in me. Perhaps that increases the older I get. There's a pain in knowing we can never go back. That we can never see or feel or experience what we once did. And the future? Well, that can look rather terrifying. Which all points to that omnipresent mindfulness advice telling us to live in the moment. Easier said than done for a writer of historical fiction!

Knowing, then, that I'm doomed to feel the passing of time with every tick of the study clock, I have given my all to these stories. This world and its characters are real to me. Their trials have been my own. My heart has ached, my eyes have filled with tears and, now and then, I have shared some small triumph with Lancelot, Galahad, Iselle and Arthur.

I pass the grail to the next author willing to drink from it. They will undoubtedly reimagine the rich and fascinating world of Arthur in their own way. Which is, of course, just as it should be.

Giles Kristian
30 November 2023

Background Reading

Of course I have dipped in and out of many reference and research books during the writing of my Arthurian Tales, but the following have remained within arm's reach throughout:

The Arthurian Name Dictionary, by Christopher W. Bruce, Garland Publishing 1999

Dictionary of Celtic Myth and Legend, by Miranda J. Green, Thames and Hudson 1997

The Celtic Myths: A Guide to the Ancient Gods and Legends, by Miranda Aldhouse-Green, Thames and Hudson 2015

Arthur and the Anglo-Saxon Wars, by David Nicolle, illustrated by Angus McBride, Osprey Publuishing 1984

Late Roman Cavalryman AD 236–565, by Simon MacDowall, illustrated by Christa Hook, Osprey Publishing 1995

A.D. 500: A Journey Through the Dark Isles of Britain and Ireland, by Simon Young, Phoenix 2006

Britain's Wild Flowers: A Treasury of Traditions, Superstitions, Remedies and Literature, by Rosamond Richardson, National Trust Books 2017

Acknowledgements

My eternal thanks to the usual suspects, without whom this book would most likely not exist, and certainly not in the form that you, dear reader, or listener, have experienced it. Bill Hamilton, Simon Taylor, Elizabeth Dobson, Anthony Hewson and Philip Stevens. You have all played a part and I hope you know how much I appreciate your advice, encouragement, wisdom and fellowship.

As always, thank you to Sally, Freyja and Aksel. You are the first words and the last.

ABOUT THE AUTHOR

Family history (he is half Norwegian) and a passion for the fiction of Bernard Cornwell inspired **Giles Kristian** to write. Set in the Viking world, his bestselling 'Raven' and 'The Rise of Sigurd' trilogies have been acclaimed by his peers, reviewers and readers alike. In *The Bleeding Land* and *Brothers' Fury*, he tells the story of a family torn apart by the English Civil War. He also co-wrote Wilbur Smith's No. 1 bestseller *Golden Lion*. His contemporary survival thriller, *Where Blood Runs Cold*, won the Wilbur Smith Adventure Writing Prize. With his *Sunday Times* bestseller *Lancelot*, Giles plunged into the rich waters of the Arthurian legend. His epic reimagining of our greatest island 'history' continued in *Camelot* and draws to a breathtaking close with *Arthur*.

Giles Kristian lives in Leicestershire.

To find out more, visit www.gileskristian.com. You can follow him on X @GilesKristian and Facebook/Giles Kristian